"I want you here,

"You never look like you need help and you never ask me for it."

"Well, I've never had to stand over the grave of one of my officers before, either. I hope I never have to do that again."

She took his hand and held it to her cheek. "It's a terrible loss. I hope you find the killer."

He hoped that her father wasn't tied up in all this but it wasn't looking good. He realized that his arresting him had broken their engagement. If and when he made that second arrest and sent him back to federal prison, maybe for many, many years, would she ever forgive him?

This might be their first and last night together.

TRIBAL LAW

BY
JENNA KERNAN

MILLS & BOON

First Published in Great Britain 2016
By Mills & Boon, an imprint of HarperCollins*Publishers*
1 London Bridge Street, London, SE1 9GF

© 2016 by Jeannette H. Monaco

ISBN: 978-0-263-91905-9

46-0516

Our policy is to use papers that are natural, renewable and recyclable products and made from wood grown in sustainable forests. The logging and manufacturing processes conform to the legal environmental regulations of the country of origin.

Printed and bound in Spain
by CPI, Barcelona

Jenna Kernan has penned over two dozen novels and has received two RITA® Award nominations. Jenna is every bit as adventurous as her heroines. Her hobbies include recreational gold prospecting, scuba diving and gem hunting. Jenna grew up in the Catskills and currently lives in the Hudson Valley of New York State with her husband. Follow Jenna on Twitter, @jennakernan, on Facebook or at www.jennakernan.com.

To Jim—Always.

Chapter One

Selena Dosela's heart beat so hard in her chest she started gasping.

"For the love of God," said her father from the passenger seat. "Where's your Apache poker face?"

She pressed a hand to her forehead and blew out a breath but still felt dizzy.

"Better." Her father, who was supposed to be home under house arrest, had crouched out of sight when they passed Gabe's police car, but there was nowhere to hide in the small cab of her box truck.

Gabe hit his lights.

"Pull over," said her dad.

She did, gliding on snow and ice to a stop on the shoulder. Gabe's white SUV pulled in behind her.

Gabe Cosen, the chief of police for the Black Mountain Apache Tribe, would spot her father the instant he reached her door, which was in about fifteen seconds.

"Tell me when he's next to the rear tire."

Selena's heart began galloping again.

She glanced in her side mirror. Gabe exited his unit, tugged down his thigh-length sheepskin jacket and put on the gray Stetson that he always wore. Now her heart pounded for a different reason. Even from a distance this man could raise her heart rate and her internal temperature.

As chief, he didn't wear a uniform anymore except for special occasions. But he still wore that hat, as if he were a cowboy instead of an Indian. He tipped the brim down and then marched toward Selena's driver's side. On any other day she might have appreciated the sight because Gabe Cosen looked good coming or going. Right now she wished it was going.

"What should we do?" she asked.

Her father cast her a look of disappointment. "What do you think? Hide. I'll be outside on the running board."

Why had she thought he meant to harm Gabe? Did her father even carry a gun? She hoped not; he would be in enough trouble if Gabe caught him and, come to think of it, so would she.

Her attention returned to her side mirror. "Okay, he's beside the truck."

The passenger door eased open and her father hopped out. The door clicked shut. Her attention slipped back to the empty seat and she caught movement through the window beyond. The large rectangular side mirror showed a view of her father crouching on the runner. She gave a little shout. He straightened just enough to peer back inside and she pointed frantically at the mirror. He disappeared like a prairie dog ducking into its burrow, hopping off the running boards and moving out of sight.

"Selena?" Gabe's voice was muffled by the glass.

She jumped in her seat, then rolled down the window to face the chief of the tribal police. The truck was old, refurbished and didn't have power anything. In fact, it even had a cassette player on the console. But she'd chosen this truck because she'd been able to pay cash for the whole thing. Unfortunately she'd had to use it and her sister's box truck as collateral against the 18-wheeler.

"Hey there," he said. His breath came in a puff of condensation that disappeared almost instantly. "Everything okay?"

Her ears were buzzing. Did that mean she was going to faint? *You absolutely are not going to faint. You can't.*

"Was I doing something wrong, Chief?" Her attempt to keep her voice level failed and Gabe pushed back the brim of his hat, giving her a closer look. How did he manage to get more handsome every single year? she wondered as she stared at his ruggedly attractive face.

"You're flushed," he said.

"Hot in here. Heater is wonky." That lie came so easily.

"I see. What's up?"

"What do you mean?" she asked, keeping her sweating hands on the wheel.

"Your route is finished and you're heading out. Usually you take the car on errands."

He had watched her that closely? She had no idea. Now she didn't know if she should be flattered, furious or frightened.

Should she go with indignation or civility? The indignation won, hands down.

"I don't think that's any business of yours."

Gabe's brows shot up as he stared steadily back at her. His long nose and flared nostrils reminded her of a wolf on the hunt. The air of authority did not come solely from his position. She felt it even now, the need to do whatever he said merely because he said it. And that mouth, oh, she had memories of that mouth on her body.

Gabe looked Apache—his brown skin, his broad forehead and his full, sensual mouth all spoke of his strength and lineage. But his hair did not. Unlike the rest of his brothers, he wore it clipped short. Perhaps to annoy his older brother, Clyne, the tribal council-man and family traditionalist. If possible, Gabe's thick black hair and stylish cut only made him more attractive. Gabe had once been approached by the tribe's casino promotion team, who wanted to use him in their ad campaigns. His brothers never let him live that one down. But they didn't want Gabe because he was boyish, like his kid brother Kino, or handsome like Clay or distinguished like his older brother, Clyne. They chose him because he made women want to take him to bed.

And she was no better than any of the rest of them because she still wanted that, too.

He narrowed his eyes. "You sure you're all right?"

She swallowed, released the wheel and gave him her stone face. The one her father said she didn't have. The one all Apache girls practiced before their Sunrise Ceremony.

"Can I go now?" she asked summoning a tone of flat annoyance and thinking her voice still sounded like the whine of a mosquito.

Gabe stepped back but kept a hand on the open window. She kept hers on the crank.

"I'm sorry I didn't bring him home," he said. "I should have been the one there today."

An apology? Selena's mouth dropped open. Gabe Cosen was the most unapologetic man she knew, except for perhaps her father. Somehow his words had the opposite effect of what he had likely intended. Now Selena was not frightened. She was pissed.

"Well, you were there when he left, so that's something."

Gabe grimaced.

"If you need anything," he said.

"I need to get going." She lifted her brows to show her impatience and gave the crank a tug for good measure. It met the resistance of his gloved hand, but he released her door. He stood there studying her. She glared back. Why wouldn't he leave? Her father couldn't get back inside with him standing there and if he tried, Gabe would see him.

"Are we finished?" she asked. But she already knew the answer. They'd been finished for nearly five years and since then all their conversations had been brief, awkward and tense. But maybe not this tense.

He inclined his chin.

"Then get back to your car. It's freezing out here."

His brow lifted to show his surprise and she knew why. No one ever told Gabe Cosen what to do. No, this man gave orders. He didn't take them.

"Please call me if you need me," he said, using that infuriating, polite, professional tone.

She needed him every night. But she'd be damned if she'd call.

Gabe hesitated, waiting perhaps for her to reply or say farewell. She cranked up the window and placed her hands on the wheel, staring straight ahead. Finally, he withdrew, melting back and away from her.

She leaned across the seat but before she could open the door her father had it open and swept back into the cab.

"Go," he said. "But not too fast." Her father ducked down below the door so as not to be visible in the wide rectangular mirrors that flanked each side of the cab, the ones that gave her a clear view of Gabe returning to his police car.

She set them in motion, then glanced to the road and then back to Gabe. Then to the road. They had gotten away with it. She grabbed a breath of icy air.

"You missed our turn when he stopped us. Turn around. And get us out of here before he stops you again."

Selena swung them around and caught a blur as Gabe flashed by her driver's side window. Then he was behind her, hands on hips as he watched her taillights.

Just keep going.

"Uh-oh," said her father, peeking at the side mirror.

Selena looked back to see Gabe had returned to the place where she had parked. He was studying the ground.

"He's spotted my tracks," said her father. "Drive faster."

Chapter Two

Gabe Cosen watched Selena go and then returned to the tracks. The snow had started again and he knew that this was his best chance to get a good read. Like all of the men in his family, he had learned to read sign, which meant he could interpret the tracks of animals and men. He was adequate for an Apache, but his younger brothers, Kino and Clay, were much better.

The prints were from a large individual wearing moccasins. That was not unheard of, but most folks wore their tribe's traditional foot gear only for hunting, ceremonies and dance competitions. The rest of the time they wore boots. He crouched beside the tracks and guessed at the person's weight—less than two hundred pounds—from the place where the person had slipped en route to the front of the truck. Who had been in the cab with Selena and why didn't that person want him to know?

His first thought was that Selena had found someone else. The white-hot fury at that prospect surprised him enough that he lost his balance and had to put a hand down to keep from toppling over. His break in concentration left the mark of his glove in the snow.

He'd know, wouldn't he? If she had a date or was dating? The community was small and he kept closer tabs on Selena's movements than he cared for her to know.

The second possibility for her unknown passenger broke through the mental fog he always felt around Selena and struck him like a rock slide. He stood and spun. The road was empty now. She had a good head start. He ran back to his unit. How long after the anklet alarm was triggered would he be notified? Someone from the Department of Corrections would have to call. They were monitoring her father, Frasco Dosela, or they were supposed to be.

He reached his unit as his phone rang. He would have sent the call to voice mail, but he saw from the caller ID that his uncle was calling. Luke Forrest was his father's half brother, an FBI field agent and he was also Black Mountain Apache.

Gabe wondered if his uncle's call was personal or business. He climbed into his unit. His wiper blades beat intermittently against the fine, powdery snow that continued to float down onto the windshield like confectioners' sugar. Gabe swiped his finger over the screen, taking the call.

"*Dagot'ee*, Uncle," Gabe said, using the Apache greeting. "What's up?" Gabe flipped the phone call to his unit so he could talk while driving. Then he took off after Selena.

"Chief," said his uncle, using his title instead of his first name. That meant this was a business call. Gabe didn't have a lot of interaction with the Feds. Mostly he dealt with state police and occasionally the district attorney. But these were troubled times, and he had more business than he and his twelve-man force could handle.

His uncle sounded rushed. "Field Agent Walker and I are seeking permission to enter the rez."

"You mean your new partner?" Gabe searched for Selena's box truck. She must be speeding, because she'd vanished like smoke.

"That's right. But I don't think she will be my partner for long. That one is a firecracker. She'll be in DC by June."

Uncle Luke was a tribe member and needed no permission. As a Black Mountain Apache, his uncle could come and go as he wished. But his partner, Cassidy Walker, was not Apache. A white woman, from the Midwest he recalled. Federal agencies needed approval from the tribal council before conducting business on the rez.

"I'll need a reason." Gabe reached the fork to Wolf Canyon. He knew that Selena lived with her family up a side road that veered to the left.

Had she headed home or somewhere else? He didn't know, but he followed his hunch and made the turn toward her house. If her father was the passenger, that would be their likely move.

"I'll fax you the official request. In the meantime, I have information on the crystal meth cooks you've been chasing."

For several years the Mexican cartels had been storing product on the rez to avoid federal jurisdiction. Last fall, Gabe and his men had taken out a mobile meth lab, thanks to the help of Clay. But there were plenty of places to hide on twelve thousand acres.

"Any information that would help narrow the search?"

"Some. Tessay wants a deal."

Arnold Tessay had been a member of the Black Mountain Tribal Council until they'd discovered that he'd had been tipping off the meth cooks whenever the authorities got close. That made Gabe sick, and so did his suspicion that there were other insiders working with the cartels, beyond the Wolf Posse, which was the tribal gang that sold and distributed drugs on their reservation, acted as muscle and took on other distasteful jobs.

"According to Tessay's attorney, the raw product is still on the rez. That syncs with our intel."

"Good," said Gabe. "What am I looking for?"

"Fifty-gallon barrels of liquid. The kind that your brothers Kino and Clay saw down on the border when they were working with the Shadow Wolves and ICE. Ask them to describe them to you. Water station barrels."

"The blue ones?"

"Exactly. We don't know how many. They might be moving them or planning another setup on our reservation."

Gabe tamped down his anger at that second possibility. He couldn't understand how an Apache could ever work with criminals. Scarce jobs or not, there was never a reason to help the drug traffickers use Indian land like some kind of home base. Though his own father had done it. But that was another story.

"The barrel contents, can they freeze?" Gabe asked.

"Yeah. Somewhere below zero, I think. Why?"

"Limits the places they can store them."

"Hmm. I'll find out for sure and get back to you."

"Anything else?" asked Gabe.

"That's it. Except we'd love to find those barrels."

"I'm on it."

Gabe gave a traditional farewell and punched the disconnect button on his steering wheel. He glanced toward the leaden sky. The snow had stopped for now, but he wondered if there would be more. They'd gotten another coating overnight, just enough to make driving interesting, as it always was in January on the rez. Especially for the tourists out of Phoenix who knew next to nothing about driving in snow.

Gabe reached the Doselas' home. He didn't need to head up the drive to see that Selena's box truck was not among the personal vehicles.

After her father's arrest, Selena had taken her father's one box truck and doubled the business in his absence. With both her and her younger sister Mia driving, they managed two routes. When Selena purchased an older box truck, Mia took over her father's truck and a longer route down to Phoenix and back. One year ago Selena had taken a loan for a used flatbed trailer and six-year-old 18-wheeler that the twins, Carla and Paula, took on longer runs. All three trucks were currently missing.

He cursed in Apache, did a one-eighty and headed back toward the town of Black Mountain.

As he drove, he radioed dispatch. Jasmine Grados responded, her smoker's voice better in the afternoon.

"Yes, Chief."

"Anything on the Dosela release?" Maybe he should have stopped to see if Frasco was home, as he should be under the terms of his early release. "Send the closest man to the Doselas' to verify Frasco's return."

"Roger that."

"And all eyes looking for a box truck."

Jasmine picked up on his line of thinking. "You mean Selena's truck or Mia's?"

"Selena's. Mia should be in Phoenix. Anything from DOC?"

Frasco Dosela had been returned to the reservation with the escort of one of Gabe's men, his parole officer and a representative from the Department of Corrections who had fitted him with a radio anklet to monitor his movements.

"Not since Officer Cienega escorted Mr. Dryer off the rez."

"When was that?"

"About ten. Um…logged at ten eighteen, Chief."

He glanced at the dash. It was past noon. Frasco Dosela had better be home on house arrest.

Gabe was already hitting the gas.

"Anything going on?" he asked, checking on the day's activities.

"One thing. Officer Chee isn't in yet."

His patrolman had been on the force for less than a year, was green as grass, inexperienced, lacked confidence but he was punctual.

Gabe lifted the radio. "You call him?"

"Yes, Chief. Home and mobile. No answer."

"Send a unit."

"Ten-four."

"Anything else?" Gabe asked.

"Pretty quiet."

"All right. Keep me posted on Chee. Out."

Wouldn't be the first time someone missed a shift. Still, it wasn't like him, and Gabe had that uncomfortable sensation that often preceded bad news. It sort of felt like there was a cold spot in his gut. He had that numbness now, though whether over his officer's absence or Selena's little mystery passenger he was not sure.

Gabe knew Selena's route as well as he knew his own. The delivery of fresh baked goods took her around the entire 113-mile loop through the reservation and usually before ten in the morning.

She should have been done and home by now.

"Where you going, Selena?"

Chapter Three

"Who are we meeting?" Selena asked her father as she hunched over the wheel of her box truck, her eyes flashing to the side mirrors as she periodically searched for Gabe.

"Escalanti's men. They're at the meth lab with a small delivery. Dryer, too."

Matthew Dryer was the man from the Department of Corrections who was supposed to have put a tamper-proof anklet on her father. Instead, Dryer had given him the easy-on, easy-off model. Not standard issue.

Her father continued with the plan as Selena kept one hand on the wheel and the other clenched in her hair. How could this be happening?

"Eventually they need a regular run. Bring a few barrels of chemicals to the meth lab each week for production. Then transport the finished product from the lab down to Phoenix."

"We can't transport off the rez."

The moment they rolled one tire off the reservation, they both lost their protected status as members of the Black Mountain Apache Tribe. Any crime they committed could be tried in state or federal court instead of in their own tribal judicial courts.

"Escalanti doesn't give a damn about our protected status. Only his."

Escalanti, the new leader of the Wolf Posse, had a reputation for never leaving the reservation. In fact, he rarely left the shabby house they called headquarters.

"So that guy from the Department of Corrections is Raggar's man?"

Her father hesitated. "Yup."

Her dad was an excellent liar, but he had that little tell, the hesitation before answering. Selena released her hair and put both hands on the wheel. So, who was Dryer really?

"Don't you think, with Gabe Cosen sniffing around, we should try this another time?"

"It's all arranged. And it's a big reservation. Besides, he won't follow off the reservation."

"He might. Or he might be waiting for us when we come back."

"You can drop me. You'll be alone. Stop worrying. You're like an old woman."

This just got better and better. She knew that her father had been approached in prison by the leader of the Raggar crime family, who was managing the business nicely from federal prison. Better access to criminals, she supposed.

"And what happens if we turn around, find Gabe and tell him everything?"

"Gabe arrests me and probably you. Escalanti tells his people down across the border that we can't deliver the product and they send killers to our home. Plus Raggar won't get the delivery and he'll be after us, too."

Selena had had this pressed-to-the-wall feeling since her father returned home this morning. It felt as if someone was kneeling on her chest.

"Where are we going, exactly?"

Her father directed her to Sammy Leekela's junkyard off Route 60, just shy of the border of their sovereign land.

Sammy Leekela had a part for everything stockpiled on his four-acre lot that was ringed by rusting fencing to keep out the scavengers of the animal and human variety.

"Here? They're cooking meth here?" she asked.

"Perfect place. Off the beaten path but close to Route 60. Lots of land. Fenced. Nothing to kill with the fumes."

"I thought it was a *mobile* meth lab," she said.

She paused at the rusty gate. Usually, if she needed a part, she went to the office. But today the gate receded the instant she pulled into the drive. Because they were expected.

She shivered with dread. Right now her father had broken parole and she had helped him. But if she continued, she'd be a drug trafficker, just like her father.

If she didn't, they'd kill her family.

"Let's go," he said.

She touched the gas and they lurched forward. Her father shot her an impatient look as they rolled in. Sammy gave them a friendly wave and closed the gate, then retreated to his office. Her father directed her to a series of abandoned tractor trailer beds. Some were rusty and dented. But now she noticed one that had an unusual addition—a stovepipe. The trailer in question sat tucked between several others, further hiding it from detection. The only other clue was the number of footprints and tire tracks in the snow. That trailer was getting a lot of foot traffic.

She couldn't believe it.

"I bought our used flatbed here. I still owe Sammy almost nine thousand dollars," said Selena, her indignation rising.

"You want me to ask for a discount?" asked her father.

"No. I do not. I want to go home."

"And we will, right after we drive to Phoenix and back."

"That's six hours, you know?"

Frasco shrugged. "I brought sandwiches."

As her father had warned, Department of Corrections officer Matt Dryer was there to meet them. He was the only one they saw. He left the center trailer carrying a blue plastic tub in two hands.

"That's it?" asked Selena. "You don't need a truck for that."

"First run. Only a few hundred thousand."

"Dollars?" she squeaked looking at the innocuous plastic storage tub.

Selena wondered how many years in prison that would translate to. Her father had enlisted Selena to make the runs because it was too dangerous for him to be out of the house so much and because she refused to involve Mia in this.

"You know there's no end to it," Selena said. "Once we start, they won't let us quit."

"Hush up now," said her father and climbed out to greet the crooked DOC officer. He wasn't even supposed to be on the reservation without an escort. No federal official was. Gabe had taught her that.

"You all set?" asked Dryer.

Frasco grabbed one side of the tub and the two disappeared from sight. Selena heard the truck doors open, close and lock. The drugs were now in her truck. She thought she might throw up.

Her father climbed in and moved to the center seat to make room for her new copilot. How much was Dryer getting to mix them up in this?

She thought of her siblings and put the truck in gear. They pulled out and had not gone a quarter mile when some idiot roared out of a blind drive right in front of them.

Selena's heart rate doubled as she hit the brakes and narrowly missed broadsiding the other vehicle. The original color of the pickup before her was impossible to determine, as it had been rebuilt entirely of salvage, making it look like the Frankenstein of trucks.

Her initial blast of adrenaline receded, to be replaced by a prickling warning as her brain reengaged, signaling her that this was not coincidence. That truck had cut her off on purpose.

Their passenger must have reached the same conclusion because he shouted.

"Reverse it," yelled Dryer and pulled a pistol from beneath his coat.

She reached for the gearshift as she gaped at this new threat and saw that the driver of the pickup was wearing a mask so that he looked like a man with a dark goatee, glasses and a black rubber hat.

The masked man was out of his truck. He pressed the rifle stock to his shoulder and aimed the business end at Dryer.

Selena had the truck in Reverse and moved her foot to the gas, but a second truck blocked her escape, pulling up fast and skidding to a halt at an angle behind her.

"Out!" yelled the masked gunman now advancing past his pickup to her right front fender and pointing his rifle at Dryer as he advanced.

Dryer threw open the door and used it as a brace to take aim with a pistol. Their attacker and Dryer both fired their weapons. Her passenger's side window exploded and Dryer dropped to the ground in a shower of shattered glass. Selena glanced to the side mirrors and saw a second gunman approaching from the rear along her side of the truck as the masked gunman continued forward at a trot toward the place where Dryer had disappeared.

Her father lifted his hands in surrender.

"Out!" ordered the masked gunman, who now stood beside the open passenger door. Selena stared at the face that was not masked. She didn't know which was more frightening, his rifle, aimed at her or the fact that he did not try to hide his identity. She had seen him before but did not know him.

A glance across the wide seat showed that Dryer was nowhere in sight.

Frasco slid across the seat and dropped to the ground as the masked attacker retreated a step. Selena heard the crunch of glass as she followed her father, sliding away from the unmasked attacker, across the warm vinyl and out into the cold air.

Dryer lay in a heap amid the shards of glass, looking as if he was just sleeping. Where was the blood?

"Move away from the truck," the masked man said.

Something about his voice sounded familiar. She looked at his hands as they gripped the rifle, brown finger ready on the trigger. His skin was the same color as hers. Then she looked past the mask to the only thing she could see. His dark brown eyes. Also familiar. She glanced back to the yard of Leekela's place. Sammy had a younger brother who had a build just like this and he was rumored to be an addict. Jason Leekela, she thought.

He came forward, rifle barrel swinging from her to her father. Her dad dropped and reached for Dryer's pistol.

"No!" she shouted, drawing the man's attention for just a second.

Then he swung the rifle around and struck her father with the wooden stock. Her father dropped on top of Dryer. Dryer's pistol skittered on the icy pavement to within inches of her boot.

She did not make a move to touch it.

"Smart girl. Always were smart, Selena," said the masked gunman.

Did he know her, too?

The second gunman had vanished. Was he waiting at the rear of the truck?

The masked gunman pointed the rifle barrel at the pistol at her feet.

"Kick that over here."

She did and he retrieved it, tucking the weapon in the pocket of his ragged army-green jacket. She was sure now. She'd seen him in that jacket in town, looking gaunt, and his eyes had been bloodshot then, too. His brother's dark double, the family's cross to bear. She'd even felt sorry for him, but that was before he pointed a gun at her.

"Now, open the truck." He motioned her to walk before him. Would he shoot her?

The fifty-foot walk was the longest of her life.

"Do you know what you're doing?" she asked.

"Do you?" he replied.

"Jason, what is Sammy going to say when he finds out his own brother is robbing his shipment?"

She heard him halt and turned to glance back at him. The rifle barrel dipped.

"How did you...? Never mind. He won't find out." His shoulders heaved as he released a whine. "Damn it, Selena. I didn't want to have to kill you."

Chapter Four

Selena's skin went cold. Not from the snow that pelted her in tiny stinging droplets, but from deep inside as she realized that Jason was just sick and wounded and crazy enough to kill her.

"Why don't we go see your brother?"

"No!" he shouted. "He's never going to know about this. He can't. Now get going."

They reached the loading doors where the second gunman waited. She remembered seeing him at Sammy's junkyard but could not recall his name. So Sammy's brother and employee had decided to steal from him, but off grounds. Did they really think Sammy would not figure this out?

"Hurry up," said the junkyard man, adding a second rifle to Jason's, and this one was aimed at her face.

"Open the truck," ordered Jason.

Her mind grasped and rejected several ideas as she stepped up onto the fender, but instead of an escape plan it provided the name of the second gunman. Oscar Hill. Selena lifted the latch that released the lock. Maybe they would just take the tub and leave her. She opened one door. Maybe they would kill her the minute they had the shipment.

Jason peered inside. "Where is it?"

That's when Selena saw it, a white SUV, no lights, closing fast.

Gabe.

GABE CRESTED THE rise and spotted a battered pickup parked close to the rear of Selena's box truck. The side door of her truck was open and something lay on the ground on the passenger side. A second pickup had the box truck pinned from the front. Selena was in the process of opening one of the two hind doors as he closed the distance. Between her and the pickup, stood two armed men.

In emergencies Gabe sank into a kind of animal brain, acting and flowing with the situation. But not this time. This time his heart thumped and his skin tingled with a feeling close to panic, because the men pointed their weapons at Selena.

One wore some kind of full head mask and both held rifles at the ready.

Selena glanced at him, said something to the gunmen and stepped into the truck's compartment and out of sight.

Good move, Selena, he thought, hoping she would think to lie flat because that truck door would afford little protection from bullets.

As the distance diminished he saw that the pile of something beside the open door was most definitely a body, possibly two. He radioed for backup, shouting the code for a shooting and the location. Then he hit the brakes and turned the wheel so his SUV formed a barrier between him and the riflemen.

"Police. Drop your weapons," he shouted.

The gunmen spun and raised their weapons at the same time the truck door swung open, sending the masked man staggering forward. Selena, evening the odds, he realized.

Gabe fired at the other man, taking him down. Selena now stood on the gate with a tire iron in her hand. He couldn't shoot the second gunman without possibly hitting her. The second shooter recovered his footing and his grip on his rifle. Selena swung the iron down, hitting the barrel of his rifle so that it dropped. The shooter grabbed Selena by her long, loose hair, dragging her down. The tire iron clattered to the pavement as Selena fell against her captor.

"Let her go," ordered Gabe.

"He has a pistol," shouted Selena.

Her masked gunman gave her a shake and she gripped the hand that threaded into her hair with both of hers.

"Drop your gun or I kill her," said her captor.

"Jason Leekela, you let me go before your brother finds out about this!"

Gabe knew Jason. He had arrested him more than once for possession.

"Let her go, Jason."

But he didn't. Instead he reached in his pocket and drew the pistol she had warned him about. Selena kicked at him. Jason staggered and Selena fell hard to her knees giving Gabe a clear shot. Jason lifted the pistol toward Gabe. Gabe fired.

Jason Leekela fell.

He landed facedown. Selena scuttled backward like a crab as Gabe came forward at a run. Selena sat on the icy road, knees drawn up to her chest.

Thank God she was safe, because he was going to kill her.

She was on her feet an instant later, throwing herself into his arms, burying her face in his coat. The familiar pull of attraction flared as her scent rose up in the icy air, like springtime in January. Still lavender, he realized. The scent was so familiar and still intoxicating, making him ache down low and deep. He drew her in, allowing himself one more full breath and the pleasure of having her arms around him again. In one hand he held Selena. In the other he held his gun.

He tried to pull her away, but she clung.

"Selena. You have to let go."

She did. Stepping back, her cheeks wet with tears. "I'm sorry."

That wasn't going to do it. He had a sinking feeling that she'd crossed a line from which he couldn't rescue her. He swallowed the lump that rose as he looked down at her forlorn, beautiful face. Why couldn't he get over her? Why?

"Who is up front?" he asked.

"My dad and Matt Dryer. He shot Dryer and hit Dad really hard with his gun stock."

"Dryer? The guy from DOC?"

Selena nodded. He ordered her to stand back by his

vehicle, knowing he should cuff her, search her for weapons. But Gabe just couldn't bring himself to do it. Instead, he retrieved the rifles and locked them in the rear of his unit. Then he returned to the gunman.

His pulse check told him he'd just killed two men. He glanced back at Selena who watched with wide eyes as she twisted one hand with the other.

"Dead," he reported and then went to check on Dryer and Dosela.

Frasco had struggled to a sitting position. He had a gash across the top of his head, sending a steady stream of blood down his forehead. He blinked up at Gabe and wiped his eyes. Dryer lay facedown in broken glass.

He pointed at Frasco. "You armed?"

"No, sir," said Frasco.

"Step back."

Frasco struggled to his feet, using the door to steady himself.

"On the ground," Gabe ordered Frasco. "Facedown. Don't move until I tell you."

Frasco stretched out, using his arms to keep his head off the pavement. Gabe hated to do this to her father, but it was that or frisk and cuff him.

"How'd you find us?" asked Frasco.

"You were spotted on Route 60. Then I saw the tracks on the turn."

If not for the fresh snow, he might have missed them and Selena might be dead. That thought made him cold all over. Gabe moved to check Dryer.

"What happened to him?" asked Gabe, motioning to the DOC officer.

"They shot him in the chest is what."

Gabe did a visual and saw no wound. Then he opened Dryer's jacket and tore open his shirt, sending buttons flying in all directions. What he found next surprised him. Dryer had been wearing body armor and the shot that should have killed him had been stopped by the vest.

Dryer groaned and his eyes fluttered open. Gabe had never caught a bullet in his vest, but understood it hurt like hell. Dryer winced. Gabe couldn't tell if he was fully conscious.

Gabe got right to the point. "Mr. Dryer. Frasco Dosela. You are both under arrest."

"That's what you think," mumbled Frasco. Then it almost sounded as if he laughed.

Gabe could not believe he was arresting Frasco Dosela again and on the day of his early release. He knew that his next arrest would likely be Selena and his heart squeezed in pain. This was the second time she had put him in this kind of position.

Chapter Five

His second in command, Detective Randall Juris, was the first on the scene followed closely by Gabe's youngest brother, Kino. Both ran without lights or sirens.

Juris pulled to a stop and exited his unit with gun drawn.

"Clear," said Gabe, and Juris holstered his weapon.

The detective paused at the rear of the truck and massaged his neck with one hand as he regarded the two dead bodies. Then he glanced to Gabe. Juris was in his midforties and had worked as an extra in several Western movies. His rugged good looks and classic Indian features had softened with age and the expansion of his middle, so he now seemed a little too top-heavy to ride a horse. As a detective, he no longer wore the gray shirt and charcoal trousers of a patrolman. Today he was in jeans, boots and a fleece-lined denim jacket.

"Where you want me?" he asked.

"Take him." He motioned toward Frasco Dosela.

Juris ordered the bleeding, older Dosela up and he made it to the front fender of the box truck unassisted. Juris searched him, cuffed Dosela's hands before him and led him to the detective's unit. Juris retrieved a towel from his trunk and offered it to Dosela with a warning.

"Don't bleed on my upholstery," he cautioned, as he put him in the backseat.

Dosela pressed the towel to his bleeding head with both hands.

Kino left his unit and stopped beside Selena. Kino was nine years Gabe's junior, newly married to a Salt River woman and was a two-year veteran of the force, so he still wore the patrolman's uniform, including the charcoal-gray jacket that had the tribal seal on one shoulder and the police patch on the other. Unlike Gabe, Kino wore his hair long and tied back with red cloth as an homage to their ancestry. But they shared above-average size, athletic frames and a calling to serve their people through law enforcement. Kino's ready smile was absent today as he looked to his chief for direction.

"Keep an eye on this one," Gabe motioned to Dryer. "Tell me if he stops breathing or comes around. And radio in an all clear."

"Ambulance?" asked Kino.

"Take too long. We'll transport."

Kino took over the watch beside Dryer.

Gabe took hold of Selena's elbow and led her to the front of her truck. Before he could question Selena, Juris reported that he had found two quart-size plastic baggies that appeared to contain crystal methamphetamine.

Gabe's heart sank still further at this news. Drugs. Selena was transporting drugs in her box truck. And she was driving. He glanced to Selena and met her gaze.

She dropped her chin. He'd never seen anyone look more guilty in his life.

He spoke to Juris but never took his eyes off Selena. "Thank you. Give us a minute, please."

Juris retreated.

"Selena?"

She reached for him and he stepped back, widening the space between them. She wasn't going to grab his weapon or pull some other stunt. He needed to start treating her as any other suspect. But he couldn't. Not Selena.

He felt sick to his stomach.

Her eyes flashed back and forth, reminding him of a cornered animal. He noted the speed of her breathing and lifted a brow in worry.

Finally she spoke, the words bursting forth in a harsh whisper. "You have to send Kino to my house. Someone." She glanced about again. "Someone you can trust. Please, Gabe."

Gabe could almost feel Selena's panic. Her entire body trembled as she spoke.

"Please. Send someone to protect my family. Right now."

"Protect them from what?"

She lifted her hands, gesturing wildly. "I don't know. More gunmen. My dad said that if we didn't do this, they'd hurt us. Gabe, please, if they find out you stopped us, they might…might…" She pressed her hand to her mouth as her eyes went wide with horror. She dragged her hand clear. "Tomas is in school. They might go there. Oh, Gabe. Help them."

"Slow down, now." He tried and failed to resist the urge to place a hand on her shoulder. She trembled beneath his touch, seemingly frightened to death. "Who threatened you?"

"I don't know!" She clamped a hand over her mouth again, then let it slip. "Someone. My dad knows. Some Mexican gang. And Escalanti. He mentioned someone… Escalanti is his name. They need Apache transportation on the rez and we have to bring barrels. Some kind of barrels."

Gabe's mind flashed to his uncle's request that he search for blue fifty-gallon drums.

"What kind of barrels?"

Selena threw up her hands. "What difference does it make? They might be headed there right now."

"Selena, if you were threatened, why didn't you call me?"

She slapped a hand over her eyes. "Because I didn't want them to kill you, too." She dropped her hand and gave him a beseeching look. "Please, Gabe. Send someone!"

He lifted the radio he kept on his hip. Selena batted at his hand and he retreated another step.

"Not the radio! They listen. Mr. Dryer said so to my father."

Gabe lowered the handset. "I already used it to call for backup and signal the all clear."

"Did you mention our names or Mr. Dryer's?" asked Selena.

"No."

"Please don't."

He clipped the radio back to his belt. Then he called Juris. The detective appeared almost immediately. "Call Officer Cienega and tell him to go out to Selena's place in our unmarked unit. Don't park where he can be seen but keep an eye on her family. Then send the closest unit to the high school. No radio contact. Tell them to use cell phones only. Finally get two units at each end of this road. No traffic in."

"I'm on it." Juris reversed course.

Selena's shoulders sagged. "Thank you."

He tried to ignore her watering eyes as he led her back to his vehicle.

"You carrying a weapon, Selena?"

She gave him a horrified look. "No."

"I have to check." He took no pleasure in patting her down. He had spent more nights than he cared to remember trying to figure how to get his hands on Selena. This had never been one of the possibilities. She was clean, as she had said.

He opened the door and she slipped in. He knew he should read Selena her rights, but he just could not summon the will.

"I'm under arrest. Aren't I?"

He gave her a grim look. "Not yet. Wait here."

He closed the door, knowing she now had no choice but to stay put. She was locked in behind the cage that separated his front and backseats, and the doors did not open from the inside.

Through the windshield, Selena cast Gabe a long look that seemed like regret.

Kino called to him.

"He's waking up."

Gabe headed over to the prison official.

Dryer now sat up, shivering in the thin nylon DOC windbreaker. Black Mountain had four seasons, something the rest of the Arizona residents couldn't seem to remember. The wind made his pale skin blotchy and pink as a strawberry. His light blond hair had been clipped in a stylish cut, but strands of feathery hair now fell over his forehead. The man was muscular and fit, too fit for a guy who pushed paper for a living. But that wasn't his only job, Gabe thought. He also arranged transportation from manufacturing to distribution. A bit of a drug-family middleman, Gabe thought.

"You frisk him?" he asked Kino.

"No. Not yet. He's just coming around."

Dryer still seemed dazed, judging from his out-of-focus stare. Blue eyes, Gabe realized. He looked like a weatherman or TV personality and stood out here like an albino puppy.

Gabe snapped the cuffs on him. Then he and Kino assisted Dryer to his feet. The man swayed.

Gabe patted him down, beginning with his shoulders. He quickly found an empty shoulder holster and a hip holster that was not empty. He relieved Dryer of his phone and an automatic pistol with a sixteen-round clip, tucking the weapon in the back of his waistband. Gabe suspected that the gun Jason Leekela had brandished belonged to this man.

"Any more weapons?" he asked Dryer.

Dryer groaned.

Gabe's search reached his hips.

"You got anything sharp in your pockets?"

"No."

"Where's your ID?" asked Kino.

Dryer snorted in a humorless laugh.

"I don't carry ID when I'm working undercover," said Dryer.

Gabe's eyes narrowed. Any federal operations on his reservation had to be cleared with his office. Kino looked to Gabe for direction, their gaze meeting for an instant before Gabe turned back to Dryer.

"Who are you?" Gabe asked.

"I'm with DOJ."

Department of Justice. But of course he had nothing to back up his claim.

"Boy, you better not be," said Gabe.

"Well, I am."

Gabe stared at Dryer, who now stood with his hands cuffed behind his back. His jacket and shirt dangled open, revealing his body armor and the empty holsters.

"You hear me?" said Dryer. "I'm a special agent."

Juris joined them, standing beside Kino to watch the unfolding developments.

"You believe him?" asked Juris.

"Easy to check."

"Does Dosela know?" Juris asked Dryer.

"I sure hope so. I recruited him."

"What about Selena?" asked Gabe.

Dryer gave him an odd look. "She doesn't know I'm DOJ. Too much risk."

"For you or her?" asked Gabe.

Dryer shrugged. "Less who know the better." He gave the three tribal officers a gloomy look.

"You going to tell her? Or should I?" asked Gabe.

"Doesn't matter. I got to tell her something." Dryer looked toward Selena and then he directed his attention to Gabe. "She's in because her dad told her that they'll kill their family if she didn't drive."

"Another lie?" asked Gabe.

"That one is true. These guys are animals."

Gabe resisted the urge to shove Dryer up against the car for dragging Selena into this.

Instead of falling in with criminals, Selena seemed to have done something more dangerous. She had fallen in with their hunters.

He glanced back at the vehicle where she waited and met her gaze. The urge to go to her was so strong he had to brace against it.

Gabe lifted the radio from his hip.

"No. No. You can't use the radio or I'm made. Nobody can know about this." Dryer scanned the scene. "Tell your guys to block traffic. A miracle no one has been by yet."

Not really, thought Gabe. He already had a man stopping traffic at both ends of this circular drive from Route 60. This little side road led only to the junkyard and then back to the highway. Nobody was coming down this road unless it was from the junkyard some half mile beyond his unit. The miracle was that Gabe had seen the box truck's tracks at the first turnoff from the highway.

"Hey, did you call an ambulance?"

"It's in Black Mountain. Take another thirty or forty minutes," said Juris. "We can transport you and Frasco to the medical center. Be quicker."

"What did you call in over the radio?"

"Ten seventy-one," said Gabe.

"Shooting," said Dryer. "That's okay. We have to make something up. But we have to get the truck out of here. Sammy Leekela cannot see this robbery attempt and we still got to make the delivery," said Dryer and swore. "Two years' work."

Gabe wasn't moved. Now he was pissed. "Next time, maybe tell us you're operating on our land."

"Yeah, right." Dryer lifted his joined wrists. "Cuffs."

"Stay on until I have confirmation." He wanted to punch him for involving Selena in this. "Who is your supervisor?"

Dryer provided the name and number. Gabe saw Dryer seated in the rear of his brother's unit but left the door open. Then he gave Kino the information Dryer had provided.

"Use your phone to call Yepa," he said, referring to his personal assistant. "Don't use the radio. Ask her to call DOJ and then ask for George Hayes." That was the name of the supervisor Dryer had given them. "Tell her not to mention the call to anyone. If Hayes exists, see if he's got an agent named Dryer on our land and tell him to call me directly or his boy is going into a jail cell."

Kino stepped away to make the call. In his absence, Juris and Dryer practiced staring unblinkingly at each other and Gabe tried unsuccessfully to keep from glancing at Selena.

His brother returned with an expression that told him all he needed to know. "Yepa spoke to Hayes, said he was rude, furious and demanded his agent's immediate release."

Juris's mouth twitched. "I guess that's a yes."

"Did you tell her about the shooting?"

"No, Chief."

Gabe's phone buzzed and he fielded an angry call from Dryer's supervisor. Gabe told Hayes his agent was under arrest, refused to let him go, hung up on Hayes and then ignored his second call.

"Turn him loose," Gabe said to Juris who removed the cuffs from Dryer's wrists.

"You going to let me go?" asked Dryer.

Gabe shook his head.

Dryer snorted in annoyance. "We need to get out of here now."

"Why's that?" asked Juris.

"We have to make a delivery. All of us. If we aren't all three in Phoenix in about three hours this operation is blown."

Juris motioned to the bodies lying in the road. "Don't you think this might be an issue?"

"I can have a team clean this up," said Dryer.

Gabe shook his head. "No."

"We can save this operation. But we have to move now."

"Is that the operation that I know nothing about that endangers two members of my tribe?" asked Gabe.

Juris and Gabe exchanged a look and Juris gave a

halfhearted shrug, leaving the decision about what to do up to his chief.

"We're bringing Frasco in. And you're coming, too," Gabe said to Dryer.

"No. You are going to let him and the girl go with me. I gotta make a call," he added.

"Who?"

"My contact who works with the distributor."

"Name," said Gabe.

He provided it, but it meant nothing to Gabe.

Dryer explained the basics. DOJ had the location of the meth lab on Black Mountain and Dryer would tell them where it was, but only if Gabe let him go. Gabe needed to know where the drugs were being received to figure out their distribution operation. Specifically where they were keeping the ingredients for production.

Gabe thought he could find the tractor trailer bed now functioning as a meth lab unassisted and from there he might locate the blue barrels. But it would be faster with the help of DOJ.

"Listen," Dryer continued. "I have the lab and I have the American supplier, Cesaro Raggar. But we want to shut down distribution *and* production. So far all Raggar's orders come through Nota. But we don't know who is delivering messages from the Mexicans to Escalanti. Nota is Escalanti's man. But I need time to connect Escalanti to the operation and find the Mexican's go-between."

"Manny Escalanti?" asked Juris, naming the head of the Wolf Posse.

Dryer nodded.

Selena had mentioned Escalanti a few minutes ago. She was terrified of him and with good reason. Manny Escalanti had become the leader of the Wolf Posse after the murder of his predecessor, Rubin Fox. Nota was a known gang member. Gabe knew the posse sold the weed they got from Mexico. He did *not* know that the gang took orders from a Mexican cartel or that they were producing methamphetamine.

Gabe returned Dryer's phone and listened while Dryer placed a call.

"Listen, we're going to be late." A pause. "Icy roads is all. Have to put chains on the tires." Another pause. "Chains. That's what they use." Dryer listened. "No, there's snow. Fourteen thousand feet, remember? It's a frozen wasteland up here." A pause and then. "Sure. I'll be careful." Dryer disconnected and tucked away his phone.

Juris gave his captain a look. "You going to let the Doselas do this? They leave the rez and we can't protect them."

Gabe didn't like that one little bit.

"Clearly someone knows your route," Gabe jerked his thumb to the back of the truck where the two bodies had been placed.

"You ID them?" asked Dryer.

Gabe provided the name of the known gunman.

Dryer nodded. "Oh, yeah. That figures. That's the junkie brother of the guy who runs the yard. Sammy must have tipped him off somehow."

"That where the lab is, on Leekela's place?" asked Juris.

"Yes. In a tractor trailer. Leekela is paid to look the other way. His brother must have found the lab and decided to make a few bucks."

"What exactly is your operation and how does it involve the Doselas?"

"It's the first delivery. If we make it, then they plan to put Frasco's family in charge of transportation, bringing the chemicals to the lab and the product from the lab. We'll have the precursor's location. But we pull a no-show in Phoenix, then these rats will scurry back into their holes. One of those holes is likely on your reservation, Chief. And it's full of fifty-gallon barrels of precursor. Enough to supply Raggar's customers with meth for years. This is big, Chief. I'm ordering you to release the box truck and the Doselas to me immediately."

Dryer's order seemed the last straw for Detective Juris. He wheeled on Dryer, aiming a finger at him like a gun as he spoke to his chief.

"He doesn't call the shots here."

Gabe lifted a hand in conciliation. "Let's take it easy."

But Juris was past that. "He can't set up a sting operation on our reservation without letting us know."

"See, now that's the trouble," said Dryer. "Every time we let you know anything, they move the operation."

"That was before we got Tessay," said Gabe.

"You got that first lab up on Nosie's land thanks to your brother Clay. But not the second mobile meth lab on the Leekela place," said Dryer.

That was true.

"The precursor? Any leads?" asked Dryer.

"I found you," said Gabe.

Dryer huffed. "An undercover federal agent. Not stellar. You can detain me, but I have immunity."

"Don't you always," said Juris, regaining his control and his stoic expression.

Dryer shrugged. "Bottom line, you haven't found that second mobile meth lab or the precursor."

"It's twelve thousand acres," said Juris.

Dryer ignored Juris and directed his attention to Gabe. Gabe knew what Dryer implied—someone was informing the cartel of their movements. Someone on the inside.

Chapter Six

The cold spot in Gabe's stomach was gone, replaced by a solid pain that shot across his middle. It felt like that bucking strap they used in the rodeo to make the horses kick.

"You think my department has a leak."

"Leak? You have a damned river. Tessay isn't the only one here on Raggar's payroll."

"Who?"

Dryer rubbed his neck. "Escalanti is the only one we're sure of." He waved a hand at the highway. "Roadblock?"

Gabe turned to Kino. "Put the cuffs back on him."

Kino moved to comply, looking much more content.

Dryer held up his hands, talking fast, trying to get it out before someone drove past and saw Selena's truck. "All right. I'll tell you. But only you. If you're the ones, we're screwed anyway."

"What *ones*?"

"There's a reason we haven't sought permission this time." Dryer rubbed his neck. "We don't know who it is. What we do know is that when there is a joint operation, they know. Nota bragged about it."

Gabe felt sick. When he had arrested Arnold Tessay, he thought he had found the one traitor here. Had that been naive?

"It's back to business, here on Black Mountain," said Dryer. "But with only one meth lab they aren't meeting supply demands. They need to expand. But since Tessay's arrest, they have moved the precursor stores twice. Just in case Tessay rolls, they're moving it again. I don't know when or where. But not here. You're too much of a pain in their asses, Chief. I hear that you've even been close a few times. They've been debating if they should move operations or just kill you."

Gabe glanced at Kino and saw him go white.

"Lucky you," said Dryer. "They're moving. Nota says it will be to Salt River Reservation."

"I have to notify my tribal council of your presence here and alert the authorities on Salt River," said Gabe.

"And he has to go. I'll be glad to show him off our sovereign lands personally," said Juris pointing at Dryer.

Dryer threw up his hands. "You need help. Admit it."

"Not your kind of help," said Juris.

"You telling me the federal authorities don't have rights to investigate federal crimes on federal land?"

"They do," said Gabe. "With our knowledge. The FBI uses the channels we established. DOJ needs to do the same."

Dryer made a face. "You think I'm alone up here? I'm not. This is a joint operation."

In spite of the doubts he felt, Gabe kept his poker face.

"You get a call about those barrels?" asked Dryer.

He had. From his uncle Luke. Gabe felt sick. Had Luke been playing him? Was it true that an Indian who worked for the Feds wasn't Indian anymore?

Gabe had aspirations to become a field agent. But not if it meant betraying his people.

"The FBI is aware of our investigation."

And yet his uncle had not notified him. Was that because Gabe was also a suspect? Frasco was back trafficking and Gabe had once been engaged to Frasco's daughter. Guilt by association. Gabe wondered.

"Before you get all pissy, your uncle doesn't know about me. It's above his pay grade."

Because his uncle was Black Mountain Apache and so could not totally be trusted? Gabe narrowed his eyes. The fury sparked, burning his carefully cultivated control.

"He should have been informed," said Gabe.

Kino's brows lifted, recognizing the potential for danger in Gabe's quiet tone.

"He's Apache. You are thick as thieves up here. Everyone is somebody's cousin. His department thought it best to keep him out of the loop. Not my call. We've been coordinating with his supervisor and his partner."

"Cassidy Walker?"

"Right."

Cassidy Walker, the one his uncle said had ambitions to transfer to DC. Gabe smelled a rat all right, but not in the Apache hierarchy.

"She's running this. Senior man, even though she's a woman."

"So you suspected my uncle?" he said.

"Seemed logical."

"Because he's Indian."

"Black Mountain Apache. Brother to a known drug trafficker."

Dryer was referring now to Gabe's father. He had been a convicted felon when he had been murdered by a trafficker who went by the name The Viper.

"My uncle went through FBI screening. He's clean."

"He's related to people involved with this case, just like your big brother, the tribal councilor."

"Clyne? You suspect Clyne? He's incorruptible."

"Everyone's corruptible, Chief. Your dad. Your tribal council...your big brother...*you*. Hey," he said his voice full of forced enthusiasm. "You back to seeing Frasco's daughter?"

Gabe was stunned speechless. How would Dryer know that he'd once seen Selena?

"I hear you two spent some quality time together. But be careful. You know the apple doesn't fall far from the tree."

Gabe spun him with one hand and hit Dryer squarely across the jaw. The DOJ field agent dropped like a stone. It took both Kino and Detective Juris to drag Gabe back. It was only after the red haze had cleared that he realized he had just struck a federal officer.

Gabe watched Dryer shake off the blow as Gabe tried to decide if he should arrest him, cooperate with his investigation or hit him again.

Dryer struggled to his feet. Neither Juris nor Kino lifted a hand to help him.

"I wish I'd done that," said Juris.

Dryer rubbed his jaw. "That was worse than getting shot," he said.

Gabe glanced at Selena, feeling embarrassed now for his outburst. How much could she hear back there through the raised windows?

She met his gaze and tried to exit the unit but found the doors locked from the outside. She was trapped. Gabe lifted a hand and she flopped back in the seat, clearly impatient with her captivity. But if what Dryer said was true, arresting her was at least a way to keep her safe.

Gabe turned to Dryer. "Do you want to press charges?"

Dryer cocked his head. "Against you?" He snorted. "No."

It was hard, but Gabe thanked him and Dryer offered his hand. The handshake was brief and halfhearted.

"Okay," said Dryer, as if getting back to business. "No comments about Selena. Got it. But that box truck. It can't be mentioned in your reports or on the radio. I know Escalanti listens to the police scanner. So, no mention of the truck, the Doselas or me."

Gabe's gaze flicked to the DOJ agent, wishing he could put him in a gag as well as handcuffs. "If there's no box truck, why did I shoot Jason Leekela and an unknown gunman again?"

"I don't know…brandishing a weapon. Shooting at you."

"So you want me to lie."

"I want you to keep a lid on the undercover operation."

"In exchange for full disclosure," said Gabe.

Dryer considered his offer. Then qualified. "To you, only. Not to the council."

"I could get fired for doing that."

"And you could catch these guys if you do what I'm telling you."

Gabe didn't like being told what to do by outsiders.

"My brother and first officer here already know."

"That's all they know from here forward, and you keep them quiet."

Both his men put their hands on their hips, clearly not liking that plan.

"Deal?" Dryer offered his hand.

Gabe thought of all the deals offered by white men to Indians and grimaced. This one didn't seem any better.

Chapter Seven

"No deal," said Gabe, and turned toward his unit and Selena.

"Oh, you're going to blow this whole operation."

Gabe kept walking.

"And you're going to get Selena killed."

Gabe stopped walking.

He turned back to Dryer, feeling trapped and angry and afraid for the first time in many years.

"You brought this here," said Gabe.

"I brought an investigation. The rest was already here."

He was right and that pissed Gabe off.

"Updates daily," said Gabe. "And you tell Selena who you are."

Dryer grinned, knowing he had won. "Sure. Sure. Mind if I release Frasco? I got to clean up his face, if I can."

"He needs a stitch or two," said Juris.

"Use snow," said Kino. "Helps with the swelling."

Dryer walked between Kino and Juris to the unit where Frasco waited.

Juris helped Frasco up out of the rear seat. Frasco still held the towel to his face.

"How you going to explain that?" asked Gabe.

Dryer glanced at Frasco. "Fell on the ice. I just told them we had to use chains."

Gabe left the men and returned to his SUV where Selena waited. He opened the rear door. Selena stepped through the gap.

"Are they safe?" she asked.

Her family, of course. They were always her first concern.

"I have units on-site."

She blew out a breath and her features momentarily relaxed.

"Thank you," she whispered.

Selena had every quality he admired in a woman. She worked hard, cared for her family, was funny, gracious and kind. But he better than most understood that a family's reputation was just as important as an individual's. Maybe more important here than elsewhere. There was a reason Apache gave their first name only after they had given the names of their tribe, parents and clan. Apache people understood that who and where you came from was more important than who you were.

But now he didn't know what to think.

Selena stood bracing her feet, with her arms folded across her chest. Her gloved hands gripped each sleeve. His gaze swept her form, taking in her work boots, tight faded jeans and that shapeless, unlined brown coat that he knew for certain was more than five years old because he had planned to buy her a new one. Why didn't she buy a proper winter coat?

But he knew why. Selena spent her money on her brother's therapy, her twin sister's driving school and her mother's medical bills. Ruth Dosela was in the midst of chemotherapy treatment again after the cancer had returned. She'd opted for double mastectomy, according to his grandmother, and doctors were hopeful.

Gabe regarded Selena and her shabby attire. This woman had no time or money for frills.

Gabe lifted his attention to her face. Her wide forehead was the perfect foil for her dark, arched brows. Snowflakes caught on the long lashes that hooded her cocoa-brown eyes. She neither smiled nor frowned, leaving her full mouth to form a perfect bow. Gabe's heart hammered, sending blood pulsing at his neck and down below his belt as he regarded that mouth. Memories stirred with the rest of him.

Even dressed as a workman, she still was the most desirable woman he'd ever known and the most exasperating. Her head was uncovered, and snowflakes sparkled like diamonds in the thick black hair that wrapped her shoulders like a curtain and framed her heart-shaped face. That angry, stubborn face that he couldn't stop dreaming about.

Gabe wiped his hand over his mouth, surprised to find sweat on his upper lip. His stomach ached. Why were they always at odds?

He met her stare, remembering when the sight of him made her eyes twinkle with joy. Now he saw only the glitter of sorrow. It still hurt to look at her, but he couldn't seem to look away. Staring at Selena was like gazing at the sun. He knew it was bad for him, but he couldn't stop.

She was clearly waiting for him to speak. Up until today, she had done her best to avoid him, which was tough because he made opportunities to see her. Had to, couldn't stop even though it hurt.

Damn her father for all he had done to break them up, and her for getting tangled up in this mess instead of coming to him.

He stepped forward, closing the physical distance that separated them. If only he could as easily leap the emotional gulf that yawned between them. What kind of woman could not forgive a man for doing what was right?

"You should have told me about this," he said.

Her mouth quirked and just that tiny gesture made his insides tighten.

"I knew what would happen if I did."

Gabe grimaced. She was right, too. He would have made arrests.

"Dryer isn't who you think. He's with the Department of Justice. He worked a deal with your dad—early release for his cooperation."

Selena's eyes widened and she looked back to where Dryer stood with Juris.

"He's not with them?"

"The suppliers? No. He's a federal agent."

"Is that good or bad?"

"I'm not arresting you. But I think I should. This is dangerous."

She drew back her shoulders and her chin came up a notch. "I know."

He was so close now that she had to crane her neck to look into his eyes. So close that he only had to lift his arms to bring her against him. Once he'd have had the right to do just that. He angled his head and imagined kissing her. What would she do if he tried?

He leaned closer, inhaling the scent of lavender mingling with the crisp, cold air. God, he missed her.

"Selena. You don't have to do this," he said.

"Yes. I do."

"Then let me help you."

She made no reply and he knew she wouldn't let him help. Instead, she tried to move past him.

"Don't go."

He reached, taking hold of her at the shoulders. She sagged and her eyes fluttered closed for just an instant. Then her eyes flashed open and her jaw set. He knew that stubborn look, and he was afraid it would get her killed.

"He could have shot you," he said.

"Or you. It doesn't stop you from doing *your job*." She said the last two words with contempt.

"This isn't a job. It's madness."

"Is it?"

"You didn't make the deal. You don't have to go along. Selena, please…"

He let his hands slip to hers. She stilled. And finally met his gaze. She seemed about to say something but instead bit that full bottom lip.

Gabe's breath caught. He tried again. "You're not a police officer. You're not trained for this."

She drew back, putting space between them. His arms dropped to his sides, one falling naturally on the grip of his pistol. Two rounds missing, he realized.

Selena tugged her hand from beneath his. "I'm not your responsibility anymore."

"That was your choice." He couldn't keep the resentment from his voice.

He saw the hurt in her expression, but he was still so angry.

"*You* returned the ring," he reminded her.

Her eyes glittered dangerously. He knew the look. Selena was done talking. She marched away, rejoining her father and DOJ field agent Dryer.

Gabe pulled his gray Stetson down tight on his head and ignored the cold wind as he watched her walk away.

Chapter Eight

Gabe returned to his office at six, having spent the afternoon at the scene being interviewed by the Arizona state police investigation team he had called in on the shooting. He'd chosen to ignore Matthew Dryer's suggestion that he lie and suppress evidence. His one concession to the DOJ investigation was releasing Selena's box truck and letting Dryer, Selena and her father drive away. That had not pleased the CSI team and Gabe would have to answer for allowing that truck to leave an active crime scene. But at least he would be able to hold his head up when it was eventually revealed that he and the gunmen were not the only ones at the scene of the shooting. Nothing was more important to Gabe than his reputation. He would not risk it, even for the Justice Department's investigation.

Once seated in his worn leather chair, Gabe checked the clock again at seven, realizing it was still too soon for Selena to have completed the round-trip and have reached home. All afternoon he had felt as though he had ants crawling on his skin. He couldn't rest or relax until Selena was back safe on Black Mountain.

En route to Selena's place, Gabe resisted the urge

to call his uncle to let him know what was happening here. If what Dryer said was true, then Luke's partner already knew.

Gabe did not notify the tribal council of the DOJ's presence here, either. He would, in time, but he took Dryer's warning to heart about an informant. Honestly, he was afraid that telling the tribal council might get Selena killed.

In the darkness, with only the hum of his tires for company, Gabe's mind pondered the disappearance of Officer Chee. A search of Chee's home had yielded nothing. The officer and his vehicle, a brown Ford SUV, appeared to have vanished.

Juris had contacted next of kin, his brother, Andre, who had not seen Dante since Monday night. Since he'd been off Tuesday that meant Chee had been missing for twenty-four hours before anyone knew he was gone and thirty-six hours in total. That was very bad.

Gabe had put Juris in charge of the search. Until Gabe knew better, he'd assume Chee was alive, possibly injured and in need of help.

Dante was twenty-two, no longer an intern, but only on his second full year on the force. He was bright, athletic and a seriously good dancer with many contest wins under his belt. He also was an excellent woodsman with survival training. Gabe hoped that would be enough to keep him safe until they found him. He feared something had happened to his man and wondered if his disappearance was somehow tied to the DOJ investigation. Dryer had told Gabe that his force had been close to discovering where the barrels were stored. Was that what he had meant? Had Dante stumbled upon the place where they stored the precursor?

He parked his unit in the intersection on Wolf Canyon Road and Route 77, knowing that Selena would have to pass this spot on her way home. While he waited, he used his dashboard computer to investigate Pablo Nota, glancing up at any passing vehicle.

Dryer had told him that Nota delivered messages from Escalanti to Raggar. Nota was Escalanti's man. Dryer said he'd been unable to connect the cartel's messenger to Escalanti. Gabe wondered if he might be able to provide that connection. Gabe knew that Nota was a known member of the Wolf Posse, which was the Apache gang that Clay had gotten mixed up with after their mother's death. Gabe had tried to talk sense into his younger brother, but Clay was in full rebellion mode and eventually Gabe had arrested Clay. After that, lots of folks had called him a hard man. But Clay had said he'd saved his life. Now Clay was running for the tribal council seat vacated by Tessay. Strange world.

Gabe glanced at the computer screen. Pablo Nota, now twenty-one, appeared to be clean. Gabe's database showed Nota had no job and that he lived with his parents. With unemployment running at 40 percent and housing in short supply, his situation was not atypical. Heck, both Gabe and Clyne lived with their grandmother.

You could be living with Selena if you hadn't taken back that ring.

Gabe saw that Nota had registered a 2015 Mustang GT with Arizona DMV. That was an expensive ride for a man with no job. Gabe stared down at Pablo's image. The face that stared back held a defiant smirk. He decided that he needed to get eyes on Nota.

Gabe's eye strayed to the glowing dashboard clock as he again compared the time the trip to Phoenix should take Selena against the actual time.

He told himself that he needed to tell her that the state police would be by to question her, but that was only part of it. He wouldn't feel right until he saw her with his own eyes.

It was close to ten when the familiar box truck bounced along on bad struts and a passenger window now constructed of gray duct tape and cardboard. That might be the best sight he'd seen all day long. She passed right in front of him and he saw her for a moment, sitting tall behind the wheel. He pulled out and followed, drawing up beside her as she came to a stop before the modest three-bedroom house her parents had been assigned by HUD before she was even born.

He was out of his vehicle before she had her lights off. Selena gave him a tired smile that warmed him like nothing else could. His heart just couldn't seem to remember that she'd broken their engagement, and it went slamming into his ribs like a giddy puppy spotting its favorite toy.

"Hello, Selena."

"Chief," she said.

She knew he didn't like it when she called him that, but she did it anyway, often.

On the other side of the cab, a door slammed. "Is that

Gabe? You about gave me a heart attack, boy. Thought it was another ambush."

Frasco appeared before the truck, a shadow in the darkness.

"Everything all right?" Gabe asked.

"They didn't shoot us," said Frasco. "Didn't pay us, either. What's happening with Jason Leekela?"

"We are only saying there was a shooting and that two parties were involved."

"They shot each other?" Frasco laughed. "Sammy will know that's not right."

Probably, Gabe thought, and they'd deal with that when it became an issue.

"What happens next?" asked Gabe.

"They'll call us."

"Will you let me know?" he asked.

"Dryer will, I expect."

"Where's Dryer?" asked Gabe.

"Dropped him at his car. Said he'd call you tomorrow."

"I look forward to that."

"You want to come in?" asked Frasco. "Ruthie has some supper waiting," he said.

"Thank you, no."

Her father arched his back and groaned. "I'm going in. Selena?"

"In a minute, Dad."

He hesitated, then left them alone in the darkness. Gabe drew closer and Selena leaned back against her box truck. Above them the stars shone bright enough to make the snow cover glow silver.

"I was worried about you," Gabe said.

"Yes?" She looked surprised. Did she really think he could just turn off the feelings he had once had for her? Could she?

Selena stared up at him with dark, compelling eyes.

Gabe stepped back before he did something foolish. More foolish than coming here in the first place.

Selena captured his hand and held it for a moment, gave it a tiny squeeze and then released him. The moonlight gilded her skin. She parted her lips and Gabe stopped moving away.

Why had he taken that damned ring back?

All his reasonable, rational thinking blew to hell beneath the smoldering gaze she cast him. He couldn't think. He couldn't breathe. He felt awkward, unsure of what to say. He was always like this around her, ever since she'd shown him the door. They'd lost the familiarity they had once shared. But not the attraction. That was blazing between them as strong as a forest fire. He stood before her under the starry darkness.

He should ask what happened in Phoenix and where she went and who she met. He should ask why Dryer had left her instead of seeing her safely back home.

She glanced at him, and all those questions vanished but one—should he kiss her? He burned like a torch in the cold air, his body pounding to life with his accelerating heart rate and rising need. Selena was like a drug to him. That was what he told himself. The only cure was abstinence.

He'd tried being with other women. There was just no comparison. And while Clyne played the field with a series of willing women, Gabe found the entire process of picking up women to be depressing, because even in the darkness he knew they were not Selena. His imagination just wasn't that good. And now she was here, and he was here, and he wondered if he'd ever have this chance again.

Selena waited.

They'd both practiced the tactic of avoidance over the years. But like two magnets, when he was near her he always felt the pull. He reached to brush the curtain of hair from her face and she didn't draw away. He used both hands to lift the silken strands back and then rested his hands on her slim shoulders, knowing how much weight she already carried there. Too much. Far too much for one woman.

Selena made the next move, fisting the lapels of his jacket with both hands and tugging. He didn't resist. If she wanted this, too, then he'd give it to her. Maybe it would help ease the ache.

Yeah, right.

It was a bad idea, start to finish. He fell forward against her, pinning her to the driver's side door with his chest. Their open jackets allowed him to feel her soft breasts and the way she pressed her hips to his. Gabe stopped thinking as the need for Selena took over.

Her hands slid under his coat and up to his shoulders. He angled his head and looked down at her. She lifted her chin in defiance and then smiled, knowing what would follow. Welcoming him. Her hips rocked against his and he was lost.

He cradled her head in one hand, controlling her as

he bent to kiss her. Selena's yielding mouth met his demanding kiss, opening as his tongue slipped inside to taste the sweetness he had missed.

She wanted this, too, and the knowledge acted on his body like gasoline on fire.

Why didn't any of the others taste like her? Why did it have to be Selena who lit him up like a firecracker on the Fourth of July? Heat blazed as the tip of her tongue slid over his and he groaned, yielding to his need and her power over him.

He tugged her shirt from her waistband and caressed the long, soft plains of her back. She wasn't wearing a bra. Selena shivered and moved closer.

The absence, it must be that, which now made it feel as if his skin beat with his heart.

He was drowning in her taste. Relishing the eager hands that turned to claws as her nails raked his back.

He slid one hand up her ribs to find the full, tender flesh of her breast.

Selena moaned, her lips still pressed to his and her body arching, twisting to give him access. She jumped and he caught her, her legs straddling his hips as his hands cradled her bottom. He sidestepped, thinking of the long backseat in his SUV and what they could do there. He had the door open and squeezed them through the gap. He lowered Selena. Then he pinned her with his hips. She ground against him and he thought he felt the last shreds of control fray and tear. He didn't know why she wanted him. Maybe only for this. He told himself he didn't care. That it was enough.

It wasn't.

But she wanted him again. Just not as a husband, and that was for the best. Wasn't it?

He braced on an elbow, wedged between her head and the edge of the narrow backseat, keeping his weight off her except for the most delicious places. Her soft breasts molded to his chest as he settled, hip to hip. She had one leg over his back and used it to pull him closer.

"Selena," he whispered. Why was this seat so small and the air so cold? Why hadn't he anticipated this might happen when they suddenly found themselves alone in the darkness?

Her teeth raked his neck, found the lobe of his ear and sucked.

The action broke something loose inside him and he could not stop any more than he could call a bullet back into the chamber. He lifted his hips to unfasten her belt. He fumbled with the button closing her jeans. She brushed his hand away and he heard the sound of her zipper.

Gabe turned to his own trousers, his hands sure now. Then a familiar voice called out from the direction of her house.

"Sa-lee-na!"

Selena stilled.

Gabe turned his head, listening. Although the voice was lower than he'd have expected, he still recognized it. Her brother sounded drunk. Only Tomas was not drunk, he had been deprived of oxygen at birth and it had damaged his brain. He had the slurring, difficult speech of a man who would always be a boy.

Selena stiffened. Gabe suppressed a groan and drew

up so his chest no it longer pressed to hers. Gabe had adjusted his cab light so it did not come on when he opened the doors. It prevented him from being backlit when exiting his vehicle, making him an easy target. But now he could not see Selena clearly. Thankfully, neither could anyone in her house. Her face was now only shadows and moonlight, but he saw the crease between her brows.

"Mama says come get you," called her younger brother.

Gabe's radio blared from the front seat, calling his name.

"Chief Cosen. This is Randall. Over."

Selena pushed up.

"Leenie! Supper!"

She called into the darkness. "Coming."

Gabe picked up the sound of Tomas stomping his feet on the icy wooden steps.

"Leenie. I'm cold."

"Go inside, Tomas."

"Okay." The door creaked open and then closed.

Juris summoned him again. Gabe cursed, reached between the seats and snatched up the radio.

"Cosen here."

Detective Juris got right to it. "Chief we found Chee's vehicle."

"Is he in it?"

"No."

Gabe turned back to Selena who had already fastened her jeans and was buckling her belt. Then she slipped from his vehicle.

Gabe felt the tug of the job drawing him away from her again, even as she retreated to her family.

"I'm sorry, Selena," Gabe said.

"Me, too."

Gabe spoke into the radio. "Location?"

Juris relayed the information and Gabe told him he was en route with an ETA of twenty.

Selena had already reached the steps when he caught up with her, clasping her elbow. She kept her head down, refusing to look at him.

"What are we doing?" she whispered.

"I don't know. It just happened."

She gave a sound that didn't seem quite a laugh. "It often does. We were always best in the dark, weren't we?"

What was that supposed to mean?

"I must be crazy," she whispered.

He wished he could think of something to say.

"I never meant to hurt you," he said. "I never meant for any of this." He wasn't just referring to the kiss. He meant everything, the entire five terrible years as he had risen from sergeant to chief. As his career had progressed and his personal life had stalled.

She glanced at him, as if waiting for him to say something else. But what?

"I just came out here to check on you. That's all."

"Well, you gave me a really thorough checking."

He let her go and she proceeded up the steps. Then he called after her.

"How did your dad get mixed up with Dryer?" he asked.

She reached the top step and turned to face him. "Dad was approached by Raggar's man in prison and so he got word to the DOJ with the help of a Salt River Apache man, just released. This all happened because of that contact."

"Dangerous game."

"Dad says less dangerous than letting Raggar recruit him. At least now he has a chance to really be free."

Or get them all killed, thought Gabe.

"Selena, the state police will be contacting you regarding the shooting of Jason Leekela and Oscar Hill."

She gripped the railing as if she needed it for support.

"But I thought Dryer said…" She stopped talking as if realizing he would not keep the shooting under wraps. "But he told you not to mention us."

"I can't suppress the fact that you were there."

"Not about my father." Her eyes went wide and she stared at him. "You didn't say *he* was there."

His silence was answer enough.

"They'll think he broke parole. They'll put him back in. If they do, then Raggar will know."

"The crimes investigation team already knows your dad is working with DOJ. They won't bring him in. They'll question you here."

"But if Raggar's people have someone in the state police, then they'll find out, something bad will happen to my family."

"He won't find out. When the state police investigation team comes, tell them everything," he said.

She gave her head a slow shake and then left him

out in the cold, with one foot on her step and one in the snow.

Had he just put his reputation above the safety of Selena and her family?

Chapter Nine

Gabe threw out the remains of the cold coffee, leaving a brown stain on the snow. They'd found Chee's car and a blood trail to Officer Chee. He'd been shot multiple times at close range. The coroner's opinion matched his own—Chee had been killed somewhere else, loaded into his car and dumped over the guardrail where he'd rolled down a steep embankment.

Gabe had found his officer, and now there were three gunshot victims in the morgue: Hill, Leekela and Chee.

Hell of a day, though officially it was already tomorrow.

They'd gotten some good footprint casts thanks to the icy cold that had preserved them. Preliminarily, it looked as though Chee had been moved in something, a blanket or tarp. The cold that helped preserve the tracks also meant the killer or killers likely were wearing gloves, so there was less chance of pulling latents.

Like all the Cosens, Gabe had learned to track from his grandfather, so he knew something about the two who'd moved the body. One was big, over two-hundred pounds and wearing size-twelve basketball sneakers.

The other person was smaller, lighter and wore construction boots.

By 3:00 a.m., the coffee wasn't keeping him alert enough for driving so he headed to his office. But he didn't release the scene because Juris wanted another look in daylight.

Gabe stretched out on the familiar leather couch where he had spent more than a few nights. He removed his tie, kicked off his boots and dragged the big sheepskin coat over his chest. When he closed his eyes, he tried to imagine Selena, safe in bed, but images of Chee kept intruding. Gabe must have dozed because he was sound asleep when Clyne woke him with a hard rap on the glass of his office door at eight. Gabe blinked against the bright sunlight streaming through his windows and checked the time. Selena would be halfway around the 113-mile loop she drove each weekday.

He wished he had more men so he could post watch on Selena's place. But not only did he not have the manpower, if there was a leak in his own department the attention would raise flags. Then instead of protecting Selena, he'd be endangering her.

Gabe swung his legs off the couch and sat up, sending his winter coat to the floor. He rubbed the bristle of his hair. It might not be a traditional style, but it sure made things easier on days like this.

Gabe eyed the coffee in Clyne's hand.

"That for me?"

His older brother handed it over.

"You ought to try food sometime."

"Grandma makes sure of that." Gabe took a sip and

sighed, sitting back on the couch for a moment with his eyes closed.

Clyne brought him back to the real world.

"You found Chee," he said.

Gabe set the coffee aside. "Yeah."

"I'm sorry," said Clyne. "Let me know what I can do."

Gabe nodded and tugged on his work boots, then yanked the hems of his jeans over the laces. Standing, he tucked in his shirt, refastened the buttons and looped the tie around his neck.

Clyne's look registered disapproval. The only thing his brother wore around his neck was Indian silver and turquoise that had been in their family for generations. The traditional designs were ancient, visually striking and protective. If it didn't support a cause or uphold tradition, Clyne wasn't wearing it.

Gabe adjusted his belt and the badge clipped beside the silver buckle that was one of many he'd won riding broncos.

"You sleep with that thing?" said Clyne, incredulous.

"More and more lately," he said. Gabe recovered the coffee and took a long swallow.

"What do you think happened to Chee?" asked Clyne.

"Something bad."

Gabe sat behind his desk and retrieved his pistol from the locked desk drawer. Then he aroused his computer with a keystroke and fired up his email.

Clyne moved to the empty chair before his desk. "What's this about Jason Leekela and Oscar Hill?"

Word traveled fast.

"I shot them."

Gabe did not mention the Doselas or DOJ. It was a breach of protocol and it bothered him. But not as much as seeing Selena shot.

Gabe continued, "I called the state police investigations team to handle it. They were on-site yesterday."

Clyne seemed to know that already. His brother also knew it was not the first time Gabe had used deadly force. The first had been in a foiled robbery, with Clay behind the wheel.

"They're coming to see me today."

"Should have cleared that with the council."

"On my list."

Clyne gave him a troubled look.

Gabe knew Clyne had been a sniper in Afghanistan. But that was all he knew, because his brother wouldn't talk about it. At least Clyne didn't know any of his kills, while Gabe had known each one. As of yesterday, Gabe had shot three men. It didn't feel good.

"You okay?" asked Clyne.

"I will be, I expect."

Clyne's mouth was tight. "Listen, I wanted to tell you last night, but you were busy. We heard from Clay yesterday afternoon."

"That right?" Gabe found himself on the edge of his desk chair, his in-box forgotten.

Clay had taken up the hunt for their missing little sister, Jovanna. Five months ago, he and Clyne had verified she had indeed survived the accident that had taken their mother's life in South Dakota nine years earlier.

Their youngest brother, Kino, and his new wife, Lea, had picked up the search in the fall and discovered that Jovanna had been adopted by a non-Indian, which had sent Clyne into a frenzy. But the adoption was closed, so they could gain no additional information. Clay was now in federal court, pursuing legal action to have the adoption unsealed and overturned under the Indian Child Welfare Act.

Gabe found himself longing for good news.

"Clay says that they served the adoptive mother with the papers that the adoption will be opened and that we are filing for termination of her parental rights to Jovanna."

Gabe sat back. "That's great. So, what now?"

"We should be getting her name and other information soon. The courts will look at our assertion that the adoption was illegal."

"How long will that take?" Gabe knew that their grandmother had already finished the loosely constructed traditional dress that their sister would wear with an ornate belt and moccasins for her Sunrise Ceremony, the Apache coming-of-age rite that marked the time when a thirteen-year-old changed from a girl to a woman in the eyes of the tribe. Jovanna was turning thirteen on June 4, and the ceremony was on July 4 each year. Suddenly, that seemed very close.

"I don't know, but the law is on our side."

Gabe's desk phone buzzed.

Jasmine, their dispatcher, did not come in until 9:00 a.m. Until then, they shared a dispatcher with the fire department and calls were routed to him if necessary. So he was not surprised to see the name of one of the firefighters, Vernon Martin, on his caller ID.

He glanced at his brother. "Gotta take this." Then he lifted the handset.

"There are some men from the Arizona state police here to see you, Chief," said Vernon.

Clyne obviously heard because he shook his head in disapproval.

"Nothing they're going to do but make things worse," he predicted, reminding Gabe of Matt Dryer's words.

Did his brother really think Gabe should be investigating the shooting he had been involved in? His brother knew everything about history, politics and Apache culture, but very little about police work.

"I'll meet them," Gabe said, and lowered the receiver.

"Have you been out to notify next of kin?" asked Clyne.

"My officers notified the Hill and Leekela families last night. I spoke to Chee's brother. He was on duty at the station." Chee's brother, Andre, volunteered at the tribal fire department.

"I'm heading out to see Chee's mother," said Clyne. "Going to invite you along."

But Gabe had a date with the state police, a cop killer on the loose and an active shooting investigation to pursue.

"Can't. Work."

"That seems like all you do anymore," said Clyne.

Why did that make Gabe think of Selena?

Chapter Ten

The roads were getting worse on Thursday morning as Selena finished her route, and she struggled to keep the box truck from sliding on the ice. She didn't have snow tires, so she took it easy on the turns, making it to their driveway after nine in the morning so her younger sister Mia could start her run down to Phoenix and back to the tribe's casino in Black Mountain. Mia was three years her junior and had been delivering foodstuffs for the four restaurants on-site for over two years, taking the route when their twin sisters, Paula and Carla, had turned twenty, passed their trucking classes and taken over the long hauls with the truck and flatbed that Selena had purchased used. Her sister normally left before Selena returned from her route. But since her mother's treatment began, they didn't like to leave their mother alone. Since the chemo, she was frail and had difficulty dressing and keeping the house.

Selena glanced at the passenger's side mirror automatically and then sighed at the sight of the clear plastic secured to the frame with duct tape. That would have to do until she could get a new side window, but she certainly wasn't going to the junkyard for one.

On entering the driveway, the first thing she noticed was the fresh tire tracks in the snow. Selena knew enough about tracking to recognize they'd had a visitor.

She had only just cut the engine when Mia stepped out of the house and hurried toward her. Her sister waited until her door was open to launch into her concerns.

"Some weird guy was here. Dad said he had hired him as a driver. Did you know about this?"

"No. I didn't."

"Oh, Selena, he's got tattoos everywhere. The scary kind. He asked me a lot of questions about the flatbed the twins drive."

"Like what?"

"How much weight it holds. How do you keep barrels from rolling around without sides and when will the twins be back. Leenie, what kind of driver doesn't know how to secure a load for transport?"

The kind who isn't a driver, Selena thought.

"Is he Apache?" she asked.

"Yeah, but trouble. Serious trouble."

"How serious?"

"Gang member for sure."

Selena's stomach dropped another few inches. Was this Escalanti's man? The promised contact who would take them to the barrels of chemicals Dryer wanted so desperately?

"Did you get a name?"

"Pablo Nota. When he asked about the flatbed, I asked if he'd ever driven and he basically told me to shut up."

"Why didn't you call me?"

"Because the weather is crappy and I knew you'd be home soon. I didn't want you answering the phone when you were driving." Mia had her arms folded, shivering in her polar fleece jacket.

Selena didn't know if she should be happy or terrified at Nota's visit. If this man was one of the gang members, then they didn't know about the shooting and they might still take them to the supplies of chemicals. Then this entire nightmare might be over. But how it might end frightened her right down to the bone.

She slipped a hand into her pocket to phone Gabe.

Mia stood in the snow, watching her older sister.

"What's going on?" asked Mia.

Should she tell her? Selena just wanted to protect Mia, but she didn't know if the best way to do that was to tell her or not tell her.

"Is he coming back?" asked Selena.

"Any minute. Dad told him when you finish your route."

Selena wondered if Gabe could really catch them or if, by involving him, she had just signed his death warrant along with her family's.

"You want me to stay?" asked Mia.

No she wanted Mia as far away from here as possible. Selena was tempted to tell her sister to pick up Tomas and their mother and drive as fast and as far as she could.

Selena met Mia's worried stare. "No. You go on."

"You know something, Leenie. Tell me."

She shook her head. "I can't."

Mia glanced at the house. "Then be careful and you tell me if I can help."

Mia lunged forward, hugging Selena tight.

"Be careful," she whispered and kissed Selena's cheek. Then Mia climbed into her truck, gave Selena a long look and then backed out of the drive. Selena hadn't even reached the front steps when her father opened the front door to greet her. The gash on his head had scabbed, but beneath it was an ugly purple lump.

"Mia tell you?"

She nodded and he stepped back, allowing her past. Then he closed the door behind her.

"It was Escalanti's guy," he said. "The lab needs regular transport. Two or three barrels a week to keep up production, or they might move the whole load with our flatbed, but that's more dangerous because if we are stopped they lose it all. They could also use our big rig to move the meth lab, though he didn't suggest that. Makes no difference because we won't be moving any of it. With luck we'll know where they're hiding it this afternoon and we can end this. That's assuming that your hotshot chief of police doesn't get us all killed before then. As I see it, Escalanti has more men in his gang than Cosen has on the force."

Selena's skin tingled as if tiny creatures walked over her skin. She tried and failed to suppress a shudder.

"Gabe said he'd take care of us."

Her father laughed. "I've been taken care of by him once already. That boy is taking care of himself and his career. He's hot as a pistol, that one. He'd be the next governor if he wasn't Apache. Only man I've ever seen rise quicker is his older brother, our future tribal council chairman. Man, I'd like to see them stumble just once."

But Gabe had stumbled, she realized. Last night with her, just as he had when he'd asked for her hand.

Selena felt trapped. She glanced toward the road, thinking of Gabe. Wishing…

Her father's voice broke into her thoughts.

"You know it's over between you two, right?"

Her heart squeezed and a cry of denial stuck in her throat. But she knew the truth of her father's words. "Yes."

"Good. 'Cause he don't want you, girlie. He's sniffing around, but not for a wife."

She was about to tell her father that Gabe was a gentleman. That he was not like that. But then she remembered his hands on her hips, lifting her up as his body pressed her down to the cold vinyl of his rear seat.

That was not the way you treated a woman you cared for. That was the way you treated a…

"Stay away from him," her father said. "They don't know about you two and if they find out they might just kill him or you or both. If they hear we were there when that stupid junkie Jason Leekela and his friend got shot trying to rob their brother's shipment…" Frasco groaned and pressed both hands to his temples.

"There is nothing between us now."

Her father dropped his hands and aimed a finger at her. "The past is between you. Keep it there."

"Yes, Dad."

"State police called." He lifted a scrap of paper.

She'd told him about the state police last night after

Gabe had told her. Her father didn't look any happier now than he had been then.

"They want to interview us both. They're coming this afternoon, which means we need to get out of here before then."

"You're on house arrest. They'll report it when you're not here."

"Let them. They already know we're working with DOJ. If they have a leak, we're dead anyway."

Her father placed a foot on the sofa and released the tracking device that was supposed to insure he stayed put and then dropped it on the coffee table.

Her father grabbed his coat and Selena followed him out. The sound of snow crunching under tires brought them both around. At first she didn't recognize the driver behind the wheel of the blue SUV pulling into their drive. But her father clearly did.

"Holy hell," muttered her father dashing past her and then scrambling to replace the anklet.

"Who is that?" asked Selena, standing in the open door.

"My parole officer. Drop-in visits, remember?"

SELENA STARED IN horror at the man she had met yesterday morning, when her father had returned from prison.

Ronald Hare was an Apache case manager from the Salt River Reservation to their south. He'd said he had more than a few parolees up here in Black Mountain and that not all his visits would be announced. But Selena had not expected him to drop by the very next day.

"What do we do?" asked Selena. Her instinct was

to call Gabe. But was he really there for her or, as her father had said, after only one thing? No, Gabe was an honest man who did his duty first, last and always.

Mr. Hare had gotten out of his vehicle and was moving toward them. He was an attractive young man with a broad smile on his handsome face. He had a small goatee. His hair was chin length and slicked back. He wore boots, jeans and an open, knee-length topcoat that reminded Selena of the dusters cowboys wore in inclement weather. But one look at the man's spotless clothing told you that this Apache did not work with cattle.

He called a greeting and her father gave a wave from the steps, his anklet now back in place. Hare was halfway to the house when a second car roared down the street, its performance exhaust system announcing its arrival before it came into view. Her father groaned.

Hare turned and Selena glanced past him as the yellow Ford Mustang made its appearance. Selena had seen the car in Black Mountain and heard it more than a few times, but she had never seen the driver because of the illegally tinted glass.

Selena gripped the railing as she watched the sports car come to a stop in the drive. The muscle car was the color of an egg yolk and just as shiny. The tailpipe extended beyond the fender with glistening chrome and the car's sides were stenciled with black detailing. The car was as practical as a parasol in an ice storm, but it certainly had flash.

The driver emerged. He was young, perhaps twenty, with a thin, angular face. His clothing was new and baggy, perfect for concealing a weapon. The dark glasses and flat-brimmed hat disguised his eyes. This could be no one other than Pablo Nota, Escalanti's minion.

He lowered the shades to check out the new arrival.

"Who's this?" he said.

"I'm Ronald Hare, Mr. Dosela's parole officer. And you are?"

It was like watching two cars slide toward each other on ice. Selena knew they were going to collide and she was powerless to stop them.

"This is my daughter's boyfriend," her father said.

Selena did not think she quite managed to hide her horrified expression.

"I see." Mr. Hare regarded Nota.

Nota hesitated, hands still in his jacket pockets.

Her father spoke to Nota.

"This is my parole officer, Mr. Hare, making an unannounced visit."

Nota's hesitation was brief. He plastered a wide smile on his face and nodded his greeting, keeping both hands in his pockets.

Selena didn't want to think what he had in there.

Hare drew back his extended hand.

After an uncomfortable silence, her father spoke again.

"She's just getting her coat," said her father and pushed Selena toward the door. "You want to come in, son?"

"Naw. I'll wait here."

Her father turned to their second guest. "Come on in, Mr. Hare."

Hare took a good look at her father and hesitated,

staring at the healing gash and lump. "Jeez. What happened to you?"

Her father didn't miss a beat. "Don't remember. Got pretty drunk last night. Woke up on the kitchen floor with this." He pointed at his head.

He did not wait for Hare to follow them but shoved Selena toward the door and followed her inside.

"You'll have to go alone," said her father.

"But…" Selena looked out the small window in the door. "Hare is on the phone." She glanced to her father. "Quick. Call Gabe."

Her father hurried to the phone and had it in his hand when Hare stepped in. Her father lowered the phone.

Ronald Hare looked from one to the other. Selena found his eyes too alert and his smile somehow threatening.

Her mother shuffled into the room still in her robe.

Her father motioned to their uninvited guest. "Ruthie, you remember Ronnie Hare, my parole officer?"

Mr. Hare greeted her mother in Apache. Her father walked Selena to the door where he gave her an unexpected hug and pressed something into her hand. She took it knowing by touch it was the tracking anklet that he was supposed to be wearing at all times.

"Take it," he whispered.

The minute she left the yard the unit would beep. It would alert Dryer that they were in trouble and tell him where they were. Unfortunately it would also cause the base unit to emit a high-pitched shrieking alarm the minute she left the yard. How was her father going to explain that to Hare?

She shoved the tracker in her pocket and drew back.

"See you soon," she said, then nodded to the parole officer.

Behind her she heard her father telling Hare to come into the kitchen for some coffee. He preceded her father who stooped and tore the wires from the monitoring unit so it would not sound an alarm if the bracelet moved out of range. They had told her father that they could track him with the anklet. Could they also track her? When she moved past the driveway, the alarm would sound only on the anklet. How was she supposed to keep Nota from hearing it?

Selena headed out to meet Escalanti's man. How long did the device beep?

"He can't come," she said. Should she just drop the tracker out the window as she left the drive?

"No kidding. Let's go." He headed toward her truck. Nota slowed as they approached the box truck. "What's up with the window?"

She glanced at the patch job and sighed, hoping it would hold until she could get a new window.

"Oh," she said. "Someone smashed my window." She didn't mention they had smashed it with a bullet.

"That blows," he said.

Selena circled behind the truck, gripping the tracking anklet in her fist.

"Where are you going?" he called.

"Have to lock the rear door or it will swing open," she said, hurrying to the rear and opened one door a few inches before tossing the tracker into the flatbed. Then she closed and locked the gate. When she returned

Nota was already in the truck. Selena climbed behind the wheel and prayed the alarm could not be heard in the cab.

"Got to move two barrels today. My man is waiting for us on site."

If she could just find out where the barrels were hidden, they might be able to shut this operation down. Selena swung the truck out of the drive and onto the road.

Dryer should be learning right now that her father's unit had been triggered. But he was three hours away in Phoenix.

She started the engine. *Please let him call Gabe.*

Would Dryer send in his cavalry or was she out here all alone with this gangster?

Chapter Eleven

Gabe was cooperative with the Arizona investigators and answered all their questions. They had released the scene yesterday and were following up today. The state police had resources that a small police force just never would, including the crime investigation unit that included the two detectives now interviewing him. Thankfully, when Dryer had been notified of the investigation he'd admitted to having been there and Dryer's testimony should corroborate his version.

Gabe's phone vibrated. He checked the caller ID and saw Dryer's name. He excused himself and picked up.

"I'm with the detectives now," he said by way of a greeting.

"Yeah, I know. Also spoke to Escalanti's man. So far he hasn't heard. Who's there?"

Gabe told him the names of the two officers.

"Anyone else?"

"No. Just three of us in my office."

"Close the door and put me on speaker."

Gabe did. Dryer raised his voice to be heard by all.

"Frasco Dosela's tracking unit just went off. That

means he left the premises. He's not answering his phone. Something is wrong."

"Where is he?"

"That's the thing, his tracker uses his mobile phone to locate. The anklet doesn't have a GPS built in, so if his phone isn't near the tracker, we can't locate him."

Even if he had his phone, they might not be able to locate him. Gabe knew that great expanses of the reservation had no cell phone reception. That was why the radios were so essential to his force.

"You lost him?" said Gabe.

"Don't know. His cell phone is at home. But the tracker isn't."

He might have left his mobile at home. Gabe gripped the phone. Something had gone wrong. Was Selena all right?

"Hold on. I think we got through to Frasco." Dryer's voice was muffled as he seemed to be taking another call.

The room remained silent until Dryer's voice again boomed over the speaker, louder now.

"He said his parole officer is there right now."

"Wouldn't he see if the tracker was missing?" asked Gabe.

"No. It can be under Frasco's sock or pant leg and I designed it to be removable."

"He took it off, but he's at his house," asked Gabe, clarifying.

"Gabe, he didn't leave the property."

But his tracker did. Someone had carried it past the perimeter to set it off.

"Malfunction?" asked one of the detectives. It was a reasonable guess. The units were not perfect.

"No. Frasco didn't answer my questions. Just kept telling me that Selena had gone out with her boyfriend. That she wasn't at home."

Gabe knew what this meant, and he was already on his feet and reaching for his mobile phone. He tugged on his hat.

"He gave the tracker to Selena," said Gabe.

"I think so," said Dryer.

"Why?" said one of the detectives.

"He wants us to know where she is. That means—"

Gabe cut him off. "Selena is in trouble."

SELENA DROVE THE truck as Pablo Nota directed. He had told her that they were meeting someone who would deliver the barrels to them and she would take them to the lab. Twice she got a glimpse of movement behind them in her side mirror, but she could not be certain.

"If it is only three or four barrels, why don't you just deliver it?" she asked.

He shook his head as if she were the dumbest person alive.

"You got insurance on your trucks?"

"Of course."

"Why?"

"In case something happens, it will be covered."

"That's why we don't deliver the precursor. Transfer of liability. We arrange transportation. We don't transport. That way if you get picked up, you go to federal prison, not me."

She was about to say that she could identify him, but thought better of it. It was unwise to threaten a man she knew had an automatic weapon in the pocket of his oversize jacket. She knew that because he'd made it a point to show her.

Again she thought she saw something behind them. Dusk came early in the mountains and this time of year the twilight descended in the early afternoon.

Nota went on. "Besides, this is only the beginning. We got lots more coming. Got to move this out to make room. Gonna be running more labs, too. A regular cottage industry." He motioned for her to turn in the direction of Piñon Lake.

Piñon Lake? There was no place out there to store anything. The lake was used for fishing and there was an old quarry. But no place large enough to store the kind of quantity of supplies they must need to make the drugs.

She stopped asking questions. She just wanted to pick up the barrels and get them to Sammy Leekela's junkyard.

When he told her to pull over, she did, still seeing nothing. Then one of the shadows moved. A big shadow, and she saw that the shadow was actually a huge man in a white snowmobile suit. He looked like a soldier on winter operations or a Yeti. When they pulled into the lot beside the quarry, she noted that he stood beside a snowmobile attached to a sled covered with a white tarp.

Nota opened the door and called a greeting.

"'Bout time," said the giant.

He stepped toward the passenger's side and she noticed that the only things not white were his high-top turquoise basketball sneakers and the semiautomatic he had slung over his right shoulder on a strap like a handbag.

"Let's load this up and get out of here."

"You're both coming?" she asked.

"No. We're both leaving. Didn't you hear a word I said?"

Selena climbed down from the truck and opened the rear doors. It took both of them to roll the barrels to the back of the loading truck. She attached her ramp and they used her dolly to get the first barrel aboard.

She glanced to the back of the truck where she had thrown the tracker but could neither see nor hear it, thank goodness.

Selena stood by as the two of them heaved and swore. But again her eye caught movement and this time she heard the crunch of tires approaching. In the gloom she just made out the white vehicle and her heart gave a little leap. *Gabe*, she thought.

That's when gunfire exploded from the approaching large SUV. Selena threw herself to the road and rolled under the box truck.

Above her, Pablo Nota screamed and toppled to the ground past the back tire, falling like a rag doll. Blood leaked into the snow beneath him, oozing outward and melting the thin coating of ice. She slapped a gloved hand over her mouth to keep from screaming and inched farther back. His partner's footsteps sounded above her as he ran farther into the box truck.

The SUV doors opened and she heard the shouts of

men, mixed with gunfire. Selena covered her ears and allowed a whimpering cry to escape her lips.

On the road beside the truck sat the snowmobile and sled, used by Nota's partner to bring the barrels. An idea formed, but as she stared at the stretch of open ground between her hiding place and escape the idea withered.

More gunfire sounded. A steady stream of shots from inside her truck and then scattered blasts from their attackers. She knew when the big man had been hit because it sounded like a refrigerator tipping over above her.

"Where's the driver?" asked someone.

Selena stiffened as the legs of the gunmen came into view. How long before they looked under her box truck and found her hiding like a ground squirrel from a fox?

Selena scrambled toward the front of the truck. If she was going to die, it would not be lying on her belly in the snow.

Chapter Twelve

Gabe accelerated toward Piñon Lake with the two state police detectives falling behind and two more units en route. His headlights flashed across the snow, showing him only the icy flakes falling on the empty road. Where was her box truck? Selena was out here. Dryer said so. He'd used the tracker and Selena's phone to pinpoint her location, and Gabe was going to find her.

Dryer was en route as well, bringing his people from Phoenix, and Gabe knew they'd be too late.

He just prayed that *he* wouldn't be.

The flash of gunfire reached him an instant before the sound of the shots. Just ahead, someone was shooting a semiautomatic weapon in short controlled blasts. A second shooter opened up to the first shooter's left.

Gabe hit the gas, flying over the snowy roads too fast. He leaned forward as if that would make his SUV go faster and he gripped the wheel, praying to reach her in time.

His headlights reached the white Ford Yukon, revealing two men. One in front of the vehicle. One to the left.

The first man turned, pointing an automatic weapon in Gabe's direction. He rammed the Yukon, sending it sliding forward at the gunman. He saw the shooter's arms go up, the automatic spraying bullets into the dull sky for just an instant before he disappeared under the grille of his SUV. The Yukon continued forward, hitting Selena's truck and sending it gliding for several feet before it came to rest.

Gabe was out of his unit and running, gun drawn.

Another blast of gunfire came from the back of the loading truck.

From somewhere beyond the truck came the whir of a motor turning over. He identified the sound of a snowmobile engine.

He reached the front of the Yukon and discovered two bodies. One lay perfectly still and perfectly illuminated in the halogen beams of the Yukon in a bright pool of blood. Gabe dismissed that threat as his gaze flicked to the man who had fallen before his vehicle. The shooter lay on his back, his weapon still gripped in one hand as he struggled to his elbows.

Gabe aimed his pistol. "Tribal Police. Put down the weapon."

The snowmobile accelerated, the engine revving louder. The man's mouth moved although Gabe couldn't hear him. But he could see him lift the weapon, swinging it toward Gabe.

Gabe fired at center mass. Two shots into the shooter's chest. The gunman went slack, his weapon rattling on the snowy pavement.

Gabe stepped forward and kicked it away. Behind him came the sweep of more headlights. The state police unit stopped just beyond his SUV. The detectives had arrived and exited in unison on each side of their vehicle.

"Two down here," he shouted. But his words were lost in the roar of the snowmobile's high-pitched motor. He waved them forward. They came one after the other, weapons drawn, covering each other's advance.

He turned back to the open box truck. Inside he saw a large lump of something that could be a trash bag or a man. Beyond sat three fifty-gallon blue barrels.

The precursor, he realized.

The snowmobile engine revved as the driver accelerated away amid another burst of gunfire. Gabe saw a small figure on the machine, the headlight bouncing wildly as the rider shifted and nearly disappeared from sight on the far side of the snowmobile. He knew then, with certainty, who the rider must be.

Selena, trying to escape, rode the snowmobile as their ancestors had once ridden their horses to avoid the bullets of the cavalry's guns. She clung with one leg thrown across the seat and her hands on the steering mechanism. The rest of her body hung off the far side of the machine.

More gunfire exploded. Gabe couldn't see the shooter who now stood before the grille of the box truck, firing at Selena who zipped past them, heading toward the woods.

Gabe moved to the passenger side, correctly guessing at the shooter's path so he was there when the man stepped clear of the grille to take another shot at Selena.

The instant he cleared the fender, Gabe shouted,

identifying himself, trying to draw fire away from Selena.

"Tribal Police! Put down your weapon!"

The man turned, a stunned look on his face and Gabe wondered if the second shooter had not heard his arrival because of the roar of the snowmobile. The man swung the automatic pistol away from the escaping snowmobile and in Gabe's direction.

Gabe fired first, two quick shots. Then he hit the ground and rolled under the box truck as the bullets sprayed over his head. He saw the shooter drop to his knees and he aimed again, considering taking out the man's knee. But the man sprawled forward, falling onto his weapon. Gabe glanced behind him and saw the detective's steady approach. Gabe rolled out from beneath the truck to check the second shooter and heard the snowmobile motor growing louder.

Selena had swung back in his direction. What was she doing?

SELENA TURNED THE snowmobile back toward the road. A glance over her shoulder had shown her Gabe Cosen's SUV.

He'd found her!

But there were two more gunmen sneaking up behind him, guns poised before them as they crept from their dark sedan toward Gabe.

She didn't think about reaching safety. Instead she thought about Gabe facing two more killers. Did he see them? He was looking toward her instead of the threat.

Her motor, she realized, the stupid, loud roaring of the machine kept him from hearing them.

She headed straight for the gunmen. They turned in her direction. One lifted his weapon.

Gabe threw up his arms and ran toward them. Why wasn't he aiming the gun at his attacker?

She saw them clearly now. White men, dressed in blue nylon jackets, zipped open to show neckties and dress shirts. Something about that didn't make sense.

Gabe was running toward the man who aimed his pistol at her. And then she saw it, the flash of gold at the man's waist, a badge, or shield as Gabe called it.

Selena sharply turned the snowmobile before it hit the two lawmen. It tipped and she threw herself clear of the rolling machine.

A SHOOTING PAIN flashed through Gabe's chest as he watched Selena rolling over and over before she came to a stop.

Gabe charged up the snowbank, floundering and swimming with his arms to clear the four-foot mound of snow. All the while he was shouting at the detectives to hold fire.

He called to her and she did not move.

The motor continued to whine. The snowmobile, on its side, sputtered and finally died. Then he reached her and rolled her into his arms.

"Selena?"

"Gabe?"

Her voice was the sweetest sound he'd ever heard.

She lifted her arms and clung to him as tears flowed down her cheeks.

"Are you hurt?" she asked.

"Me?" He blinked at the moisture at his eyes. "Did he hit you?"

"No. I don't think so."

He eased her back, searching for injury, his hands moving down her face and through her hair as his gaze swept over her. And then he saw it, the tiny hole in the shoulder of her coat.

"Who are they?" she asked, glancing back at the two men who had moved to the back of her truck.

"State police, detectives. Investigating yesterday's shooting." He pushed his finger into the hole in the fabric, feeling down through the brown workman's coat and coming out the other side. "Take this off."

He helped her draw it back and checked her shoulder. The bullet had missed her. Gabe blew away a breath.

"You were clear. Why did you come back?"

"I thought they were with the others."

He dragged her against him and she clung. "Oh, Selena. You scared me. You can't do this. It's too dangerous."

She didn't say anything. But a high-pitched cry emerged from her throat. He drew back and saw her shoulders begin to jump. He remembered what that signaled. Selena was weeping.

He held her close, stroking her head as she cried into his coat.

"I'm s-sorry."

"Oh, sweetheart." He rocked her. "You have to stop this. We have to get you and your family out of here."

From behind him came the shout of Detective Spencer. "Clear."

Gabe lifted his cheek from the top of Selena's head. Had he really just failed to clear the scene of gunman?

Selena wept against his chest. He needed to get her out of here and then he needed to do his job. Four more men killed in a gun battle on his reservation.

How could he protect her and still break this meth ring? He couldn't, he realized. He would have to choose.

Chapter Thirteen

"I'm taking Selena home," Gabe said to state police detectives Spencer and Murdy. He wasn't asking their permission.

Selena had had enough. He knew that much.

Three hours had elapsed since the shooting at Piñon Lake. And he was now surrounded by his men, representatives from the state police and a team from DOJ. The FBI was en route. Clyne had arrived alone, as requested by DOJ, without the other members of the tribal council. And from the look he cast Gabe, he was mightily pissed that Gabe hadn't kept him in the loop.

Selena had been questioned and from that he had learned how she came to be out here in a restricted area with two known gang members.

It was Dryer who identified her two attackers, rival gang members from Salt River. How they had known Selena's location and that she would be transporting barrels of precursor remained a mystery that Gabe planned to unravel.

Dryer lifted a brow. "Thought you'd like to be here when your boys track down the origin of the snowmobile."

The snowmobile that had transported the barrels and therefore would likely have left a trail leading to the location of the rest of the precursor. Gabe glanced at the snowmobile, still and silent on its side, the trail of packed snow behind it so clear that it was visible in the starlight from twenty-five yards. Then he looked at Selena. She stood beside Detective Juris, her arms folded across her chest as she stomped her feet to stay warm.

Gabe looked back at Dryer. "Yeah, well, I'll be back."

Dryer shrugged and Gabe continued toward Selena, who spoke to Clyne and Detective Juris.

"Come on," he said to her.

"Who needs to speak to me now?" Her voice was dull with weariness.

"I'm driving you home."

Selena knit her brows. "My truck?"

"Part of the crime scene," said Gabe.

"We'll notify you when it is released," said Juris.

As Gabe started walking, Selena shuffled along beside him like a sleepwalker. He could almost feel the exhaustion weighing her down.

"Where?" she said, as if forming a complex sentence was just too much effort.

"Home," he answered.

"Mine or yours?"

He blinked.

"Yours," he said automatically, and then wondered if Selena had just asked him what he thought she had.

She forced a smile that cut across her full mouth like a knife blade. He'd never seen her look more miserable.

The photographer from both the state police and his department had already finished with his SUV, which now sported a freshly damaged front bumper. Would he have hit that gunman's vehicle if he had known that Selena had been hiding under hers?

The picture of her box truck tire rolling over her body sent a shiver through him.

Gabe ushering Selena toward his vehicle, opened her door and pulled her safety belt across her waist. She sat like a tired child, allowing him to fasten the clasp. He hesitated then, leaning over her as the sweet scent of lavender mingled in the air close to her exposed neck. He shifted his gaze and found her dark eyes fixed on him. Her lips parted. His stomach dropped.

He leaned in to kiss her, but before their mouths met, he stopped. Her eyes opened and she gave him a quizzical look. He stood and glanced about to find Detective Murdy regarding them with quiet, hawkish attention.

Gabe hadn't done anything wrong. But he felt like a child caught with his hand in the cookie jar. Kissing the only surviving witness at a crime scene was skirting pretty close to the kind of unprofessionalism he usually had no trouble avoiding. But this was Selena. He'd always had trouble avoiding her.

"You ready?" he asked.

She nodded and he closed her door, feeling guilty for almost kissing her and feeling guilty for not kissing her. As he rounded the creased front fender he tamped down his desires and focused on her. Selena had been through a terrible ordeal. What did she need now? A shoulder to cry on? Food? Sleep? Someone to listen to her? He didn't know. But whatever she needed, he wanted to be there for her.

Gabe started the vehicle and reversed course, turning them in the direction that would take her home.

Selena had been allowed to call her parents, so they knew she was delayed. Had she told them everything or nothing?

From the time they left Piñon Lake until he pulled onto Wolf Canyon Road, he heard only the hum of the tires.

"Are you all right, Selena?" he asked.

"I…I'm so sorry to hear about Officer Chee, and about what happened to Jason and Oscar, and for today." Her voice rose, cracked. She struggled with the last two words. "Just everything."

The lump in his throat rose so fast that he thought he might choke. He'd been so involved in the investigation that he hadn't allowed himself to feel anything. Until now. He was nothing but feeling around Selena.

"How did you hear about Dante?"

"On my route this morning. Folks were talking about it. And then I saw Andre Chee," she said, referring to Officer Dante Chee's brother, who worked for HUD and volunteered at the fire house.

"Where?" asked Gabe.

"He was at the convenience store in Black Mountain when I made my delivery."

Oh, God, was he tearing up? He swiped at his cheek and clamped his jaw against the ache in his chest.

He pulled into her driveway, threw the SUV into Park and switched off the headlights. On the other side of the front steps was a yellow Mustang GT. Gabe tried to ignore the dead man's car, but realized he had to talk to Dryer about it. Likely they'd leave it, as its location temporarily corroborated the cover story he'd devised for tonight's shoot-out. Dryer wanted Gabe to report the shooting as it occurred with one small change—Nota was driving and he was alone.

The car ticked and then went still. He didn't want her to leave but did not know how to make her stay.

Selena sniffed and he turned toward her.

He could see from the dashboard lights that she was crying. And he just sat there like a chunk of wood, wishing he could take her in his arms. Knowing what would happen if he did.

She reached out and he clasped her cold hand, his thumb rubbing over her knuckles. Her fingers were smooth and elegant, and devoid of the wedding band he had promised her. The lump in his throat moved to his heart.

This touch was not sexual and yet, somehow, it felt more important. They'd always had the physical attraction. Fierce and alive as an electrical storm. And for a while they'd had the intimacy, too. But that had all changed after her father's arrest. How he missed it. Being able to tell her everything, anything, and knowing what she was feeling, too.

Had he lost that because of his job or because of her father?

Selena spoke again, her voice intimate in the closed compartment. "Andre invited me to the funeral on Saturday."

"Will you go?" Gabe asked, resisting the urge to bring her soft fingertips to his lips. What would he give to have her run her fingers over his face and through his hair?

"Of course. And he told me you'll be speaking."

Gabe felt a stab of sorrow slicing through his middle.

"I've never given a eulogy before."

He'd never needed to. Dante Chee was the first of his men to be killed in the line of duty.

She brushed her thumb over the back of his hand. "You'll be wonderful."

He didn't remind her that he wasn't the family orator. That was Clyne.

"I'd rather be locking up his killers." Though it seemed that the two gang members who had been killed tonight might be the shooters. A preliminary check indicated the footwear worn by Nota and the second man might be a match. If their shoe treads and the tracks at the site of the body dump were the same, the police might right now be zipping Chee's killers into body bags. Too good for them, he decided.

"Andre told me they still don't know who killed his brother."

"We've got some leads." He said nothing else.

She cast him a sidelong glance. Was she waiting for him to say more? He had always avoided speaking about his police work with Selena. Up until today, he had believed he was protecting her from the darker side of his profession. Now it felt more as if he was just shutting her out.

Back when he had discovered what her father had been doing with his delivery truck, he'd been very glad that he'd never divulged anything that might have compromised an investigation. Could he have been using his job as a way to keep Selena from getting too close?

Gabe shifted uncomfortably. He glanced over to see her staring out at her house.

Could his silence feel like distrust to her?

Selena had stopped stroking his hand. His gaze snapped back to her. She studied him with her brows raised and he scowled.

"What?"

"Nothing." Her hand slipped from his and she turned away, staring out at the snow that glistened under starlight.

Gabe glanced at Nota's car parked beside her sister Mia's box truck and then at the empty place where Selena's truck should now be parked. She had no truck for tomorrow's run.

"I know you'll find Dante Chee's murderer," she said, her voice filled with a sort of world weariness. "You never let anything stand between you and an investigation."

And that included her. They both knew it.

"What will you do tomorrow?" he asked, pointing at the place her truck should be.

"I'll take Mia's truck. She'll have to wait until I get back. We did it that way for a long time, remember?"

He did.

She glanced toward the front door. His heartbeat accelerated. He wanted to keep her here, if only for a moment more. Every moment with Selena was worth the pain that came afterward, when he was without her again.

"My little sister might be visiting soon," he blurted.

Her attention returned to him as she cast him an odd look. "Jovanna? That's good. Your grandmother told my mother that you had found her."

"She's been adopted by a white woman."

Selena drew in a breath. "Clyne must be furious."

She knew his brother well enough to know that. Of course, she knew his family, or *had* known, them very well. His heart ached again at the losses, one upon the other.

"Clyne wants her to know her roots, of course, become part of her tribe, and my grandmother wants her to be home for the ceremony."

"What do *you* want?"

No one had ever asked him that. His first thought was that he wanted Selena. But he just couldn't think how that could happen. Because of her actions tonight she was now part of another active investigation. That alone meant she was off-limits. Would they always be on opposite sides?

"I want Jovanna happy. But I worry about her losing a second mother."

"Yes. I understand that. Being forced from her adoptive mother might be very hard on her."

Selena echoed Gabe's thoughts, but as of yet, he had not raised them with his family.

"I hope she will want to know us and learn about being an Apache woman. And I wonder if she even knows about the Sunrise Ceremony."

"She'll need a sponsor. A woman to teach her what she must know. Has your grandmother asked anyone yet?"

"Probably." But he didn't know. The woman who was selected must be a close friend, but not a relative. So it couldn't be either Lea or Isabella, the new wives of his younger brothers. He looked at Selena, thinking she would be perfect.

"What?" asked Selena.

"I wish it were you," he said, and then lowered his head, thinking he shouldn't have said that.

She rested a hand on his forearm and his muscles twitched beneath the gentle pressure. He met her gaze.

"I would be honored," she said in Apache.

He responded in the language of their birth. "It would be our honor, Sunflower Sky Woman."

Her mouth gaped as she blinked up at him. Was she surprised that he remembered her Apache name? She shouldn't be. He remembered everything about her. Couldn't seem to forget a single thing.

"I wish things were different, Selena."

"I wish that, too."

The silence stretched. He closed his eyes, praying for some path that would bring him to a place where he could be with her and still keep his position as chief of the tribal police. Selena zipped her coat closed. It had grown so cold inside the interior of the vehicle that he could see each exhalation she made. Her breath and his breath mingled, fogging the windows, obscuring the outside world and leaving them in an icy cocoon.

"Gabe, I have to go in." But she didn't move to do so.

"Soon," he said.

"How did those men find us?" she asked.

He had no answer.

"I don't know." He shifted in his seat. He needed to tell her something.

She turned toward him, so that her back was to the passenger's side window, giving him her attention.

"When I reached your truck and I saw someone lying inside, I thought…" Here his voice failed him. The squeezing pressure across his chest grew too great. He dragged in a breath and blew out frost. "I thought I'd lost you."

She smiled. "I'm right here."

He had lost her once before, but the permanency of this, of realizing that she might have died, frightened him so much.

"I don't want you to go inside."

She cocked her head. "I don't understand."

He didn't know how to explain it. He just knew he needed to get her away from this house.

When he said nothing, her gaze strayed toward her front door.

"I wish I could be like you. Believe in something so much that it came before everything else. For me it's always been a balancing act. What's best for Tomas? What does my mother need? How can I get enough business to pay the loans, keep us fed and keep my sisters happy? And now my father. I want everyone safe."

And that love for them was going to get her killed, he thought.

She gave him a beseeching look now. As if wanting

him to understand something. He got that cold feeling in the pit of his stomach again.

"Selena, don't let him drag you any farther into this. Please." He was about to ask her to come with him. To let him protect her from her family, which he now believed to be the biggest threat. Her love for them put her in danger. But Selena cut him off.

"You have your job. I have my family. My sisters, my mom and my little brother all need me. My father needs me, too, in his way. They are everything to me."

"But you're not safe here. Come with me. I can protect you."

"Protect us, my entire family? With twelve men? Or just me?"

She waited.

"Just you."

Her smile was so sad. She leaned forward and he followed, filled with a fragile hope. She stroked his cheek and then her fingers slipped away.

He didn't want her to put him through this again, making him choose between doing his duty and protecting her family.

He knew what he'd do if she forced him to choose and it scared him to his core. He'd choose her and lose it all.

"I'll find the precursor," she said. "Then you can arrest them, and things can go back to the way they were."

"Is that what you want?" he asked. It wasn't what he wanted. Not anymore. He wanted Selena back.

This time her father was working with DOJ, but he'd

still managed to drag Selena into the line of fire twice in only twenty-four hours.

He wished he could throw him back in prison.

"So you're willing to stick to Dryer's story?" he asked.

"That Nota took the truck because Dad's parole officer stopped by? Yes. Nota didn't call anyone. So Escalanti wouldn't know I was with him, and his car is still here. Plus it explains the bullet holes in my truck. The story works."

It might work. Or it might get Selena killed. If Escalanti thought she was working with the federal authorities, would he kill her or just call off the deliveries?

It was a huge risk. One he didn't want Selena to take.

If he were Escalanti, he would either move the lab and call things off, or kill the Doselas on the suspicion they were playing him.

"I should arrest you," he said. The threat was half-hearted. "At least then I'd know you were safe."

To arrest her was to blow the investigation wide-open. He chafed at the need to do his job and his instinct to keep Selena with him.

"I just want this to be over," she said. "Good night, Gabe."

She shifted and the door release clicked, then Selena slipped from his unit.

She hesitated. He knew he should say something. But words failed him. Selena closed the door and he let her walk away, waiting until she was inside before starting the engine. Had he thought she might change her mind and come back to him?

She wouldn't. She had her family and he had his job.

He stared at Nota's muscle car, which gleamed yellow under the light from the Doselas' living room window. It wouldn't be long before the Salt River gang missed their two gunmen and Escalanti knew that Nota and Martinez were not coming back.

Chapter Fourteen

Gabe returned to the crime scene after dropping off Selena and met with his lead investigator and Murdy, who had bad news. His men had run the snowmobile's trail and hit a dead end. The precursor had been off-loaded at the shoulder of the road that ran parallel to Piñon Lake Road. They could determine nothing of the delivering vehicle or vehicles. In other words, they had not found the location of the storage site for the precursor.

"Another dead end," said Gabe.

"Seems so," said Detective Juris.

"Any notion on how the Salt River gang members knew about this delivery?" asked Detective Murdy.

Gabe shook his head. "Love to know that myself."

Unfortunately the ones who could tell them were both dead. He stayed until the scene was released and then drove back to the station to jot down some notes.

When he was finished he was too tired to drive home, so he once again stretched out on the wide leather sofa. His last thought before slumber stole him away was of Selena sitting at his side, her thumb caressing the back of his hand.

There was a gentle rapping on his door. Gabe startled to a sitting position, catching his big sheepskin jacket before it hit the floor. He rubbed the sleep from his eyes and glanced up to see Detective Randall Juris looking at him from beneath a creased brow.

"That's two nights in a row," said Juris, pointing to Gabe's choice of sleeping arrangements.

"It saves time and it's quiet."

Juris looked around at the Spartan little box of an office. Filing cabinet, minifridge, desk, chair and couch. Gabe knew that Juris had been married many years and thought his smile looked indulgent.

"Quiet might be good, but when Dora goes down to see her folks, it drives me a little crazy. You know?"

Gabe understood. Too much quiet was not good, especially compared to having a woman you loved share your home and your bed. Gabe thought of coming home to a family, as Juris did every night, and felt an unexpected surge of envy.

"All ready for tomorrow?"

He meant the funeral. The assemblage would be tremendous. Bigger even than some of their festivals.

"Thanks to Yepa, we are. She has been coordinating with the family. Arizona law enforcement will be here. US Marines, state politicians and representatives from the Apache tribes in Salt River and Oklahoma. Chee had family up there." Gabe had never given a eulogy and in his heart he knew he was not up to the task.

"I thought he was army," Juris said.

Juris massaged his neck with one hand and gripped the latch with the other. Gabe recognized this as a sign that whatever news Juris had, he was not anxious to deliver it.

"Salva asked me to come get you, Chief," said Juris. "They're all assembled."

Gabe's gaze flicked to the wall clock. It was almost time. First shift would be gathering in the conference room. But today was different because they had located Chee's body, confirmed he was dead. So today all twelve officers in the brotherhood of tribal police would assemble for roll call. Gabe corrected himself. Only eleven officers, now.

He and Juris exchanged a grim look.

"I'll be right there."

Juris left him. Gabe headed to the bathroom to throw some water on his face, his bones suddenly weary. When he entered the briefing room a few minutes later, all the men stood.

Sergeant Franklin Salva addressed him. "Chief Cosen, would you like to call the roll?"

"No, Sergeant. It's your honor."

Although the funeral was tomorrow, today they would perform a private ceremony for Officer Chee. The men remained standing, responding, as always, as Salva took the roll, but with one exception. He left their fallen officer for last. When he called Dante's name all the men stood in silence as their sergeant called for Dante Gerald Chee again, and again and one final time. Then Salva turned to his chief and said, "Officer Dante Gerald Chee, end of watch."

The gathering of men remained standing in somber

silence until Sergeant Salva broke through their contemplation in a voice thick with determination.

"Okay, listen up because I have some information…" Salva launched into his briefing, concluding with a warning. "And I will personally kick the butt of any man who is not wearing his Kevlar."

Gabe headed back to his office and was on the phone with the state's evidence lab when Parole Officer Ronnie Hare stopped by a little before ten.

Gabe motioned him to a seat. Ronnie relaxed back into the chair before Gabe's desk, glancing around the room until Gabe returned the handset to its cradle. The two spoke in Apache for a while, just exchanging pleasantries and news from each reservation. Salt River was connected to the southern border of Black Mountain reservation. But each reservation had its own government. Ronnie's reservation was a mixture of several different Apache people, while Black Mountain was almost exclusively Mountain Apache.

Ronnie switched to English. "Hey, I'm real sorry to hear about your guy. That's terrible."

"Yeah. He's the first man we've lost."

"Just awful. You got any leads?"

"We're running forensics. I'm sure we'll find something."

"And you had some gang violence."

Gabe's brow lifted. "Where'd you hear that?"

"I was chatting with Yepa. Her husband is a classmate of my cousin."

"Were you?" But he offered nothing more.

He recalled Dryer's complaint that everyone here

was related to everyone else. Gabe forced a smile and resisted the urge to look at his watch.

"Think they're connected?" asked Hare.

"It's early in the investigation. Can't rule anything out."

"Sure. Sure. Anyways, I went out to visit Frasco Dosela yesterday," said Hare. "Unannounced visit. So that's why I'm here. I was getting a vibe. You know? Like something was going on. Thought I'd let you know."

Gabe believed that what Hare had noticed was that his untimely arrival had kept Frasco from riding along with Selena, as they had planned.

"A vibe?" asked Gabe.

"Yeah. I've been at this a while and Mr. Dosela seemed agitated at my arrival. Really restless."

"Interesting," said Gabe.

"And I didn't like the looks of his daughter's boy-friend."

Gabe's antenna went up as he realized the weakness in Dryer's cover story. Here was a witness to Selena being at the house when Nota arrived. Had he seen them leave together in her truck?

"Why not?" Did his voice still sound casual? He wasn't sure. He needed to get to Dryer. Let him know.

"He seemed a little young for her. Plus that car. And he was dressed…" Hare waved his hands as he struggled to come up with a description. "Like one of my parolees."

"That's not good."

"Plus they took the box truck instead of his car."

Gabe's heart sank. Nota's car was still at the Dosela's. He needed to get it out of there before Hare saw it again.

"Why would they take that truck?" asked Hare.

Gabe rubbed his neck. "Better traction?"

"Maybe. It was weird. Anyway, Yepa said gang violence, so I thought I'd mention it to you."

What would Hare think when he learned that one of the victims was the man he had seen leaving with Selena?

"Hey, next time I go out there, would you like to ride along?" Ronnie asked.

Gabe did look at his watch this time. "Not unless you feel you need me there."

"Oh, no. I can handle my job. Just, well, as I said. Something seemed off." Hare's eyes drifted, turning to the files on Gabe's desk before sweeping back to him.

"You going out there today?" asked Gabe.

"No. Seeing another release." Hare provided the name.

Good, Gabe thought, because if Hare were going, Gabe would need to speak to Selena first. Likely impossible now as she'd be on her run and her phone got no service on much of the route. Still he'd try until he got through to her.

Gabe stood, signaling an end to the chat.

"Well, if anything seems wonky with Dosela, I'll let you know." Ronnie rose and Gabe walked him to the door. They shook hands and they said their farewells in Apache.

Gabe waited until Ronnie Hare was out of sight to call Juris and explain the problem.

"I'll run a check on him. But if he's got a big mouth, that could be a problem. I can send a unit to stick with him," said Juris.

"No. That will just make him suspicious."

"Okay, then." Juris turned to other matters. "We have positive ID on all of the shooters. Red Hawk down in Salt River helped with the ID of the ones who attacked the truck. He knew them on sight."

"Maybe Nota's death will flush Escalanti out of his burrow," said Gabe.

"Hope so. Oh," said Juris. "I spoke to Sammy Leekela about his brother's death. Routine interview. He seemed more nervous than grief-stricken. Think they might move that meth lab?"

"Dryer's got men watching it."

"That's good, I suppose." Juris certainly didn't sound pleased with that news. "I hate that they're on our land."

"I know," said Gabe. "But it's too big, Randall."

"We need to nail Escalanti," said Juris.

Once the prospect of taking down the leader of the Wolf Posse would have filled Gabe with anticipation. What he was feeling now was more like dread.

Yepa buzzed him with a call, which Juris could easily hear.

"Later," said Juris, ending the call.

Gabe picked up the call from Detective Murdy of the Arizona state police crimes investigation unit. Murdy had been one of the two men on-site at last night's shooting.

Murdy told him they had a match between the tracks at the site of Chee's body and the ones of Nota and the second man, Alfred Martinez. Initial results indicated they had found the killers of his officer.

He'd only just replaced the handset when Yepa buzzed him again. She had another call for him and asked if he wanted it patched through. He needed to call Selena. Tell her about Ronnie Hare.

"Is it important?"

"I don't know. But it's Selena Dosela."

Gabe's heart fluttered as if it was considering stopping. Selena never called him. Not once since she handed back his ring.

"Put her through."

Chapter Fifteen

Gabe waited, clutching the handset so tight that his wrist started to ache. Still, he couldn't release his grip. There was a familiar click.

"Gabe? You there?" It was Selena's sweet voice.

He'd forgotten to say hello or even identify himself.

"Here," he said, his voice sounding harsh, like a dog's bark.

"Uh, hi." There was a long pause. Gabe could hear the clock on the wall ticking away the seconds. He should say something.

He didn't know if he should launch into his business or ask her what she wanted or tell her he enjoyed seeing her, but that seemed wrong because of the shooting. As he was dithering he realized she wasn't speaking, either. He waited, phone now pressed tight to his ear listening to the silence.

"Selena?"

"Yes. I'm here."

Another long pause. Gabe wiped his brow and discovered he was sweating. Yepa peered in from the doorway and gave him an odd look. Her brows rose.

She whispered to him. "Want some water?"

He waved her away, fanning the air so hard it looked as if he was under attack by a swarm of hornets.

"Um, Carla and Paula are home," said Selena.

Gabe sat back in his chair because he knew who she meant. Her youngest sisters, the twins, had returned from their long haul.

That meant a truck big enough to transport the load out of here was now on Black Mountain. They had to find the precursor pronto.

"Gabe?"

"Yes. I heard," he said. "The twins are home safe."

"Yes."

"Thanks for telling me."

"Sure."

The silence stretched.

"You need me to come out there?" he asked.

"No. We're fine."

"Okay, then. Where are you?"

"Finishing my route. Why?"

Because mobile phones could more easily be tapped.

"Maybe you should come in. We could have lunch."

There was a long pause. "What's going on?"

"Your dad's parole officer was here. He's worried about your new boyfriend."

"He's not my...oh." More silence. "I see."

"I'm heading out that way." He hadn't been, but he was now.

Her breath became audible for a moment. "See you later, then."

She said goodbye and he heard the click. He stared

at the phone as the image of Selena stroking his hand rose. He stood and headed for the door.

Yepa buzzed him. Juris was on the line wanting to review initial findings.

"Switch it to my mobile." He set his hat on his head and made a beeline for his unit.

His phone rang and he took the call, switching it to speaker as he drove toward Wolf Canyon. Juris reviewed initial findings, evidence collection, identification of the two Salt River shooters.

"I'll call Chief Red Hawk in Salt River," said Gabe, referring to the chief of the tribal police in the Apache reservation to their south. "See if he has any more details on those two than what's in the database."

"Good."

Gabe told Juris about the visit from Hare and the hole in his story.

Juris cursed. "Well, he's not going to talk to Escalanti."

"He's got ex-cons to check on all over both reservations."

"Could be a problem," said Juris.

Understatement of the year, thought Gabe. "I'm heading out to the Doselas'."

"Might be best not to be seen coming and going. A police unit parked in her drive is the worse of the two threats."

"We have to pick up Nota's car. Gives me an excuse."

"Fine."

Gabe called a tow truck and met him at the Doselas'. They had Nota's car off premises when Selena appeared, driving Mia's box truck, hers having been seized for evidence.

Gabe waited beside the parked 18-wheeler with the flatbed trailer while Selena opened the driver's side door of the box truck. Then he did what he used to do— reached up, clasped her by her small waist and lifted her down in front of him. Her arms slipped naturally around his neck. She grinned up at him. Did she remember how they used to laugh together? Her smile faded by degrees and she removed her hands from the back of his neck. Suddenly he felt the cold there more acutely.

"I didn't talk to anyone," she said, and stepped back making some space between them. "And no one mentioned the shooting. I don't think word is out yet."

It would be, and soon.

"Juris thinks I should stay away from your place. I just removed Nota's car for processing."

She glanced to the empty place where the car had been.

"That's good."

"I can meet you somewhere if you want to talk to me. Or you can call me. Please call me if anything seems wrong."

"I will." Selena glanced toward the house. "I better go. Mia is waiting to start her run. We're down to one truck now."

"I'll try to get yours back to you as soon as possible."

She cast him a smile. "I'd appreciate that."

"May I call you later?"

She cocked her head. Was she wondering if this was business or personal? With Selena it was always both.

"Of course."

And then she lifted on her toes, angling to press a kiss to his cheek. But he turned to intercept the kiss, taking her mouth with his, giving her the kind of kiss usually reserved for the darkness. She relaxed against him, letting him deepen the contact. Suddenly the day seemed more spring than winter. He reluctantly eased back, brushing his lips over the soft skin of her fluttering eyelids and then holding her tight.

"What are we doing?" he asked.

"Catching bad guys," she murmured.

"Oh, right."

She released her hold and inched away. He let her go.

Gabe headed back to his freezing-cold vehicle as Selena disappeared into her house. The day was gobbled up with the two investigations and the barrage of the usual disturbances, including one domestic dispute with shots fired. There were numerous auto accidents because of black ice.

He finally dragged himself home, looking forward to having his grandmother fuss over him. Clyne was out, he knew, because it was Friday night and he had mentioned that he had plans to take a girl to a place in Salt River for dinner and dancing. Gabe wished he could take Selena dancing. Why hadn't he when he'd had the chance?

Work, he remembered. Always work.

Gabe called a greeting as he entered and was met with a banquet of aromas that set his stomach rumbling. He deposited his hat and coat by the door and found his grandmother busy in the kitchen. Glendora Clawson was an excellent cook and tonight she had outdone herself with a wonderful chicken-and-rice casserole that smelled delicious. His grandmother stood at the stove, flipping her fry bread so that the golden-brown side bobbed in the oil in the cast-iron skillet like a duck on water. At her elbow was a large plate draped in several paper towels, waiting for the next batch of hot bread.

No church function was complete without his grandmother's fry bread. The organizers of the annual Fourth of July rodeo had even tried to get her to set up a booth for the tourists, but his grandmother, now in her seventies, had declined, leaving that to the younger women in the tribe.

"Smells amazing in here," said Gabe, dropping a kiss on his grandmother's soft cheek and stealing a piece of bread in a deft move.

She scowled and brandished the wooden spoon at him. "Those aren't for you."

He already had taken a large bite out of the bread. That was when he saw the cooling apple pie and his ears went back. She didn't cook pies, except for special occasions.

"Who's coming for dinner?"

"No one."

"Is Clay back?"

"He's in court Monday. You know that. He and Isabella are taking a long weekend. Do her good to get away from her herd for a bit."

The adoption hearing. He must be more tired than he realized.

"Who's the food for, then?"

"The Chee family."

Gabe lost his appetite and the warmth that always came from his grandmother as much as from her kitchen. She was cooking for the gathering after tomorrow's funeral—of course.

His grandmother glanced his way and seemed to sense his sorrow.

"Guess who I saw at the clinic today?" His grandmother had begun volunteering two days a week at the Apache health clinic.

Gabe ran through all the people who might be at the clinic. It was a long list, but his mind latched on to one particular name and he felt his chest constrict.

"Ruth Dosela," Glendora announced, confirming his guess. His grandmother made a small *tsk*ing sound. "Poor thing is skinny as a rail. She's just started another round of chemo and her hair hasn't even grown back from the last time.

"Oh, I was telling them about how you had gone on up there to South Dakota to find your little sister. How you used your detective skills to track her down and find the man who rescued her from the car. How she got lost in the foster-care system and was alive all this time, even though we didn't even know it, poor little lamb. I can't wait to get my hands on her. I've finished the beading on her ceremony dress. I'll close those seams on the side when I see how big she's gotten. Wait until you see. Oh, it's beautiful, if I do say so myself. Yellow as corn pollen. I think I used every ribbon from here to Phoenix on the yoke. Now I've got to work on the moccasins."

There might not even be a ceremony because they didn't have custody of their sister and might never get it. But he knew better than to suggest that scenario to his grandmother. She was determined that this would happen and was acting accordingly. At least they knew that their sister was alive and well. And if Clay was successful, they would know more about where she lived and who had adopted her. And Jovanna would soon know who she really was. An Apache of the Black Mountain Tribe.

"Ruthie offered to bring food to the ceremony, which is good. Give her something to look forward to."

"You invited them to the ceremony?" Gabe couldn't keep the shock from his voice. He was so good at keeping his stone face at work, but his grandmother knew just how to stir him up.

"Of course. I've invited them. They were almost family. When are you going to ask that girl out again?"

"Grandma, she gave back my ring." He found himself touching the medicine bundle that always hung about his neck. Inside were many sacred objects including the diamond solitaire she had returned that awful day. "*She* broke the engagement. Remember?"

"Of course I remember. I also remember how happy you both were until you were testifying in federal court against her father. *Of course*, she tried to return the ring. You didn't have to take it."

"Yes, I did."

"You haven't seen any other girls."

That was not true. He just had not brought any of

them home to his grandmother's table because that was just a whole different level of seeing a woman.

In the past few months, both he and Clyne had become a great disappointment to their grandmother. Everything had been just fine until Clay and Kino had settled down. Now his grandmother had ramped up the pressure to get him and Clyne wed.

The only thing she spoke about more often was the return of Jovanna, but that was something on which they all agreed.

"Well, one thing I know for certain. You'll never find a girl in that police station or your police cruiser."

Gabe changed the subject. "Any word from Clay?"

"I forgot you slept in the station last night. Yes. He did it! The judge ordered the adoption opened. He's hoping we'll have the name of the mother and some details on Jovanna within the week. The judge gave them seven days, and Clay's attorney says they will use every bit of it."

"Does that mean we can see her?"

"Not yet. But soon." His grandmother clasped her hands together. "I'm so excited. I cannot wait to get my hands on that girl."

When Gabe stuck his head in the refrigerator, his grandmother took pity on him, heating a bowl of chili to go with his half-eaten piece of fry bread. Gabe ate at the kitchen table as his grandmother cooked. When he finished his meal he announced that he was going to bed. She cast him a look of disappointment. Likely Clyne was spinning some pretty woman around the dance floor about now. Meanwhile, Gabe would be ironing his uniform for tomorrow's funeral service.

He wondered what Selena was doing. Was she home with her family or out on the town? Gabe drew out his phone. Before he knew it he had made the call.

"Selena?" he said.

"Mia. Who's this?"

Gabe drew a breath. "Gabe Cosen."

There was a long pause.

"May I speak to Selena?"

"Um. I'll see if she's here."

Gabe smiled. Their house was smaller than his grandmother's. Surely Mia knew if her big sister was home, but the white lie would give her time to ask Selena what to do. A moment later Selena said hello.

"Hi, Selena."

"Hi."

She sounded so good.

"What's up?" she asked.

"Is everything okay there?"

"So far. Is everything all right with you?"

He didn't know exactly why or what he said, but he told her about his day and about the funeral preparations. How there would be a motorcade before the flower car and about coordinating the service with the family and how his speech wasn't good enough to do justice to the loss or to the man Chee had been and might have become. He said his grandmother had made another casserole and he'd be at Chee's home after the funeral. Before he knew it he had told her that now he had to interview for a new man and that he'd never had to hire a new officer to replace a fallen one. Finally he told her about the ceremony this morning for end of watch. When at last he finished talking he was met with silence and he wondered for a moment if she was still there.

"Selena?" he said.

"I'm here." But her voice sounded choked and strained. Were those tears?

"Selena, did I make you cry?"

She cleared her throat. "No. It's just… I'm so sorry for all of this. I wish I could do something. Except make a casserole. We made one, too. Mama insisted. We'll be at the Chee home after the funeral, as well."

It was the first bright spot in his day.

"I'll see you there, then."

"Yes. And Gabe?"

"Yes?"

"Thank you for telling me about your day."

He had, hadn't he? And it felt natural as breathing.

"You're welcome."

"Good night, Gabe."

He whispered good-night and disconnected, recalling a time when he had imagined what it would be like when the good-night wishes were not whispered over the phone but over the pillows in their marriage bed. Gabe pressed the phone to his forehead as the terrible ache made him fold at the middle. How had he let this happen?

Chapter Sixteen

On Saturday, after the funeral, the home of Officer Chee's parents was filled to bursting with members of the tribe. Tables groaned under the weight of casseroles and platters of cold cuts. Some had brought drinks, desserts, flowers. No one came empty-handed. Chee left behind a father, mother and brother. Andre stayed close to his mother, straying only a time or two to speak to his friends. On the top of the television was a framed photo of Dante Chee in his Black Mountain police uniform and one of him looking much younger in his US Marines uniform.

Selena stood beside Mia, who elbowed her in the ribs and inclined her head toward the door. The Cosen family had arrived. Selena lifted to her tiptoes to see them parade into the crowded room. Glendora Clawson, Gabe's grandmother, carried a casserole wrapped in tinfoil. She was dressed all in black, except for her open pink parka and the stunning turquoise-and-sterling necklace. Her hair showed only a sprinkling of gray and there was no doubt where her grandsons had gotten their looks. Behind her came the oldest Cosen brother, Clyne, wearing a black woolen topcoat. Snow stuck to his neatly braided hair, which he had dressed with silver beads. He looked every inch the tribal leader, from his bear-tooth bolo to the distinctive toe tab of his traditional moccasins. Next came Kino, still in his police uniform and escorting his pretty new wife, a Salt River woman named Lea. He wore his long hair in one single braid down his back. Clay was absent. Still in federal court down in Phoenix, she knew. Kino closed the door and Selena lowered herself back to her heels.

"Where's Gabe?" asked Mia.

"I don't know."

Clyne approached Brenda Chee first, representing the tribe as he spoke. He was formal and eloquent, and she was glad she had never been interested in Clyne. The woman he chose would have to represent the tribe as well as he did and be the model of all that was good in an Apache woman.

By the time Glendora and Kino had finished speaking with the family, the door had opened again and Gabe stepped in from the cold, still wearing his blue dress uniform. The sight of him made her catch her breath. Her hand went to her mouth, pressing the pads of her fingers to her lips. Judging from the women standing about her, she was not the only one who noticed his arrival. Old and young watched Gabe steer through the crowd. It was not only his striking good looks or the uniform that he filled in all the right places, it was the elegant way he walked and the air of authority that was as much a part of him as his skin. Heads turned and the room quieted again as Gabe spoke first to Mr. and Mrs. Chee and then to Andre. His words were sincere and heartfelt. Like in his eulogy, Gabe spoke of honor and duty and his genuine grief at the loss that was shared by the entire tribe.

"You have to catch this man," Brenda Chee said, clutching Gabe's hand.

"Yes, ma'am. We will," he said, and Brenda released his hand, mollified.

Gabe left them and found his brothers. Mia poked her again.

"What?" she said.

"Go over to him."

"Why?"

Mia rolled her eyes. Selena bolstered her courage and made her way across the room, but Violet Norris got to him first. Her giggles sounded like the call of a screech owl. Selena paused and Amelia Bush cut in front of her to join Violet, who appeared less than pleased with Amelia's arrival. Selena glanced back to Mia who held up both hands in surrender. Selena noted that Kino, newly married, was the only Cosen not drawing a gathering of female admirers. And why not? The older Cosen boys were two of the most eligible men on the rez and definitely the best looking.

Clyne was now speaking to four women and Gabe had three. Martha Moses had elbowed her way between Amelia and Violet.

Her younger sisters Paula and Carla flanked her.

"Want us to run interference?" asked Paula.

Selena smiled. "No. It's okay."

"You sure?" asked Carla, casting Selena a sympathetic look.

"Positive," Selena forced a smile and scanned the room.

Glendora sat with Mrs. Chee. Selena went to greet Gabe's grandmother and they had a nice chat. Glendora had never treated Selena differently after her father had been arrested. Perhaps it was because her own daughter had been married to a man who had been in and out of prison for much of their troubled marriage. Her mother had been close friends with Gabe's mother and had told her some of what had happened. It was Selena's opinion that all the Cosen boys had a mission to redeem the family name. But, more than that, they seemed determined to be what their father had never been—honorable men.

Selena wandered back to her sister and noted that their mother looked wilted from the long day and the chemotherapy.

"Ready to go, Mom?" she asked.

Her mother nodded wearily. Her mother and sisters went to make their farewells to the Chee family as Selena slipped out to start the car and turn the heater up to full blast. She returned to the foyer where Mia helped her mother with her coat. Carla held her mother's gloves and Paula gripped her hat. Selena glanced back to see Gabe staring at her over the heads of two women before she stepped out into the night.

Her sisters all climbed into the back of the car and pulled the doors closed while Selena saw her mother seated. She was heading toward the driver's side when a familiar male voice called to her.

"Selena!"

She turned to see Gabe trotting out to her. Mia's window buzzed down as Selena stepped out of the headlights' beam to meet Gabe.

"I didn't get a chance to speak to you."

"Yes. I know." She thought that answer showed restraint. Did it mean anything that he had called her last night? That when he was stressed and harried he had turned to her? Perhaps it was nothing, but she felt a connection growing again.

"I wondered if I could…if you'd like to go for a cup of coffee?"

There was coffee inside, of course, but no privacy.

"Now?" She glanced back to her vehicle where her mother and sisters waited.

Gabe rubbed his neck.

Mia climbed out of the backseat and opened the driver's side door.

"See you at home," she said and closed the door, making Selena's decision for her. A moment later her car was pulling away, leaving Gabe and Selena alone beneath the stars.

"I guess you're driving me home," she said, and then remembered that his family was inside. "Did you come with Clyne and Kino?"

"Kino and Lea have their pickup. Grandmother and Clyne are together, and I have my unit." He motioned out toward the road and the line of cars and trucks that sat bumper to bumper. "I came right from work."

On a Saturday. Of course he had.

"Shall we?" Gabe said, indicating the direction.

They walked in silence toward his SUV where he

opened her door and clasped her elbow as she climbed up. She usually would not need the assistance, but tonight she wore a simple gray woolen dress and black shoes with low heels that had absolutely no tread whatsoever. Once she was up, he reached and pulled the seat belt across her body and clasped it at her hip. His hand lingered there and her whole body began to tingle and tighten. Suddenly she was glad she had gone to the trouble to comb out her hair and clip it back from her face. She'd even put on light makeup, mascara and a raspberry lip gloss.

She glanced from his hand on her hip to Gabe's face. His eyes glittered and his jaw clenched tight. She tried to remember why seeing him was such a bad idea. Something to do with him breaking her heart, but here was her heart pounding wildly and urging her on as if it had never been torn to pieces.

He was going to kiss her again, and she was going to let him.

Chapter Seventeen

Gabe wished he hadn't strapped Selena into the passenger's seat. Now that they were kissing and she was tugging at the shoulders of his uniform, he wanted to drag her out of the car and take her…where?

Gabe stood beside her open door at the shoulder of the road before the Chee family's home where anyone might see them. He pulled back, ignoring her groan of protest as he rested his forehead against hers.

"I've missed this. I've missed you," he said.

She stroked her hand through his short hair, and finding no purchase, she laced her fingers behind his head and sighed.

"I wish things were different," Selena whispered.

"We could make them different."

She released him and gave him a sad look that told him nothing had changed. In fact, her father's return had only made things worse. He shouldn't even be seen with her because he did not know who was watching her. He should take her home.

"Did you say something about coffee?" asked Selena.

Gabe drew back. She let her fingers glide down his neck and over his shoulders before sitting back in her seat. By the time she'd released him, he needed the cold air to bring himself back under control.

Gabe left her to return to the driver's side, moving his coat out of the way to take his seat. He'd left it in his vehicle before going in, but now he draped it over Selena's lap. That darn threadbare coat she wore over her pretty gray dress was just not warm enough on a night like this.

She snuggled under the sheepskin and he started the engine, whisking them away from the gathering and his family.

When he sat beside her, he was glad for the intimacy of darkness that hid them from the view of all the people who pulled them apart.

Gabe drove toward Black Mountain, trying to think of some way to change things while the smell of lavender drove him crazy.

Memories surfaced. They had not waited for marriage to explore each other's bodies, but he knew he had been Selena's first. He did not know if she'd had others since then, but he knew there'd been none here on the rez. So she'd been discreet or gone without. Perhaps she'd been the wiser, because he'd gone out and tried to find her replacement. He never could. There was no one like Selena anywhere.

Had she missed him deep down the way he'd missed her? They'd been so good together.

Her words stretched out across the space that divided them.

"You were wonderful today," she said. "Your words were very…heartfelt."

"It was difficult."

"You didn't show it. And your call for action, for the tribe to return to the old ways and not let ourselves be used by outsiders. I wish my father had been there to hear you."

Her father, who could not attend as he was under house arrest. Her father who had cut a deal with the DOJ and not bothered to tell Selena, and then let his daughter drive out alone with a member of Escalanti's gang. Gabe gripped the steering wheel in a stranglehold as the anger settled in his guts.

"Has your dad been contacted by anyone new?" Escalanti would have to send a new contact or come himself.

She glanced at him. "Is that what this is, another interview?"

Gabe cursed himself for a fool. He finally had Selena alone and he was blowing it again.

"No. It's not. Just coffee." He focused on the road and not the way Selena's scent filled the warming air in the cab. But when they got to the town of Black Mountain, they found every café and restaurant closed.

"I didn't realize it was so late," he said.

"There's the casino," she suggested.

That never closed. But the bright lights and the horde of outsiders held no appeal. Weekends were always crowded. But the casino did have a hotel and hotels had restaurants and beds. His body went hard at that and he fought a mighty battle to resist his needs. He'd only just gotten her to agree to go for coffee.

"Too loud," he said.

"And too many people we know work there."

That was certainly true.

"There's my office. I have coffee." Why hadn't he thought of that earlier? It was quiet and the dispatcher on call was over at the firehouse tonight. He'd have her all to himself.

But Selena had not agreed. In fact she was scowling.

"Or the casino," he offered. "If you want."

Idiot. His office made it sound like what it was—an ambush.

"Your office," she said.

Had she just agreed to what he thought? Oh, he hoped so. He turned them back toward the station, parked in his usual spot and showed her in via the back door, walking the familiar route through the squad room.

"It's creepy in here after dark."

They threaded between his men's desks.

"Let me get the lights." He stepped into his office and flicked on his desk lamp, leaving the fluorescents off.

"Better?"

She nodded and turned as he took her brown work coat, sliding it from her shoulders to reveal the trim gray dress that clung just enough to make a man interested.

Who was he kidding? Selena could be dressed in a paper sack and he'd still be interested. He hung her coat on the coat tree beside the door and added his jacket and hat to the adjoining hooks. When he turned she was already seated on his couch, one leg crossed over the other at the knee, one shoe dangling from her toe.

Oh, boy, he thought. He was in trouble.

Gabe headed toward the coffeepot.

"Do you have tea?" she asked.

He thought Yepa drank tea, so he raided her top drawer and returned with two tea bags wrapped in white paper envelopes. He preferred coffee but he'd drink dishwater if it meant sitting beside Selena. He filled the carafe and sent the water through the coffee machine.

"Sugar?"

"One."

The water heated, dripped, and when he had enough, he poured the water into two paper cups. Selena left the couch and came to stand beside him as he added one packet of sugar and a tea bag to her cup. She accepted the offering and dunked the tea bag. He felt just like that bag, bobbing up and down and unable to get out of the hot water.

Finally she lifted the liquid to her mouth. Gabe stared as Selena blew on the hot tea. She might have managed to cool it, but her actions heated him so much that he unbuttoned the collar of his uniform and loosened his tie.

Selena cast him a knowing smile and headed across the room where she sat on his leather sofa and sipped her tea. He set aside his cup and followed her, sitting close, but not too close.

"How is your mom?" he asked.

Selena uncrossed her long legs and planted her feet on the ground as she edged toward the front of the cushion. She told him about the treatment and how it stole Ruth's strength.

"My father said that Raggar would find out soon about the shootings. That he might not want to take delivery from the lab because of it. He also said that it's

Escalanti's job to take possession of deliveries of the chemicals from the Mexicans and store the chemicals for the labs. And that it was his men's job to protect me and the barrels. He asked me to ask you if those two who attacked me were Mexican cartel."

"No. Tell him they were from a gang in Salt River."

Selena frowned. "That's bad, isn't it?"

He nodded. Shootings were always bad.

"That means they knew about the barrels," she said. "How did they know we were moving it, and how did they know where we would be?"

"We are working on that now."

Gabe wondered if there was a leak in Escalanti's organization.

"Why would the Salt River gang attack the Wolf Posse?" she asked.

"We're not sure. Maybe to steal the chemicals."

"Or take over Escalanti's operation?"

"Yes. That's possible. They also might just be shopping for material to cook down in Salt River."

He tried to puzzle it out, but the scent of lavender intruded. Nothing and no one could compete with the chase and with the job. Until now. Tonight he didn't want to know why the Salt River gang had crossed into Wolf Posse territory or if Raggar had learned of the attack on the shipments or how they had found Nota and that truck. He wanted Selena. He turned toward Selena and tucked her hair over her shoulder.

"Thank you for coming to the service and then the grave. I knew you were there and it helped."

She gave him a quizzical look. "You never look like you need help from anyone and you never ask me for it."

"Well, I've never had to stand over the grave of one of my officers before, either. I hope I never have to do that again."

She took his hand and held it to her cheek. "It's a terrible loss. I heard you promise Brenda that you would find the killer. I hope you do."

"We already have."

Her eyes widened. Was that because of his revelation or because he had confided in her?

"That's good."

"We have evidence that the body was moved by Nota and the other man. The one on the snowmobile. His name was Alfred Martinez."

She nodded, her eyes still huge.

"Why did they kill him?"

"We don't know if they did yet. But it's likely. I'll know soon." He turned to her question. "Chee was hunting the morning of his disappearance. We think he might just have seen something he shouldn't have. Stumbled on to something."

He wished he knew where they had shot Chee and what his officer had seen before he was killed. He didn't have ballistics back yet. Just the match on the prints. Nota and Martinez had moved Chee's body. Whether they had shot him was still in question. But he thought it likely that the slugs in Chee's chest would match the ones fired from Nota's pistol.

"Poor Dante," she whispered.

Selena moved closer. Her cheek pressed against his and he drew her in. She felt so good in his arms.

"We should have gone to the casino," she whispered, and then nipped his ear.

"Maybe," he said, drawing her tight. Nothing had changed; in fact, things were worse. She leaned in so that their bodies pressed together.

Everything but Selena dissolved in the yawning desire. He kissed her neck and she arched back, giving him access to her throat as her fingers kneaded his shoulders.

She straightened and took a firm hold on the back of his neck, her fingernails raking through his short hair as their lips met. When she finally pulled back, Gabe had to resist the need to keep her close. It was hard, as always, to let her go. But he did. She eased away, panting, her eyes wild with the heat that burned him up inside.

"Chief Cosen," she said, "are you sure you know what you're doing?"

He didn't. His thoughts where all jumbled up, tangled in the long strands of her dark hair, pushed aside by the enticing scent of her warm body.

"Are you?" he asked.

"*I'm* not the chief. What do I have to lose?"

"I should stay away from you," he said.

"Why don't you, then?"

He grimaced. "I can't."

Her gaze flicked to his and held, her face serious. Just the sight of her made his entire body quicken with need and readiness. He needed to hold her again. But he waited for Selena.

She gripped his hand and gave a little squeeze. She rose and her fingers slipped from his. She walked toward the door. Gabe edged forward, but he somehow remained where he was, though his heart was hammering and he had to bite down to keep from calling her back. She made it to the coatrack and reached. He held his breath, but she did not lift her coat. Instead, she closed and locked the door. Gabe exhaled his relief. She was staying.

Selena moved gracefully to his desk and flicked off the tabletop lamp.

Chapter Eighteen

For a moment Gabe could not see her, but gradually his eyes adjusted to the light that filtered in through the blinds from the hallway beyond the squad room.

She turned to face him.

"You're staying?" he asked.

She shrugged. "I never was very smart where you were concerned. And I'm sure I'll make worse mistakes than this."

A mistake. That's what he was. He should stop this, but he waited for her to come to him.

She didn't.

Instead she faced him as she slipped off her boots. She reached behind her back. He heard the sound of her zipper descending. Then her hands moved beneath the hem of her dress and she drew the opaque black tights down, exposing a peek of lacy under things and her firm thighs. She stepped from one foot to the next and the tights came off. Selena straightened, her hand now moving to the shoulders of her dress. She lowered the garment to her waist and let it drop, stepping clear of the puddle of gray wool, revealing herself to him. He stopped breathing.

The black lace panties and matching bra accentuated her lovely breasts, exposed her trim middle and clung to her full hips. Selena wore no slip, just the enticing under things. Was it possible that she was even more beautiful than his memories of her?

His breath came fast now, and his fingers itched to take her.

Selena bent to retrieve her dress. The movement, the play of light on satiny skin and black lace, made him twitch. He had to remember this, how she looked and smelled and tasted.

He reached her in two steps. Her cool fingers glided over fevered skin as she unbuttoned his uniform, exposing his chest. She hung his shirt neatly on the rack and startled when he scooped her up in his arms. Selena clung and laughed, the sound sweeter than birdsong to his ears. He stretched her out on the couch and sat to unlace his boots. She used her foot to stroke his back and then scissored him between her long legs. He tugged her up and she slipped onto his lap. He read the hunger in her eyes and something else. Did she also fear it couldn't last?

Was she also collecting memories for the cold nights ahead? His heart ached as he looked at her. Why couldn't he have her? Not just tonight, but every night?

The answers crowded his mind until Selena pressed forward, rubbing up against him and stroking his back. All objections fell away. He slipped the narrow straps down her shoulders, savoring the feel of her warm skin beneath his fingers and the shiver of excitement she gave as his hands moved back up and over her chest.

Selena. His mind and body were ablaze with her earthy scent and sweet taste, and the arousing sounds she made as he kissed her breasts. Only his trousers and the thin scrap of lace separated them.

She pulled back. "You have protection?"

Of course he did. In his wallet, which was in his coat across the room. Why were they across the room when Selena was finally here in his arms?

He motioned with his head, unwilling to release her lovely round bottom. He considered carrying her across the room again, but she slipped off his lap, freeing him. He dashed over to his coat and rummaged. It gave him just a moment to think, but all he could think was to hurry back to her before she changed *her* mind. He turned to find her sitting on the couch, shadowy and mysterious. He went to her, wondering why he could never banish this woman from his heart, wishing she was not the daughter of Frasco Dosela and hoping that this evening would not come back to bite either of them in the ass.

"Stop," she said.

He did, sure that she had come to her senses and would get up and leave him. She should. It would be better for them both. What would happen if they started this all up again? He knew enough to know that one night with Selena would not be enough. But what if it was just tonight?

The panic at that thought made him realize something. He didn't just *want* to sleep with Selena. He *had* to sleep with her. She was why he could never find a wife. Somehow, some part of him, the part that was not careful or wise, had chosen…

"Selena?"

"Take off your pants," she whispered.

He didn't argue but moved slowly, watching her as she watched him. He lowered his trousers. Her eyes caressed his flesh as he removed every stitch.

He offered her the condoms and waited as she selected one, tearing the packet and stroking his ready flesh.

Gabe wanted to go slow, but that didn't happen. If anything, Selena was more frenzied than he was. It seemed as if she also knew this time between them couldn't last and that this moment was only a sweet pause in their troubled relationship.

Afterward, as he held her, their flesh still damp, their breathing labored, he wondered how he could make this work. How he could do his duty, keep his position and the respect of the community, and still have Selena.

He looked down at her, naked, on her side. She lay next to him on the leather sofa, one arm and one leg flung over him and her hair fanning across his chest like a black silk curtain. Her breathing slowed and her eyes remained closed, but her lips were parted. He felt himself stirring again. Wanting her already.

He should take her home before morning. Get back to his work. Instead, he pressed one hand over his forehead as his mind and body battled.

Already he was wondering what would happen if word reached Escalanti that Selena had spent the night

in his office. Could he keep her safe with only his small
police force?

He just wanted her safe. No, he realized. He wanted
so much more. But her being here with him tonight—
this was unwise. He stroked her stomach, watching
the muscles tense. She shivered and her skin turned
to gooseflesh.

They had been so good together. Still were. And they
were even better now. So why had she called it off, cut
him loose, shown him the door?

His grandmother said she had to give his ring back
and that he didn't have to take it. He'd regretted taking
it. Still did. But at the time their troubles seemed insur-
mountable. They were worse now.

"Selena?"

She stirred, swiping the back of her hand over her
forehead.

"Hmm?"

"Why did you give me back my ring?"

Selena opened her eyes, blinking at him. He felt her
stiffen before she swept her leg off his thighs and she
moved off and away from him.

"I have to go." Selena brushed back the curtain of
hair.

"Selena? Answer the question."

Her expression changed as the urgency to flee ebbed
and she settled to hold her ground. She lifted her chin,
giving it a defiant tilt.

She pushed herself up, swinging her feet to the tile
floor. She retrieved her bra and fastened the clasp

under her breasts before expertly slipping back into the garment.

"This was a mistake," she said. "Take me home."

"No. Not until I get an answer."

She stood and drew on her panties. He reached out to clasp her hand. She turned, facing him.

"Selena?"

Her breath hissed between her teeth. "I gave you your ring back for the same reason you brought me here tonight instead of the casino. You don't want to be seen with the likes of me. Isn't that right?"

He straightened as her words struck him like a slap. Indignation rose like a wave.

"I never said that." He sat up, his bare feet joining hers on the cold floor.

"Didn't you?"

He raked his hands through his hair and then glared at her.

"Just like last time," she muttered.

What was that supposed to mean? And then he remembered. After she had broken it off and the trial had ended, he'd gone to her, determined to change her mind. But instead the encounter had led them both to the bed of his pickup and they'd spent one last evening tangled in each other's arms. Why hadn't he offered her the ring then, as he had intended?

"Hey. You're the one who said that we should call it quits. I was just doing my job."

She gave a humorless laugh. *"Your job."*

He didn't care for the way she spit the words, as if they were some foul taste in her mouth. His job was everything to him. It had to be. Otherwise he never would have let her go.

"I never blamed you for his arrest."

"Of course you did," he said, but he was suddenly uncertain and that cold place in his middle, the one that warned of threat, was icing up again.

"I was offering you a way out."

Confusion filled him and he frowned.

She wouldn't look at him now. "I thought if you loved me that…"

"What?"

She met his gaze, her eyes now glittering and as cold as the abandoned tea that sat on the side table.

"I thought you'd fight for me. That you would argue. Tell me I was wrong. That we could make it work." She glared. "Do you remember what you *did* say?"

He shook his head as the cold place turned to a tight knot.

"You said, 'Maybe you're right.' You were relieved."

"No. That's not true." But his voice had lost its conviction.

"Because…if we were together, people would wonder about you. Question your choice in a wife and then, well, I just never wanted to hold you back. And look how well you've done. Promoted again and again. Solving big cases and now police chief. But it still hurt. That's how I knew I was right."

"Right? This whole thing is wrong. I never argued because you said that you couldn't be my wife."

"But not because of my dad or your part in his arrest. Because of you. A tribal officer can't have a wife like me. You know it. I know it."

"Selena, you're wrong."

"Am I? You didn't come see me much during the trial."

"I was busy."

"And you only saw me at my home. You stopped taking me out in public."

Had he? Yes. He had.

He'd even made an excuse not to take her to the Fourth of July rodeo. Made sure he was on duty the entire three days of the tribe's big event. Gabe swallowed, seeing things differently. Was this really all his fault?

"How will you feel when everyone knows my father was working with the Feds? That Raggar picked him because he knew he could get him to move drugs again?"

"This is ridiculous." Gabe grabbed his trousers and jerked them on.

"Answer the question," she said.

He met her probing gaze and he knew that she had her answer.

"The story will make the newspapers and be on the Apache radio station. They'll talk about it at the tribal council meetings. Everyone will know. They'll know that the chief of police is seeing that woman again, the one whose father is an ex-con, a criminal. Such a shame." Her eyes dared him to say differently.

It was true. There was talk when their engagement broke up, but mostly it was along the lines of, "It's probably for the best." And, "He's too good for the likes of her."

He'd been thankful that the firestorm of scorn and disapproval had not touched him. He'd been thankful because nearly everyone thought he'd done the right thing. And until this very minute he had never considered himself a coward. But now, suddenly, he thought that taking back the ring she offered him was the most cowardly thing he had ever done.

"I heard them," she said. "The things they said. 'Not a good match' and 'What could you expect from a girl from Wolf Canyon? Bunch of thieves and criminals up there,' isn't that right, Chief?"

"I don't know what they said."

She snorted. "I was glad when they took him. Did you know that?"

"Glad?" But that didn't make any sense. She'd given him back his ring right after Gabe testified against her dad in federal court. That very same night. And she'd said...what? Not that she blamed him or that she couldn't forgive him. She said that she could see "it wasn't going to work." And she'd left the rest unsaid. What she had meant was that their marriage was not going to work *for him*. Not for them or for her. Not even between then. She'd done it for him, to protect him, and he had taken the damned thing when she offered it.

Her gaze held a thinly veiled fury. He hadn't fought for her. Hadn't stood by her side when trouble came as he had for Clay and Kino. What had he done?

Nothing.

And his inaction proved her right.

"It wouldn't have worked. You were right to take it back," she said. "The job comes first for you."

Because, without her, what did he have? Had he really chosen his job over Selena? He hadn't meant to do that—had he?

She pressed her lips thin and then exhaled a long breath.

"It's an important job. It's just…" She paused.

"What?"

"I let you do it to me again. Bring me here where no one would see us."

Gabe felt as if she had kicked him in the stomach. Had he made Selena feel like a dirty little secret? He had never intended that. He just didn't want them to be the cause of gossip or put her at further risk by being seen with her. He'd been protecting her, hadn't he?

Or had he been protecting himself again?

She stood now, giving him her back, her lovely shoulders hunched in shame and he knew he had done that to her, too. Selena's words were a strangled whisper.

"Take me home while it's still dark."

He didn't know if he should chalk the evening up as the stupidest thing he'd ever done, or if taking back that ring was the stupidest. He was all tangled up inside like a ball of barbed wire.

Chapter Nineteen

Just one more night in Gabe Cosen's arms.

Selena had thought that this was what she wanted. Now, standing in her bare feet in his office as she zipped up her dress, she knew she longed for so much more.

There had been pleasure. But not the joy she'd once felt. Not when she knew that she shamed him.

Now, alone with the chief of police, her ex-lover, Selena knew her night with Gabe had only left her more aware of how much she missed him and how much she lacked when it came to being the sort of woman he wanted.

All her work making a family trucking business legitimate—she hadn't done it for her sisters or her family. She'd done it to win Gabe's approval. To finally be good enough.

She marveled at her own stupidity.

And the worst part was she still admired him. Gabe never dithered about his duty or what was right. He shouldered his responsibilities and he did it at the expense of all else, his safety, his family and the company of the woman he had once professed to love. Was he right?

She turned toward him, his form illuminated only by his desk lamp. She allowed herself the joy and the sorrow of watching him dress, noticing how he seemed to fill up the room.

He dragged on his dress uniform shirt and swiftly tucked in the tails before fastening his trousers and buckling his belt. He adjusted the gold shield that was the symbol of everything he was. Then he checked the grip of his pistol, now nestled in the worn black leather holster. She admired those long muscular legs as he pushed his feet into the highly polished black shoes and knelt to tie the laces. Finally he slipped into his coat.

Gabe turned to face her. He had a predatory stillness about him and she felt the hairs on her neck lift as she met his gaze and found herself the object of his steady stare.

His short black hair glistened, and she resisted the urge to run her hand up his neck to the back of his head, drape her body across his as she once had. The aching in her chest grew more painful.

Why did he always look so damned appealing?

How she would miss this. But she would not come to him again. It hurt too much.

He turned to his coatrack and lifted her jacket from among all the rest. He held it out and she turned her back on him, lifting an arm to repeat the ritual he had performed for her so many times so long ago. She slipped one arm and then the other into the coat, but instead of dropping the garment onto her shoulders and stepping back, he moved in, drawing the coat across her chest, his hands meeting and crossing as he embraced her. Gabe leaned in, inhaling the air at her neck. Her eyes fluttered closed as his lips brushed that sensitive place beneath her earlobe.

"I'm sorry, Selena."

She squeezed her eyes tight. Was he sorry for hurting her or sorry for tonight? It didn't matter. She could not let this go on.

It would be so easy to let him back into her life. But she couldn't because he didn't want her. At least, not in the daylight.

Selena stepped out the door and he followed her out into the cold, dark night. Had it really only been hours that she had come here with him? She did not speak to him in the car on the long drive to her home and kept her head turned toward the passenger's side window to keep him from seeing the glint of tears on her cheeks. When he finally pulled into her drive on the road that cut off Wolf Canyon, he broke the silence.

"I'll walk you in."

She said one word—"No"—before getting out. She couldn't bear to have him walk beside her and abandon her on her front step yet again as if they were still teenagers. Or, worse, try to kiss her in the darkness where none but the stars above would see them.

She had little left of her shredded dignity, but she would preserve what remained.

Tonight was a mistake. She needed to move on.

He was out of the SUV and stopping her before she cleared his front fender. So much for a painless escape. The ache only grew.

"Selena," he said. "Wait."

Her tone was sharp. "No, Gabe. I won't wait."

He gave her a quizzical look, and her heart sped up just to be near him. Only this time the attraction that usually made her miserable made her angry.

"I am done waiting for you. Done with waiting for you to think I'm good enough. I love you, Gabe Cosen. I have been in love with you since I was in seventh grade. And I probably will always love you. But I am done waiting. If you don't want me, then I will find a man who does. One who is not ashamed to be with me. A man who does not see our relationship as a conflict of interest."

Now his jaw dropped open.

"That's not how I feel."

"That's the trouble." She pressed a finger deep into the dress coat directly over his heart. "You don't feel. You act on reason and judgment and duty and law."

"What's so terrible about that?" he said.

He was even more handsome when he was angry. But she had reached her limit.

"Goodbye, Gabe." She spun and marched away. Her heart heavy and her body shaking. But at least her head was up.

GABE STOOD BENEATH the cold starlight a long time after Selena shut the front door behind her. Somehow this time was worse than when she had offered back his ring. Then he had felt vindicated by her apparent unwillingness to forgive him. Now he knew she had never blamed him for doing his duty, only for choosing his career over her.

And he had.

Selena had broken the engagement and he had made all the right moves. His uncle had even encouraged him to apply to the Bureau. If he married Selena, they'd likely never take him. The background checking process used by the FBI was secret, but he knew that having Frasco as a father-in-law would not help his application. He had always known that. Now it seemed that his ambition had become an all-consuming glutton that devoured his personal life.

But he was a success. Gabe trudged back to his car and paused by his door. He was also living in his grandmother's house and spending more nights sleeping on his office couch than in a bed.

Gabe did not want to face his grandmother or Clyne tonight. He needed time to think. So he headed for his office.

On the way he phoned the officer who was currently watching the Leekela place and got a report that all was quiet.

His force was small and stretched thin, but he still managed to have a twenty-four-hour watch on the junkyard. He wanted to be sure that meth lab stayed put and feared that with Jason's and Oscar's deaths, Sammy might correctly guess that his brother's death was related to his illegal activity. He also had patrols swing by Selena's place on rounds to be sure all was quiet at her home.

As he sat in the dark, alone with his computer and his work, he wondered again at the choices he had made.

How could he span the gap that stretched between

them? He wondered what would happen if he told Selena that he was ready to put her first?

Somehow he didn't think words would be enough, but he was baffled when it came to knowing what to do.

How did you show a woman you needed her more than anything else?

Gabe dozed but failed to find steady sleep and finally gave up at five in the morning and headed to his grandmother's home for a shower. There was one at work, but he needed to change out of his dress uniform.

When he pulled into the drive in the dark on Sunday morning it was to find the porch light still on, which was bad. It meant his grandmother had expected him home.

Before leaving his unit he checked in with his patrols and got the all clear. Once he reached the house, he let himself in and headed to the bathroom, showered and changed into jeans and a dress shirt cinched at the neck with a bolo fashioned from a turquoise cabochon tucked beside a bear claw. His grandmother attended church every Sunday and Gabe thought he would take her today. Selena attended church, or she used to. Would she be there this morning? He slipped into a blazer and had his head in the refrigerator when the overhead light snapped on. He straightened so fast he nearly hit his head on the freezer door and was surprised to find his grandmother appear in her blue zip-up robe and bed slippers a moment later.

"Did you take her home?" she asked.

Gabe felt like he was suddenly sixteen again.

"Who?"

She made a face. "Selena Dosela. Her mother called and said you had taken her for coffee."

Who else saw them leave together? His stomach tensed as he realized he was doing exactly what Selena had accused him of, damage control.

He shifted uncomfortably.

"Yes. I took her home."

"This morning or last night?"

"Grandma, that's not really your business."

"Grandson, that girl's mother practically grew up in this house. And I love that girl as if she were my own. So if you hurt her again I am going to take a switch to you, no matter how old you are."

"If *I* hurt *her*?" His words were indignant. "I don't hurt women."

She made a noise in her throat that sounded like *humph*.

He pictured Selena when she had slipped out of his SUV in front of her house. He had offered to escort her in, but she had refused. She had walked to her front door with her chin up against the wind and she had not glanced back at him even once before letting herself in.

He looked at his grandmother's stern face and was about to speak the same words he had said so many times that they had become a chant. *She gave back the ring. She gave back the ring.* The words that absolved him of all responsibility, preserved his reputation and made it so damned easy to play the wounded one. The gift she had given him that he had not even had the manners to acknowledge. He knew it. Even then. Deep in his heart and in places he didn't examine too hard, he had known all along what she had done.

Selena hadn't given back the ring out of anger; she had done so out of love. "Last night, Grandmother. I took her home last night."

Glendora nodded and brushed him away from the refrigerator.

"Breakfast or a sandwich?" she asked.

"Sandwich sounds good."

She pulled out all the fixings including the carved remains of a turkey breast.

He sat and his grandmother began assembling a meal, then she offered him a generous sandwich on a plate and a paper towel for a napkin. As he ate, she cleaned up the counter. She had just gotten out the sponge to mop up when he finished. He hadn't realized he was that hungry.

His grandmother used a rag to wipe up the dampness left by the sponge and then hung the cloth on a peg beside the sink. Satisfied, she turned to face him, leaning back against her spotless counter.

"Clay called last night. He has the name of the parents."

Gabe's brows lifted and he pushed back his chair.

"What did he say?" Gabe carried his plate to the sink.

"Her father was a US Army captain named Gerard Walker. He died in 2011 in Afghanistan when Jovanna was seven years old."

Gabe did the count in his head. "Four years after her adoption."

"Yes. That's right."

"Her mother?" asked Gabe.

"Her adoptive mother's name is Cassidy Walker."

Gabe's skin began to tingle. It couldn't be *that* Cassidy Walker. Where had his uncle said his partner came from, again?

"Do you know what she does for a living?"

"Yes. She works for the Federal Bureau of Investigations out of Phoenix. Clay said they wouldn't tell him more than that."

"Does Uncle Luke know?"

His grandmother frowned. "Uncle Luke. No, I haven't called him yet. But I was tempted because I think he might know her. But he's your father's brother. If you think we should contact him, then it should be you or Clyne who makes the call."

"Not Clyne," he said, rubbing his neck, which was suddenly tight as a bowstring.

"Why not?"

"Because I think Cassidy Walker is Uncle Luke's partner."

Glendora sat heavily on a kitchen chair, absorbing the news that Gabe's uncle's associate had adopted her granddaughter. "I had no idea." She pressed a hand over her heart. "My goodness, I've met her. And to think, all this time…"

Gabe met her gaze. "Did you tell Clyne?"

She shook her head. "Not yet. Clyne was out when he called and I haven't seen him…" Then her hands came over her mouth and she stared wide-eyed at Gabe as the realization hit her. Cassidy Walker was white, really, really white, and Clyne was a staunch objector to the long-time practice of placing Indian children with white families.

"What should we do?" she asked.

Gabe gave a slow shake of his head as he sank into the chair across from her.

"We have a strong case. We'll have her back soon. Then it won't matter."

But it mattered. Jovanna had been raised by a white woman. She would know little to nothing of who she was or where she had come from.

"But even if we win…what if Jovanna chooses her mom?" his grandmother asked, knitting her brows together.

His face went hard. He knew exactly what she meant. Their attorney had explained it to them all. Under the Indian Child Welfare Act, there were three reasons a child could be adopted by a non-Indian. One of them was if a child, over twelve, chose to be adopted away from her tribe. His sister would turn thirteen in five months. Gabe knew instinctively that Jovanna would pick her adoptive mother over the family she had never met.

"We have to get her back before June," said Gabe.

Chapter Twenty

The crunch of snow and gravel in the drive alerted Selena to a visitor. Her route made her a perpetual early riser even on Sunday morning, her one day off. So she was alone in the kitchen at a little after eight in the morning when she heard someone pulling in.

She lifted the living room drape, peering out into the gray gloom. Who would be calling at this hour?

Her reflection obscured her view, so she pressed her cupped hands to the window pane. A chill of foreboding slithered up her spine as she spotted Ronnie Hare climbing out of his vehicle.

What was he doing here?

Another drop-in visit? But this was odd timing and something about his appearance didn't feel right.

Selena's heart began walloping in her chest. She reached for her phone to call Gabe as Hare parked beside the flatbed.

The parole officer straightened, wearing his slate-gray ski jacket unzipped and no gloves, scarf or hat. His step was quick and he looked over his shoulder twice as he hurried toward the house.

Her mother shuffled up beside her, squinting as she

peered out the window, nearsighted without her glasses. "Who is that?"

"Mr. Hare."

"I'll go wake your father." Her mom reversed course, leaving Selena alone.

Selena stepped back, dropped the drape and retrieved her phone from the charging unit.

Outside, the parole officer's boot heels drummed on the wooden steps and his knock sounded loud as the crack of a rifle on a still afternoon.

She lifted her cloth coat, the one with the fleece lining and the bullet hole in the sleeve. Then, she stepped outside to intercept Hare. She planned to tell him that drop-ins or no drop-in visits, he had no right to wake her family out of a sound sleep. She stepped onto the porch, pulling the door shut behind her.

"*Dagot'ee*, Miss Dosela."

"Mr. Hare." She spoke in English instead of Apache. "It's very early for a visit. My father is still in bed."

"That's all right." He glanced about the yard, then back to her. "Because I'm not here to see him."

Her mouth went dry as she wondered at the purpose of this visit. One of the icicles behind her on the gutter broke loose, fell and shattered on the glassy ice pack below, making her jump.

"Easy there," he said.

He glanced toward the road again. What was he looking for? Or perhaps she should wonder *who* he was looking for.

When he turned back he held his steady, affable smile, only now there was something about him that made the hairs on her neck lift.

"Grab the keys to the 18-wheeler."

"Excuse me?"

"Keys. Get them. Now."

His tone seemed indulgent as if he were speaking to her brother Tomas instead of her.

"I'm not working with the parole office today. I'm running an errand for some friends in Salt River."

"I don't understand."

"They need a driver for that." He pointed to the flat-bed truck. "My friends think they should be in charge of distribution. The suppliers have been slow to accept them, so we're taking over Escalanti's operation. First step was disturbing his supply line. Second step, procure the product. Product, transport, driver." He pointed at her.

Selena backed toward the door. "I don't know what you are talking about."

"No?" he said, with a cold smile. "That's hard to believe. Thursday's attack. You were there and your police chief was there. Ruined our raid, but he helped me convince my contacts across the border to go with Salt River instead of the Wolf Posse. Better location. Better protection. When I saw Nota show up here, it all fell into place. Escalanti's man tells me they had secured transportation for their operation and next thing I know your dad gets early release and…"

Selena peered back over her shoulder, wondering if she could get inside and lock the door before he grabbed her. She caught movement at the window and saw a glimpse of her mother's blue robe before the drape fell into place.

Hare cleared his throat. When she looked back at him, he wore an impatient look.

"The point is we need a driver and you can drive. All four of Frasco's girls can drive big rigs. He told me. He's very proud of you. You answered the door, so you win! Get the keys."

"I'm not leaving with you."

Hare made a *tsk*ing sound. "I think you'll reconsider when you hear my offer. You drive or I shoot everyone in your family, beginning with your mother." He pointed toward the living room window where she knew her mother watched. It seemed Hare knew, as well.

The chill that had slithered down her spine now seemed to be squeezing her ribs so she could barely breathe.

"And your sisters are all home, I hear. Folks are so nice hereabouts. Catching me up on all the news. Like you and Chief Cosen. An item again. That's not good for business. Transportation and law enforcement. Bad match. Yet another reason to move the operation."

He pushed past her and entered the house. Every hair on Selena's head lifted as she rushed after him.

Ronnie Hare left the door wide-open, letting the cold air fill the room.

"Selena?" said her mother.

"Don't worry, Momma."

"Your daughter was just getting her keys," Hare said and then smiled at Selena.

She did exactly as he said.

"Where are you going?" asked her mother.

Hare had Selena's elbow and hustled her outside. He leaned back to call to her mother in Apache.

"Call the police and you won't see her alive again."

Her mother's screams were cut short by the slamming of the front door.

"Phone," he said, extending his hand.

She gave it to him and he threw it. The rectangular device spiraled through the air and vanished into a snowbank beside the house.

"Get in the truck."

She did and made sure she hit the snowbank on the way out of the drive. If anyone was looking for her, she wanted to leave a trail of bread crumbs.

Gabe, she thought, *come and find me.*

GABE CALLED CLAY and he confirmed his fears. Jovanna's adoptive parent was the same Cassidy Walker who was their uncle's new partner. Clyne was going to flip.

He had just disconnected when his phone vibrated again. He checked the caller ID and recognized Selena's home number. He picked up.

"Selena?"

But it was not Selena.

He heard a woman shouting. Something about them saying not to call the police. The next words came in a wail and were very clear. "Don't. Don't. They'll kill her."

Gabe clutched the phone. It was Selena's parents and her mother was screaming.

"Frasco? Ruth?" he called. They didn't seem to hear him.

He understood only two words—*taken* and *Selena*—but that was enough.

Gabe retrieved his badge, holster and pistol. Then he headed for the door.

Chapter Twenty-One

Gabe had tried to call twice en route with no success. He reached the Dosela home with Kino, Dryer and Juris all behind him.

As Gabe pulled into the gravel drive, he saw immediately that the tractor trailer and flatbed were gone and felt a moment's relief. Perhaps the twins were already gone on another run and Selena was safe. But the cold lump remained in the pit of his stomach as he skidded to a stop and threw open the door to his unit.

Where was Selena?

He dialed her phone again and heard it ringing nearby. Gabe retrieved her mobile from the snow. He judged the distance from the porch and the plowed drive and decided the mobile could not have just slipped from her pocket. It seemed to have been thrown there. Gabe tucked her phone into his front pocket.

The front door swung open and a very anxious Ruthie Dosela appeared, her tattered blue terry-cloth robe flapping open to reveal her flannel nightie and worn pink slippers. His heart gave a little jolt at her complete disregard for her state of undress as she motioned Gabe back.

"Go away," she shouted.

Her husband emerged behind her, his high-topped moccasins tugged over his sweatpants and his hooded winter coat also flapping open. The gash and bruise on his hairline had turned his forehead purple. Ruth grabbed at him, but he brushed her off. He was followed closely by Selena's three sisters who poured down the steps, passing their parents at a run. Behind them her mother paused on the steps.

"Go away!" wailed Ruth from the bottom step. "They'll kill her."

Mia and Carla were both talking at once to Detective Juris, and Kino was trying to make sense of Paula's babbling. Tomas appeared on the steps in his pajamas crying and clasping his stuffed frog to his chest. Ruth retreated up the steps to hold him, rocking as they both wailed.

Gabe intercepted Frasco as he reached the drive.

"What happened? Where's Selena?" Gabe asked Frasco.

"He took her. My parole officer. I should have known. Coming back here two days in a row."

"Ronnie Hare?" Gabe asked.

"He took her."

Gabe straightened, stunned. He had chatted with Ronnie Hare in his office, trusted him...because he was Apache.

Dryer trotted up to join them. Gabe didn't have time to fill him in.

"Where did they go?" asked Gabe.

Frasco flapped his arms. "I don't know. Only know he took her and the rig."

Gabe glanced at the empty place where the 18-wheeler should be parked.

"He must know you'd call me," said Gabe.

"Who are we talking about?" asked Dryer.

Frasco filled him in. "Hare took Selena about forty minutes ago. Maybe an hour. I'm not sure. Found out when I woke up and found my wife crying in the living room."

Dryer frowned. "The guy who was here the day we discharged you?"

"Yeah. You met him," said Frasco.

"Hare would be a perfect messenger for the cartel. He's all over both reservations and he's got legitimate reason to talk to all kinds of ex-cons," said Dryer.

"He warned Ruthie not to call you. Said they'd kill her."

He looked to Frasco whose face was now drawn and pale. He knew as well as Gabe did that it wouldn't matter if he called or not. They were going to kill Selena either way.

"He took the truck and a driver," said Dryer. "He's moving something."

"Precursor. Got to be," said Frasco.

"Gambling that you wouldn't call me or knowing he has time to move it."

"Takes more than a few men to ready that kind of load."

"And move it where?"

Frasco gave him a bewildered look. "I don't know."

But Gabe had to know. He had to get to Selena. Because he knew what they'd do with her when she finished her run.

"Who is Hare working for?" asked Gabe.

"Not sure," said Frasco. "Could be the Mexican distribution organization or someone else."

"Takeover," said Ruth. "Salt River instead of the Wolf Posse. Better location."

The all turned to Ruthie, who had both fists gripped in her graying hair.

"What?" asked Frasco.

"I heard him. Something about Escalanti's men and…they need a driver." She pointed at her husband. "Why did you tell him that all our girls can drive?"

Frasco moved to his wife, reaching for her, but she batted away his hand and turned to Gabe.

She was babbling now, her words coming fast, choking past the tears. "They said if I called the police they'd…they'd… I was… And he said he'd kill her… He threw her phone… They left. He has her." She looked to her husband. "Do something!"

"Which direction?" asked Gabe.

Ruth Dosela pressed her hand to her forehead, glancing frantically about the icy front yard. "I don't know," she wailed. "I don't know."

Frasco gathered her in his arms and gave her a little shake. "Think, Ruthie."

"West," said Ruth. "They turned to the west, towards Black Mountain."

Gabe's heart sank. That was the direction from which they had just come and they had not encountered Selena and her flatbed tractor trailer. That meant Selena had either passed the station before they left or she had turned north in the direction of the restricted area and Wind River settlement. If they were an hour behind, Selena might already be off the reservation, unless they had to first load a flatbed with fifty-gallon barrels of precursor.

Kino spoke to Ruth Dosela, clasping her elbow and steering her back to the house where he turned her over to her daughters before he backtracked to his unit.

"We're moving out," said Gabe to Juris, Kino and Dryer.

"I'm going with you," said Frasco.

Gabe hesitated. He didn't take civilians into danger.

"I'm working with DOJ. Dryer told you that," said Frasco.

Precious seconds ticked by.

"She's my daughter, Gabe," said Frasco. "I got her into this. Let me help get her out."

"Get in," Gabe said, motioning toward his SUV.

They left behind his sobbing wife, son and frightened daughters.

Gabe returned to his unit and reversed out of the drive with Juris, Kino and Dryer all following in their vehicles. Once heading west on Wolf Canyon Road, he radioed to Jasmine, putting out an all points on the trailer. He wasn't hopeful, however. It was a big territory with so many little back roads to hide a tractor trailer. But not all of them were plowed. Could a trailer make it over roads with half a foot of snow pack? He feared it could.

He saw where Selena had clipped the snowbank on

the right side sending a spray of ice into the road. The snow left a clear wet tire print for about ten yards and then disappeared. Both the warmth of the day and time were working against him. The next intersection was four miles up. He knew he would have to turn toward Black Mountain or head north toward Wind River. Since they had not seen them going to Black Mountain, Wind River was the logical choice. But if she had turned off any of the side roads before Black Mountain, then he'd be heading the wrong way.

Chapter Twenty-Two

Gabe's gut churned as he clenched the wheel and continued to search for some sign that he was still on Selena's trail.

Frasco pointed. "There!"

Gabe looked in the direction Frasco indicated and saw the large double tire track where Selena had clipped the snowbank as she made the turn to the north in the direction of Wind River. And then he knew. Selena was an excellent driver. This hadn't been an accident on her part. The last time had been intentional and this was, as well. Selena was leaving them an ice trail. A trail that any Apache tracker would find simple to follow. She was in trouble and he could read her call for help in the crushed snowbank as clearly as any sign he had ever seen.

Gabe picked up the radio and called ahead to see if any of his men were in the vicinity of Wind River. Only Officer Cienega was nearby, at Broke Bow, north and west of Wind River on Route 260. He spoke to Cienega and told him to head east toward Wind River, keeping his eye out for Selena's truck.

At the next intersection, Gabe spotted Selena's turn

before Frasco did. She'd entered the Piñon Lake area where she had been previously waylaid by members of a Salt River gang. This area was closed to all but Apaches and was used for ceremonies and retreats, and was a popular hunting spot among the tribe. Why had the traffickers chosen this spot? There was no cover. No building large enough to store the precursor and keep it from freezing.

And then an idea began to form in his mind. The caves. He'd explored them as a boy. They were always the same temperature inside, but in the winter no one went up there except a tribe member who might be bow hunting—like Dante Chee. Was this his secret spot that he would not share even with his brother?

Gabe felt a cold sweat as he realized he might have figured out the place where the barrels of precursor could be safely stored from the freezing temperatures and the site of Chee's murder.

He used his mobile to call Juris and explain his theory. His second in command thought he might be on the right track.

Gabe continued along the narrow road, following Selena's tracks as the snow drifts rose, penning them in on both sides. His heart was now pumping so hard that his chest ached. This was not the usual adrenaline rush that accompanied a chase. This was something low down and gut twisting. Worry, he realized, blinding worry over Selena's safety.

He saw the place where the truck tracks indicated she had stopped.

Gabe halted the string of vehicles well before the

imprints and exited the SUV with Frasco. Dryer pulled in next. A moment later they were joined by Kino and Randall Juris. The five saw the prints of Selena's truck and a second vehicle following behind.

"Company?" asked Kino.

"Large truck or a large SUV," said Juris. "Anyways they were here first and Miss Dosela now has an escort."

Gabe stared at the beaten-down snow on the bank that was wide as a sidewalk.

"Foot traffic," said Frasco.

The bank had been crushed flat.

"They moved the barrels with a snowmobile," said Kino, crouching down for a better look. "Dragged them on something from the looks of it."

"Tarp, maybe," said Juris. "Not a sled or board."

It took more time than Gabe would have liked, but they saw the imprints of six men. One had been in the truck with Selena and five distinct tracks came from the second vehicle.

"Snow machine went that way. Toward the cave," said Juris.

Gabe radioed the new information. They were looking for one or two men on a snowmobile in the Piñon Lake area and an SUV and a flatbed, possibly together.

"What are these marks?" asked Juris, pointing at the flattened snow at the parking area.

"I'd say that's the bottom of the barrels of precursor," said Gabe. "Do the marks match the barrels you saw down on the border?"

Kino squatted and took a closer look. "Yes. Fifty gallons each."

They'd stacked them by the truck and loaded them onto the trailer.

"How many trips?" asked Juris.

Kino studied the scooped-out place that led uphill as Gabe cursed at the delay.

"I'm seeing at least eight. Can't say how many barrels per load, but on a tarp, maybe two to six."

Gabe did the calculation. "Say ten trips of four. At least forty barrels. They can't be far ahead of us."

"Road's too narrow to turn around," said Juris. "They went past the lake and will come back out on the main highway."

Gabe looked to Kino. "You think they made it out of the closed area yet?"

Kino studied the tracks of the departing tractor trailer, judging time by the condition of the tracks, and shook his head.

"Narrow roads up ahead and there's a steep grade up and down."

Selena would be driving a heavy load on dangerous roads. That alone was enough to terrify him, but she also likely had a gun pointed at her.

If he could only get there in time, save her, he'd tell her what he should have said when she offered him back his ring.

They headed out, Gabe in the lead. He radioed Jasmine and told her to send everyone to the Wind River entrance to the lake.

Time seemed to drag, but it was only eleven endless

minutes before he spotted her tractor trailer followed by a large black SUV. The load on her truck was wrapped in camouflage tarps and strapped down. Selena knew how to secure a load, so Gabe was sure the barrels were battened down tight.

Gabe stared at the truck rumbling downhill in low gear. They had found them on the most dangerous part of the drive, a thirty-degree incline on a narrow road that curved around the other side of the quarry cliffs. On the left was a wall of stone sheathed in a frozen cascade of glacier-blue ice. At its base lay a field of large boulders that had sheared away. To the right was a sharp drop-off, beyond which rose only the tops of the tallest pine trees. If he had tried, he could not have chosen a worse place to engage them.

Gabe lifted the handset. "Kino. Call for backup."

"Roger that," said Kino.

Dryer's voice emerged from his radio. "I'm calling DOJ and FBI for backup."

"Affirmative," said Gabe.

The cavalry was coming, but just like always, it was the Apache scouts who would be there first.

Gabe drew his pistol and lowered his window. He didn't shoot at the SUV. Instead, as the truck turned almost broadside to his position, he aimed high and shot at the load. He had the satisfaction of seeing a spray of liquid shower the tailing vehicle before the SUV skidded to a halt across the road and the shooting began.

His windshield exploded and Frasco screamed. Gabe's vehicle slid. They skated toward the embankment between the road and the drop-off. Gabe had to steer into the slide or risk sending them into a spiral. The SUV fishtailed but stopped short of the embankment.

"Grab my rifle behind you," he said to Frasco.

Gabe used his car door and front fender as a shield. He looked toward the truck and saw Selena looking back at him in the large rectangular side mirror, her eyes wide. He knew someone was sitting next to her. He didn't know for sure, but he suspected it was Ronnie Hare. He had just a moment of eye contact, meeting her gaze, and then she disappeared from sight in the mirror.

The gunmen in front of them exited their vehicle from both sides, gaining defensive positions behind their SUV. The men carried semiautomatic weapons, meaning that Gabe's team was outnumbered and outgunned. But they had to get past the gunmen to reach Selena.

The air brakes of the truck shrieked and they all turned, showdown suddenly forgotten as the trailer began to turn on the narrow snow-covered road. There wasn't room. Selena must know that.

"Oh, no," he whispered, and then he could only watch as the drama unfolded in slow motion.

"Please, God," called Frasco.

Driven by momentum and the steep incline, the tractor trailer jackknifed. The trailer left the road first, spraying snow into the air in a cascading wave of white. Gabe's heart stopped as the straps failed and the barrels broke free, tumbling off the falling trailer. The loose load now bounced and rolled toward the incline, and Gabe knew that Selena had done this all on purpose.

She was ditching the load and distracting the shooters. She was doing this to save him and in that moment he knew that the most important thing in his life was not his job or his duty to his people.

It was Selena and he was about to watch her go over that cliff.

Chapter Twenty-Three

Selena's ears rang with the shriek of the air brakes, the scrape of metal on ice and the scream of her passenger, Ronnie Hare. Ronnie was not belted in and so when the truck teetered and slammed to its right side, he hit the door now below him so hard that he released his grip on the gun that he'd had pointed at her most—but not all—of the afternoon. When she'd been securing the load, he hadn't seen her put the tire iron in her coat.

The trailer twisted and barrels spilled off the flatbed like bright blue beads. The trailer left the road, spinning out into space and then dragged them backward toward the incline. The truck skidded on the door where Ronnie now lay in a heap. Selena tried the door above her but could not lift it against gravity, so she cranked down her window as they continued their slow-motion glide to the embankment.

"Wait," shouted Ronnie, lifting a hand toward her.

She didn't. Instead, she unfastened her belt and tugged herself out, riding on her door panel like a surfer for just the time it took to seize the tire well and pull with all her might. She slid over the metal like grease on a griddle and bounced over the tire, dropping into space as the truck rolled upside down and fell from sight. She landed on her side in the deep snow just past the road. From the incline came the shriek of man and metal as the truck and trailer crashed into rock and trees on its deadly descent.

Her first thought was that Paula and Carla were going to kill her. Her next was of the five Mexican cartel killers shooting at Gabe.

She reached into her coat sleeve and came up empty. Where was that tire iron?

GABE AND FRASCO started running toward Selena, as another round of gunfire cut over their heads. Frasco scrambled back toward the SUV, but Gabe continued on, exposed, out in the open, but he was now so close to the shooter's position that the men behind the vehicle had not yet spotted him. When they did, he would be an easy target. But he had to get to Selena and that meant getting past these men.

The shots volleyed over his head. A spray of lead from the SUV and then a shot or two from a rifle behind him. Kino was the best shot on the force. But even an expert marksman could not outshoot the barrage of bullets spewing from the automatic weapons.

Frasco gave a shout and Gabe saw him limp behind his SUV holding his leg. Gabe's rifle lay on the ground in front of his unit.

Kino, Dryer and Juris moved forward, one by one. Dryer was in the lead with the rifle, followed by Kino and Juris with pistols firing.

Gabe couldn't see the truck and the sound of it tearing through the tree branches had stopped. Where was Selena?

Gabe looked under the six-passenger SUV and saw the lower legs of two men. He fired, hitting them both in the shins. Both went down, giving him much better targets. He aimed for mass and hit them in the chest— one and two. The men lay still and the others shouted, moving behind the wheel wells. One of the men inched around the rear bumper and shot past Gabe at his men who opened fire, driving him back. Gabe heard cursing in Spanish. Were these men from the Mexican cartel coming to retrieve their product from Escalanti's care?

Behind him Kino shouted. "Dryer's hit."

Gabe turned to see Kino dragging a limp Dryer toward cover. Wasn't he wearing a vest? Kino was on the radio in Gabe's cruiser, reporting an officer down.

Kino shouted to Gabe. "Highway patrol, DOJ and FBI are en route."

That got the gunmen's attention. One of them peered under the vehicle at Gabe. Gabe rolled, coming to his feet behind the gunman's SUV. He drove them toward the front end with a steady stream of lead to where he hoped Juris or Kino would have a shot. One man kept Gabe pinned, but judging from the shots, the second and third shooter still fired at his men.

"Hit," shouted someone.

Gabe's stomach clenched as he recognized it was Kino.

"How bad?" he called.

There was no answer.

"Juris?"

Juris answered in Apache.

"Here. I'm out."

Gabe used Apache, too. "Kino's weapon?"

"Can't get to it."

The gunmen only had to kill Gabe and they could take off with no obstacle between them and the main road. From there they could disappear into the Salt River rez or hole up here on Black Mountain, maybe hightail it all the way to the border.

Shots continued, but they were coming closer. Gabe sucked in a breath and peered around the fender. He had a shot and he took it, dropping one of the final three men. *Two targets remaining*, he thought and aimed. Then he fired at the one behind the fallen man. His pistol clicked. Gabe reached for his clip, but he knew he wouldn't be in time.

His next thought was that he had failed Selena. Not his duty, not his tribe—Selena, because she was the only one who mattered.

One of the two men stepped out from behind the front fender with a smirk on his face. A rifle shot cracked and the man dropped to his knees clutching his chest. His eyes rolled back and he toppled to the ground. A glance back showed Gabe that Frasco had recovered the rifle and used it.

Gabe faced the final man who aimed his automatic weapon as Gabe's clip clicked home too late. Sixteen rounds and not one was going to save him.

A small figure in a familiar worn brown coat stepped behind the shooter. Selena lifted the tire iron and brought it down so hard on the gunman's head that

Gabe winced at the crunching sound. The cartel gunman squeezed off the trigger as he fell, but his eyes were no longer focused and his aim had drifted. The bullets went wide and the man sprawled facedown on the icy road.

Gabe rushed to Selena, scooping her up in his arms. "How?" he said.

She was crying so hard that he didn't recognized the sound at first, but it grew louder. The *womp, womp, womp* of helicopter blades. They turned to see the chopper heading straight for them.

Gabe released Selena.

"Kino!" He ran over the frozen ground to find Randall cradling Gabe's brother's head in his lap. Juris's hand was clamped across Kino's neck, but the blood spurting from between his fingers scared Gabe to death.

"Nicked the artery in his neck."

Selena knelt beside Kino and added her hand to Randall's.

"Dryer?" asked Gabe.

Juris motioned with his head. Gabe saw Dryer lying on his back, staring wide-eyed at the sky. His necktie was flung over his shoulder. There was a hole the size of a cherry stone in the shoulder of his jacket.

"Went through his arm and under his armpit. I checked," said Juris. "Bullet's in his chest somewhere. Dead when I reached him."

Gabe checked Dryer's neck and confirmed what Juris had said. Dryer had no pulse.

Frasco stood unsteadily on one leg in an open spot on the road, waving one hand at the chopper, the rifle still gripped in the other. The bird touched down, and Frasco limped away in the opposite direction.

The pilot remained in place, but two familiar FBI agents dropped to the ground—his uncle Luke Forrest and his partner, field agent Cassidy Walker.

Chapter Twenty-Four

Gabe sent his brother and Frasco Dosela by chopper to the hospital in Phoenix escorted by Detective Randall Juris. Then he called Clyne, telling him that Kino had been shot and instructing him to find Kino's wife and drive her and their grandmother to the hospital.

"Is he going to be all right?" asked Clyne.

"I don't know."

Clyne told him he'd call later and then he was gone.

Gabe's men had arrived, followed by men from DOJ. Together they began the descent to the tractor trailer. The EMTs pulled in and checked Selena. She was bruised in the shoulders and ribs but was otherwise miraculously uninjured. Still, he felt the need to keep her close. The final gunman, Ronnie Hare, was still unaccounted for.

"Do you want to go home?" he asked Selena.

She nodded but clung to his arm. He wished he could gather her up, but the EMTs were checking the gunmen, his men were diverting traffic and there was so much that needed to be done. He didn't want to do any of it. He just wanted to take Selena away.

"Won't you want to question me?"

"Eventually." He would have to because it was his job, but right now he saw the pure exhaustion on her face.

"You ditched that truck on purpose," he said, not sure if he should be angry or grateful. Mostly he was amazed.

"What if I did?"

Why was he talking to her when he wanted to be kissing her and holding her and telling her how stupid he had been to ever take back that ring? He glanced at his uncle and his uncle's supervisor and recalled that he had not yet told Clyne who she was.

It didn't matter. Not now. He turned back to Selena.

"You could have been killed." He managed to sound stern.

"I think you have that backwards."

She was right. At the time when she had turned that trailer, the Mexicans were taking his patrol car apart with their semiautomatic weapons.

"You saved my life," he said.

She smiled. "You're welcome."

"I don't want you to do that again." That came out wrong.

She wrinkled her brow.

"Take a risk like that, I mean."

"Because you're indebted to me? You don't have to worry, Chief. It can be our little secret."

That was what he'd made her feel, he realized, as if she were nothing, when the truth was she was everything. Better than he was in every way. She had understood the power of love all along. She hadn't tried to control it or ignore it. Instead, she had accepted it and him with open arms. And when trouble had found her family and his feet went as cold as the snow beneath them, she had still given him what she thought he wanted—his freedom. And, fool that he was, he'd taken it and lost the best thing that ever happened to him.

"I'm an idiot," he said.

Cassidy Walker joined them at the spot where the guardrail was broken and now stood twisted back upon itself like ribbon candy.

"Well, we found the snowmobile hidden in the empty cave back at the lake. The shooters all dead." She glanced at Selena as if looking at a bug. "Is she hurt?"

"Bruised," said Gabe.

"We'll want a statement from her and from you." She glanced at Selena clinging to his arm. Gabe knew that in the past he would have stepped away. This time, he pressed Selena's hand closer to his side. She released him and started to withdraw, but he captured her arm and pulled her back.

"Not right now," he said to Walker.

"Sooner is better," she said, pressing.

Did Cassidy Walker know of his relationship to Selena? He thought that very likely. This time, instead of embarrassment, he felt a strong surging of protective instinct toward Selena. She'd defended him with her life and he'd be damned if he'd turn her over to the Feds.

"She'll be giving her statement to me."

"You don't see a conflict of interest there?" Walker asked.

Gabe didn't answer. Of course he was conflicted. And why in the wild world had he ever thought he wouldn't be conflicted around Selena? He'd been delusional for years. Even back then he had known that, if forced to choose between his duty and Selena, he'd pick Selena. But now that seemed exactly as it should be.

Walker moved on, peering over the embankment. The tops of several trees had been shorn off by the trailer's descent.

She stood on the road beside his uncle. He figured he and his uncle would be having a heart-to-heart soon. Right now he wanted to know if the final gunman had survived the fall.

"Who was in the cab with you?" Cassidy asked Selena.

It seemed she was planning on doing the questioning without his permission. She had guts, this woman. Normally he'd admire that.

"My father's parole officer," said Selena.

Cassidy Walker snorted in disbelief. "What?"

"Ronnie Hare," said his uncle Luke. "He's Salt River Apache."

"Really?" Cassidy thought a moment, looking down over the cliff. "An Apache parole officer. Perfect cover for moving messages between the cartel and gangs. He was your father's contact?"

Selena glanced from Gabe back to this aggressive woman.

"Contact? All I know is that this guy shows up at my door with a gun and threatens to shoot my mother. So I drove." Selena pointed down the mountain. "That."

Gabe looked at the truck. He knew it had been Selena's

pride and joy, and even though both the truck and trailer had been purchased used, it was the most amount of money she'd ever spent and likely still owed on the loans.

Walker took out a pad and started scribbling notes.

"What time was that?" she asked.

Gabe held up his hand. "That's enough now. Selena's going to the local hospital. This can wait until tomorrow."

Walker extended a card to Selena. "Call me if you feel up to talking."

Gabe picked up his radio and asked for one of the EMTs to take Selena to Black Mountain Hospital. Below them the barrels lay scattered over the snow. Some had rolled all the way to the bottom of the slope. Others had cracked open and the contents had bled into the snow.

Gabe's men had reached the cab of the truck.

"Ask them what they see," said Walker.

Gabe didn't. Instead he faced off, squaring his shoulders.

"Do you know who I am?" he asked.

She made a face. "Chief of Tribal Police."

"No. I mean, do you know who I am to your daughter?"

Gabe saw his uncle looking uncharacteristically nervous.

Walker went stiff and her blue eyes turned frosty.

"I'm here to do my job, Chief. Not to discuss my personal life."

"I see. And your job involves telling me how to do mine and sending a DOJ agent onto my reservation to spy on us while keeping your partner in the dark. I have to say, Mizz Walker, you are not making us Indians feel any more comfortable about trusting the federal government."

"This has been going on under your nose. Those men," she indicated the bodies strewn across the road. "They are using this reservation like a child uses home base in a game of tag. You can't stop them."

"Perhaps not. But I can stop you."

"This is a federal case," she said.

"On Indian lands."

"You're going to need our help."

"If I do, I'll ask."

"We are not leaving until that precursor is all accounted for."

Gabe waited a moment. "I'll ask my tribal council what they think about that."

His radio came on and Officer Cienega's voice emerged loud and clear.

"Cab is empty. There's a blood trail."

"Where's Hare?" asked Walker.

Gabe smiled. "Looks like that rabbit has gone for a run."

With a forty-minute head start, Gabe figured, on foot in deep snow.

"Cut for sign," he said, ordering his men to find Ronnie Hare's trail.

"A helicopter might come in handy in a search like that," said Walker.

Selena started shivering. He didn't know if it was from the cold or from the stress. But it didn't matter. He needed to get her out of here.

"I have to call my mother," she said as he walked her

back down the road. She rubbed at her face and then spoke through the fingers that covered her mouth. "I still owe nine thousand dollars on that tractor trailer and rig."

He took hold of Selena as they walked past the dead men. She shuddered and buried her face in his coat.

"You're going to the hospital," he said to her.

This time she didn't argue.

"Who is that woman?"

He told her. She straightened up, moving away to look up at him.

"She's Jovanna's mom?"

Gabe felt his stomach hitch. "My mother was her mom. That's the woman who illegally adopted her."

"But it wasn't illegal. They thought Jovanna's only relative was killed."

"Well, they didn't do a very good job looking for her kin, now did they?" What was he doing, arguing with her? He looked at her sad expression and pale complexion and felt terrible. "I'm sorry. I just think none of this should ever have happened."

"Still…" She stopped walking and glanced at the imposing little blonde woman at the cliff's edge.

"What?"

"That woman took your sister out of foster care, gave her a home. It might not be the home you would have liked, but she adopted her and she might be the only mother that your sister remembers. She's raised her for nine years."

Gabe hadn't thought of that. He'd been so busy trying to find his sister, it never occurred to him that his sister might not want to be found. She might be happy and might even love that bristly porcupine of a woman. The notion made him cross.

"What kind of a mother works as a field agent? Do you know how dangerous that job is? A mother has responsibilities. Plus her husband is dead, so it's just her. If anything happens to her, Jovanna will be right back in foster care. She ought to consider that before she goes charging around with a gun on her hip."

Selena studied Walker. "That's sad. What happened to her husband?"

Gabe was about to say he didn't know and didn't care. But instead he said, "I only know he was in the armed forces."

"Oh. Just like your uncle and your older brother."

"Just like that." Only they had both come home alive.

Andre Chee found them. The brother of his fallen officer was there with several other volunteer fire and rescue workers and said he'd be driving Selena to the hospital.

"Can't I just go home?" she asked.

"Hospital first. I wish I could come."

Selena gave him a sweet smile. "Duty first," she said.

He wanted to deny it. And for the first time in his life he was tempted to leave an active crime scene. Selena made him want to do that, but instead of feeling frightened by his love for her he felt both lucky and stupid. He should have trusted her to help him do the right thing.

But he was still the chief of police. Now, suddenly, that felt less like an honor and more like a burden. But if he wasn't a police officer, what was he? He'd done this job since he was twenty-two years old. The only other thing he was good at was rodeo and he was too darned old for that.

He stood with her for a moment, feeling lost as his job began dragging him away from the woman he loved—again.

"Will you be all right?" he asked.

"Yes. If they let me, I might drive my mom down to Phoenix to see Dad."

"Let Mia, Carla or Paula do the driving."

She nodded.

He had so much he needed to tell her. So many mistakes he needed to make right. But all he could think to say was, "I'll call you."

And then she was gone.

Chapter Twenty-Five

They had all parties accounted for except Ronnie Hare.

Cassidy Walker offered the Bureau's tracking dogs, but Gabe declined. There wasn't a dog on the planet that could track better than his men. They had found where Ronnie Hare had been thrown or had jumped clear of the rolling truck. He had not been more than twenty feet down on the embankment. He had been bleeding but managed to get to the road and wave down a man in a pickup. He'd stolen the truck at gunpoint. The stranded driver, unaware that nearly the entire police force was around the bend, had been found walking back down the mountain with his dog.

The Feds had taken action then, sending out alerts and positioning road blocks at all roads leaving the reservation and Salt River.

But Gabe knew Hare and he knew Apache. Ronnie was not leaving the reservation and the protection it afforded to its members. He'd be making tracks to Salt River but likely not on any of the roads. If he reached his home reservation, he would find someone to help keep him hidden deep in some burrow. Instead of road blocks, Gabe made a call to Jack Red Hawk, the chief down in Salt River, told him what was happening and included the information on the stolen truck.

"Think he's still in that truck?" asked Red Hawk.

"Would you be?" asked Gabe.

"I'd lose that vehicle at the first opportunity."

"You know him?"

"Not yet," said Red Hawk, "but I'm looking forward to getting acquainted with him and all his kin. Small place, Salt River. Someone will know someone. *Ashoog*, Gabe," he said, using the Apache word for thanks.

"Don't mention it. You take care now."

As the bodies were photographed and bagged, Gabe said an Apache prayer over Matthew Dryer. Then his body was zipped away and carted off to the fire rescue truck with the others. The man was a hero and Gabe hoped his spirit would know peace.

At dusk Gabe sent Juris and Franklin Salva to the Piñon Lake caves to see if the barrels had been stored there.

Gabe called Clyne at seven but he had no information except that Kino was in surgery and the family was on their way to Phoenix.

"You got time to give me an update?" asked Clyne.

"A quick one." Gabe briefly told him what had transpired. "The gunmen were Mexican cartel. They were moving their product to Salt River. Selena was driving. She'd been taken captive by her father's parole officer. Looks like he's been delivering messages from the Mexicans to both Salt River and the Wolf Posse."

Clyne cursed.

"You got Hare?"

"Not yet."

"What about the second lab?"

"Still on Leekela's place." Gabe figured he'd give it to him all at once. "Clyne? FBI and DOJ are on-site. Luke and his partner are headed over to pick up that second lab with a team right now."

Clyne muttered something in Apache.

"And I'm bringing in CID," he said, referring to the state's criminal investigations division.

"Keep me informed," said Clyne. "Doctor's here. Gotta go."

"When you see Kino, tell him…" Gabe's throat was burning and the words just stuck.

"Yeah. I'll tell him. Stay safe."

Gabe looked at his mobile and the next thing he knew was calling Selena. Her phone rang in his front pocket. He'd never given it back to her. He disconnected, wondering if they had made it to the hospital all right.

Clyne called in at ten in the evening with a report. Kino was out of the OR. A thoracic surgeon had repaired the damaged artery in his neck. Kino had lost a lot of blood but was stable and alert. His wife, Lea, and his grandmother were both fussing over him.

"Where's Clay?" asked Gabe.

"Here with his wife. First ones here."

Because they were already in Phoenix, Gabe realized.

Clyne said that Frasco had a through-and-through in his upper thigh and was under armed guard until they could sort out what had happened. Clyne had stopped in to say hello and spoken to his family, all four of his girls and his wife.

"Where's Tomas?"

"I didn't ask."

Salva called in from Piñon Lake, verifying that the barrels had been stored there. Juris had seen some evidence of old tracks and they were expanding their search.

Through the night, Gabe received updates. His uncle called to say they had seized the meth lab and made arrests with no shots fired. Sergeant Salva and Juris returned from the cave site to lend a hand at the scene. The new snow and the darkness were making tracking difficult and so they had decided to wait for morning. It was a long, cold, tedious night collecting evidence at the Piñon Lake road site. At sunup, his uncle returned without Agent Walker. She was pursuing leads to locate Hare and now working with Tribal Chief Red Hawk. *Better him than me*, thought Gabe.

A little later, his men were joined by CID. Arizona's criminal investigations division had a specialized unit just for narcotics investigations. His department would be using their labs for all evidence processing.

Another agent from DOJ showed up, making it a three-ring circus with Gabe as the ringmaster.

The rising sun was turning the snow pink when Salva phoned from the cave site. Using a metal detector, his team had found bullet castings just outside the entrance, a tree with several bullet holes and depressions in the snowpack where someone might have fallen.

Had they found Officer Dante Chee's secret hunting spot?

"What do you need?" he asked.

Salva requested an additional team from CID to help collect evidence.

They were wrapping up at the scene and there were still a hundred things that needed doing. But Gabe didn't want to do any of them. Instead he felt an unexpected detachment from the investigation. It didn't seem as important as visiting his brother, seeing his grandmother and telling Selena that he was the biggest fool in Black Mountain. He called Detective Juris over.

"You okay?" asked Juris.

"Yeah. You're lead. I've got to go see a man about a horse."

"Chief?"

"I'm going to Phoenix."

Detective Juris nodded. "Tell Kino we're thinking about him."

"Will do."

IT HAD BEEN almost twenty-four hours since Selena had nearly slid off that embankment. She sat in her father's hospital room in Phoenix with her sisters and mother, waiting for someone from the Department of Justice to verify that her father was not in violation of his parole. She rolled her sore shoulder and shifted, trying and failing to find a comfortable position. The clinic said her ribs and shoulder were bruised from the accident. She considered herself lucky to have walked away with only bruises.

Her father was in high spirits. His leg was bandaged and they learned that the bullet had just punched through muscle, narrowly missing the main blood vessel. He had an IV drip of antibiotics and a Phoenix police officer stationed outside his room.

"And you're a hero," said their mother to her father.

Her father smiled. "I don't think Gabe Cosen will forgive me. Sneaking around behind his back."

"He might." They all turned to see Gabe standing in the door.

Selena was so surprised she was speechless. He was in the middle of the biggest, most important case of his life. What was he doing here?

Gabe stepped forward and shook Frasco's hand. "I'm glad you're all right, sir. Thank you for your help last night."

"How's Kino?" asked her father.

"I just came from his room in ICU. He's going to make a full recovery."

Selena breathed out a sigh of relief.

Gabe turned to her family. "I need a moment alone with Mr. Dosela."

Selena felt a stab of sorrow. He was here on business, of course. Why had she thought he had come all this way to see her? Mia, Paula and Carla headed out the door. Selena lingered a moment and then followed. He heard Gabe tell her mother that he would like her to stay.

Mia was hungry, so they headed to the vending machines in the waiting room down the hall.

"Will the insurance pay for our truck?" asked Paula.

"She was transporting drugs," said Carla, her tone exasperated.

"At gunpoint," said Mia, her words muffled by the large bite of chocolate bar she had stuffed in her cheek.

"I don't know what will happen," said Selena. "I'll call them in the morning and put in a claim."

"The Department of Justice should buy us a new one. It's their fault. You could have been killed," said Paula.

For some reason, though she had known that all along, the entire thing hit her right then. Her knees went rubbery and Carla just managed to grab her elbow and guide her into a well-worn sofa.

Selena cradled her head in her hands as the crash replayed in her mind. She trembled and Mia sat down next to her, then gathered her up.

"We got you, Leenie. We've all got you."

Selena sagged against Mia and let the tears flow. Paula patted her knee and Carla furnished a wad of paper towels so she could mop her face and blow her nose. The tears didn't last long. And when they were past she looked up at her wonderful sisters. She felt so lucky to have them.

"It's just a stupid truck," said Paula. "We'll get another."

"The important thing is that you're all right and Dad's all right," said Mia.

"And he's not a criminal," said Carla.

"He's a real live hero," added Paula.

"Not everyone thinks working with the Feds makes you a hero," said Selena.

"Well, I do. He stopped that poison from reaching its destination," said Paula.

"Selena did that," said Mia.

Paula continued as if Mia hadn't spoken. "I can't believe that his parole officer was working with the cartels. I hope they catch him and revoke his membership in the tribe," said Mia.

"And lock him up," added Paula.

"And throw away the key," said Mia.

Their mother joined them, her face seeming younger now, as if all the stress of the last few weeks had finally passed. She looked happy.

"Girls, could you come with me?"

They stood to follow, but their mother turned to her oldest daughter. "Not you, Selena. Wait here a minute. All right?"

What was going on?

Selena's sisters filed out after their mother. Mia looked back, her brow wrinkled and lines of concern flanking her mouth. It was only then that Selena had a terrible thought.

Was Gabe here to arrest her?

Chapter Twenty-Six

Selena watched her sisters depart, trailing behind their mother toward her father's room. They passed Gabe who was heading in her direction. Selena's mother only nodded at him in passing. Gabe continued on, turning his attention to Selena and fixing her with an intent stare that straightened her spine. His grave expression only increased Selena's rising panic. She *had* driven that truck. It had been loaded with barrels of chemicals used in making drugs. What if Ronnie was dead and there was no one to corroborate her story?

Selena's breathing came so fast she grew dizzy again and had to drop back down on the sofa before she fell. Tiny spots swirled before her eyes like snowflakes. Maybe she should tuck her head between her knees.

"Selena?" Gabe said, his voice serious. "I have something I need to discuss with you."

The slammer, she thought. Handcuffs, police lights, her name in the paper beside her father's. She couldn't go to jail. But maybe Paula and Carla could take over her morning route now that their truck...

"Selena?"

Her head popped up from her hands and she stared

at him. He was standing right before her so she had to crane her neck to see his face. What was he saying?

"Are you listening to me?"

She hadn't been. She'd been too busy wondering what she'd look like in an orange jumpsuit.

"He made me drive. Hare. He had a gun. It wasn't my fault."

The harder she scrambled for solid ground, the farther she slipped backward. It was like running on ice.

Gabe cocked his head. He looked so handsome in his blazer and jeans. He's cinched up his turquoise-and-silver bolo and removed his hat. He gave the Stetson a little spin and then dropped it on the sofa beside her, brim up. Then he offered his hand. She took it, hoping he wasn't going to slap a steel handcuff on her wrist. Instead, he led her to the window. Her knees were a little rubbery, but they carried her. They were on the fourth floor and so the windows gave them a view of the parking lot and emergency room entrance beyond. The world down here at lower elevations was completely devoid of snow, and the trees and vegetation ringing the lot all looked dry and thirsty.

He kept hold of her hand.

"Shouldn't you be back at the crime scene?"

"Yup. I should be. I ought to be leading the investigation and fending off the Feds who are trying to take over. I should be helping Clyne take on an FBI field agent who looks like she could eat us for lunch and who happens to be the woman who adopted my little sister. I should be looking for a fugitive. But I'm not, because this can't wait."

"I didn't know about the drug stuff. Swear to God."

Gabe actually smiled and her heart did that little twist it always did when he looked at her like that. She had to squeeze her free hand into a fist to keep from reaching out to caress his handsome face. Selena noticed the fatigue now, there in the circles beneath his dark eyes.

"Selena, I want to start with an apology. Five years ago, when you said it wasn't going to work, I should have argued. I should have fought for you. But I was afraid."

Afraid? Had she heard that right? Gabe Cosen was not afraid of anything or anybody.

"I don't believe it."

"It's true."

She angled her head, trying to understand. "Afraid… because of your reputation?"

He nodded. "That was part of it and I'm ashamed to admit that. After I arrested your father, I was more concerned about what others would say about us. That our relationship would compromise the trial. I was so sure that I couldn't do my job and have you. I thought I had to choose."

And he had picked the job. She lowered her head.

"It's an important job," she managed to say.

"No, it's not. Not as important as loving you. Selena, I thought my work was everything. But seeing you almost go over that cliff, well, it shook things into place. The job is nothing if I lose you. You don't threaten me or make me vulnerable. You make me…" He switched to Apache. "Sunflower Sky Woman, you are my heart."

Tears leaked down her cheeks. "I am?"

He nodded. "And I'll spend the rest of my life trying to earn your forgiveness for the time it took me to recognize what you knew all along."

"You're not here to arrest me?" she asked in a quavering voice.

He blinked down at her and then he had her by each elbow, his touch light and firm. His scent filled her senses and made her dizzy with need.

"Arrest you? Selena, I'm trying to propose to you."

"Pro...pr..." She couldn't get the word out.

Gabe released her and sank to one knee. She looked down at him with amazement as he reached around behind his neck and under his collar. He untied the medicine bundle he always wore. Then he held the small beaded leather pouch in one hand. She knew his mother had made it for him. She had made one for each of her boys when they were still too young to undergo the initiation into the Black Mountain tribe.

He upended the pouch. Into his palm tumbled a clear, naturally faceted stone, the claw of a bear, the tooth of an elk and a familiar diamond engagement ring. He plucked the solitaire from his palm and returned the other sacred objects to his medicine bundle. He had kept her ring here, beside his heart, all these years.

He held the ring between his thumb and index finger, extending it to her.

"Selena, will you marry me?"

She reached for the ring and then hesitated.

"Selena, I have thought about you and dreamed about

you and longed for you every day since I took this back. I need you. Please take it."

"Me?" she squeaked.

"Yes. I need your wisdom. Your love for your family. Your pride. I am not weaker with you. I am stronger because you give me balance. I need more than my job. I need joy, too. Be my joy." He offered the ring. "Say yes."

"But your reputation. You're the chief and I'm…"

"A hero. A miracle. The bravest woman I've ever met. I know why you gave this back, Selena," he said, lifting the ring. "It was to help me in my career. And, fool that I was, I let you and it worked. I've done well. But none of it matters without you."

"What about your job?"

"I don't need it. I need you. I told Clyne the same thing when I resigned."

She stepped back. "You did not!"

He nodded. She stared at him, in shock. He'd resigned his job as chief of police for her. But she didn't want that. Everything she had done was to prevent that very thing.

"Can you take it back? Your resignation?" she asked.

He smiled. "If that's what you want."

"I do."

He held up the ring and the diamond flashed in the light.

"I love you, Selena. Be my wife."

She offered her left hand and he slipped the ring over her knuckle. It still fit.

"Is that yes?" he asked.

"Yes!" She threw herself into his arms and he stood,

sweeping her into a spin as he whooped for joy. Then he lowered her until their lips met. Her toes curled with the delicious pressure of his mouth possessing hers. He deepened the kiss, rocking her over his arm so she arched back, letting his tongue dance over hers. Finally, when she had begun to tug his shirt from the waistband of his jeans, Gabe groaned and set her aside.

It took a moment for the cloud of lust to recede and when it did, she leaped back into his arms again.

"We're engaged," she chirped. "Again."

"But this time we're getting married. The sooner the better."

The phone on his belt vibrated and she glanced at him. He didn't reach for it.

She lifted her eyebrows.

"What? I have a second in command. He can handle it for a few more minutes." He offered his hand and said, "Let's go tell your parents."

And then it made sense. Why he'd wanted to speak to her father and mother.

"You were asking them for my hand, weren't you?"

He nodded. "I can't believe you thought I was here to arrest you. You have a guilty conscience."

She grinned up at him and they walked down the hall. "You know what would be great?"

"What?"

"If you gave me something to feel really, really guilty about."

Gabe blew out a breath. "I'd like that. But after we get married."

She groaned. "Killjoy."

"Hey. This time I'm doing it right. I want that marriage certificate and a church service and a reception with the entire tribe so that everyone knows you are mine."

Everyone? That sounded perfect to her.

"Oh, so you *are* here to detain me."

He grinned. "I'm taking you into custody—my custody."

"I deserve it." And then Selena kissed him again.

* * * * *

"Are you sure that it's okay if I stay, Kevin?"

"I can go. I'm sure that I can stay with—" She stopped before she said Brittany. Her only other friend didn't have a place in her life for Heather's mess. She had her hands full dealing with the fire at her house. "I can stay at a hotel or something."

"You're not staying at a hotel." Kevin set her bag next to the wall, but his movements were awkward and tight. "You're welcome to stay here as long as you need."

"Kevin, I. . .Thank you." She didn't know what to say. *Thank you* just didn't seem like enough when what she really wanted to say was that he was part of the reason she had the strength to leave.

He had shown her there could be more in the world. That there could be something besides heartbreak and the constant thoughts that she could be doing something more to make someone else happy, even if that meant being miserable in her own skin.

Kevin had saved her life and he probably didn't even realize it.

SMOKE AND ASHES

BY
DANICA WINTERS

First Published in Great Britain 2016
By Mills & Boon, an imprint of HarperCollins*Publishers*
1 London Bridge Street, London, SE1 9GF

© 2016 by Danica Winters

ISBN: 978-0-263-91905-9

46-0516

Our policy is to use papers that are natural, renewable and recyclable products and made from wood grown in sustainable forests. The logging and manufacturing processes conform to the legal environmental regulations of the country of origin.

Printed and bound in Spain
by CPI, Barcelona

Danica Winters is a bestselling author who has won multiple awards for writing books that grip readers with their ability to drive emotion through suspense and occasionally a touch of magic. When she's not working, she can be found in the wilds of Montana testing her patience while she tries to hone her skills at various crafts (quilting, pottery and painting are not her areas of expertise). She always believes the cup is neither half-full nor half-empty, but it better be filled with wine. Visit her website at www.danicawinters.net.

This book is dedicated to those men and women who have lived through the turbulent cycles of abuse. May this book help you find your voice, live your truth and experience the love you desire.

This book would not have been possible without the support from a multitude of firefighters and law enforcement agents, including: Sergeant Ryan Prather, Retired Training Officer Jerome Kahler, and the men and women of the Frenchtown Rural Fire Department. Thank you for taking the time to help answer questions and making sure that events portrayed in this novel were accurate. You make this world a safer place.

A thank-you cannot be complete without thanking Lane Heymont, Denise Zaza and the Harlequin team. Thank you for helping to bring this book to life.

Prologue

He looked down at Heather Sampson as he pulled the matchbox from his pocket. The box dropped from his hand, spilling matches onto her bedroom floor in a heap of deadly promise. Crouching down, he scooped them back into the container, careful to move quietly, afraid that at any second she would awaken and find him standing over her.

Her eyes were closed and her lips slightly parted, as if she waited for a kiss from her Prince Charming. She should have known better. There was no such thing as Prince Charming. There were only toads and a precious few men like him—men who worked to make everything just.

The sad truth was that there was no justice in marriage—at least not in any of the marriages he had witnessed. No. Marriage was one lie after another. One hurt feeling masked with a fake smile, only to have another lie strip it away. It was an endless cycle of pain.

What was the point? What was it all for?

As far as he could tell, it was for nothing more than ego and some idealistic hope that if they acted happy, if they faked it well enough, maybe they could finally believe it themselves.

He was here to make her a martyr, not that she would understand, but this was his chance to show her and the world what her marriage truly was—nothing more than smoke and ashes. A fire that had yet to burn itself out. But at last the time had come. The hour was here for him to stoke the flames and let them consume every crumb of her failing marriage.

The inferno could have it all.

He walked out of her bedroom and made his way downstairs, where the glorious scent of gasoline filled the space. Unlike the others, Heather's house would go up in a flash. In one giant fireball the whole charade would be over—the secrets, the lies, the fake smiles and the hurt feelings. It would all be gone and all her pain could be for a higher purpose.

The night air blew into the house, diluting the gas's perfume. He made sure to leave the door open as he stepped out and walked toward the garage. A puddle of gas sat on the sidewalk, just waiting for him.

He struck the match.

It was so much easier this way.

The fire's smoke curled skyward, creating a trail that led to the heavens. If he had his way, life would be better and she would be free.

Chapter One

A few days earlier

The note had been simple. Two little words. Two haunting, terrifying and humbling words. Words that had the power to rip out Heather's heart.

I'm leaving.

The paper sat on the kitchen counter where David had left it, a glass of water as a paperweight. The condensation on the glass had dripped down, leaving a ring of water. Like her tears, it was long dried, but it would never disappear.

She fought the urge to turn around and leave the kitchen, lunch be damned for the second day in a row, but the pressures of the day and her nagging hunger drove her forward, past the stained note on their newly installed granite countertops to their perfectly polished stainless-steel fridge.

David had been adamant that they have the finest of everything—the finest appliances, the finest table, all the way down to the silk table runner they'd had specially made and shipped from India. Now, in the lifeless kitchen, the bloodred runner made the entire room seem like a picture out of a home decor magazine, but nothing like a home.

None of it had ever really mattered, not when all she was left with was an empty kitchen and anger in her gut.

Opening the fridge, she was met with its cold, stale air. The only contents were a single bottle of Perrier and a half-eaten piece of week-old cheesecake. God, she loved cheesecake. The way it melted on the tongue, leaving behind the luxurious texture of butter. David hated for her to have it, complaining it made her gain weight.

She grabbed the plate and folded back the plastic wrap. David could hate the cake and her all he wanted. He had made it clear he was *leaving*. If she wanted to eat cake, she could. He wasn't here to stop her.

Grabbing a fork, she stabbed the tines into the cake and lifted it to her mouth. The scent of cream cheese filled her senses, making her mouth water. David would have hated this defiance.

She threw the fork and the uneaten bite into the sink and dropped the cheesecake, plate and all, into the garbage bin. David would come back. He always came back. And when he did, he would know she had gone against his wishes.

She stared down at the garbage. David would notice the plate was missing from the stack of exactly eight.

She had every right to be angry, but she would pay if he thought she had done something to intentionally upset him.

Reaching into the bin, she retrieved the plate and scraped the cheesecake off the edge. She couldn't disappoint him no matter how much he disappointed her.

She stood at the sink and washed the plate as she

stared outside. There had been so much more that she had wanted to do with her life. When she'd been young she had dreamed of helping people, of being a nurse. She smiled as she thought of her old teddy, Mr. Bear, who'd always stood in for a tragic victim of some terrible accident. She would use Band-Aid after Band-Aid fixing his wounds. Now he sat at the top corner of her closet, a reminder of a path not taken.

Because of David, she had given up everything,

There was a knock on the door and she set the plate in the drying rack. Reality was calling. Grabbing David's note, she stuffed it into her pocket.

There was another knock, this time harder, more urgent.

"Coming." She made her way out to the living room.

Looking in through the window in the door was her neighbor Kevin. He smiled and his eyes lit up as he saw her. As he moved, his sexy, prematurely graying hair sparkled in the sunshine. Heather tried not to notice the wiggle of excitement she felt at seeing him.

She opened the door. "How's it going?"

"Great, but I need your help," Kevin said. "I just got called to work. Do you think you could keep Lindsay for a while?" He pushed his daughter out from behind his legs.

Lindsay clutched the straps of her pink backpack. "Hi, Mrs. Sampson."

"Hi, sweetheart. Why don't you come in?" Heather dropped her hand onto the girl's shoulder and gave it a reassuring squeeze. "I'm glad you're here. I got a bunch of new craft supplies. There's a new bracelet designing kit you'll love. And I needed a friend today."

"Awesome!" Lindsay beamed.

"Thank you so much, Heather. I don't know what I'd do without you." Kevin reached out. "Lindsay, can I get a hug before I go?"

Lindsay threw herself into her father's arms. Kevin closed his eyes and squeezed her as if no one was watching. "Love you, honey. Be good, okay?"

"Okay, Daddy." Lindsay let go.

"Don't forget you have a peanut butter and jelly sandwich in your backpack if you need a snack."

Lindsay nodded.

Kevin turned to leave and Heather couldn't help but glance down at his black uniform pants. As he moved, they seemed to hug the muscular shape of his body. Warmth rushed through her.

"Wait," she called out to him, hoping to see his handsome, slightly mischievous grin one more time. "Where's Colter?"

He looked back and the grin reappeared, making the heat in her core intensify. "He had baseball this afternoon. He should be done in time for the Millers' barbecue. You going?"

Weeks ago David had promised they would go, but now, with everything that had happened between them, he would never agree.

"I'm not sure." Heather forced a tight smile.

"I hope you do. It'd be nice to catch up." Kevin paused. "I'll be back to pick her up as soon as I can."

Heather nodded. "No rush." She needed all the excuses she could get to keep from having to focus on her life, and a nine-year-old girl and her much-too-handsome father were the perfect distractions.

"Thanks!" Kevin rushed off, heading toward his

white truck that was emblazoned with the golden words *Fire Inspector.*

Heather pasted a smile on her face as she closed the door. Everything would be okay. "You ready for some fun, Lindsay?"

"I need to do my homework. It's due tomorrow."

"Homework? You only have a few weeks of school left."

Lindsay shrugged as she sat down in her regular spot on the couch. She took out her worksheets. "It shouldn't take long."

"You need me to go over it with you?" Heather silently wished she could help.

"Nah, I got it. Thanks, though."

Her hope deflated. "Okay. I'll be in the kitchen. Let me know if you change your mind. When you're done we can make those bracelets."

"Okay," Lindsay said, sounding preoccupied.

Heather walked back into the lifeless kitchen, picked up her cell phone and unlocked the screen. She tapped in David's phone number and when the phone rang her stomach twisted with nerves. He would pick up, wouldn't he?

It rang again.

"Why are you calling?" he answered.

"No 'hello'?" Heather asked, trying to keep her anger from seeping into her voice. "I thought maybe by now—"

"By now what? That I'd want to come back to the house?" David growled. "Listen, Heather. We can't keep doing this. Did you get my note?"

Her fingers moved to the letter in her pocket. "I did, but I was hoping—"

"What?" he interrupted. "That I didn't mean it?"

"David, we can work this out. We just need to go to counseling. I would do it for you." She pulled the note from her pocket and flattened it on the island.

"If we went to counseling that would imply that there's something to save. At this point, Heather, just seeing you makes me sick."

Her knees gave out under the weight of his words and she fell onto a barstool. "I'm sorry, David. I didn't mean—"

"Sorry doesn't cut it, Heather. I told you that you weren't allowed to talk to Andrew anymore. I see the way you look at him. And the way he looks at you. You're having an affair." David paused. "Don't you care how it makes me look that you're sleeping with another doctor?"

When she'd seen Andrew at the Easter fundraiser for the American Heart Association, he'd been overly friendly—maybe even approaching flirtatious with her—but it had been nothing more than banter. If David hadn't kept bringing up the incident, she would have forgotten it by now, but David wouldn't let it go, no matter how much she pleaded.

"I'm not. I never—"

"If you're not having an affair, then why did I see you talking to him outside the hospital the other day?"

She stared at the wrinkles in his note. "He stopped me. He just wanted to ask about you. I told him you didn't want me to talk to him, but he wouldn't listen."

"Was he trying to find out the next time it was safe to come into our house and screw you?"

Hot, unwelcome tears rolled down her cheeks. "It was nothing like that. He just wanted to know if you're okay."

"What did you tell him?"

"Nothing. I didn't tell him anything."

"Do you think I'm stupid? That I don't know when someone's lying to me?"

"I promise. I never lied. Just come home," Heather said, her voice like that of a trapped animal. "Tonight's Brittany's barbecue. Please, you have to go…"

"First you have an affair, and now you want me to come home? You are nothing, Heather. Why would I want to be seen with a woman like you?"

She crumpled his note in her hand. She wasn't weak…but it was hard not to be crushed when the world around her was collapsing.

Chapter Two

The windows of the sage-green house were intact, and a basket full of half-dead pink flowers waved lazily in the breeze as Kevin parked his truck. Aside from the flurry of motion and yellow caution tape, it would have been hard to tell this had been the location of an active fire.

Something about the place reminded him of Heather. Maybe it was the way it seemed so perfect, so put together on the outside, but if he looked a little deeper he saw whispers of turmoil within. Yet, with the house, he could open its doors and uncover its secrets, whereas with Heather there were too many things standing in the way—he could never truly know her.

A fire crew milled around the yard as they mopped up the scene, and the battalion chief, Stephen Hiller, was writing something in his notepad. Kevin killed his engine and the BC turned and gave him an acknowledging tip of the head. Hiller's face was pinched and his eyes tired, as though he was just waiting for him to arrive so his crew could hand off the chain of custody.

On the porch of the neighboring white row house a little boy, his thumb in his mouth, sat in a turquoise patio chair. The boy smiled and waved at him, his chubby arm wiggling.

Something about how the boy's eyes lit up reminded Kevin of Colter when he'd been younger. Colter used to love waiting on the porch for him to come home. The second he'd arrived, his son would rush down the steps in a hurry to welcome him.

How things had changed.

For the millionth time, he wished he could turn back the clock, but life was fickle and moments fleeting. If he'd only known then what he knew now, he would have run to Colter and scooped him up in his arms and carried him inside to where baby Lindsay had been. He would have spent every spare moment he had with his wife and his perfect little family. Yet, most nights, he had just pat him on the head as he brushed past him on his way toward the fridge and a cold beer.

Allison had hated his routine, the way he was so wrapped up in his job when he'd come home from work. She had never understood how badly he'd needed a moment to wind down, to relax after a crazy day fighting fires. Then again, he had never really understood what it must have been like for her, waiting for someone to come home, only to have him arrive in body but not in mind.

There was no going back.

The little boy's mother opened the door and hustled the boy inside. After a moment the curtain in their living room shifted slightly as if the woman was watching.

Hiller walked up to the truck and tapped on the window. "Glad to see you could make it, Jensen."

"Sorry I'm late. I had to find someone to watch Lindsay." His thoughts moved back to Heather, the way her hair had haloed her face and her jeans had hugged her perfect hips when she'd answered the door.

Hiller nodded, but it was easy to see from the puckered look on his face that he didn't really understand—or care.

"We've been waiting an hour."

"I'm here now."

"Next time be quicker about it. Some of us have work to do."

"What, do you have a girlfriend waiting?" Kevin joked, but Hiller's face remained motionless. Kevin coughed, trying to dispel some of the tension. "Anyways… Ya wanna fill me in?"

"The crew arrived on scene at 5:03 a.m. I arrived a few minutes after. Fire started on the second floor. They managed to get the homeowner—one Elke Goldstein—out of the house in a matter of minutes."

"Anyone else in the house at the time of the fire?"

Hiller scanned his notes. "She was the only one. I asked her a few questions, but Ms. Goldstein wasn't especially forthcoming with information. She seemed relatively unharmed, but was adamant she had to leave."

"Do you know anything about her? Does she work? Is the house underwater?" There were no for-sale signs in the yard and the grass was well-kept, but it was amazing how good a house could look even when the owner was only a piece of paper away from losing it.

"As far as I know, everything was on the up-and-up, but she didn't really want to talk to me."

"Making friends again?"

"What the hell's that supposed to mean?"

"Just that you're popular."

"Why don't you stop worrying about me and start worrying more about your investigation?"

Kevin chuckled. "You know where Ms. Goldstein went?"

"She said she had to go to work. Someplace called Ruby's."

Kevin grabbed his clipboard. "What else can you tell me about the fire?"

"Fire was small. Confined to the second floor. Extinguished quickly. There was a suspicious mark in the upstairs hallway."

"Was anyone seen running from the scene? Anything suspicious?"

"One of her neighbors…" He pointed to the white house where the boy had been sucking his thumb. "They reported seeing a man leave the house a few minutes before the smoke started."

"Ms. Goldstein didn't tell you about him?"

Hiller shook his head. "Not a word." He handed Kevin a copy of the fire report. "Here're my notes. I've been more than thorough."

"Great." He clipped the report in his clipboard.

Hiller turned around to face his crew. "Let's go, guys. Now this is someone else's problem."

"Wait. Leave me a couple of guys. I need them stationed outside the door until I'm done."

"How long you want to keep the scene intact?"

Chief Larson's words echoed in his mind—*Things are tight, Jensen. We need to cut costs.* If he didn't watch it, he would be getting the ax. But he had to get back to Heather's to pick up Lindsay, and he had promised Colter he would swing by his baseball practice. Heather would help him, if he needed—she always did—but something in her beautiful, hazel eyes told him that today was one of those days that she needed him. He couldn't let down her or his kids.

"I'm going to need at least a day or two."

"Jensen, time costs money—money the city won't give us. What little we have would be better spent on something other than chasing down a ghost. You know the chance of finding whoever is behind this is slim to none. Don't waste my time and the taxpayer's money. Let the insurance company write her a check."

"I'm trying to save the taxpayer's money by stopping this from happening again."

"You haven't even been in the house yet, Jensen. Who the hell knows? Maybe it was just some kid playing around. Why do you always have to assume the worst?"

"Hoping for the best is a rookie mistake."

Hiller slammed his fist against the truck. "This is coming out of your budget."

"No problem," he lied.

The fire inspector's budget was closer than a hair on a gnat's ass every month. If he found adequate evidence of arson, maybe he could convince the chief to cover the cost of keeping the chain of custody going for the next thirty-six hours, but probably nothing more.

"You need to step into line with the rest of the department, Jensen," Hiller threatened. "It's been long enough since Allison died. You're starting to cost us money because of your inability to do your job."

He cringed. Why did Hiller have to remind him? The weeks and months after Allison's death, he'd get into the flames and all he'd been able to think about was his wife, sitting in her hospital bed as the chemo burned through her veins.

Three years ago, after Allison's death, the department had taken him out of the fire and put him in an office chair, but even as fire inspector things weren't going as they should be. He'd been taking too long on investigations, but he rationalized it by telling himself that he was holding his responsibilities to a higher standard than his predecessor—a senior firefighter who had been happy playing by the unwritten rules while he sat back and waited to collect his pension.

"I've got this, Hiller."

"Time is money, Jensen."

"Do I need to remind you of our motto: *protecting lives and saving property?* Lives come first, Hiller. Money isn't even in the equation."

Hiller glowered at him but said nothing.

"Just give me the men I need."

Hiller looked out at his crew. "The rookies can stay behind." He pointed at two twentysomethings that had just been hired. "You guys monitor the house!"

They nodded and walked to the front of the yard.

Hiller turned back to him. "Get this handled. I need my guys. Our work actually makes a difference." Then he stormed off.

Kevin ignored the retreating cavalry as he looked down at Hiller's notes. At least he had a description of the man—dark haired, around six feet tall and an average build.

His handset sat in the window, and he stared at it for a moment before deciding to leave it there. He wasn't a real firefighter; nothing he did was an emergency. As Hiller was more than happy to point out, his job rarely made a difference. He was little more than a glorified desk jockey, filling out paperwork and teaching kids about smoke detectors.

He stepped out of the truck and slipped into his bunker gear and boots, making sure to grab his investigation kit and helmet before he made his way toward the house.

There was less than an hour before Colter's practice was over. He had to make a pass through the scene and take some notes, but then he could get across town to the high school to catch the tail end. If he hurried, Colter wouldn't notice he'd been missing. Maybe he would even get a chance to talk to Heather and thank her for her help.

Perhaps he could convince her to come to the barbecue. She always looked beautiful at those things—her naturally tan skin finally exposed after a winter hidden away. Last year, she'd worn her dark hair down. It had looked so soft, so touchable, just like her lips.

Those lips. He'd love to make those lips his.

He laughed at himself. Those lips, just like the rest of her, could never be his.

The only thing he could ever be to her was a friend, and that was only if he hurried.

He made his way around the back of the house, taking pictures every few feet. The door to the garage was unlocked and, as he opened it, the smell of burnt chemicals swirled around him. Thick black residue coated everything, including the woman's car, but nothing was burned.

On the wooden steps that led to the house, there was a pair of discarded women's flip-flops and beside them was an oily black shoe print. The print had a star pattern at its center and rectangular squares around the sole's edges. He snapped a picture. It was probably a leftover of someone walking through the oil slick in the garage while they'd made their way inside. He took a swab of the substance and tagged it as evidence to be sent to the crime lab.

The whole downstairs dripped with water and his footsteps sounded like suction cups as he made his way through the kitchen. The small rectangular room was typical of a low-income home, linoleum on the floor, cheap oak cupboards and an apartment-sized refrigerator.

In the living room, there was black, sticky ash on the walls where the smoke had billowed through the house. A thick layer of oily soot covered every surface making it impossible for him to be able to lift fingerprints.

He followed the smoke pattern up the stairs, and the acrid smell grew stronger. In the center of the hallway, between two bedrooms and in front of the burned-out bathroom, was a black circular pattern.

Another V-shaped pattern started at the floor, and at its center was an electrical outlet. He looked up. The light had melted and it pointed like a finger to the blackened circle.

There was no doubt about it, he'd found his ignition point.

He crouched and wafted the air toward him as he took in a long breath of the oily, dirty smoke. It had a faint chemical smell.

Around the edges of the charred circle was a ring of white powder. He took another picture. Opening his bag, he pulled out an evidence can and scooped some of the white residue into it.

This fire was no accident.

An event like this, one started with chemical oxidizers, wasn't the work of a novice. This was someone who knew the chemicals required to start a fire. Plus they likely knew most chemical reactions took several minutes to ignite—giving them enough time to flee the scene.

If he had to bet, this was a person who would do it again.

According to the notes, Elke had been in her bedroom at the time of the fire. If the perp had wanted to kill her, they would have built a fire that she couldn't escape, yet they had kept it small, manageable.

He turned to his clipboard and wrote: *Suspect may not have meant to kill victim.*

He glanced down at his watch. Fifteen minutes before the end of practice. He was never going to make it to the baseball field in time to see Colter.

He put away his clipboard, labeled the evidence and dropped it into his kit.

The burden his job put on him was fine, but bit by bit and day by day, he could see Colter pulling away. It was even evident in the way his son walked, no longer the fumbling steps of a boy, but the saunter of a young man. Every time Kevin had a call lately, he had watched as Colter used this newfound gait to walk as far away as possible. After today and his broken promise, it would only get worse.

Chapter Three

David stomped into the house and slammed the door, the sound making Heather jump. The sweat on her palms made her hands stick to the edges of the kitchen counter, and they peeled off with a wet sound as she stood up to greet him.

His dark hair was perfectly shaped and his eyes bright, as if he hadn't had the same trouble she had sleeping last night. The only thing that gave away his anger was the slight tic of his lip, as though he was holding back a snarl.

"Hi, David," she said, trying to sound cool and indifferent but failing as fear and desperation crept into her voice.

"Don't talk to me. Don't think I came home for you."

"Are you going to come to the barbecue with me?"

"We'll both be there. I would hardly say we're going together."

Heather glanced over her shoulder toward Lindsay, who was sitting on the couch weaving thread around her bracelet.

"You look like crap," David said as he walked to the fridge and grabbed the unopened bottle of Perrier.

She closed the door to the kitchen. Lindsay didn't

need to hear anything David had to say right now. She would get the wrong idea. David wasn't a bad man, just stressed. Stress always brought out the worst in people.

"I should've known you would go to seed without me around." He smirked as he looked at her. "I don't know what you're going to do without me."

His words were like a fist slamming into her gut, but she tried to ignore the pain. She needed to fix this and get him back. She couldn't let herself fall into the same cycle her mother had—a life built around a husband who only came home when it was convenient and who was more than happy to use her love as a tool to manipulate her. She was better than that.

For a moment her mind moved to Kevin—he had never treated Allison the way David treated her. Yet that was in public. Who knows what happened behind closed doors. Perhaps all marriages were the same—one person always bending to the whims of another for the sake of commitment.

"I don't understand this, David. I don't even know where this is coming from."

"Do I have to remind you about Andrew?"

Heather flicked a glance over her shoulder. "Don't. Lindsay's here."

"You afraid she's going to find out what you've done?"

"I didn't do anything." The second the words fell from her lips, she wished she hadn't spoken back. Her insolence would only make things worse, and she needed him back—she needed to hold her family together.

David glowered. "I don't care what you say anymore. You're a liar and a cheat." He slammed the bottle on the granite countertop so hard Heather couldn't believe the emerald-green glass hadn't broken.

She slumped onto the stool as tears welled in her eyes.

David pushed back from her in disgust. "Save the waterworks for someone who gives a damn." He strode out of the room. "Lindsay, when you grow up don't be like her," he said as his heavy, angry footfalls thundered through the living room.

Heather moved to follow him, but stopped in the doorway. Lindsay glanced over at her but looked away when she met her gaze.

Heather wiped away her tears. "Don't worry, Lindsay." She tried to smile, but the simple action pained her. "David's just upset."

Lindsay just nodded.

"Really." The lie made her voice quake. "Everything will be okay."

"Okay, Mrs. Sampson." It was clear from Lindsay's averted eyes that there was no way to make her feel better or forget what had happened.

"Can you do me a favor, Lindsay?"

She finally looked up. "What?"

"I don't know what you heard, but can you please not tell your dad anything? I don't need him to…" She paused. He had so many things in his life that needed his attention. She couldn't let him sacrifice his time by helping her to deal with the storm in her personal life. No doubt, this storm would pass, just like the others that had preceded it.

"You don't need him to what?"

"I don't want him to worry."

Lindsay shrugged. "Okay, Mrs. Sampson."

The pipes clanked as David turned on the shower in the master bathroom.

"How's the bracelet coming along?"

"Fine." Lindsay lifted it for her to see. "You know, if you wanted, you could come with me and Dad to the Millers'."

Heather's smile came a little easier. "That's really nice of you, but you don't need to worry. I'll have to go up and talk to David, but I would guess that we're probably going together. Fighting is just what married people do."

KEVIN MADE HIS way toward Heather's house where Lindsay waited. David's Porsche was in the driveway. Hopefully everything was going okay. Every time he was around, David treated him like the village idiot, and he always wrapped his arm around Heather as if she was some high school conquest rather than his wife.

He had always hated men like that.

There was no reason for two people in a healthy relationship to hover and mistrust one another. When Allison had been alive, he'd never needed to claim her. No. Anytime they had been together it was like they were magnetic. It hadn't mattered whether they were alone or in a room filled with people, he only saw her.

They had *fit*.

It was dumb luck he had found such a once-in-a-lifetime love.

Maybe it was stupid of him to compare what he and Allison had to anyone else. Maybe they hadn't had just a simple once-in-a-lifetime love. Maybe they were soul mates, their love created by the gods.

Either way, he appreciated Allison way more than David seemed to appreciate the special woman he had found in Heather. His neighbor didn't deserve such a woman—a woman so beautiful that the first time Kevin had met her she'd taken his breath away, a woman who put up with David's possessiveness, a woman who accepted the hours that a cardiologist worked. Who knew what else she was forced to accept. Bottom line—Heather deserved better. Whether she knew it was another thing.

Regardless, it was none of his business. And he shouldn't be thinking of his neighbor and his daughter's babysitter this way. Though, truthfully, she'd been in his thoughts way too often lately.

He parked the truck and walked toward the house. Every bush along the walkway was perfectly shaped into a little sphere—it was like a trail of bombs just waiting to explode.

He knocked on the door.

It creaked open. Heather's long brunette hair was pulled half up, making her look like one of those models from the Victoria's Secret catalogs that he kept hidden in his bedroom like a teenager. Quickly he envisioned her in the skimpy lingerie and his gaze drifted to her breasts, but he wrestled his attention away. He hardened at the thought of her undressed.

What was wrong with him today? There were so many other things he needed to be worried about besides how a friend looked naked.

"Hey. I'm glad you're here." She smiled, but it didn't reach her eyes. Something was wrong.

"Lindsay good?"

Heather's face tightened.

At the sound of his voice, Lindsay poked her head around the corner and smiled. "I gotta grab my backpack."

He turned back to Heather and looked into the darkness that seemed to fill her hazel eyes. "Are you okay?"

"I'm fine. Really. Just tired," she said, maybe a little too insistently.

"I appreciate your taking Lindsay, but if you have other things that you need to take care of, I can find something else to do with her. Colter's sixteen—he could be helping."

Heather leaned in close. "No teenage boy wants to babysit his sister. I'm sure he has other things on his mind." Her breath brushed his cheek. He breathed in, trying to control his body, but she smelled like flowers and the scent only made him harder.

"Yeah. Other things on his mind," he said, stumbling through his words. He tried to take that advice and thought about baseball and who won the 1996 American League pennant.

"Are you okay, Kevin?" Heather frowned.

"Yankees," he blurted out, trying to look anywhere but at her.

"What?"

"Nothing." He leaned in, through the open door, brushing lightly against Heather and her not-to-be-noticed-by-him breasts. "Lindsay, let's go!"

"Coming!" Lindsay said in a sing-song voice.

David came down the stairs and stopped beside Heather, barely giving her a sideways glance. He smiled. His teeth were straight with long, oversize canines. "Hi, Kev, how's it going?" He slapped him on the back. "Heading to the Millers' tonight? It's going to be a good one."

"Thought I'd pop in. Probably won't stay too long." The lust he had been feeling disappeared as he stared at David's predatory smile.

"Long day?" David wrapped his arm around Heather, but she seemed to freeze under his touch.

"Brutal."

When Lindsay made her way to the door, David turned and gave her a warm smile. "Thanks for coming by, hon. Great to have you here keeping the old ball and chain happy."

Lindsay stared at David, a confused look on her face. "Sure, Dr. Sampson." She slid past David, giving him plenty of space. "Bye, Mrs. Sampson. See you soon." She rushed to the car.

From Lindsay's befuddled look, he couldn't help wondering what he had missed.

He turned to Heather. "Everything go okay?"

"Of course. Always." Heather looked to David as though she was checking to make sure she was saying the right thing.

"We have a few things to discuss." David pushed Heather back and moved to close the door. "Talk to you later, Kev."

"It's Kevin."

David didn't seem to notice; instead, he turned toward Heather. As the door closed, Kevin could swear his face was contorted with rage.

Chapter Four

The teak chair pinched Heather's leg as she perched on the edge trying to make her legs look sexy. David wasn't even looking at her; instead he stood chatting away with Heather's beautiful friend Brittany. He brushed back Brittany's blond hair and whispered something. Her laughter cut through the air.

The grill sizzled and smoke poured into Heather's face, making her look away. A group of teenage boys were splashing around in the pool as the teenage girls sat on the side whispering behind their hands and texting on their bubblegum-pink phones.

Life had been so much simpler at that age. Days consumed with flirting and laughter. Nights filled with dreams of things to come. When she was close to that age she had been consumed with thoughts of the charming, too handsome, college-aged David—the man who had started their relationship with flowers and love notes and now couldn't even look her in the eye.

She walked over to him, but only Brittany looked at her. "Hiya, Heather. David was just telling me about his day. He's so funny!"

He hadn't been funny with her in a long time.

She suffered through a smile. "Yeah."

Brittany turned to David and laid her hand on his shoulder. "Did you tell her what happened?"

David finally bothered to look at her, but his eyes were pinched into a glare. "She doesn't like to hear about my job."

"What? Really?" Brittany giggled, the sound mimicking the titters coming from the poolside. "I think it's fascinating." She ran her finger down David's arm. "You have such a noble job—saving lives."

Heather couldn't stand the way David's face transitioned from a glare to a smile as Brittany touched him.

"I need a drink," Heather said.

Everything would be okay. She just needed to fake it and get through this day without breaking down and having everyone find out about her failing marriage.

"I'll go with you. Nathan's made the best strawberry margaritas." She looped her arm through Heather's and made her way toward the tiki bar.

Heather glanced back at her husband, but he'd already started to talk to another woman. Across from her, poolside, was Kevin. He sent her a sexy smile as he waved.

"Two margaritas, *por favor*!" Brittany called to her husband.

The winter-pale Nathan had on a coconut bra T-shirt, red hibiscus-covered Bermuda shorts and a party store straw hat. "Coming right up."

He shook his chest, making the coconuts jump. "Where's the smile, Heath?"

"I...uh..."

"She just hasn't had a drink yet. That'll make everything better. Isn't that right, bestie?" Brittany giggled and pushed her into a seat.

"Lime in the Coconut" came on the speakers and Nathan did his best impression of a hula dancer as he flipped on the blender. But not even the goofy Nathan could make her laugh today.

He poured the mix into a bowl-sized glass. As he sat the glass in front of her, the scent of tequila was strong in the air.

"Little heavy-handed with the tequila, huh?"

Nathan laughed. "I just want you to get to feeling better. Remember, it'll be better tomorrow."

She doubted it.

One of her neighbors, the woman from three doors down who always walked her Pomeranian in the mornings, stepped to the bar and drew Nathan's attention.

"So what's going on?" Brittany asked.

"Huh?" Heather took a long sip from the delicious, strawberry drink.

"You've barely spoken to David all day."

Brittany thought that his avoidance was *her* fault? Brittany was her best friend, but if Heather told her what was truly going on and how close she was to divorce, the gossip would fly faster than cottonwood fluff in spring. Then again, if she didn't explain, Brittany was likely to assume something far worse than the truth.

"We're going through a rough patch."

"I got that. I don't think I've ever seen you look at David like that before."

"Like what?"

Brittany chewed on her lip. "Well… You looked *desperate*." She said the word as if it left a foul taste.

She could hardly admit that she was desperate, or

Brittany wouldn't just carry the foul taste for the word, she would have a foul taste for her, as well. She couldn't lose her only girlfriend.

"It's hard, Brittany. One minute I can't imagine my life without him, and the next I'm so angry. I'm so confused."

"What do you want?"

"I don't know, but I can't give up." She may not love him at the moment, but her mother had always told her that love varied in marriage—now was just a low.

Heather took a drink, letting the tequila soak into her tongue. "How can I get him back?"

"You're talking to the right woman." Brittany wiggled her finger. "I've got just the thing."

"Have you seen Colter?" Kevin asked, handing Lindsay a juice box.

She shaded her eyes as she looked up at him from beside the pool.

"Uh-uh. You think he's still at practice?"

Kevin glanced down at his watch. "He should've been done an hour ago."

"He's gonna come. It's okay, Daddy."

He nodded as he took out his cell and called his son. It went straight to voice mail.

"Colter, this is Dad. Sorry I missed your practice. I had a thing with work. Lindsay and I are at the barbecue. Where are you? Give me a call. Love ya, bud."

He slid the phone into his pocket and walked toward a long table filled with food. He popped a stuffed mushroom into his mouth, savoring the flavor as Bob Marley & the Wailers sang in the background.

His phone buzzed. "Colter?" he asked without looking at the screen.

"No, Kevin. It's Detective Lawrence. I got your message."

"Thanks for getting back to me. Did you get a chance to run by the house?"

"Yeah, your guys showed me around. Thanks for waiting."

"Sorry. I had a meeting."

"A meeting where they play Bob Marley?" Lawrence sounded annoyed.

"You know how it is," Kevin answered with an awkward laugh. He didn't need Lawrence to think of him as anything less than professional, and he was already on his last leg after leaving in the middle of an investigation. "Did you get a chance to pull up Goldstein's record?"

"She has a few citations, but nothing major. Certainly nothing that would make me think she would be behind an arson. Then again, it's the ones you don't see coming…" Detective Lawrence sighed. "You got any suspects?"

"I'm looking into it."

"You haven't spoken to Goldstein yet?"

"Not yet."

Kevin's breath caught in his throat as Heather made her way out of the back door of the Millers' house with Brittany close at her heels. He couldn't help notice she'd changed clothes. A pink miniskirt now hugged the round arch of Heather's hips and she wore a white shirt with a cut so deep that it exposed her navel. For a moment, everything and everyone at the block party went silent. The only sound was the lapping of the pool.

Lawrence said something, but Kevin couldn't make out his words.

She was so beautiful standing there with curves he never knew she had. The wind fingered the edge of the V-neck top, exposing the roundness of each of her breasts.

What would it be like to kiss that skin—that gorgeous, fresh skin? His mouth watered as he imagined running his lips over her body.

"Kevin, you there?"

"Huh?"

He tried to look away.

"Are you listening?"

"Sorry, what did you say?"

"I *said* let me know if you need anything."

"Sounds great. I gotta run," Kevin said, forcing himself to stop staring.

The woman was his neighbor. She was married. No matter how badly he wanted her, she was off-limits.

Chapter Five

Her mind swam in the relaxing surf of her second margarita. The world around her had mellowed; there were no more harsh whispers or judging stares. Just a hot pink miniskirt and Brittany by her side.

"You *have* this," Brittany whispered.

"You think he cares?"

Brittany rolled her eyes. "David's going to eat this up. You look beautiful."

Heather reached down and tried to inch the skirt lower. David always gawked at the women who wore this type of thing. Hopefully he'd be just as happy to see her in such an outfit.

"Here he comes." Brittany nodded toward David, who was staring wide-eyed at her. "I told you this would get his attention. From the looks of things, you got everyone else's, as well. I wish I got that kind of reaction." She giggled and gave Heather a quick side hug and then walked away. David strode over.

"What in the hell, Heather?" he seethed through a smile of gritted teeth. He grabbed her by the back of the arm and moved her so their faces were concealed.

She looked back over her shoulder. Every adult was

staring at them—even Kevin. His mouth was open, as if he wanted to say something, but she quickly looked away.

"Don't I look nice?" she said loudly, hoping David would catch the hint that they were on display.

"You look great," he said, but the way his fingers dug into her soft flesh said exactly the opposite.

He turned and nodded toward Nathan. "Thanks for dinner. We have to be going."

Nathan nodded and waved with a paper umbrella in his hand.

"What in the hell do you think you're wearing?" David dragged her out of the gate and toward his Porsche.

"You're hurting me. Please, let go," she said, her drink-slowed words coming out of her lips as though they were coming from someone else, someone bolder.

"I'm hurting you? Do you know how much you just embarrassed me?"

He'd been embarrassing her for years—when he hadn't shown up to dinner dates, when he had forgotten to come home at night and when he had called her names in front of their friends. Now he was telling her she was embarrassing him?

It might have been the margaritas, but she couldn't even look at him.

He pushed her into the passenger seat of his coupe and then went to his side and got in.

"You're such a slut."

A feeling of sickness rose in her throat.

"I'm not a slut," she said under her breath.

"What was that?"

"Nothing." She swallowed back the urge to vomit.

"Did you think Andrew would be there? Were you

parading yourself for him?" He looked her up and down. "He can do better."

"I don't know how to prove to you that I've never cheated."

The road buzzed by. "So you're a liar and a whore? Real classy. I married you to be a pure wife and a whole-some mother. First you couldn't give me the children I wanted, and now you're a cheater. There's no reason to keep you in my life."

"I..." She tried to swallow the sickness back, but it was no use. She threw her hands over her mouth. She tried to tell him to pull over, but it was too late. She was sick all over his black dashboard.

He'd never forgive her. He loved the car more than anything, and definitely more than her.

"What the hell!" He pulled the car to the side of the road. He reached across her and opened the door. "Get out! I'm never going to be able to get your stench out of the leather."

They were only a few houses away from theirs, but distance didn't matter... She was sick. If he'd been sick, she would have spent the rest of the day being the duti-ful wife her mother had taught her to be. Yet he cared so little, he was kicking her out on the side of the road.

"I can't believe you, David."

"Get. Out." His fingers tightened on the steering wheel.

She grabbed her purse and stepped out of the car. He slammed the door and sped away with a spray of gravel.

Once again, she was alone, just as she had been as a child when her parents had fought. Sometimes it fright-ened her how much David reminded her of her father. They were cut from the same cloth, constantly berating and putting down their wives—and this time, instead of her mother, it was Heather being demeaned.

David stopped at their house. He didn't pull the car into the garage; instead he got out and walked in through the front door.

What would happen if she didn't go home?

David would probably love it. He'd never have to see her again. He'd get everything. All he'd need was a new wife. A wife to give him the family he'd always wanted—something he was only too happy to remind her she'd failed to give him no matter how hard she'd tried.

She stepped up onto the sidewalk and made her way toward the house. Before she could go inside she needed to clean herself up. She walked around the side of the house and washed up with the hose.

When she entered the kitchen, David threw a manila envelope at her.

"I've had the divorce papers written up. All you have to do is sign them. Do it now."

She stared at the envelope that lay on the counter just where his note had been only hours before. She didn't dare touch the paper out of fear that, if she did, it would make everything real.

"David…no…"

"Just sign the papers. You have to be as unhappy as I am."

For the first time in memory, she agreed with him. She wasn't happy. In fact, she couldn't remember the last time she had been happy with him. But that was what marriage was, right? It had ups and downs, and the job of both people was to make it work. Wasn't it?

"Things will get better. We just need to work together. Maybe you could take some time off. I don't remember when we spent real time together."

"Did it ever occur to you that I was avoiding you? We should've put a stop to this relationship a long time ago, but I know you're nothing without me. It was an act of sheer kindness that I've allowed you to be my wife this long."

Something inside her broke.

"You've *allowed me* to be your wife? Hasn't it occurred to you all I've given up to be with you? I gave up my education for you. I gave up my hopes of a job."

"A job," he said with a smirk. "That would take dedication."

"Just because you don't see it doesn't mean that I'm not dedicated—if I love something, I give it everything... Even if my love turns out to be misplaced." She looked at him and tried to control the hatred that welled within her.

"If you loved me so much, maybe you should have tried a little harder." He reached into a drawer and pulled out a pen and laid it on the envelope. "Just sign the paperwork. It's over."

She stared at the envelope but didn't move. "We made a promise to each other. You told me you never wanted to get a divorce. That marriage meant something to you."

"Marriage does mean something to me, Heather. It means fidelity, trust, honesty. You haven't given me any of those things."

She shook her head, trying to get rid of the ringing of his words. "Why do you always accuse me of something I haven't done? I've never given you reason to think—" She paused as a terrible thought came to mind. "Are you cheating on me, David? Is that what all this is about? Are you accusing me out of your own guilt? Are you trying to make yourself feel better about something you've done?"

"How dare you accuse me. I spend my days saving people's lives. I'm a damn hero." He ripped open the envelope and pushed the papers in front of her. "Sign them."

Her hands shook. It wasn't that she hadn't imagined the possibility of him asking for a divorce; she had just never thought it would be today.

There was no coming back from this—not right now. He was too angry. There was only one thing to do that could make it any better—she had to hold him off.

"I'll have a lawyer take a look."

"Don't you trust me, Heather?"

"If you had asked me two hours ago, I would've said yes. But now, it would be stupid if I did."

She picked up the papers and her car keys and walked out.

Chapter Six

After Heather's forced disappearance, Kevin hadn't been interested in the Millers' party and he'd found an excuse to leave. He shut his daughter's door. Surprisingly Lindsay had dropped into her bed without protest, just as she'd easily agreed with him to leave the party.

Colter sat behind his computer in his bedroom as Kevin made his way down the hall.

"Where were you, Colter?"

His son shrugged as he faced his screen. "I dunno."

"Try it again, bud. Where did you go after baseball practice?"

"Baseball practice ran long." He didn't turn around. "When I made it to the Millers', the party was over."

"You mind looking at me? I'm trying to talk to you."

His son shifted a few degrees in his seat. "What? I'm talking to you."

Kevin had never been much of a disciplinarian—that had always been more Allison's job. God, he wished she was here.

Once again he was reminded how badly he wanted a woman in their lives, someone he could share the ups and downs with, someone he could hold in his arms at night—someone like Heather.

"Is Heather going to come to my game?" Colter asked, as if he could somehow sense what was on Kevin's mind.

"I don't know. If you'd made it to the party, you could've asked her yourself. Where were you?"

"God, don't you get tired of asking the same questions? I told you… Baseball practice ran late. When I got to the party it was shut down. I didn't stick around."

"You don't expect me to believe that baseball practice lasted that long, do you?" Kevin leaned against Colter's door frame, half in and half out of the bedroom, just far enough in to let him know that he had his full attention, but far enough out that it wasn't a confrontation.

Then again, everything with Colter these days was a confrontation.

"Were you with a girl?"

Colter tapped at his keyboard. "No."

He was getting nowhere. "I would appreciate it if you would do as I ask. It's important that I can count on you, or else this free-for-all is going to come to a screeching halt. No more baseball. No more girls. No more friends."

His son spun around and cursed.

He twitched at the sound of his son's language. That was a new one.

"If you want to talk and act like a big man, that's fine, bud. But you need to know you're causing problems. I'm trying to do my best here. I'm sorry I can't be everywhere, but you aren't making this any easier. I need to trust you, okay?"

Colter's expression remained blank. He would make one hell of a poker player.

"Fine."

"Will you let me know when baseball practice runs late again? Please?"

"Fine."

"I love you, kid, but this attitude needs to come to an end." Kevin pushed off the door frame. "Get to bed. You have school in the morning."

Colter turned back around in his chair to face his computer. "Got it."

Kevin closed the door and walked into the living room.

Every day since Allison had died, some more of Colter seemed to fade. No matter how hard Kevin had tried, no matter how many parenting books he had read, he had failed at helping his son—just like he'd failed to save Allison. He couldn't help but feel as though he was on the brink of losing someone else he loved.

There was a knock at the door and he went to answer it, wondering who was calling on him now.

Heather stood on the top step. Her hair was disheveled, her eyes were red as if she'd been crying, her deep V-neck shirt was wet and soiled.

"What happened?" He motioned for her to come inside.

"I'm sorry. I didn't know where to go. Brittany wasn't answering."

"Come on in." He stepped aside. He would have asked her what was wrong, but after what he had seen at the barbecue there was no point.

She stumbled to the couch and sat with her feet curled beneath her. "Thank you." She dabbed at her eyes. "I hope I didn't wake you."

"No. I just put the kids to bed." He pointed at her shirt. "You want something clean to wear?"

She looked down and her mouth dropped open. "Oh, my God… Those damn margaritas."

"Be right back." He went to his bedroom and came back with a shirt. "Here, you can have this." He handed it to her and turned his back as she slipped off her V-neck. In the mirror by the door, he caught a glimpse of her naked breasts. He stiffened as he looked away. No matter how much he wanted to look at her, to take those puckered pink nipples into his mouth and make them his, she belonged to someone else.

"I'm done," she said. "Thanks for the shirt."

He turned but didn't know where to go, so he just stood there. "You're welcome."

Normally around women he was cool and collected. Yet with Heather, it was different. She was different. And no matter how badly he tried to break into work mode, treating her as though she was just another victim, he couldn't. He didn't feel right taking her by the hand and telling her it would all be okay. If he touched her, he might not be able to let her go.

"You want something to drink?" He moved toward the kitchen.

She stared into space. "David wants a divorce. He has the papers ready. I don't know what to do."

"What?" Kevin stopped and turned to her.

"Don't make me say it again. It doesn't feel real. None of this feels real."

"I get it." He felt like a moron, but he couldn't think of the right thing to say.

In a way, he'd been in her shoes when he had found out about Allison's death. A part of him had died in that moment. No matter how many times people said "I'm sorry," nothing could staunch the pain.

"I never thought this day would come. I mean…we've been unhappy. I thought maybe, but…I thought we'd make it through this. I should have seen this coming."

"When you love someone, sometimes you don't see what's staring back at you."

"What do you mean?"

He thought back to David hitting on Brittany at the barbecue. If Heather hadn't seen it, he was the last person who should tell her.

"Nothing. I just mean—"

"You think he doesn't love me?"

"I didn't say that," he said, mentally trying to back-pedal.

"It's okay. I know he doesn't. It's been a long time since…well, since I think he felt something other than contempt toward me. A divorce seems like the only answer."

"Is that what you want—a divorce?" The question came from a place inside him where he begged that she would say yes.

She didn't answer. Rather, she looked broken, as though she was a pane of glass that had been waiting for the strike of a hammer, and now that the blow had been struck, she'd come to him to help find the pieces.

He saved lives, but he'd never been good at rebuilding them—not even when the life was his own. He tried hard, but despite his efforts, Colter was a mess and he didn't spend nearly enough time with Lindsay. Everything he did was a struggle. Every choice was wrong or surrounded by guilt. He could never give Heather what she needed.

She wiped the tears from her eyes as she stood up and moved to him, her hips swaying with purpose.

What was she doing? She'd never looked at him like that before, with such intensity. If anything, she'd been overly insistent that they were friends...*good* friends, but that had been all. But that look, that light in her dark eyes, said there was something more—something he'd felt since the first moment he'd met her.

He must have been reading her wrong. He stepped back until he bumped into the table beside the door. "Heather..."

She put her finger on his lips, quieting him. Rising to her tiptoes, she swept her tear-dampened lips over the skin of his neck. Sparks of electricity shot down his body and reawakened a part of him that he had written off.

"What're you doing?" he tried to say, but it came out barely above a whisper thanks to the soft pressure of her finger against his lips.

She slipped his earlobe into her mouth and sucked.

Oh, God... He wanted this. He wanted her.

He wanted to sweep her up in his arms and carry her to his bed. He wanted to wake up covered in her scent, to lick her flavor off his lips. Her kiss moved lower. Her tongue traced the neckline of his shirt. Her hands moved up his chest.

"Heather..." he moaned. "I want you..."

Before he could say another word, her lips met his. She tasted sweet, like warm berries right off the vine. How could a woman taste so good?

He wrapped his arms around her as he relished their kiss. He could do this forever...hold her forever...*be* with her forever.

The scent of sweetened alcohol wafted from her.

Kevin pulled back. Those lips, those pink, full lips weren't berry flavored—they tasted of margarita.

If she had been sober and come to him willingly and openly, it would have been hard for him to say no, but as it was, with her judgment skewed and muted by booze, there was only one choice.

"Heather…" He unwrapped his arms from around her body. "We can't do this. You can sleep here. You can have my bed. But tonight… *This* can't happen."

Chapter Seven

Heather rolled over in bed. Where her clock should have been was a glass of water and two red capsules she assumed were ibuprofen. The sides of the glass were beaded with sweat, reminding her of the letter that David had left behind.

The letter... The divorce papers... Oh...

She sat up but was forced back down by the *thump, thump, thump* of the bass drum beating in her skull. She picked up the pills and swallowed them down, anything to stop the pounding.

Light streamed through unfamiliar white curtains and she looked down at a dark gray shirt, underneath which was a miniskirt. She remembered Brittany's skirt but where had the T-shirt come from?

The bedsheets were yellow and soft, but those, too, were foreign.

She sat up more slowly, and this time the pounding of the bass drum changed to the *tom, tom, tom* of a timpani.

She pushed down the miniskirt and the simple action brought back a flash of her kissing Kevin, her hands sliding over the muscles of his stomach, her lips tasting the salty flavor of his skin.

Her body ached from what felt like gallons of tequila sloshing through her veins. At the very least she hadn't had sex with him—if she had, she could have never faced him again.

Hopefully he didn't think that her feelings were just some attempt at a drunken rebound. She had been foolish, but for her, it had sometimes felt as though there was more than a simple friendship between them.

She was such an idiot.

She tiptoed to the door and peered out into the empty hallway. This early in the morning everything was still. She slipped through the house and made her way outside, making sure to grab her shoes and purse by the front door.

The grass dripped with dew and not a single house's lights were on, with the exception of her and David's perfectly white house, where every single window was alight. He must have been awake all night, waiting for her.

Her stomach lurched, forcing her to run to the hedges that acted as a fence between the houses. She made it there in time to be sick.

There was a squeak of hinges as a door opened. She looked in the direction of the eerie, disquieting sound. David stood on their front step and glowered out at her.

His arms were crossed over his chest and his jaw was set, making him look like a dictatorial tyrant peering down upon his subjects.

"Get in the house."

She made her way to the door, carefully sidestepping him as she went inside. She could feel his glare upon her.

"Your catting around just saved me a lot of money."

KEVIN TRIED NOT to think about Heather slipping away. He should have known that was exactly what she would do when she woke. Regardless, it still bothered him that she would run away as soon as she realized how badly he had wanted her.

Hopefully they could still be friends. Hell, maybe something more if her divorce went through, but something like that had to be months, maybe years, away from happening. For all he knew, last night had been her attempt at a one-night thing. Maybe she only wanted to get back at David. Maybe his was just the closest door.

Maybe, when it came to him, she didn't really care.

He wouldn't know how she felt until he saw her again. He didn't know whether to look forward to it.

Meanwhile he walked into Colter's room. He made his way through the mess and stopped at the side of his bed. Colter's chin showed the nicked signs of a recent battle with a razor. He reached up and pulled fuzz from a hair that had been missed. The hair was barely enough to be called a whisker, yet it was just another sign of the changes in their lives.

He leaned in and gave Colter a kiss on the head and drew in a breath, the way he used to when his son had been a baby. He no longer smelled of milk and baby powder, but rather he carried the odor of sweat with a pungent sock-scented kicker.

"Hey, bud," he said softly, trying to rouse him. "Time to get up."

Colter opened one eye and, seeing him, answered with a forgiving, sleepy smile.

There was still a chance to fix what was broken.

AFTER COLTER LEFT for school, Kevin dropped Lindsay off and made his way to the diner. No matter what was going on in his personal life, work awaited. At least in an investigation there was a chance he could get answers. It was black and white. Not like his mess of a private life.

His phone rang as he pulled the truck into a parking spot.

"Hello?"

"Inspector Jensen, this is Chief Larson."

"Hey, Chief, how's it going?" He tried to sound nonchalant.

"Not so great. I heard you and I may need to have a little meeting."

Kevin forced a laugh. "Come on now, Chief. I didn't do anything that bad, did I?"

"You were at last week's meeting, correct?"

"Yes, sir."

"Then you may have some idea why you and I would be having a problem."

"I'm aware that we're trying to cut back on costs. I understand and would love to comply with your request. However, sir, I must be able to do my job in a professional manner. *Protecting lives and saving property*— am I right, Chief?"

"Absolutely." There was a rustle as the chief moved the phone. "However, as I was made to understand, your investigation was impeded by your need to go to a neighborhood barbecue. Correct?"

His stomach clenched. How did Larson know?

"I did need to attend a social event with my family. It was an unavoidable situation." He tried his damnedest to make it sound like brain surgery instead of a party.

"So let me get this right, Jensen. You took two rookie firefighters and had them sit on an investigation that should have been buttoned up in one pass so that you could go to an *unavoidable social event*? Do you know how much you cost us? I had to call in two more firefighters and give them time and a half to cover for the ones you needed to retain your chain of custody."

"That wasn't my intention, sir."

"Your intention or not, this has to come to an end or I'm going to have to start cutting. We'd hate to lose you, Jensen."

"I'm working on the investigation now. I'll have this wrapped up soon." He walked up to the diner. Near the door was a newspaper kiosk where a picture of Elke's yellow-taped house blared out from the front page.

"I don't see why you need that much time."

"I've come to believe this may be the work of a serial arsonist. I'm hoping to pin down the suspect before there are any other fires."

"What makes you think it's a serial arsonist?"

"It's just my gut, sir."

"Your gut is going to cost me thousands…and possibly cost you your job. You need to get your butt over to that scene and pull the men off the lines."

He stared at the picture on the front page of the *Missoulian*. "I would, but I'd hate for the press to get the idea we aren't doing our best to keep the public safe. I mean it would look bad if there was another fire, a fire where someone was killed."

The phone rustled. "You've got thirty-six hours."

The line went dead.

He slid his phone into his pocket. The pressure was on.

Smoke and Ashes

Kevin walked inside and a sixtysomething waitress strode up to him.

"Can I help you, sonny?" she asked in the raspy voice of a lifelong smoker.

"I'm looking for an Elke Goldstein. She work here?"

The woman frowned. "Waddya want with her?"

"I'm just here to talk with her. I'll sit down and wait, if that's okay."

She grabbed a menu and led him to a table close to the kitchen door. "She'll be right out. Coffee?"

He mostly wanted answers, but coffee would do for now. "Sure. Thanks."

"Take it black?"

"Unless you can pour some of your sweetness in," he joked.

"Oh, we got a charmer, do we?" The woman strode into the kitchen with a wide smile on her lips.

A minute later a mousy, brunette woman walked out and stopped beside his table. She had a nice face, but her eyes told him she was a woman who worked long hours and dreamed of something more.

"I'm Elke." She scowled at him as she poured his coffee. "I know you?"

"The name's Kevin Jensen. I'm a fire inspector for the city of Missoula." He took a long drink of the ashy tasting coffee. "I was called to your house last night. Nice to meet you."

She took a step back from the table and looked over her shoulder. "How'd you find me? I thought y'all weren't going to bother me," she said, her voice tinged with a slight Southern drawl.

"Battalion Chief Hiller told me you worked here."

She nodded, but her body tensed and the pot in her

hand shook slightly, sloshing the coffee. "He had no business tellin' you. I didn't have nothin' to do with that fire."

In the fire academy, one lesson had been drilled into him over and over: It didn't matter what words came out of a person's mouth, body language and demeanor were a much better indicator of someone's guilt or innocence. Right now, Ms. Goldstein looked guilty. All he needed to figure out was whether she was guilty of setting the fire or guilty of something else.

"I'm sure you didn't have anything to do with it," he lied. "I just need to ask you a few questions so we can make sure you get the money you are entitled to from your insurance company." He paused as he let the bait sink in. "You do have insurance, don't you?"

"Yeah, I think so…" She looked away as though she was trying to catch a memory that had drifted out of reach.

If she had started the fire for the money, she would have known her house was insured, and for how much. But she wasn't innocent. She knew something.

"Miss?" A woman three tables down lifted her coffee cup.

Elke nodded. "I need to get runnin'. Want something to eat?"

He ordered the special, and as she turned to leave she said, "I get off in an hour. Meet me at the coffee shop 'round the corner. Sit in the back. Okay?"

"Got it."

"Good," Elke said.

SHE BARELY LOOKED at him while he sat and savored his breakfast, taking his time to dip his toast in his egg and drink three cups of coffee. Elke needed to feel the pressure. She needed to see that he wasn't going anywhere.

His phone buzzed.

"Hello, Mr. Jensen?" said a woman's nasal voice. "This is Ms. Farmer from Big Sky High School."

He stabbed his fork into his egg. "What did Colter do?"

"Colter hasn't arrived at school today. I was just calling to let you know that I will need a note to excuse his absence. Are you aware he is not in attendance?" There was a tremble of excitement in the woman's voice, as if she was thrilled that finally, among what was undoubtedly dozens of phone calls for delinquent teens, she'd caught one troublemaker red-handed.

"Ms. Farmer," he said, "I waved at him this morning when he left for school. He may have been a few minutes late, but I'm sure he's there." He tried to have faith in Colter. Sure, the kid had been acting out lately, but what sixteen-year-old didn't? Maybe the attendance secretary had it all wrong. Colter wouldn't have screwed up twice in two days.

"I assure you, Mr. Jensen, he has not arrived. His homeroom and first period teachers have reported him in absentia."

In absentia... If Colter had to deal with her type all day, it was no wonder he skipped class.

"I'll take care of it."

"I'm glad to hear it. As things stand, I will be marking him down as unexcused. Two more and he will be in considerable trouble."

"Don't worry. He's already in *considerable trouble*." He hung up the phone and turned back to his cooling eggs.

He couldn't just pick up and leave Elke now. She would run. He could see it in the way she kept glancing over at him as if she was the rabbit and he the hound. If he left now, it was likely he would never get answers.

He picked up his phone and dialed Colter.

"Hello?" Colter answered.

"Where in the hell are you?" He tried to ask quietly, but based on the wide eyes of the retirement-aged woman in the booth next to him, he'd failed.

"What?" Colter paused. "I'm at school."

"Then why did I just get a call from the attendance office?"

"That's bull. I'm here, Dad."

"Is that right? Then walk down to that office right now and let me talk to Ms. Farmer."

"But…Dad, I'm in the middle of a test."

"A test so important you answered your phone?" Kevin growled. "You better have your butt in Ms. Farmer's office in less than ten minutes." He hung up and glanced down at his watch. Elke didn't get off for another thirty minutes.

There was little to no chance Colter was at school, or would be at the school in ten minutes, but if Kevin left to check on him, he'd be putting his job and the investigation in danger. The parenting books always said he had to "be consistent" and "follow through." How was he expected to be consistent and follow through when he had a job that pulled him in an opposite direction?

He took a pull of his coffee. Colter was going to have to wait. This job paid the bills. This job was the only thing that held the family—or at least what was left of the family—together. Colter was acting impulsively and whether he meant to do it or not, he was pulling apart what little family they had left.

He thought about calling Heather, but after last night…he couldn't. Not with so many unspoken things between them. For all he knew, she hated him.

He had to go at this one alone. It was his job as a father to make sure he drew the family together.

If he hurried he could make it to the school and back to meet Elke in thirty minutes. That was, if Colter did as he was told.

Kevin stood up and pulled out his wallet. He went to grab a twenty to pay for breakfast but stopped. His cash was gone.

Damn that kid.

Elke brushed by him.

"Hold on a sec," he said. He couldn't lose track of Elke, if he did, he would miss his chance to find the perpetrator and he'd be back to square one. "I have to go, but you better be at that coffee shop or you will be suspect number one."

Chapter Eight

If Heather had been asked to describe a lawyer's office, this would have been the last thing she would have envisioned. The little room was hidden in an office building in the middle of downtown, seemingly content to disappear in mediocrity. The black melamine doorplate blended in with the shadows, barely making it possible to read the sign: Phyllis Kohl, Attorney at Law.

Everything about the place, from the hand-worn doors to the squeal of an unseen radiator, made Heather want to turn around and leave.

Everything she had tried to do for the past year had ended in failure; her marriage had crumbled and nearly all of her friendships had disappeared. She had even failed at her attempt to finally act on her feelings toward Kevin.

She tapped on the antique door.

"Hello?" a woman replied, her voice muffled as though she was in the middle of eating.

"Ms. Kohl? May I come in? It's Mrs. Sampson. I called earlier?"

There was a rustle of paper. "Yes. Come right in."

Heather opened the door and was met with the scent

of onion and liverwurst so strong that she stood outside until she could summon the will to continue.

A woman in her early twenties with stringy blond hair and a wrinkled black suit sat behind a desk covered in paperwork. A water cooler gurgled in the corner of the room and beside it a stack of paper cups and a box of tissues.

"Thanks for seeing me. I know this was short notice, but…well…"

Ms. Kohl dropped her lunch into her desk drawer. "I completely understand, Mrs. Sampson. These things have a way of sneaking up on us, don't they?"

Her divorce hadn't exactly snuck up on her. If she had been smarter, if she had paid more attention to the signs—the late nights, the terrible notes and the effort he had made not to touch her. No, this hadn't just snuck up on her; she'd just been too stupid to see it coming.

But now wasn't the time to argue.

There was only a single picture on the wall and it was a degree from the University of Montana Law School. The date at the bottom was last spring.

Ms. Kohl must have just passed the bar. She was probably full of hopes and dreams, and yet, she was just another victim to be taken down by Heather's husband.

Unfortunately, after calling law offices all morning, this newbie was all she could afford.

A lifetime of trying to please a man and all it had amounted to was a few thousand dollars and a crappy lawyer.

"Would you like to take a seat?" Ms. Kohl motioned toward the folding chair.

"Thanks." Heather sat down, the folding chair creaking as she moved. She tried not to notice the way the cheap seat cut into her legs. Comfort didn't matter. Nothing about what was going to happen in the next few hours would be comfortable.

"So you mentioned that your husband... Daryl?"

"David."

"Yes. *David.*" Ms. Kohl made a note on a napkin. "You said David has asked for a divorce. You mentioned you had a prenuptial agreement?"

Heather pulled the manila envelope out of her purse. "Here's the prenup and the documents he gave me. I signed it a few months before our wedding, seven years ago."

"That's great," Ms. Kohl said as she took the envelope. She pulled out the paperwork and scanned the pages. "It looks like he has gone ahead and already filed for the divorce." She flipped over the next page. "Everything seems pretty straightforward."

Only a new lawyer would have made the mistake of calling a divorce straightforward. Nothing about what was happening around her seemed to be clear-cut. Everything, from the way she brushed her teeth to the roads she drove, seemed hard to remember. Everything was fuzzy, as though a haze of emotion had engulfed her and clouded even her most mundane, habitual actions with a fog of confusion that had her questioning her sanity.

"He's accused me of having an affair. Will that affect our agreement?"

"Were you having an affair?" Ms. Kohl looked up at her. "Wait, let me rephrase that... Is there any direct *evidence* of you having an affair?"

"I've never cheated on my husband. So, no, there

can't be any evidence. But he's… Well, David doesn't let things go."

Ms. Kohl set the papers down on her desk and glanced at the prenuptial agreement. "You have some things in here that may protect you, but without having a closer look, it's hard for me to say exactly how much is going your way. However, one thing I am seeing is that it looks like you are on a vesting schedule."

"A vesting schedule?"

"Yes, you don't remember this being discussed before you signed?"

She didn't want to admit to the lawyer that she'd read the contract over with nothing more than a glass of wine and a desperate desire for marriage. She hadn't paid attention to too many details. At the time, David had been her lifeline, a heroic doctor coming to rescue her from her dysfunctional family in his white Porsche. He had made promises that he would never act like her father, who came and went as he pleased—not coming home at all some nights—and then demanded they revere him. It was a cycle of love and hate, emotional manipulation at its worst.

Then she had been daft enough to fall for David's promises—only to have him repeat the cycle. She had been so naive.

She'd trusted him and the promises he'd made. She'd trusted that the prenup he'd given to her was fair.

"Well, Mrs. Sampson, a vesting schedule is basically a division of assets based on the length and/or reproductive success of your marriage."

"Reproductive success?"

"Yes, basically you are given more money if you

have more children." Ms. Kohl looked up at her with a quizzical expression. "Do you have any children?"

"We tried. I lost one. On and off since then we've tried, but we haven't had any luck."

"Hmm…" She looked back at the paper. "What did your lawyer say when you signed this document?"

Heather chewed on her lip. "Uh, well, I didn't have a lawyer."

"You signed this without a lawyer's review?" Ms. Kohl's face was awash with horror. "You should never have signed this. Who knows what else he's snuck into the pages. I'm going to need a few hours to go over this."

What else could David have put into the agreement that would be worse than paying her for having children? It was as if she was nothing more than a brood mare—worse, an unsuccessful brood mare. Thanks to her poor reproduction ability, he was basically sending her off to the glue factory.

Without a fair settlement, she would have to go to work at a glue factory. Who else would want to hire a woman with only a high school education and a broken past?

She tried to swallow the lump that had formed in her throat. Now wasn't the time to cry.

"He'll pay me alimony, won't he?" Heather asked, her voice thick with poorly harnessed emotion.

"Hmm…" Ms. Kohl tapped her finger on the paper. "Here it says, basically, that you will be getting no alimony for any marriage that lasts less than fifteen years. However, based on the length of your marriage—seven years—you will get 15 percent of all assets accrued during the time you were married."

"What about premarital assets?"

"Whatever was achieved before marriage remains in the hands of the original owner and isn't to be split or taken into consideration in the calculation of assets accrued."

She and David owned three homes, but two he had bought the week before they were married. The sudden rush to buy homes had seemed strange, but he'd brushed her concern off by telling her it was all an investment. He'd failed to mention the investment was only for him.

The only house she had any right to, then, was the one in which they lived. Even then, it would only be 15 percent of the sale value. They were in debt on the home up to their eyeballs, maybe deeper, but she couldn't be sure. She hadn't seen their account in months. They had a man to do that. David had always kept her on an allowance—no more than five hundred dollars per month.

"So, I'm getting nothing?"

"Well, you will get the 15 percent," Ms. Kohl said in a reassuring tone.

There was no reassuring her.

"Here," Ms. Kohl said as she pointed at another sheet of paper from the envelope. "In the letter from his attorney, it says he's willing to give you the house and a settlement of ten thousand dollars. Does that sound like it's about 15 percent of your assets?"

Her throat tightened. "I have no idea."

Ms. Kohl's eyebrow rose. "You don't know?"

"I don't have access to our accounts. Well, *I did*, but I didn't have anything to do with them. I just gave him my receipts at the end of the month."

"It sounds like you've been a very trusting woman, Mrs. Sampson."

Yes, very trusting and, looking back, very stupid. Now her trust was coming back to bite her.

"What do I need to do?"

Ms. Kohl pressed her hands together and laid them on the desk. "Do you think you would be happy with the house and the ten thousand dollars?"

"I don't work. I wouldn't be able to afford to pay the mortgage on the house for more than a few months. And then there would be nothing left."

"What if we let him have the house? What if you just took the money? Maybe we could negotiate for more."

She shook her head. "I need alimony. At least until I can get on my feet. Maybe go back to school…" Or maybe even think about finding someone who wanted to have a future together, someone who loved her for exactly who she was—someone like Kevin.

"We can try." Ms. Kohl sighed. "But unless we can find a way to prove this contract is null and void, it's likely this will hold up in court."

David was going to leave her with nothing and with no way to live—all because of his crazy paranoia and the fact that she hadn't given him a child.

Ms. Kohl leaned forward. "Are you sure that this divorce is something you really want?"

Chapter Nine

"What were you thinking?" Kevin growled as Colter flopped down in the seat next to him in the attendance office.

"What?" Colter crossed his arms over his chest and slouched so low in the chair that his chin rested on his chest. "I'm here. Ain't I?"

"You just got here. Where were you?" Kevin whispered, he didn't want to draw the attention of Ms. Farmer, who was talking on the phone.

"I told you… I was here." Colter kicked his backpack as though the bag was proof he'd shown up to class.

"Don't treat me like I'm stupid. Your car wasn't in the parking lot. I had to walk out on an investigation to come and deal with this. The least you can do is tell me where you were."

Colter jumped to his feet. "I can't believe you're coming down on me like this. You're the one who doesn't show up."

Kevin stopped him. "You need to get to class." He looked his son in the eye. "Do I need to escort you there to make sure you make it?"

"I got it." Colter picked up his backpack and made his way out of the office.

"And get your butt home straight after school!" he called after him. "And the twenty dollars that's missing…it better find its way back into my wallet."

Kevin hated the way Colter stared at him, with contempt in his eyes. He'd always tried to do the best he could and now here he was in the seventh level of hell—frozen, unable to stop his son's self-destructive path the past few months. The worst thing was that he didn't understand why Colter was acting up.

Kevin stood up and walked to the secretary's desk, where she still jabbered away on the phone. "Please mark Colter Jensen as present." He motioned toward the door. "He's on his way to class."

The secretary nodded and hung up the phone. "I have a note here from Colter's baseball coach." She handed him a sealed envelope with *To the parent(s) of Colter Jensen* written across the front.

He took it and fled from the office. Getting to his truck, he stared down at the envelope but he couldn't open it.

He threw the letter on the dashboard.

Whatever the coach had to say could wait. All he could hope was that Colter's coach wasn't having the same problems he was with his son. Colter got decent grades, but his future hinged on his baseball. That would be his gateway to college, his chance to break away from Missoula and make something of himself. If he screwed this up, Kevin couldn't bail him out.

Their lives would be so much easier if only Colter's frontal lobe would just kick in and help him realize there were consequences to every decision.

Kevin snorted. *Consequences* were something he knew entirely too much about… After last night with

Heather, his own personal consequences were about to rain down.

His head ached. He would deal with those flare-ups later. Now, he needed to get back to work.

THE COFFEE SHOP was awash with sound as people sat talking and others tapped away on their computers. Kevin sat down at an empty table in the corner and nursed a coffee as he waited for Elke. Hopefully she would come. He hated that his investigation hinged on a woman he might never see again.

The door to the coffee shop opened. Elke looked around, her gaze moving from one patron to the next. As she spotted him, she balled her fists as if she was summoning her resolve to face him.

She stomped over. "I didn't like ya showin' up to my work like that. You don't know what they been sayin' all day." Elke plopped down on the seat beside him. "I bet I lost twenty bucks in tips 'cause of you."

"Sorry, I didn't mean to get in your way." That wasn't entirely true. He'd wanted to be a visible presence, to let her catch a glimpse of what her life would be like if she refused to help him. "I just need to ask you a few questions. Now that you're not in your home, it's tough to catch up with you. You have a cell phone number?"

She shook her head. "Those things are a waste of money. The people who want to talk to me, they know where I live—or at least where I normally live. How long is it gonna be before I can get back into my place?"

"That's all up to you, Ms. Goldstein."

"Whatcha mean?"

"The quicker you answer my questions, the faster I can let you back into your house. As it is, I'm going to have to keep it off-limits until my investigation is concluded."

"Well, I don't know nothin'." Elke shuffled in her seat, picked up the roll of silverware off the table and inspected the pieces. She went off on a long soliloquy about the silverware at Rudy's.

Kevin listened. Sometimes the best way to get a person to answer the questions he wanted to ask was to not ask them at all. Rather it was better to lead them to the answer he wanted without them knowing they were giving him information. People, especially those who were stressed, had a way of talking too much. They would go on and on, each time they spoke giving away a little more about themselves and what they knew. Patience was the key.

"How long have you been at Ruby's?"

"Goin' on ten years. I make real good tips. My regulars, they love me."

"You get along with everyone you work with?"

"Yeah. Ain't got no problems. But mostly everyone keeps themselves to themselves—except the cooks. Those cooks are hornier than a rooster in a henhouse. You should hear some of the things they say." Elke frowned and shook her head as if she was appalled, but the gleam in her eye told him she enjoyed the cooks' lewd attentions.

"Dating any of them?"

"God, no." She laid the silverware on the table as a waitress stopped beside their table.

She ordered coffee.

"So you are dating?" Kevin asked, leading Elke back to the conversation once the waitress walked away.

"I'm always dating. Haven't found the right one yet.

Seems whenever I start gettin' to like a man he up and disappears. Ah well, that's life, right?" Elke looked at him as though she hoped he would lift her out of her endless cycle of dating.

An image of Heather flitted into his mind. He wouldn't mind dating her. He roped in his errant thoughts and focused on his investigation. "Would you say your relationships have dissipated or have some ended on a more tumultuous note?"

"Tumultuous note?" Elke gave him a confused look.

"I mean is there a man or anyone else upset with you?"

"I've never been good at pleasin' everyone."

"Was the man at your house the morning of the fire someone who wasn't pleased?"

Elke smiled and leaned in. "Oh, he was pleased."

"Was he?" Kevin asked, trying to hold back his excitement that he'd finally gotten her to admit there had been a man at her home. She'd fallen for the chatting trap.

"This old dog has learned a lot of tricks over the years." She leaned back, folding her arms proudly over her chest. "I'm not popular with the men for no reason."

"I just thought it was your good looks that had them coming around," Kevin said, playing into her flirtation.

Elke giggled.

The waitress walked to their table and set down a cup of coffee. "Anything else I can get you?"

"No," Elke said, shaking her head.

"Okay, well let me know if you need anything else." The girl smiled and left.

"She shoulda brought you a refill. It woulda saved her a trip." Elke pointed at his half-drained cup. "The young ones never understand that ya gotta work smart in this business. You need to save your energy for when you get home." She winked.

Kevin laughed. "I bet *your friend*—" he paused, hoping she would say the man's name, but she didn't take the bait "—appreciates your conservation of energy."

Elke laughed, her sound the coarse warble of a smoker. "You better believe it."

"What did you say his name was?"

"Anthony."

"And his last name?"

Elke chewed on the corner of her lip as if she was trying to remember. "I don't know. I don't think he ever said."

"So I'm guessing you hadn't been together long?"

She shook her head. "That was the first time I had him over. He'd come to Rudy's for dinner and ended up gettin' a little dessert."

"Do you think he was behind the fire?"

Elke took a long drink of her coffee. "In my line of work ya get to know people. I can tell you before a person sits down whether or not they are gonna stiff me or leave me a tip worth savin'. Do you think I would bring home a man who would start my stuff on fire? I work hard for my money."

She may have learned to read people in her business, but Kevin had, as well. And the first thing he'd learned about people is that given the right circumstances— most often need and opportunity—people were capable of anything.

"Can you describe him?"

She stared up at the ceiling. "Well, he was pretty average."

"Age? Hair, eye color?"

"He never said how old he was, but if I had to guess he was about forty, maybe forty-five. Dark hair. Brown eyes. Strong. Lean. Said he liked to work out."

Kevin thought back to the report. The neighbor had said the man coming out of the house in the morning had dark hair and an average build. It was possible this Anthony was the man they had seen, but at the same time, it was possible that it wasn't.

"Do you know where he works?"

"He never said. He's just been coming around the restaurant pretty regular. Always leaving me a twenty. A twenty five days a week can make a big difference."

"So you took him home to thank him personally?" Kevin asked, being careful to ask in a way that didn't ring of judgment.

Elke smiled. "I bet that's how you work. You help a woman and then end up taking her home."

Elke was wrong. His mind shifted to Heather, the last woman he'd taken home. No, he corrected himself, she'd come to him on her own. Still, he'd done nothing to help her; instead, he'd made her a victim of embarrassment by stopping her come-on. If only she hadn't been drunk... He could have finally done what he'd always wanted. He could have shown her what she was missing with David. He could make her feel how she deserved to feel.

If her reasoning hadn't been compromised, he wouldn't have stopped. Rather, he would have made the move; he would have taken her in his arms and kissed the curves of her lips, pulled her hips against him and caressed her over her clothes until she begged for his soft touch in more forbidden places.

He shook away the images.

"This conversation isn't about my dating history, Ms. Goldstein," Kevin said, trying to turn their conversation back to the business at hand.

"You might try to tell yourself that, but I know it ain't true. Everything we do in this world is pushed by our relationships—past and present. Who you are now is because of the people who've hated or loved you."

"I'm a professional inspector, ma'am. My investigations are based on science not on emotion."

Elke smirked. "Even for a man like you, everything comes back to feelings."

"Feelings can be the basis for many things, Ms. Goldstein, but an investigation isn't one of them." He readjusted the sleeves of his uniform. "Now, would you say Anthony left with particular *feelings* that would give him a motive for starting this fire?"

"Not that I know of." Elke shrugged.

"Did he spend the night?"

"I'm not the kind for sleepovers."

"So what time did he leave?"

She swirled the spoon in her coffee. "I don't know. I wasn't looking at my watch, but I would say sometime around two." She sipped her coffee. "And I ain't seen him again."

Things didn't align. The fire wasn't reported until 5:00 a.m. If the man left her house around two it either wasn't the same man the neighbors had seen or he had come back. Only one thing was for sure, he had one hell of an investigation on his hands.

Chapter Ten

Heather sat in her car as the tears flowed. They streaked down her face and her nose ran, but she let the ugly sobs take over. David was a jerk.

How could he have done this to her? She had given him everything—her life, her future, her heart.

What had he given her? Shame. Embarrassment. Regret.

She hated him for that. Despite that, her lawyer had pushed for her to reconsider the divorce—as if she had a choice. David was running this decision, just like he ran everything else.

She slammed her hand against the steering wheel, driving pain through her palm, but it was nothing compared to the pain in her soul.

What was she going to do?

She dabbed at her tears. She looked out the window. Around her, the city flowed like a river as people rushed through their lives.

Her eyes lit on a woman in the crosswalk, waiting until it was safe to cross. A little boy held her hand and under his arm was a blue bunny. The bunny's ears were gray, bits of a black gooey substance stained its fur, and its black plastic nose was askew. The boy's arm relaxed and the bunny dropped to the ground as the boy's mother tugged on his hand, urging him to come along as she crossed the street.

The boy's eyes widened and he dropped to his knees, protesting about his lost friend. His mother spotted the toy and, gathering the boy in her arms, retrieved the bunny. The boy pulled his toy tight under his arm, protecting it with the strength of his love.

A renewed wave of tears flooded Heather's cheeks. What it must be like to be loved like the bunny, to be wanted regardless of the dirt on its ears and the wear on its fur. What she would give to be loved like that… especially by a child.

She would give anything to have that moment. To be given the gift of motherhood. To be able to pull a child into her arms and fix all the wrongs with a simple kiss. To love wholeheartedly without the fear of being abandoned. Or to know the child in your arms loved you with every thread of their being.

It wasn't just her vanity that made her want a family. No. It was so much more. It was a deep ache in her gut, a feeling in her core every time she thought of a child. Like an amputee felt a lost phantom limb, she felt the loss of her child, who had never had a chance to exist more than a few weeks in her inhospitable womb.

Every ounce of her love had ended in loss.

Heather sobbed as the mother and her boy made their way across the street.

What she would have given to still have her mother around. Her mother had been tough, but she'd always been there. It was in moments like these when she missed her the most. She missed everything about her, from the way her hair always smelled like hair spray to the way she would wrap her arms around her and tell her the things she needed to hear. Alone, she wasn't strong enough to make it through. She would never make it through to the other side.

She would prove a broken heart could be fatal.

She needed a friend.

Heather drew her phone out of her purse and stared at the screen. Kevin's face greeted her as she looked at her recent calls. God, she wished she could call him. To confide in him what the lawyer had told her. It would have felt so good to be back in his arms, listening to the soothing beat of his heart, to feel the strong touch of his lips.

She'd stepped too far over the boundary of friendship. He had pushed her away. If he felt as she did, he wouldn't have been able to stop.

She needed to talk to someone neutral. Looking to her phone, the only other two people on her recent calls list were David and Brittany. She clicked on Brittany and the call went through.

"Are you busy?" she asked when her friend answered.

There was a short pause. "Um… No. What's up?"

"David wants a divorce."

"What?" There was an odd strain in Brittany's voice.

Heather couldn't bring herself to repeat the words and the phone crackled and buzzed with the silence between them.

"Where are you?" Brittany asked.

"I'm outside my lawyer's office."

"So you already went to see someone. That's good. Has David filed anything yet?"

"He had the papers ready last night."

"Damn. I didn't think he was going to do this so fast."

"What? You knew he was going to ask for a divorce?"

There was a long pause. "Well, no. But things have been so rocky with you guys. I thought maybe it was possible he would pull something stupid like this."

The word *stupid* didn't seem to cut it. This was more than stupid. It was irrational, terrifying and horrific. More, it was life shattering.

Her mind was a muddled mess of thoughts, like a painting that she was standing too close to so that the colors streaked in no discernible order. Unlike the painting, however, she doubted that if she stepped back she could make sense of the mess in her life. There was no beautiful picture, no passion behind the madness.

"Heather?"

"Huh?"

"Why don't you come over?"

"Okay," she said, her body numb.

She drove on instinct, bobbing and weaving through traffic and turning down the streets that she had driven a thousand times. She pulled into Brittany's driveway where, only yesterday, she'd come to celebrate. The pink metallic party streamers were still hanging on the porch and they fluttered in the breeze as though they were beckoning party-goers. In her, they would find only disappointment.

Heather made her way up to the streamers and, without thinking, reached up and pulled them down. The wispy foil crinkled in her hands as she balled it up in her fist.

"Hey now, they didn't do anything to you," Brittany said as she opened the door and motioned her inside.

"I just thought—"

Brittany stopped her with a wave of her hand. "No worries. They needed to come down anyway. I'm just glad you're here."

False felicities. Women spoke in them all the time, offering a kind word and a smile when inside they were thanking God that something wasn't happening to them or, worse, snickering at their friend's misfortune as though it was some kind of karmic retribution.

Heather was just as guilty as the rest. She'd lost count of the number of times she had congratulated a pregnant woman with a fist in her gut. Now Brittany was welcoming her with the same double-edged greeting. No one wanted to spend their day with a blubbering mess. Brittany was just trying to do what she thought was right, but the strain in her smile spoke louder than her words.

"Thanks for having me. I didn't bring your clothes back. I'm afraid your shirt got a bit ruined, but I'll make sure—"

Another wave. "Don't worry about those silly old clothes. Just throw them away."

Heather nodded. Of course Brittany didn't want them back—they were not only tainted with last night's margaritas, they were also tainted with failure, and failure wasn't a going commodity in her world.

Heather shook her head to try to squash her thoughts.

She's trying to help. Why can't I just appreciate it? Why can't I just let her love me like a sister? Not everyone is out to get me.

"Come on," Brittany said, motioning her toward the kitchen. "I have a cup of coffee waiting. I even put in the creamer you like." She sent Heather a smile.

Brittany handed her a fresh cup of coffee, the white cream billowing and swirling like a cloud of sweetness.

"Thanks. I appreciate your having me over. I know you've got better things to do."

"Stop it. You know I've got your back." Brittany walked to the other side of her granite island and poured herself a cup of coffee. "Why didn't you come over last night?"

Heather smiled as she thought of where, and with whom, she'd spent last night, and she tried to cover her reaction by taking a long drink.

She couldn't tell Brittany about Kevin. It wasn't that Brittany wouldn't understand; no, she would slap her back and praise her for her ability to go after the man she really wanted. Brittany had been through more than one breakup before settling down with Nathan. Every time her heart had been broken, she always landed on her feet—and in the bed of the next man. The same couldn't be said of her.

"You know I'm here," Brittany continued. "If you ever need me, you just have to call."

"I tried, but you didn't answer. With your party and all, you had enough going on. I didn't want to bother you."

"I can't believe you didn't come over. I mean I get it if you didn't feel like talking, but you could've at least slept in my guest room. You didn't have to be alone."

I wasn't alone. She bit back the words.

Heather looked around and tried to focus her attention on anything other than the pain and guilt that roiled within her. "Where's Nathan? He at work?"

"It's Friday, remember?"

"Oh…"

In truth, she had forgotten this was Nathan's day off.

Brittany smiled. "He needed to get out of the house. This is his golf morning. Afterward he normally hits the nineteenth hole. Most of the time he doesn't come home until dinner, and sometimes not even then. It's great. We both get a break."

"A break? Is everything going okay?"

Brittany nodded, maybe a bit too fervently. "Absolutely. But you know how it is." She smiled. "Absence makes the heart grow fonder."

Heather stared down at the mug in her hands. The white rim was stained with her pink lipstick, lipstick she didn't remember putting on.

"Maybe somehow your hiccup will end up helping," Brittany continued. "Maybe you guys just need a little break. Maybe he'll come around and see what a wonderful woman you are."

"I'm not wonderful."

"Stop that, Heather. You are. What other woman would do what you do for David?"

"I'm hardly the first woman to take care of the household." Heather looked up. "You do the same thing for Nathan."

"Hardly. You're the perfect wife. Every day David comes home from work to a hot meal. *Your* house is always clean." Brittany motioned to piles of letters, empty paper plates and last night's red Solo cups that littered her counter. "You volunteer everywhere and you watch other people's kids. You're one step away from being Mrs. Cleaver. In fact, the only thing keeping you from being the picture of a 1950s super wife is that you don't bring David his slippers and paper."

"He doesn't like sweaty feet."

Brittany's face pulled into a disgusted pucker. "See? You even know *that* about your husband. I couldn't tell you anything about Nathan's feet other than he has short toes. Really short toes, actually. They're freakishly troll-like. They're even hairy."

Heather giggled as she imagined Nathan, the bra-shirt-wearing griller with hairy troll feet.

Brittany reached over and squeezed her hand, reassuring her. "Look, every marriage goes through a rough patch. It's normal, especially after everything you guys have gone through. Maybe you just need to take this time to figure out who you are and what you want."

She ran her thumb over the smooth glass of the coffee mug.

Her thoughts moved to Kevin and the spark she'd felt last night when his eyes had met hers. She hadn't felt that want, that raw desire for David in a long time. Yet, if she was the super wife Brittany claimed, she would have felt nothing. She would never even have found her way to Kevin's front steps.

She was far from perfect—especially if someone asked David. No doubt he wanted a woman who would come to him in the night, lips parted and body needing. In the bedroom, she had played the part of a dutiful wife, but even then the feelings hadn't come close to what she had always felt for Kevin.

"Don't take this the wrong way," Brittany continued. "But maybe you've been *too* good at being a wife."

Heather choked on her swig of coffee, coughing until she could get the liquid out of her lungs. Tears streamed from her eyes and she dabbed at them with a napkin.

"If I was that good, then why would he want to leave me?" Her voice was thick and rough.

"You made life too easy. People don't appreciate things they don't have to work for." Brittany sighed. "Think about it. David had to work to get everything he has. He may not admit it, but he loves the chase. He loves having to tear his way to the top to get what he wants."

A knot of jealousy and confusion tightened in Heather's gut as she stared at Brittany. Her friend seemed to know more about David and what he wanted than she did. Sure, Heather had talked about David a lot over the years of their friendship, but there seemed to be something more than hearsay or simple familiarity in the way Brittany spoke.

What was she thinking? There couldn't be… She flushed the thoughts from her head.

"Do you want the divorce?" Brittany continued.

The question sat in the air like a heavy cloud.

"The lawyer asked me the same thing. To be honest, Brit, the only thing I know for sure is that I don't want things to keep going as they are."

Brittany nodded, but for once didn't say anything.

"There's a prenup," Heather said, looking down at her hands. "As things stand, if I go through with the divorce, I get ten thousand dollars and the house."

"That's it?"

"I'm lucky if I'll get that. The last time we spoke, David threatened to take everything. He thinks I broke the conditions of the contract. My lawyer thinks I'm in the clear, but I don't have a whole lot of faith in her."

"What did you do?"

Heather paused. Did she really want to tell Brittany that David had caught her sneaking out of Kevin's house? Brittany was her friend, but she doubted she

would believe she'd done nothing with the handsome Kevin. Over the years, they'd laughed and talked about what it would be like to be with a man like him, but it had been nothing more than girl talk—until now. All of a sudden, with the proclamation of divorce, all of those talks had a new weight.

"He's accusing me of all kinds of things," Heather said, carefully sidestepping what and who was really on her mind. "He's even accusing me of cheating on him with his coworker, Andrew."

"Andrew Bosche—the one who has the huge nose and the piggish eyes?"

"The one and only."

Brittany laughed. "You could do a lot better than Andrew. Why would he think you'd ever go for someone like that?"

Heather explained David's convoluted thoughts, all the time trying to stop her hands from shaking. "I swear, Brittany, I've never slept with another man."

"I know, sweetheart. David's just the jealous type." Brittany sat her coffee cup down on the island and ran her finger over the rim. "Don't take this the wrong way, but do you think that he's accusing you to take the heat off him?"

"I considered that, but I don't know."

"It's kind of classic. A cheater always accuses the innocent to make themselves feel better. If they're not the only one cheating, then what they're doing isn't so bad. They feel justified in having an affair."

Until recently she had never thought David was the type to cheat. He was a doctor—a man held to a higher moral code. He'd always made a point of telling her how much his reputation mattered and reminding her that how she acted mattered. She had to be a good, upstanding wife so that he could appear to have the perfect life.

She had never let him down. At least not in her mind... That was, until last night when she'd kissed Kevin.

Instead of regret, empowerment flowed through her.

If what Brittany was saying was true, David was the one to blame. He was the one who was stripping down their marriage, leaving behind only tired flesh and fragile bones.

Right now, the dying beast wasn't worth saving.

"I'm sorry, Heather. I didn't mean to upset you. It's just... I just feel so bad seeing you go through this. You don't deserve this."

"It doesn't matter what I deserve. I just want—"

The front door slammed, rattling the lights in the kitchen and stopping Heather midsentence.

"What was that?" Heather jumped to her feet. "Was someone here?"

Brittany stood up. "No." She rushed out of the kitchen toward the door, Heather close behind. "Hello?"

There was nobody at the door, but the curtain on the window was drifting back into place. Brittany opened the door and they looked outside. The front yard was empty and everything stood still.

"What in the hell?" Brittany turned back to her. "Did you see anyone?"

She shook her head.

The faint aroma of chlorine stung her nostrils. "Are you bleaching something?"

"Huh? No." Brittany frowned. "Why?"

Heather sniffed, pulling the scent deeper into her

nose as she tried to follow the smell. She walked toward the stairs to the second floor.

A white haze filled the stairwell. It billowed and roiled as it hit the ceiling and started pouring downward. A tongue of orange flame wrapped around the wall at the top of the stairs. It spread, its blue maw stretching and gaping upward in its ravenous consumption of oxygen.

For a moment, she just stood staring as the orange tips rippled over the ceiling. In a disturbing but primal way, the fire was beautiful.

Heather forced herself to turn away. As she moved, something stirred behind the back window. A man stood staring at her, his face hidden in darkness. As quickly as she noticed him, the dark-haired man disappeared.

Brittany stepped around her and looked upward.

She screamed.

She tugged at Heather's arm, tearing her from her trance. "Heather, let's go!"

Stumbling through the door and out into the front yard, Heather couldn't help but emit a low, joyless laugh. She had come here for comfort, to see a friend and talk, yet no matter where she went, she left only destruction.

Chapter Eleven

Kevin sank back into the turquoise patio chair as the little boy ran across the porch and down the stairs, his plump little feet pounding on the wood as if he was beating a drum. The scent of smoke lingered in the air and strengthened as the wind drifted from the direction of Elke's house next door.

For a moment it was as though he had gone back in time and was watching Colter. Maybe if he tried hard enough he could look over to the neighbor's house and see Heather in the window. He smiled at the thought, Heather looking out at him…the feel of her against his body.

The door slammed behind him.

"Mr. Jensen, I'm surprised you're here. I thought they, you know…the investigators, were done questioning me," the blonde said, but her body language was soft and welcoming in direct incongruity with her words.

"I am sorry for the intrusion, Miss…" He looked down at his notes, searching for the woman's last name.

"Mrs. Jones. Tracy." She looked toward her son. "And he's River."

"River? Cool name." Kevin smiled. "I have two kids of my own. They grow quick, don't they?"

She nodded.

"How old is River?"

"He's two, and full of piss and vinegar, just like his father." Mrs. Jones smiled, pride lighting her eyes.

"What does his father—your husband—do?"

"He works for the railroad. Lays rail."

"Was he home the morning of the fire?"

Mrs. Jones glanced over at the house next door as though she was recalling everything that had happened. "Yeah, he gets up early for work. Most of the time he's out of the house by five. He's the one who noticed something was wrong."

Kevin took out his notepad and made a note. "Do you know what he saw?"

"At first he noticed the smoke, and then he came upstairs and woke me up. By the time I made it out of bed and to the window, there was a man standing on the front porch."

"Are you sure it was a man? Did you see his face?"

"I had been up most of the night with River, so I was pretty tired, but I'm pretty sure it was a man." Mrs. Jones sat down in the patio chair next to him as she carefully kept a watch on River. who was playing with a yellow truck in the grass. "I didn't catch his face, but it was too big to be a woman, and he had dark hair, short, cropped."

"Was it dark outside when you caught sight of this man?"

"Yeah. It was dark at five. But Elke's porch light was on."

River roared, mimicking the sound of a dump truck's engine.

"How well do you know Elke?"

"Mostly in passing. She keeps different hours than us, so our relationship pretty much consists of waving."

They sounded like typical neighbors. "You don't have any animosity toward Ms. Goldstein?"

"Nah," Mrs. Jones said, waving him off. "We get along. She's even offered to watch River for me." Her face tightened. "You don't think what happened over there will continue happening, do you?"

"You mean arson?" Kevin asked.

"Well, yeah. You don't think we're in danger, do you?" She looked worriedly toward River, her fingers gripping the edge of her patio chair.

"No, ma'am." He tried to sound reassuring, but if she had been listening well, she would have been able to hear the lie in his voice. The truth was that he didn't know who was behind the fire. Elke had been helpful, but he wasn't any closer to finding the person responsible. He could only hope he'd been wrong about this arsonist being one who would strike again.

There was a long pause as he tried to think of something reassuring to say to the mother.

Mrs. Jones looked at him. "Oh, I just remembered something…"

"What?"

"The man wasn't driving. I remember him walking off, down the side of the road, and I thought it was strange. I mean, what grown man doesn't have a car?" Her face pinched.

Kevin made a note: No getaway vehicle.

That could mean one of several things. Maybe the man had planned to set the fire and didn't want to be easily identifiable. Or maybe the man didn't have a car.

Could he have been a transient? Missoula was known for having a sizable population of homeless people.

"Did you see what the man was wearing?"

She closed her eyes like she was trying to recall a memory. "I think he was wearing black pants. And he had on a T-shirt. White."

"Did the T-shirt have any logos on it? Any identifiable features?"

She shook her head. "I don't remember. Like I said, I was pretty tired. He had on hiking boots, though. You know, like the ones that loggers wear."

Kevin made another note. He thought back to the footprint he'd seen in Elke's garage. It had been made by a boot with a star pattern. That had to belong to his suspect. Finally a lead, but it wasn't much.

"How old would you say the man looked?"

"I don't know. It was hard to tell."

"Did he look to be in his forties?"

Mrs. Jones bit her lip. "Maybe, I didn't really get a chance to look too closely at his face. For all I know, he could have been a twentysomething or he could have been fifty. He was a little heavy, though. Kind of a paunch belly."

Elke had described Anthony as being in his midforties with a trim build. This man, the man Tracy was describing, didn't fit the description.

He needed to question Anthony, but it suddenly seemed unlikely he was the man who'd set the fires.

Did the possible arsonist see Anthony coming out of her house and get jealous? Could it have been one of Elke's former lovers?

From what Elke had said, there were plenty of them.

But he knew he couldn't jump to assumptions. He had to follow the evidence—regardless of how little there was.

There was a crash of two plastic trucks hitting one another and River making the sound effects of some poor imaginary victim.

"Is there anything else you or your husband noticed? Anything at all?"

She gave him a tired look. "I told you everything."

"Sorry, just trying to get as many facts as I can. I appreciate your patience in aiding with our investigation."

"Isn't there something you can do? You know, some CSI stuff?"

Kevin smiled. Mrs. Jones had an idealized vision of what power he wielded. He didn't live on the set of *NCIS* or whatever crime-drama television show she watched after River went to bed. He worked on a shoestring budget, where even having men maintaining the chain of custody was a cost his department didn't want to absorb.

He imagined taking the request to the crime lab to run shoe prints for a simple arson with no fatalities. If the chief heard about something like that, he would be canned for sure.

His phone rang, "Eye of the Tiger" sounding from his pocket. His thoughts instantly turned to Heather. "Excuse me," he said to Tracy.

"Hello?" he answered, hoping to hear Heather's voice.

"Kevin, this is Hiller. You busy?" the battalion chief asked.

"Well, actually, I'm in the middle of questioning a witness. What can I do for you?" He smiled over at Mrs. Jones who, nodding, stood up and made her way down the patio steps and to River's side.

"We are on another call. Upper Miller Creek. We have another fire you might want to look at."

He wasn't going to be able to continue his investigation on this fire if he was chasing after another one. If he walked away, the chain of custody would be broken and, if he returned, any evidence he found would make the case harder to prosecute. He'd promised himself he'd help Elke and that he'd find an answer. It wasn't just a simple investigation anymore. It had morphed into something else the moment he'd first seen River, the little boy who reminded him so much of Colter. What happened if this arsonist was targeting this block? What if the boy was in danger? He couldn't let the boy be hurt.

He couldn't stand the thought of someone getting hurt at the arsonist's hands; he'd seen too much pain between Allison's death and the multitude of cases he had investigated. This was one case where, if he just worked hard enough, if he just dug deeper, he'd find the answers he needed. If he just did his best, maybe he'd have the power to save a life.

"Isn't there someone else who can take that one? I have my hands full," Kevin said, trying to think of another, more urgent reason for him to refuse to bow out and leave this case unsolved.

"Actually, that's why I called," Hiller said. "This fire looks as if it may be tied to the other. We have what looks to be the same oxidizers used, but it's hard to say for sure."

He knew it. He knew another fire would happen. He'd failed.

"Was anyone hurt?" He braced himself for the answer.

"Two women were in the residence at the time of the

fire, but they made it out unharmed." There was a line of tension in his voice.

"What aren't you telling me, Hiller?"

Hiller cleared his throat. "Well, Jensen, they asked for you. Said they're friends of yours."

There was the echo of feminine voices on Hiller's end. "Hold on, ladies. I'll let him know." Hiller sighed with annoyance. "It's a Brittany Miller and her friend Heather Sampson."

Heather and Brittany?

Hiller had to be kidding.

"They're both okay? How's Heather?"

Hiller chuckled. "They're both fine. Including Heather."

Thank God she hadn't been hurt. After what had happened between them, he would have never forgiven himself.

"Where was the fire?"

Hiller rattled off Brittany's house number. A sense of relief drifted through him—at least it wasn't Heather's house.

"I'll be there in fifteen minutes."

KEVIN PARKED ACROSS the street from Brittany's two-story house. He looked over the mass of trees and lights that was the city below. Most days he would have enjoyed the hillside view, but right now all he could think of was Heather.

Heather. He shouldn't have been so worried about Heather. She couldn't be his. No matter how much he longed to kiss her pink lips, feel her warmth pressed against his body.

She had been so warm…

Damn it. Knock it off, Jensen.

Two fire engines and the battalion chief's truck were parked in front of Brittany's house where, only yesterday, he'd suffered through her annual neighborhood party. The only bright spot of the barbecue had been seeing Heather walk out of Brittany's house in her sexy miniskirt and low-cut top. He needed to write to whoever invented that shirt a thank-you; seeing her in that top was one image he would never forget—no matter how much he should.

Hiller was standing over by his crew, directing them in their attack on the smoldering blaze.

His breath hitched for a second as Heather stepped out from behind the ambulance. Ash smudged her cheeks and her eyes were shadowed with what he could only assume was fear. Even frazzled, she was beautiful.

Kevin made his way over to her. "Are you okay?"

She turned toward him and, before he had time to react, she threw her body into his arms, pressing hard against him. Her hair smelled of acrid smoke, but underneath the pungent smell was the heady floral aroma of her shampoo. Something about the smell, the safe beneath the dangerous, made some of his concern for her dissolve. She would be okay. She would make it through this. She hadn't been physically hurt. Only the memories of this would remain.

"You sure you're okay?" Kevin asked again, leaning back so he could look her in the face.

She nodded. "Fine. I…I'm sorry about last night. I—"

He stopped her with a shake of his head. "Don't worry. Let's not talk about it here." As he said the words, he instantly regretted them. He didn't want to forget what had happened between them—or at least what had almost happened—and he didn't want her to, either.

They both just needed time. And she needed time to figure out what was going on with her life.

She let her arms drop from his waist and the cool evening air robbed him of her warmth. The hard edges returned to her face and she stepped back from him.

He tried not to notice the way her body, which had only seconds before been open to him, closed.

"What happened?" he asked her. "Where's Brittany?"

"Don't worry. Brittany's fine. She's just getting checked out by the EMTs." Heather looked toward the ambulance. "As for what happened, I don't understand it. We were standing around in the kitchen, talking. Then we heard the front door slam. Then the smoke started pouring from the second floor."

Another second-floor fire and perhaps another fire started with an oxidizer. Assuming it was the same type of ignition source, it had to be the same arsonist. But why was this man starting all the fires on the second floor? Why not where they would be more deadly? Why not the kitchen or somewhere he could easily get away from?

Whoever had set the fire must have known Heather and Brittany were in the house. If he'd wanted them dead, he would have never started the fire in a place where it was unlikely to trap them. If he'd wanted to hurt Brittany and Heather, he would have set a hotter, more explosive fire at escape points.

Just like Elke's, this fire wasn't set to hurt. No. It

was set to send a message. But what did Brittany and Elke have in common?

"Is that where Brittany's bedroom is?" He pointed toward the second-story window above the front door.

"Huh?"

"Is her bedroom on the second floor? Near where the fire was started?"

"That's her bedroom, but I don't know exactly where the fire started. We never went up there. We just saw the smoke." Her eyes clouded over, as if she was suddenly gripped by thought. "When I turned I think I saw a man looking in the window."

"What? What did he look like?"

"I don't know." She shook her head. "He was in shadows."

"Anything you remember about him, anything at all?"

"He…he had dark hair. I couldn't see his face. But I could feel him watching me." Heather hugged her body. "Kevin… I have a feeling this guy isn't done."

He moved to hold her, but stopped as Hiller looked over toward them. "Don't worry, Heather. If I have my way, this will all be over soon. I won't let anything happen to you."

Chapter Twelve

She shouldn't have allowed herself to run into Kevin's arms…not after last night. Then again, he had taken her willingly. Maybe she was seeing things that weren't there, but she could have sworn he hadn't wanted to let her go.

Heather collapsed onto the grass of Brittany's front yard, which was wet where the firemen had sprayed water, quickly dousing the flames.

The fire hadn't been huge, but thanks to the phalanx of firefighters, EMTs and neighbors, it had blown into a full-scale event. Even the news crews had arrived, and the perky brunette from the ten o'clock news was interviewing neighbors.

Kevin was talking to a man he'd introduced to her as Stephen Hiller, his battalion chief. As he spoke, Kevin kept looking over and giving her reassuring smiles.

She was so confused. All she should have been thinking about was the fire and her burned-out marriage. Instead, all she could think about was the way it had felt to be in Kevin's arms.

After last night, she had convinced herself she wouldn't let it happen again, that she wouldn't let herself run to him. Yet she had allowed herself to fall into the arms of her hero.

That's exactly what he was—a hero.

It had nothing to do with the fact that he was a firefighter. Not anymore. No. He was so much more. He had such a good heart. There had been so many little things he done over the years, moments of selflessness, that showed her how much he cared. Once when she'd been sick, he had shown up with a bowl of chicken noodle soup. After she had lost the baby, he had the kids bring her flowers as a reminder that they loved her, that they would all be there.

He was so different from David. In fact, he was exactly the opposite of her narcissistic, demeaning, jerk of a husband.

She slapped her hands over her mouth as though she'd said the words aloud, though no sound had escaped her lips.

She hadn't meant that.

David wasn't a bad man. There had been a point early in their marriage when he'd been the picture of the perfect husband—bringing her flowers, coming home early and telling her every spare minute how much he loved her—but time had passed and it had all changed. As the months and years passed, the nice side of him had slipped away, only returning when they were in the presence of others. At home, she'd been left with nothing but the hatred and bitter, angry words that he kept hidden from the outside world.

There was no fixing things. There was no going back. There was only moving forward.

Maybe that was why they had never been given the

gift of children. In fact, maybe it was a message that they should never have been together.

Brittany's impish laugh cut through the air from the direction of the ambulance. Heather looked over at her friend, who even in the face of destruction was smiling as if she was on stage at the Miss America Pageant. She touched the arm of the twentysomething EMT and tilted her head back with another hearty laugh.

She wished she could be more like Brittany, beautiful and majestic even in moments of turmoil.

Kevin made his way over to her. A large black bag was draped over his shoulder. It was unzipped and inside were empty evidence bags. "Still doing okay? Do you need something?"

She needed a lot of things. First, she wanted to escape the spotlight. She hated this—this sideshow for the public. She didn't want her life, or even her day, to be scrutinized. She just wanted to go home and bury her head in a pillow or, better yet, to climb into Kevin's warm arms and forget everything.

"I'm fine," she lied, staring at Kevin's biceps, which pulled hard against his white uniform shirt. His badge sparkled in the sunshine, drawing her gaze to his chest.

"Before I wrap up here, are you feeling up to a couple more questions?"

Heather nodded even though all she really wanted to do was escape.

"Did you see anyone parked outside at any point during your visit?"

Heather thought about the moment she'd pulled up to the house. "I don't think so. Then again, I wasn't really paying attention. I had my mind on…" She paused as she thought about the last time she saw him.

"I completely understand," he said, a soft knowing smile on his face. "I—" He stopped and looked down at his notes.

What had he intended to say? What had he held back?

She warmed as she imagined him telling her that he had been just as torn about their night together or, rather, their almost night together. More than likely, however, he was thinking about a way to do his job and help her once again.

She thought of what it meant to be a true hero. It wasn't someone who ran into a burning building; a sociopath could do that. Rather, a hero was someone with great fears. They were the ones who feared the fire, who had dreams of the heat and woke up smelling imaginary smoke, yet who each day ran into those buildings, compelled by the need to help and refusing to be beaten by nightmares. In an odd way it made her think of the battle she faced. If only she could refuse to be beaten.

He smiled as she looked him in the eyes, and she could have sworn she caught a glimpse of his heart. This hard, battle-worn hero had turned gentle, made himself vulnerable, all for her. Whatever he had held back from saying didn't matter.

Kevin shifted from one foot to the other, looking away. "Did you see anyone near the house, other than when you saw him at the window?"

"I wish I could help you more, but all I saw was the shadow of a man." She shook her head. "We had no idea anyone was in the house with us. I don't even know why anyone would want to hurt Brittany."

"Do you think someone would want to hurt *you*?" He glanced in the direction of her and David's house.

She swallowed the gasp that lodged in her throat. "You don't think David would want to hurt me, do you?"

Kevin looked up, worry in his eyes. "Is there anything he has said or done to make you think he would target you in this type of act?"

"He's said so many things." There was a quake in her voice. "Lately, the things he's been doing to me have come as a surprise. I never thought he would hurt me like he has."

"He—" Kevin stopped. "Has he hurt you *physically*?"

She shook her head. "He's done a lot of things, but he's never raised a hand."

Kevin nodded, a frown darkening his face. "Are you afraid to go home?"

If she told Kevin the truth, that she was afraid, there would be no going back to the way things were. Undoubtedly, David would be moved up on Kevin's list of suspects. He would be questioned. No doubt he would quickly realize why he'd been put there and he would be even angrier.

If she told Kevin the truth, her world would be forever changed.

"I don't want to go back home."

"Do you have somewhere to go? Somewhere that you'll feel safe?"

She only had Brittany and Kevin.

"I'll just go back. Maybe he's gone."

"You need to stay away. Let me figure out what's going on. Maybe he's nothing to worry about, but maybe he is. I don't want you walking into a hornet's nest."

Everything with David was a hornet's nest.

"Okay. I'll look into getting a hotel room or something."

"Do you have any cash? You can't pay with a credit card. If you do, he can easily find out where you are."

She hated to admit how little money she had access to. For all she knew, David had already cancelled her credit and debit cards. Her stomach lurched at the thought.

Kevin reached out toward her. "Are you okay? You look pale. Why don't you sit down?" He motioned to the ambulance.

She shook her head. She would be fine; she just wasn't used to her world crashing down on her.

"I need to get some cash."

"You haven't done that yet?" He frowned. "You're a trusting woman. I know more than a few spouses who made it a personal mission to clear out bank accounts when they were planning a divorce."

The blood rushed from her head.

"Are you okay?" Kevin asked.

"I'm fine…" In truth, she was numb.

Kevin motioned toward the battalion chief. "Hiller, you can pull your men off Elke's house. I need them here instead. Got it?"

Hiller's face puckered. "I told you—" He stopped midsentence as he looked toward Heather. "Fine. Twelve hours, Jensen. But that's it."

There was a wave of tension between the two men, making Heather wish she was anywhere other than standing between them.

"Fine," Kevin said.

Hiller spun on his heel and yelled at one of the firefighters who stood near Brittany's front door.

Kevin turned to her. "I'll take you to the bank."

"You can't do that. You have to stay here and finish your investigation."

"I can take a short break." He looked back at the house and his face went rigid.

She was interfering in his work.

"Thanks for the offer. Really. But this is something I'm going to have to do on my own." She thought about how she would react if David had robbed her of everything. Kevin didn't need to see her sink any lower. "Would you just let Brittany know where I've gone?"

"No problem. By the way, I have an extra bedroom. It even has a lock on the door." He tensed. "I mean, if you don't want to get a hotel. I could use the help. I would pay you to take care of the kids."

She was tempted to take him up on his offer, but she shook her head. No matter how much she dreamed of a life with him, dreams rarely became reality.

IN ALL OF Kevin's studies, the motives for arson varied from revenge to fraud to some sociopathic impulse, and the list went on and on, but serial cases were different. Serial arsonists lived for the thrill. They reveled in the strike of the match, the smell of the smoke and the feel of power and control when they watched a fire ignite. Many serial arsonists were proud of their work—and that pride was what often got them caught. Many returned to the scene of the crime hours, days or weeks after the crimes just to see their devastation.

Kevin couldn't wait for that pride to get his perp caught.

Now that things had quieted down, he wanted one more chance to get a look at the scene. It was easy to miss something in the rush of firefighters—and it was easy to lose evidence. He'd given up the chain of custody at Elke's, so Brittany's was his only chance.

With a stiff nod he acknowledged the rookie firefighter who was stationed at the door and made his way upstairs. The fire was eerily similar to Elke's. The black burned-out circle sat exactly in front of the master bedroom's door. Again, the light was melted and it pointed like a finger to an ignition point. The only difference was that Brittany's upper floor was larger, with more places for an arsonist to hide.

He took a photo.

The man must have been trying to draw attention to Brittany's bedroom, just as he'd tried with Elke's. What about this room in particular was upsetting the arsonist? Had something happened in both of the women's bedrooms? Or did the arsonist randomly pick his victims?

He started to build a profile of the perp. Perhaps he was a man who felt inadequate in his sexual abilities. Maybe he'd been sexually abused as a child. Maybe he had been picked on as a child or rebuked by women as an adult. Therefore, in order for him to find fulfillment, he found a way he could control women and punish them for the mistakes made by the women of his past.

Kevin shrugged. Sounded logical, but he wasn't a professional profiler.

There was a ring of white powder around the scorched carpet, and he took another picture and a sample. Like before, it had a faint scent of chlorine. This time, however, there was a liquid, an oily substance staining the carpet outside of the powder. Grabbing a swab, he took a sample. The liquid was clear and had a distinct petroleum-based scent.

He'd smelled the odor before. He wafted the swab under his nose. He couldn't put his finger on that scent.

He stared at the white powder. Smelled like chlorine. Probably a pool shock treatment. It was easily attainable. Hell, Brittany even had a pool in the backyard. She would likely have something like that on hand.

Chlorine was a hell of an oxidizer. All that had to be added was brake fluid—

Brake fluid.

Why hadn't he figured it out before? It was so easy. Heather and Brittany had both said they witnessed a white smoke and then combustion. It made perfect sense. When the chlorinated isocyanurates from the shock treatment reacted with the ester in the brake fluid, it generated heat, causing the hot liquids in the fluid to give off a mist, and as the heat increased, flame to erupt.

He'd seen these types of fires in several of his practice burns.

Finally he could figure this out. He had the modus operandi narrowed down. The man entered women's homes when only the women were at home and waited for the right moment, when they were asleep or preoccupied, to start the fires. Given that this time there were two women in the house, Kevin had a feeling the perp was growing less afraid of being caught.

The signature of his crime, the way his actions reflected his needs and his personality, was coming to light. This was a man who thought he was above the law. He wanted to watch. He took joy from controlling and dominating women.

The fires weren't an act of rage. They were well planned, well executed and extremely ballsy.

Kevin imagined the man standing where he stood now, in Brittany's master bedroom, calmly waiting, listening to the women talk. Maybe he even took some kind of sexual pleasure in it.

Kevin had the source and a growing profile of the man responsible. He just needed to get his suspect.

On Brittany's dresser was a picture of her and Heather. They were holding wineglasses and pink streamers were strewn around behind them. Heather's hair was longer and she wore a bright blue shirt that made her eyes stand out, but the most beautiful thing about the photo was the smile on her face. Even though it was only a picture, he could sense her joy.

Ever since he'd moved to the neighborhood, he'd noticed Heather. She would always smile and wave and act happy and nice when he'd spoken to her, but it wasn't until last night, when he kissed her, that she'd really seemed to come to life. When she had looked at him, he'd seen that woman, the happy woman in the photograph. It was as though she had forgotten herself and her burden while she was in his arms.

He would do anything to have her look at him like that again. To see the sparkle in her eyes, the heat of her fingers as they rolled his shirt into a ball and she pulled him closer, hungry for more. Something had happened in those precious seconds, something irreversible. At least for him.

Until last night, he hadn't realized how lonely he had become. How badly he wanted a woman. Not just any woman. He wanted Heather.

He picked up the picture and, for a moment, thought about putting it in his pocket. If he hadn't been standing in the middle of a crime scene he would have taken it.

He sat the picture back. Heather was another man's wife; not even a picture of her could belong to him.

On the other hand, he could be a friend. After they had spoken, it had been easy to see that she needed, more than anything else, someone she could trust. Hopefully she would take him up on his offer of staying at his house. Sure, it would be odd at first after what had transpired, but they were both adults. Last night had been nothing more than too much alcohol and too little self-control. They could just slip back into their roles as friends. No big deal.

He would just have to ignore the way she walked… and the way her hair always smelled like flowers…and the way she always said her *R*'s as if they deserved an entire syllable just to themselves. He loved that about her.

Then again, there were so many other things that he loved about her. She was so selfless. She always seemed to care about others more than herself. She had taken such good care of the kids—especially Lindsay. She had been like a mother to her. He could do most things, but Lindsay had needed the guidance of a woman. Lindsay would need even more in the years to come and, without a doubt, Heather could be the woman to give it.

That was, unless he screwed it up. Or if she had to leave town after her divorce.

He couldn't bear the idea of her a thousand miles away, leading a life separate from him. Lindsay would be equally as heartbroken. And Colter, though he may not always have shown it, especially in the past few months, loved Heather, as well. In Colter's world, baseball came first and Heather had always made a point of coming to every game. Sometimes, when she could, she had brought Lindsay down after school and they had sat through the practices. Whenever she sat in the bleachers Colter lit up, his face glowing with pride.

Kevin had depended on Heather so much. Throughout the years she had always been there when he needed an extra hand. After Allison's death, she had taken Lindsay at least once a week. He hadn't realized until now what a huge role she had played in their lives.

But now was not the time to dwell on these thoughts. He had a job to do. He turned back to the task at hand, trying to focus.

Brittany and Nathan's king-size bed was covered in a faux leopard-print fur, complete with pink sheets. There were two walk-in closets, and he entered one. Clearly Brittany's, it was full of shiny clothes and accessories, and one entire wall was covered in shoes of every color.

Nathan's closet was only half-full, but everything was meticulously hung on wooden hangers. His shirts, pants, jackets and belts were kept separate and then further organized according to color. On the floor beneath the clothes was a line of shoes, just as carefully arranged. At the end of the closet, in the far corner, sat a pair of boots. They lay on the floor askew, as if someone had taken them off and thrown them in. They looked out of place in the meticulous order of Nathan's closet.

He took a picture and then carefully lifted the left boot. The toe of the boot had a faint white residue on its tip and he took a sample. The sole was covered in stars, the outside edge sported rectangular squares. And it was a size ten. Kevin scrolled back in his camera, searching for his picture of the print he'd taken in Elke's garage. When he found it, his pulse jumped.

He had his match.

He studied the boot further. It had been well-worn, the star and rectangular edging worn thin near the big toe and the heel, and the sole had been forced flat, the rubber permanently squished out of the sides. Whoever had worn these had been a heavy man, heavier than Nathan Miller.

He turned back to the closet and picked up one of Nathan's shoes. Size twelve. Either Nathan's feet had shrunk or the boots belonged to someone else, someone who hoped to hide evidence in plain sight.

The brand was one Kevin recognized from the local chain department store where thousands of the same type of boots had likely been sold over the past few years. There would be no way he could trace sales back concisely enough to be of any use. Yet the owner must have been the type to be on a budget. These weren't the expensive boots worn by loggers as Tracy, Elke's neighbor, had assumed. They were cheaper, more common, though they did match her description.

He carefully slipped the boots into an evidence bag and set it in his duffel.

It was strange, the one solid lead he had on his suspect had been discarded on the scene. Why? Why hadn't the boot's owner kept them? Thrown them in some random Dumpster where they would have never been found? Was the arsonist purposely leaving clues behind, leading Kevin on a trail of breadcrumbs? Or was he confident he would never be caught?

The thought pissed Kevin off, but he tried to keep his emotions in check. He didn't have time to be angry.

He glanced down at his notebook. His notes were finally starting to take shape:

Dark-haired man
Average build
Midforties
Sets fires outside of master bedroom doors
Chlorine/brake fluid fires
Heavier man
Size 10 boot
Likes to control
May watch the fires
Enjoys reaction

There was one note that still bothered him and, as he stared at it, it seemed to fade and sharpen like a blinking neon sign.

Motive?

He had no idea how the two victims were connected. Elke was in an entirely different socio-economic bracket, different education background, single and, though Elke was pretty in an average way, she couldn't compete with Brittany's appeal.

It seemed unlikely that whoever was behind this was sleeping with both women, but he could be wrong. Maybe the women had upset the suspect in some way while they were having an affair. Or maybe it had nothing to do with their bedroom behavior, and the fact that the suspect set the fires outside their doors had something more to do with mommy issues.

He had so many questions and so few answers.

Patience. Study. Evaluation.

He would get his answers.

He made his way downstairs. The carpet squelched as he walked through the area. The walls were blackened, the paint was scorched and blistered, and the air smelled of acrid, chemically laced smoke.

He made his way into the garage, hoping there would be another clue. Brittany's car was in the garage, the keys hanging loosely on a rack. Nathan's keys and truck were gone, substantiating Brittany's claim of his being at the local country club at the time of the fire. He'd still need to talk to the club to verify his alibi, but he doubted Nathan had any part in the fire.

There was no clear point of entry. All the windows in the house were intact. It was hard to say how long the suspect had been waiting in the house but, according to Heather, she'd been in the home for at least thirty minutes and had heard no one come in. Yet at some point the suspect had entered the house and made his way upstairs. It must have been before Heather's arrival and after Nathan had unlocked the door when he'd left. Perhaps when Brittany had been in her room to get dressed after Nathan had left. Which meant the perpetrator must have been in the house for almost an hour.

Why had he waited to start the fire? He couldn't have known Heather was on her way over unless he was close to Heather or he'd heard Brittany inviting her.

If he had heard Brittany's invitation and chose to wait, did that mean the suspect knew Heather? Or was there another reason? Did he want to send a message to both women?

Kevin took his time as he looked around the yard. There was nothing out of place in the front, so he made his way around back to the pool's shed. The doors were locked so he peered in through the window. In the darkness, he could make out the rows of well-organized supplies, brushes and hoses. Everything seemed in order and undisturbed.

He made a note: "Suspect likely supplied powder. None stolen from Brittany's pool supply."

A long row of bushes ran along the side of the garage and under the house's back windows. In a bush beneath the back window, something white caught his eye. Putting on his gloves, Kevin took a picture and then picked up the object. It was a long white bottle with a red-and-blue label. Brake fluid from Truck Boys, a local auto parts store.

He carefully slid the bottle into an evidence bag. Perhaps the lab could pull prints. Then again, asking them for another test meant more money.

At least he finally had concrete evidence—evidence that backed his hypothesis on the ignition source.

Yet, assuming this bottle had held the fluid used to ignite the fire, why was it in the backyard? This was where Heather had seen the man standing. Was it possible he had dropped it by accident, or had he intentionally planted another clue?

Kevin would be a fool to underestimate his suspect.

There was nothing in the grass or dirt near the bottle, nothing to give away the suspect's intention.

He looked up, through the window. The front door was directly in view. A chill ran down his spine. The man had watched as Heather and Brittany had rushed to the door, watched as they must have questioned what had happened.

He must have wanted to see the results of his work; that was, until he'd seen Heather looking at him.

His crimes weren't going to stop, but God only knew what direction his next crime would take. A man like this, a man who got excited watching the fear and pain of others, was dangerous. If he thought Heather could identify him, that put her directly in danger.

It was hard to say what this perp was capable of. All Kevin could do was set a trap the egomaniacal suspect couldn't resist.

He called Detective Lawrence.

"We just had another fire. I'm sure it was started by the same man from the other night, but I haven't got a handle on who he is yet."

"So what do you want me to do?"

"I want you to call a press conference. We need to pull this guy out into the public eye."

Chapter Thirteen

Heather stood in the bank teller's line. Her stomach ached as she anticipated what she might find. She kept her eyes on the man who waited in line in front of her. The way he wrung his hands and stepped from one foot to the other made Heather think of David. If he'd come in, would he have had the same washed-out pallor, sweaty brow and squashed facial expression?

She doubted it. David wasn't the type. He was the kind of man who would step up to the Devil with a haughty grin. If he made his way through these doors, he'd probably saunter to the desk and charm the teller while he stripped their accounts bare. He'd probably even get her phone number on his way out the door.

"Ma'am?" one of the tellers called from behind her. "May I help you?"

Heather stood there a moment. If she found out David had not touched their accounts, she would feel crazy. Her suspicion would only validate David's opinion that she was the problem. Yet, if she didn't check her accounts, Kevin would think her a fool.

She had learned enough in the past few days to know she couldn't trust David to be fair or just. He could only be trusted to do the wrong or hurtful thing. She needed to protect herself. She needed to be strong and safeguard herself.

Her hands shook violently as she turned and made her way to the counter. "I need to check my accounts." She handed the teller the slip where she'd written her account numbers. "Could you print out the balances?"

"No problem," the woman said, tapping away on her keyboard.

As she waited, her heart beat so loudly she was almost positive the teller could hear it.

"Okay," the teller said, her face pinched slightly as she held out a printout.

Heather took it and looked down at the paper that would tell her her future.

Account Summary
Savings Balance…$150
Checking Balance…$50

Heather sucked in a breath. Her head swam in a chilling fog.

He had done it.

He had cleared their accounts.

She had nothing.

"Can you print me out a record of all account activity for the past six months?" Heather asked, her voice barely making ripples in her trance.

The woman nodded. "Are you okay, Mrs. Sampson?"

She nodded, afraid that if she spoke tears would start to flow.

The woman tapped another button and handed her a small packet of papers. "Is there anything else that you need, Mrs. Sampson?"

She shook her head, turned away and rushed to her car.

She gripped the printout as if it was the edge of a cliff, and it crinkled in her hand. The world was giving way under her feet as she collapsed into the driver's seat, letting her pounding head rest against the steering wheel.

He'd screwed her. Again.

She had proof. Proof that he cared nothing for her. He didn't care whether she had nothing. He had made a point of keeping her from her life, telling her that college was for "other women" and not her. He had wanted her to concentrate on starting a family. If things were different, she could have been a nurse by now—she could have had everything she needed to start a life on her own. Instead, she had nothing, only the wreckage she had allowed him to create.

She hated him for what he'd done to her and the agony he was inflicting.

Unable to be held back any longer, tears poured from her eyes, coming so fast they splashed into her lap.

Let them pour. Let them rain down and purge her of the pain and shame she felt. Maybe if she cried long enough and hard enough, she would shrivel up and collapse in on herself like a spent balloon. David would be happy to see her gone. His life would be so much easier.

Maybe that could be her last gift to him—to disappear.

She envisioned his life with her dead. He would collect her life insurance. Then, he would find another woman. Take her on vacation on the profits of Heather's death. They would drink. Make love. Tell each other their passions. He would tell her the tales of his childhood. He'd tell her secrets he'd once whispered in Heather's ear after a long night of making love until their bodies ached and their sheets were dewy with sweat.

Rivers of tears sluiced down her cheeks, contorting her face in the rearview mirror. It was the perfect picture, her face ripped apart by pain. David would have loved to see her now. The mess he'd created.

He had played God with her, just like he did with everyone else.

She couldn't let him do this. She couldn't let him play God anymore. He needed to be stopped and she was the one to do it. She had nothing left to lose.

Wiping the tears from her face, she dialed her lawyer.

"Have you had a chance to look over my prenuptial agreement, Ms. Kohl?" she asked when the lawyer responded.

"Oh yes, Mrs. Sampson, I was just about to call you."

From the trepidation in Ms. Kohl's voice, Heather doubted what she said was true.

There was a rustle of paperwork before the lawyer continued. "Actually, I did find some things that are rather interesting. However, there are several amendments that may be upsetting."

She had already had enough for one day, but she steeled herself. Once she heard what she had to hear, it would be over.

"What?" Her tone was tight, like a bullwhip cracking in the air.

"First there is a clause that states if either of you is to separate and leave the home for more than seven days, that person will be held liable for all legal costs accrued during the divorce settlement." Ms. Kohl exhaled. "I've been in contact with Dr. Sampson's lawyer, Mr. Deschamps."

Heather cringed at the name. He would have been her first choice if she could have afforded him. The grayhaired lawyer was known statewide for his role in most high-end divorce cases. David was pulling out all the stops to make sure she got nothing.

"Mr. Deschamps said, in no uncertain terms, that Dr. Sampson will not be gone from your residence for longer than that seven day period. In short, Mrs. Sampson, Dr. Sampson will soon be moving back into your home, where he must reside for two uninterrupted weeks before he may leave again. If he doesn't stay for those two weeks, or if he should fail to return to your main residence, he will be responsible for not only his legal costs, but yours, as well."

She let the news sink in. David was going to come home. He wasn't the type to let the knife sit at the surface, he always pressed until he drew blood.

"May I leave?" The thought of living in the same household with David again made the bile rise in her throat.

"You may, but the same rules apply. If I may, Mrs. Sampson, I recommend you stay in your home. Let's keep things as civil and quiet as we can."

"Civil in the sense that we have an amicable divorce? That we don't steal each other's money?" Heather said, her voice coming from somewhere so deep it clawed at her throat.

"Has he done something I need to know about, Mrs. Sampson?"

"He took everything he could from our bank accounts." He'd left only the bare minimums, so that he didn't need her signature to officially close the accounts. "I have no money and no liquid assets." She twisted in her seat at her admission and the fear Ms. Kohl would quit after finding out that, for the moment, she wouldn't be paid.

"I'm new to divorce law, but I've seen this before. For now, send me your financial records and I'll try to prove he is misallocating your marital assets. At the very least, I can get you some funds to help you get back on your feet."

Finally, there was a glimmer of hope in the darkness. She would still be at others' mercy, but now it would only be until she could get her money back.

"Do you think you could get a job, some source of income while I work with Mr. Deschamps in getting some funds returned?"

She thought of Kevin's offer to watch the kids after school. He'd even offered her a room.

"I can."

"Great," Ms. Kohl said. "Now, there's another section here about extramarital affairs and their impact on the validity and terms of your agreement."

A man got into the truck that was parked next to her. He glanced over and looked at her as though he could hear her conversation. Heather couldn't bear the weight of his gaze and she looked away.

"What does that mean, Ms. Kohl?"

"As it reads, if it is proven you have an extra-marital relationship you get nothing, but if your husband has an extramarital affair, your prenup will be null and void."

"Okay." She thought of her kiss with Kevin. His lips had been hard and wanting, searching for more but resistant to taking things toward the bedroom. "What constitutes an extramarital affair?"

There was another rustle of paper as Ms. Kohl must have flipped through the prenup. "There's nothing that clearly defines what actions shall be defined as an extramarital affair, so that could be a way to get the entire prenup dismissed. If we can do that, we have a chance of getting you a fair and equitable division of assets."

"Would a kiss be considered an extramarital affair?" Heather asked, her voice low.

"Is there any evidence of the kiss? Photos? Videos?"

"No. Not that I know of."

"Well, unless there is evidence of Dr. Sampson kissing another woman, then there is little we can do. We need to find either some sort of proof or a credible witness to the event in order to pursue legal action."

Heather's cheeks burned. Ms. Kohl had misunderstood her meaning. She gave a light cough and looked around to make sure no one in the bank's parking lot was paying her any mind. "What if *I* kissed someone?"

"Oh… Well…" Ms. Kohl paused for a moment as she must have collected herself. "It would weaken our case, even though Montana is a no-fault state. I would recommend you don't put yourself in a position that would adversely affect any possible settlements."

If she found herself alone with Kevin again, she couldn't repeat her mistake. She couldn't allow her body to overrule her mind. "Not a problem, Ms. Kohl."

"In the meantime, you may want to start doing a little digging on your husband. You can do this yourself or you can hire a private investigator. If you can, we need to find direct evidence of an affair. That is, if David returns home. For now, the ball is in his court."

As usual David held the power position. At least she had a play. She could go home and get to work on building up her life while trying to analyze the fine details of his.

"Thank you, Ms. Kohl."

"You're very welcome. Please don't hesitate to contact me should you need anything else."

"Thank you."

"And Ms. Sampson?"

"Yes, Ms. Kohl?"

"I look forward to taking your husband down. Have a good afternoon." She hung up, not waiting for Heather's response.

For the first time since she had met her lawyer, she truly liked the woman. Maybe Ms. Kohl's being a new lawyer wasn't such a bad thing. As a newbie, she still had the passion to work hard to bring down her adversary. And she was still building her reputation. If she could win this case against the infamous pit bull, Mr. Deschamps, it could be a strong foundation for her career.

A career. That was something Heather was lacking. Until the two lawyers could come up with some agreement, she needed to come up with some way of making money.

Heather looked down at her phone and scrolled through her contacts. She dialed Kevin.

"Oh, hey, Heather. How did it go at the bank?" he said as soon as he answered.

She swallowed back the lump lodged in her throat. "Not as well as I'd hoped. He took everything."

"Are you okay? Do you need me to do anything?"

God, just hearing his voice made her want to run to

him, but she couldn't. She couldn't risk the damage an affair would cause with her divorce.

"Actually, you can help me."

You could hold me. Tell me everything is going to be okay.

"What do you need?"

"Actually, I was thinking maybe I could take you up on your offer and come to work for you for a while... maybe I could help with the kids?"

She couldn't control the insecurity that welled within her. If she had ever asked David for a job at his office, or in any part of the hospital for that matter, he would have told her to find something else.

"That would be great." Kevin sounded excited. "You'd be saving me. Having you full-time with the kids would really help me out."

She didn't know if she entirely believed him. She had been helping out with his kids for a while, spending an hour here and there after school, but he'd always made things work. Regardless, she was thankful.

"I'll pick the kids up from school today, okay?"

"That would be great," he said. "I have a meeting tonight. I don't know what time I'll be home."

"You want me to keep them at your house?" Heather wasn't sure what David would think, but that didn't matter anymore.

"You're not getting a hotel?"

"I... My lawyer didn't think it was a good idea."

"Oh. Well, I guess at least if you stay at my place for a while, you can make sure the kids get to bed at a reasonable hour." He sounded tired, and maybe a little upset.

After the kids were in bed, she would be nearly

alone, waiting until he came home. Her thighs tingled with unwelcome desire.

"That's fine, but…" She tried to think of something that would keep her heated desire at bay. *David.* Just the thought of having to go home to him turned her emotions cold.

Chapter Fourteen

Kevin stepped out of the crime lab, the evidence bag hanging limp from his shoulder.

He should have been concentrating on what he would say at tonight's meeting, and how he would play his hand; instead, all he could think about was Heather's dark hair. Everything about her seemed fragile, as though, if he reached out too fast or too hard, he risked breaking her or—worse—pushing her away.

There had been something in her voice when she had called, a supplicating tone with an undercurrent of tension, which reminded him of their kiss. The way her lips parted, inviting him to go deeper, to open his heart. Yet their kiss had been flavored with the forbidden.

She deserved someone better than David—someone who would treat her like the beautiful princess she was—even if that man wasn't him.

He imagined her in another man's arms and a strange, unwelcome wave of jealousy coursed through him.

He gripped the strap of his evidence bag so hard that it cut into his hand. He hitched the bag farther up his shoulder. Work needed his attention, not things he couldn't change.

He glanced back at the crime lab where he had dropped off his samples. The techs there had assured him the samples from Elke's house would take a few more days to analyze, and the new set from Brittany's maybe a week. Every moment that slipped by was upping the chances the perpetrator was going to get away. Maybe the fires would stop, maybe the arsonist would get scared after his run-in with Heather, but Kevin doubted he would get that lucky.

The perpetrator was getting bolder, looking in the back window of Brittany's home—and nearly being identified.

A couple walked by Kevin as they made their way out of the crime lab, the man's face pinched and the woman's eyes red. They reminded him of the many victims he had seen during his tenure. He couldn't let another fire happen. He couldn't let someone get hurt.

Kevin walked toward his truck. Detective Lawrence was leaning against the driver's door, his arms were crossed over his chest.

Lawrence used to work for the Drug Task Unit. To most, the man would have been an intimidating presence as he was built like a Mack truck on steroids, his neck disappearing between his boxy head and wide shoulders. To Kevin, he would always be the man whose favorite coffee mug had a picture of Hello Kitty.

Kevin stopped beside him. "Hey, Detective. Did you get the meeting set?"

"Seven o'clock, on the courthouse steps." Lawrence unfolded his arms. "The mayor wants to make a big show of it for the media. By the way, in case you were wondering, your battalion chief is a pain in the ass. He always so helpful?"

Kevin smirked. "Hiller's about as accommodating as a porcupine, but once you get to know him…" He paused as he thought about the BC. "Scratch that. You're right—he's always a pain in the ass."

Lawrence laughed as he pushed off from the truck. "So what do you have on our suspect? Anything I can help you with?"

Kevin pulled out the fire investigation report, the camera and his notebook and laid them on the hood of his truck. "Feel free to take a look."

Lawrence stepped beside him and picked up the fire reports. He studied them for a moment, flipping through the pages.

"Do you think it's possible your perp had been sleeping with both women, or at least been attempting to seduce them?"

Kevin thought of Brittany, her long blond hair draping like a curtain over her face, hiding the secrets in her eyes. She was beautiful and she seemed to have a good relationship with her husband, but that didn't mean that their marriage was perfect or that they didn't have secrets.

"It would be a strong motivator." Kevin leaned against the truck. "But so far this investigation is going nowhere."

"It's fun to be thrown a curveball once in a while, ain't it?" Lawrence said, glancing up. "Keeps us on our toes."

This case was doing that, but rather than being on his toes, Kevin felt more as if he was in a free fall with the ground nowhere in sight.

"I suppose. And hey, I appreciate your taking the time to lend me a hand. It's nice to have another set of eyes on this."

Detective Lawrence waved him off. "Taking bastards down is what keeps me going. We'll just have to make sure the district attorney will want to move on this. Right now, with everything you've shown me, there hasn't been much damage, no loss of life. Even if we file charges, she may decide to pass on this one."

"You think so? Even if this is a serial arsonist?"

"Two doesn't make a serial arsonist. If there were three on the other hand… But it all depends on the DA's mood. You know how it is. Sometimes they're busier than hell, other times what they take on is completely dependent on politics and the budget."

It seemed crazy to him that justice could only come at the price of loss of life or another person's home. Then again, he shouldn't have been surprised. He'd been a firefighter long enough to know that those who deserved to be caught and punished were often the ones who had enough experience with the legal system to know how to evade its grasp.

"This budget crap sounds familiar. Hiller has been on my back with these investigations. I think he shares the DA's opinion of the importance of prosecution. The only thing he's worried about is the department's bottom line."

"At least you have the media on your side. If they weren't covering this, it would've already been swept under the rug."

"I'm hoping it's going to help smoke out our perpetrator."

"What do you make of this guy?"

"He likes the control, the manipulation and the thrill."

"Then your subject will be there tonight." Lawrence nodded. "How do you think we can get an ID on him?"

"We need to bring up the ass-pucker factor. Give him something that only he'll see and realize the true meaning of. Something he won't be able to take his eyes off."

"I like it. You have something in mind?"

"I'm thinking the bottle of brake fluid." He grabbed his camera, flipped through the pictures until he pulled up the photo of the bottle stuffed under the bush. "We should take this picture, blow it up and make sure it gets plastered somewhere at the meeting that's out of the line of sight—somewhere the perp would have to make a special effort to see."

Lawrence took the camera and scanned through the rest of the pictures. He stopped at one of Brittany in her yard. "We should blow this one up, too. Then have the Miller woman come up and talk about her loss. The media will love it. Plus, it'll build the pressure for your department to get a hold on this perp and give you more time. You're going to need it."

"In the meantime, I want to speak to Elke. See if I can dig a little more information out of her. Maybe I can get her to come." He took the camera from Lawrence. "Can you help me get all the pieces in place for the meeting? I'll email you the pictures. Can you get them printed?"

"No problem. Tonight, when we get things rolling, I'll talk for a while. Give you an intro and the mayor a little lip service. While I'm working, you look for your man."

Kevin nodded. "Let's get this bastard."

Chapter Fifteen

Heather sat in her car, waiting for Lindsay in front of the elementary school. Once the bell rang, children poured from the doors. They swarmed toward the parking lot in a wave of dropped papers and swinging backpacks. Near the back, with her pack sagging from her shoulders, was Lindsay.

She waved at the girl, catching her attention, and Lindsay made her way over.

"Am I riding with you today?" Lindsay asked.

"Yep, your dad asked me to pick you and your brother up," Heather said.

Lindsay opened the back door and thumped down in the seat. "We don't have to pick up Colter."

"Why?" Heather checked to make sure Lindsay was buckled in before she merged into the meandering stream of cars leaving the school.

"Colter has a game today."

"I totally forgot."

"It's okay. Dad forgets about the games all the time."

Heather glanced in the mirror at Lindsay. "Do you think that's upsetting Colter?"

"I dunno, but he and Dad have been mad at each

other a lot." Lindsay shrugged. "Does that mean Colter's going to leave?"

"What do you mean, Lindsay?"

"Well," Lindsay said, looking at her. "You know. You and David fight. That's why he left. People fight and then one of them leaves."

"No, Lindsay," Heather said, her heart lurching. "When people love each other, they don't leave just because they fight. Colter and your dad love each other. I promise."

"If Dad loved Colter, he would come to all the games, just like you do."

She had to get Kevin to come. She couldn't stand seeing the disappointment etched in Lindsay's face, disappointment that would be echoed on Colter's face when he realized his father wasn't there.

"Your dad loves you both—there's no doubt in my mind. But I'll talk to your dad about coming to the game. I'm sure he's probably already on his way," she lied.

Lindsay shrugged. "Whatever."

Once Heather was parked in the high school lot, she dialed Kevin, but the call went to voice mail. She left a message, telling him she and Lindsay hoped to see him at the game.

Then she took the girl's hand and went to find a seat on the risers. Her eyes scanned the first players who came out of the locker room. A sensation crept through her, telling her something was wrong when she didn't find Colter among the last players who stepped onto the field.

Heather made her way down the risers and toward the dugout.

Mr. T, his coach, had his back to her. His wide neck had been sunburned early on in the season, but now, after a month in the sun, it had taken on a nice toasted caramel color.

"Coach T?"

He turned slightly, like moving his entire frame was too much of an effort. "Mrs. Sampson. What can I do for you?"

She stepped closer. "Hey, Coach, I was just noticing Colter wasn't out of the locker room yet."

Mr. T frowned. "He's not *in* the locker room. I took him out of today's game. He's been missing too many practices."

"What?"

The coach must have had it wrong. Colter wasn't the type to miss baseball. It was his life. So much so that she wouldn't have been surprised if Colter slept with his mitt tucked under his pillow.

"I sent a note home." He stabbed his toe into the dirt.

"But, Coach—" she started to argue, but he cut her off with a wave of his hand.

"Hated doing it. But he was a bad example for the younger players. They need to see that just because you're a top player doesn't mean you can cut practice and expect to play—even during semifinals."

She could understand, but this wasn't like Colter. He wasn't cocky and caught up in all the trappings that came with being a star athlete. He was better than that. He'd always kept his humility.

"I'm sure he isn't cutting practice because he thinks he's some hotshot. He…he isn't that kind of kid. I know him. I swear."

Mr. T nodded, but he stared at the dirt. "I wouldn't

have thought so either, but lately there's been something going on with him. Hasn't been acting right. Tried to talk to him. Didn't get much. Just said he was busy."

Busy? For his entire life Colter had only been busy with two things—baseball and homework.

"I'll talk to Colter. Good luck with your game."

"Let him know I'm looking forward to getting him back, but he needs to show me he's serious. I know there're a few college scouts that have got their eyes on him."

She nodded. Colter had been talking about going to Washington for baseball since he first started playing. That had been his dream. Whatever was going on must have been major if he'd let it hold him back, but what could it possibly be?

"I'll let him know." She tried to smile, but her lips barely registered her attempt. Between her life's upheavals, Brittany's and now Colter's it didn't feel right to even try to fake happiness.

She made her way back to the stands where Lindsay looked up from the book that had kept her busy when Heather was gone.

"What's the matter?" the girl asked.

"Nothing, sweetheart, everything's okay."

Maybe she couldn't control the storm in her own life, but she vowed to be there for Colter, Lindsay and Kevin. They needed her.

THE FRONT DOOR of Kevin's house was unlocked when they got home, but there was no sign of Colter anywhere, not even in his room, according to Lindsay who'd run to check.

"Is there anywhere else you think he'd go?" Heather asked her, but the girl only shook her head.

"I'm going to run to my house and give your dad a call. Will you be okay for a few?" From there, she could talk to Kevin openly.

"I'll be fine," Lindsay said.

Heather walked to the front door just as Lindsay clicked on the television and the sound of children's voices filled the empty house.

She made her way to her house. In the middle of the living room was David. His scrub bottoms were heaped in a pile by the foot of the couch and his top was thrown over the table next to the door. He sat on the couch wearing only his black skintight boxer briefs. He looked up at her with shock on his face.

"I thought you were at the baseball game. It's Friday." His look of surprise was quickly replaced by anger.

She didn't know what to say or do. The last thing she had expected was to find David nearly naked on the couch.

She couldn't stand looking at his sweaty, personal-trainer sculpted chest, and she quickly looked away. "I needed something."

"Now isn't a good time, Heather." He looked toward the steps leading upstairs.

"This isn't a good time? You may have been forced to move back in, but this is my house."

"How dare you talk to me like that?" David said as he stood up and slipped on his scrub pants. "I paid for this damn place. Without me, you'd have nothing."

"Stop it, David," she whispered.

"What did you just say to me?" He stormed toward

her, his face so close she could see the sweat oozing from each pore on his nose.

She stood still, afraid that if she dared to move a muscle, David would lose control. "I said…" She spoke slowly, the words curdling in her fear.

"What?" He grabbed hold of her arms and squeezed her. "Just like I thought. Nothing. There's nothing in your damn head."

She stepped back, out of his grasp, and out of the anger-laced scent of his hot breath. "Aren't you supposed to be at work? And why are you half-naked?"

"I took the day off." He turned away from her and grabbed his shirt, slipping it back on. "I'm moving back in."

"I know." Trepidation churned in her belly. She didn't want to share this house with him. The truth hit hard. She wanted to be in Kevin's house, with him. Kevin would never treat her the way David had. Instead, he would worship her, just as he had when he'd kissed her.

She recalled that moment in his arms, his lips against hers… When he had pulled away, it hadn't been to shame her, it had been to save her from regret. In that moment, he had saved her in the only way he could. And now, when she needed even more help, he was there for her again, offering her a job, a safe place to stay and a distraction from the agony of her life.

She would give anything to be with a man who would raise her up instead of break her down. For so long, she hadn't realized how badly David treated her, how wrong it was when he grabbed her beneath the arm, pinching her until her flesh bruised. She had blindly loved him. She had forgiven him his trespasses. She had taken the blame and accepted fault for his actions.

Every time he'd lost his temper or raged, she had accepted responsibility—if she just hadn't said what she said, or worn what she'd worn, he would never have lost control. She was living the cycle of abuse and now was her chance to start to break free.

David looked at her, his icy gaze filled with contempt.

"If you're going to stay here, I'm not," she said. "At least not until I have to, as the prenuptial agreement stipulates. For the next few days, David, the house is yours."

David's jaw went slack. "What?" He looked at her with confusion.

She turned away from him and made her way upstairs. Grabbing her suitcase, she threw it on the bed and started packing. Now was the time to rekindle her dreams, remember who she was and stop living a life that was no longer her own.

Chapter Sixteen

Kevin pulled up to Elke Goldstein's house. He'd tried to call her, but there had been no answer and, once again, he found himself running after shadows.

The windows were open, probably in her attempt to rid the scent of smoke from her house until she could get the money from her insurance company to pay for a restoration company. The neighbor Mrs. Jones and her son were out in the front yard watering the garden, and she waved as he made his way to Elke's front door.

"She's not home," Mrs. Jones yelled.

"You know where she went?"

"Some guy in a white car came to pick her up a few hours ago." She stopped watering for a moment. "She didn't say where she was going, but I've seen the car there before… In fact, I think the guy driving it was the guy she had over the night of the fire."

Elke had told him she hadn't seen or heard from the man since the day of the fire and that she didn't have his phone number. Now, all of sudden, they were meeting? He had told her to contact him if she heard from the man again. His hackles rose. Elke knew more than what she had told him, but why had she kept the truth from him?

Kevin made his way down the steps and toward Mrs. Jones. "Do you know the model of the car?"

"Well, it was white. Small." She shook her head. "My husband is the one who knows cars."

"That's fine, no worries. Can you tell me if the car was a sports car or a sedan?"

She looked back toward him. "Sports car. Pretty flashy. You don't see them a lot."

Kevin's mind went to David and his white Porsche Carrera. There was only one like it in Missoula. He shook off the thought. Just because someone he knew drove a car that somewhat resembled the one described didn't mean David was his man.

Then again…

"Was the car a Porsche by chance? Has an emblem on the hood that's yellow, red and black with a horse."

"Yep." Mrs. Jones smiled with relief. "That's it. Looks like a family crest kind of shape." She made the shape with her fingers.

Elke had admitted the man was her lover, which meant David was cheating on Heather.

His anger flared, but he tamped down his emotions as he struggled to remain logical. Now wasn't the time to let his emotions cloud his judgment. It never ended well.

For a moment, he was back at the last fire he'd fought three years ago. He was standing in the doorway of the burning house, tongues of fire licking the walls around him as he made his way inside. A child had been on the second floor, an eight-year-old girl, and her screams were nearly drowned out by the whipping crackle and roar of the beast.

Many nights he'd heard that voice in his dreams. He'd awaken to the smell of smoke, a scent that had invaded his dreams and spilled out into his reality. He'd run down the hall to Lindsay's or Colter's room, only to remember that the smell and the sounds were nothing more than a dream.

That was the moment he'd lost his edge.

He couldn't let that happen again.

Just because David had been with Elke didn't mean he was having an affair, and just because David was at the scene didn't mean he had started the blaze. It just meant maybe he knew something, something he had been trying to keep hidden. Or maybe the man Mrs. Jones had seen wasn't David at all, maybe she was just mistaken. Elke had made a point of telling him the man who'd been to her house had been named Anthony, not David.

There were so many possibilities. He just needed to follow the leads and hope that he could find his arsonist and stop the fires. But what if the investigation led him straight to David? What if David *was* the one responsible?

In many ways, David fit the profile. He liked to be in control and dominate women. Liked to play God. Thought he was above the law. The fires had been thought out and extremely ballsy. The only thing that didn't fit the profile was the fact David wasn't sexually inadequate—he didn't fit the bill as a man who was regularly turned down by women. David was confident and, from the way he'd soaked in Brittany's attentions at the barbecue, easygoing when it came to women. Well, all women except his wife.

He treated Heather as though she was a possession he owned and could use as he wanted, or throw away when he found something better.

No matter how much Kevin despised the man, it

didn't make him the arsonist. With Mrs. Jones's sighting, it made him a suspect. And Kevin's only solid lead.

He turned to Mrs. Jones. "Thanks for your help. If you see anything else, please let me know. I appreciate your cooperation."

Kevin rushed back to his truck. He would need to talk to David to find out exactly why he had been going to Elke's house and to see if he could find something that would tie David to the fire at Brittany's. If everything went well, he could nail David.

He got into his truck and dialed Elke. No answer.

He looked down at his screen as a voice mail popped up from Heather.

Had she found out something about David?

He went to his voice mail and was met with Heather's voice. She sounded somewhat frantic as she reminded him about Colter's game.

Damn it. Not again.

He was so sick of failing his son. Erasing the message, he threw his phone on top of his dashboard, pushing the envelope from Colter's coach into view.

He picked up the envelope and ripped it open. Each word seared into him.

Dear Mr. Jensen,
I'm writing to let you know that due to Colter's recent uptick in absences, his dropping GPA (the only class he's currently not at risk of failing is auto shop) and his overall disregard for authority, I have made the decision to bench him…

The letter continued, but Kevin stopped reading. He glanced at the clock. He had three hours before tonight's meeting. Between now and then, he needed to question David and talk to Colter about what was going on.

If he went to see David first, he would be failing his son again.

He was tired of getting pulled in a thousand directions. Tired of always making the right choice for one, but the wrong choice for another. Well, this time, he was going to do what was right for his family. His son needed him.

He turned the truck around as he dialed Colter.

"Hello?" Colter answered, sounding annoyed. "Why is everyone calling?"

"Because everyone's worried. I just got a letter from your coach. You want to talk to me about it? What's going on with you, Colter?"

"Damn it, Dad. I don't have time for this."

"Really? I would think that if you aren't at baseball and you're failing your classes that you would have plenty of time." The moment the words passed his lips he wished he could take them back. He'd get nowhere if he was confrontational.

"I have to go, Dad. I have crap to do."

He tried to control his anger. "What are you doing?"

"I—" Colter paused. "I'm studying. I have a Spanish test tomorrow."

He wanted to believe him even though every bit of him thought Colter was lying. "Really?"

"Look, Dad, it's not like I wanted to be taken out of the game. I just have to deal with some stuff and then everything'll be fine. Now, I have to go study. Okay?"

"Okay, but be home before five. I'm not done talking with you. We need to figure some things out, bud."

"Fine."

The line went dead.

Heather's car was parked in front of his house when Kevin got home. Lindsay was sitting on the front porch with a book in her hands and she looked up as he approached. Her eyes were full of storm clouds.

He knelt beside her, taking her hand in his. "You okay, sweetheart?"

"Yeah, Daddy." She smiled, but the movement of her lips didn't match the look in her eyes. "Colter isn't here. Mrs. Sampson's worried. I shouldn't have told her that he wasn't in his room."

"Sweetheart, it's not *your* fault."

Lindsay nodded, but her gaze moved to the ground. "But, Daddy, I got Colter in trouble. He's gonna be so mad at me."

"You didn't get him in trouble. Colter got himself in this mess. He's not mad at you."

"Yes, he is. The other day I walked into his room without knocking. He screamed at me, Daddy."

He smiled as he thought of all the reasons a teenage boy would be angry at his sister for barging into his room. "Don't worry. But maybe next time knock. It's no big deal. Really. He loves you."

"That's not what he said. He said he wished that I was never born."

That didn't sound like Colter. Ever since Lindsay had been born, he had doted on his baby sister, and when Allison had died, Colter had picked up where she had left off, taking on a role of the other parent and helping to raise his sister.

Maybe that was where everything had started to go wrong. Maybe Kevin should never have let his son take on so much responsibility. Maybe he should have just let him be a kid.

Kevin squeezed Lindsay's hand. "I'm sorry. I'm sure Colter didn't mean what he said. I'll make sure that he talks to you. Okay?"

Lindsay nodded, but he could feel from the way her little hand tensed that she didn't really believe him. Would a mother have handled the situation better? What would Allison have done?

It had been so long since she'd left him that he could just barely remember her face, or the sound of her voice, but he knew she would have done the right thing, something that would have ended with a hug and Lindsay smiling.

No matter how many years passed or how much experience he had, he always felt inadequate as a father. Would it ever change?

"Is Heather still here?" he asked.

"No." Lindsay shook her head. "She had to run back to her house. She's been gone for a while."

He looked over to Heather and David's white house. The lights were on in the living room and David's Porsche was in the driveway.

He gritted his teeth. David had better not have touched her.

"Why don't you go inside, Lindsay?" He helped her stand up and wrapped his arms around her, pulling her into his chest. "I love you, baby girl." He let go of her and lifted her chin so he could look into her eyes. "No matter what happens, that will never change. Everything's going to get better. Trust me."

Lindsay smiled. "I love you, too, Daddy."

It was amazing how fast a few sweet words could mend the spirit.

"I'll be right back."

She walked to the door and twisted the handle. "Okay, Daddy."

He went to his truck and took out his notepad and investigation report and then turned to the Sampson house. The television's blue light flickered in the windows. As he made his way across the yard, he felt like a dead man walking.

Logic. Logic had to be his plan. He couldn't go in there and let David see how he was really feeling. And he certainly couldn't go in there and punch the bastard in the throat like he wanted to.

He rapped on the door, the hollow sound reverberating in the empty street.

"Heather, answer the door!" David yelled from somewhere inside the house.

She didn't answer, but at least she was there.

"Damn woman," David growled as his footsteps moved toward the door. It opened with a creak. His frown tightened. "What're you doing here? Didn't get enough of my wife the other night?"

"What are you talking about?" Kevin took a step back, but forced himself to stop retreating.

"I caught her doing her walk of shame. She tried to lie to me. To tell me nothing happened between you two, but she's always been a terrible liar."

His fists tightened at his sides, but he didn't move. "Nothing happened, David." The man's name felt like ash in his mouth. "Heather's just a friend. Nothing more."

His thoughts flashed to her lips pressed against his, the sweet flavor of her kiss and the heat of her body.

"You're just as bad a liar as she is, Kev. The good news for you is that I don't care. Not about her and definitely not about you or what you do to her. She's not my problem anymore."

"Funny you should talk to me about lying, *Dave*. Where were you last Wednesday night?" He opened his notebook.

"Why do you care?" David leaned against the door. "Need to know my schedule so you can have more time with my wife?"

Kevin reached into his back pocket and pulled out his wallet. He opened it to the badge he kept for moments like these. "Dr. Sampson, my name is Kevin Jensen, I'm the Missoula City fire inspector and I'm here to ask you a few questions."

"Are you kidding me? You're really going to pull the *inspector* crap with me?" David laughed. "Well, I haven't done anything and I don't have any information to give you."

"I'll be the judge of that. You just need to answer a few questions."

"What right do you have to ask me anything?"

"Dr. Sampson, you can answer my questions willingly or I can have a detective show up to your door and take you into custody. Right now, we have reason to believe you are a suspect in an arson."

David's face drained of its color and his eyes shifted to the left. "I've done nothing."

Kevin closed his wallet and slipped it back into his pocket. Maybe Kevin couldn't punch him in the throat, but he could still make him suffer. "If you answer my questions willingly and to the best of your knowledge,

I will make sure to note your cooperation in my investigation report."

David's gaze fell to the notepad in Kevin's hands. "I don't know what you're talking about."

"Let's start again. Where were you on Wednesday night at about 8:00 p.m.?"

David stepped back, recoiling from the question. He looked back over his shoulder as if he was looking for a place to run, but there was no running. There was no hiding. There were only questions and answers.

"Like I said, Dr. Sampson, if you choose, I can have you taken into custody. Knowing you and your reputation as an upstanding doctor within the community, I'm sure this would be the last thing you'd want anyone to know about."

David turned back and faced him. His eyes were dark, like two black holes absorbing all the energy and matter that sank into them. Kevin looked away, an illogical part of him fearing that if he looked too long, those gluttonous holes would consume him.

"Wednesday… I had a full schedule of fresh caths that day and my rounds."

"What time did you leave the hospital for the day?"

"I don't know. Maybe five." David continued to lean against the door frame, but his body stiffened, almost defensive.

"Then where did you go?"

David opened his mouth to speak then shut it and gave an exasperated sigh. "I'm sure Heather told you I asked for a divorce. Is that why you're doing this? To act like her knight in shining armor? Think you can help her by coming after me?"

"I assure you, Dr. Sampson, my actions have nothing to do with my personal life. I have a job to do, and right now that job involves questioning you."

David grumbled.

"Now, if you had left Heather, I assume that means you didn't come home after work on Wednesday night?"

"I went to dinner. There's a place not far from the hospital. I go there all the time."

"What restaurant was it?" Kevin pressed.

"Er…" David looked away. "Ruby's."

"Do you remember the name of your waitress?" Kevin quelled his excitement at taking one leap forward in his investigation.

"I think her name was Deer or something."

"Elke?"

"Sure." David glared at him and he shifted his body as if he was a snake trying to slither from danger.

"Where did you go after leaving the diner?"

"I—" David stopped and pushed himself away from the door frame. "Look, do I need to have a lawyer present?"

"Right now, Dr. Sampson, you are not under arrest. I'm merely asking you some questions to help further my investigation. Should you be arrested, you can obtain a lawyer at that time. But if you have not taken an active role in any arson, you should have nothing to worry about."

Sometimes he loved amping up the ass-pucker factor and making someone step into a box that they themselves had built.

"Well, like I said, I didn't *do* anything."

"Then this little tête-à-tête shouldn't be problem." Kevin made some notes in an attempt to increase the pressure. "So what time did you leave Ruby's and where did you go?"

"I guess it was about seven."

"And?"

David stepped outside and closed the front door behind him. "If I tell you the truth, it would be confidential. Wouldn't it?"

"What you tell me is confidential, unless there is a reason for further law enforcement to become involved."

"You won't tell Heather anything?"

His stomach clenched. He needed to be a man who could be trusted to do the right thing, even if that meant withholding something from the woman he cared about.

"Dr. Sampson, it is my hope that nothing you tell me will put either you or me in a compromising position."

David stared at him, crossing his arms over his chest. Kevin had seen a hundred men do the same thing when they were about to admit guilt. The simple action of crossing their arms was instinctual, a primordial urge to protect the core.

He didn't need to ask the question to know the answer, but he had to hear David answer it. "Where did you go when you left the diner?"

"Elke and I went back to her place."

"And?"

"We played Twister. Come on. Do you need me to spell it out for you?"

He could never tell Heather. Unlike David, she couldn't just cross her arms and protect her heart. No. Her heart was already broken—he'd seen it in her eyes, felt it in the way her lips searched his. David's infidelity would only make it worse. He couldn't even stand the thought of inflicting more pain.

David's secret was a weight he could shoulder, a weight he could keep from bearing down on her.

"So you had sex with Elke. What time did you leave?"

"I don't know. It had to be about 2:00 a.m."

"You played Twister for six hours?"

David's lips turned up into a smirk. "What can I say?" He shrugged.

"You can't expect me to believe it went on for six hours."

David laughed. "No, we watched a movie first. Some stupid romantic comedy." He shrugged. "I turned in my man card for a few hours but it got me laid. I guess it worked out."

For a moment, he imagined holding Heather in his arms, her body resting against his as they watched a movie. It was such a simple thing, those minutes spent together, not speaking, just enjoying the story before them. Those moments were something he could only wish for.

He stared at David and, for the first time, he really noticed the fine lines around David's eyes and the wrinkles on his brow.

Kevin could never understand how Heather fell in love with him—then again, most of the time David hid his real self behind a line of crap a mile wide. When he'd first met the man, Kevin had thought he was all right, even kind of funny. There was no going back to that; he'd seen the monster behind the lab coat.

"Did you return to your house at any point after you left at 2:00 a.m. on Wednesday?"

"I stopped by to pick Heather up for Brittany's barbecue and then I dropped her off. After that I left and got a hotel room. Haven't been back to my house until…"

"Until today?" Kevin tapped his pen on his notebook.

David jerked. "Yeah, until today." His body tightened and his jaw clenched.

"Why did you tell Ms. Goldstein your name was Anthony?"

He answered with a tight laugh. "Look, I thought I would have a little fun. There's no harm in that, right?" He looked at Kevin and seemed to mentally backpedal. "I only gave her a fake name because I never thought I'd see her again."

"But you did. Why did you go to see Elke again today?"

"I heard about the fire and I thought I'd talk to her. Set her straight. Tell her the truth about who I was. I didn't do anything. I thought I could make her feel better."

It struck Kevin as funny that this man, who cared nothing about the woman he'd married, seemed to care more about a woman he'd met in a diner. Just when he thought he couldn't like David any less, David surprised him.

"Where's Elke now?"

"I got her a hotel room near mine," David said. "Her house hasn't been fixed up yet. I thought it was the least I could do."

Kevin jabbed his pen into the paper as he thought about how David had emptied his bank accounts so Heather couldn't have access to any funds, only to, a few hours later, spend money on a hotel room for his mistress.

"Is there anyone who can vouch that you left Elke's house at 2:00 a.m. Wednesday morning?"

"Sure. Call anyone working in the Heart Center. I was the on-call doctor and was called into work at two-thirty. I had to come in for a fifty-six-year-old woman with a MI, a myocardial infarction. I had her in the Heart Center until about five-thirty."

Kevin flipped back in his notes, where it said the fire had been reported at 5:03 a.m. So, the jerk had an alibi. Of course he would have to verify David's whereabouts, but he had a feeling it would be rock solid. Surely David knew the hospital was under constant video surveillance. No way would he lie about being there.

David was guilty of many things, but no matter how much Kevin wanted to arrest him and send him to prison, David probably wasn't the arsonist he was looking for.

Then again, maybe David was lying. He had one hell of a reputation for it. Plus he had to know that, at the very least, it would take Kevin a few hours to pull enough strings to check his alibi.

Chapter Seventeen

Heather watched from her bedroom window as Kevin walked back across their lawn and toward his house. Just as he was about to make his way through the hedges, he looked back, almost as if he could sense her watching. Catching his gaze, she couldn't help but notice the dark circles under his eyes and the pain in his expression. She tried to wave to him, but he had already turned away. Her heart ached to see his face again, even if it was only a glance.

For a moment, she considered running outside, catching him and asking him exactly what was wrong to see if she could help.

What had David said?

She grabbed her filled suitcase, heavy with the mementos of her past and hopes for the future, and she made her way downstairs.

"What did you do, David?"

"What did *I* do? What in the hell are you talking about, woman?" David growled, slamming the door shut.

"What's the matter with Kevin?"

David laughed, his sound low and menacing. "Of

course that's who you would care about. You don't care about me. You never have and you never will."

"Sorry, David, I'm just following your example. You haven't cared about me in years."

"What is wrong with you, Heather? These past few days, you've been different." He stared at her as though he was trying to find a loose thread in her resolve, one he could pull until she steadily unraveled. Well, he could search all he wanted, but he wouldn't find it. "I know what you did. You've been having an affair with Kevin. You can't deny it. I can see it on you."

She let out a shocked laugh. Who was David to call her out? He'd left her standing on the side of the road. He'd made her feel worthless. He'd called her every name that he thought would degrade her not only as a woman but as a person. And now he was going to chastise her?

No more.

"How *dare* you, David. You have no right to say anything to me. You may have thought I wasn't good enough, but all I've ever tried to do is make you happy." Her hands shook with anger. "The best thing you ever did for me was to empty our bank accounts. If it hadn't been for that, David, I would've kept on being your fool. I would've kept listening to your lies when you didn't come home. I would've believed you when you told me you'd been at work even though I could smell another woman's perfume on your skin."

The hard lines around David's mouth softened and his mouth pulled into an O.

She lifted up the handle on her suitcase and rolled it to the door. "While I'm gone, I want you to move into the guest room. You're no longer welcome in my bedroom or in my bed. This marriage is truly over."

She opened the door and stepped outside.

"Heather, wait!" David's voice was a tone too high. "The second you walk out that door, you're going to have nothing and no one. No one is ever going to love you."

She slammed the door on everything that was David. If he was what love was, she didn't need it.

She wheeled her suitcase down the driveway and toward Kevin's house.

There was no going back.

Excitement raced through her, but fear was close on its heels.

She would have no one, but how would that be different than what her life had been? The nights David had sat down with her for dinner, the mornings they'd been together in bed, he'd not really been there. His mind was always on something else. For the past few years, she had been alone. She just hadn't realized it.

She made her way up Kevin's driveway as his front door opened. The light from his dining room was on behind him, making him look as though he was basked in golden rays.

"Are you okay, Heather?" Kevin asked.

She nodded.

He took her suitcase from her, his warm hand brushing against hers. "I'm glad you're here."

"I can't believe it… I walked out on him." She looked at Kevin, but no matter how hard she tried, he wouldn't meet her gaze. "What did he say to you?"

"Don't worry, everything's okay." He turned away from her and led her inside.

She wanted to stop him, to turn him around and have him face her, to have him tell her why he couldn't look her in the eyes.

Why did David have to ruin everything? Couldn't he just let her have one thing that wasn't going to hell? Everything he had touched in her life, all the way down to her spirit, he had broken.

"Are you sure that it's okay if I stay, Kevin? I can go. I'm sure that I can stay with—" She stopped before she said Brittany. Her only other friend didn't have a place in her life for Heather's mess. She had her hands full dealing with the fire at her house. "I can stay at a hotel or something."

"You're not staying at a hotel." Kevin set her bag next to the wall, but his movements were awkward and tight. "You're welcome to stay here as long as you need."

"Kevin, I... Thank you." She didn't know what to say. Thank you just didn't seem like enough when what she really wanted to say was that he was part of the reason she had the strength to leave.

He had shown her there could be more in the world; that there could be something besides heartbreak and the constant thoughts that she could be doing something more to make someone else happy, even if that meant being miserable in her own skin.

Kevin had saved her life and he probably didn't even realize it.

She moved toward him. She wanted to take in his scent, the safe edge of soap mixed with the dangerous perfume of smoke. She'd loved that heady mix since she had met him. In truth, she wanted so much more.

For a moment she imagined him lifting her into his arms and taking her to his bedroom...and showing her exactly how good she could feel. She warmed as she imagined his lips running down her body, his hands cupping her curves…

What it would have been like to be utterly his.

She stepped closer, hoping he would wrap his arms around her, pull her in tight and make her feel whole.

He didn't move; instead he looked down the hallway toward the children's rooms. A look of concern flickered over his features.

Lindsay's door was closed and her music was playing, but she could just make out the sounds of his daughter talking on her phone.

"Is Colter home yet?" Heather asked.

Kevin shook his head. "Not yet. He said he's studying."

From his tone, she could tell he was worried.

He looked down at his watch and his face darkened.

"Is everything okay?"

"He should be home by now."

"Don't worry. I'm sure he'll be home soon."

"I'm not. I think he lied to me. I don't think he had any intention of listening. He's been lying a lot lately. But what am I supposed to do?"

She thought of Colter and what his coach had told her. "Has he given you any clues about what is going on with him? Did he break up with a girl or something?"

Kevin finally looked at her. His eyes were filled with a tempest, and as she stared she could have sworn there was a flash of lightning somewhere deep within the squall.

"Colter hasn't talked to me in months." He looked away. "I don't know my own son."

"That's not true, Kevin." She took his hand in hers. "You're a great father."

He shook his head. "No, I'm not. That's the problem. I've been focused on everything except my kids. This week just proved it."

"Stop. That's not true. Just because you're busy doesn't mean you aren't focused on your kids. You do the best you can do."

"Clearly, that isn't enough." He motioned toward Colter's room. "If it was, Colter would be at home or on the baseball field right now, not running off to God-only-knows-where and doing God-only-knows-what."

"Being a parent isn't about being perfect, Kevin. Every teenager goes through a hard time. It's a rite of passage."

"But I don't even know why he's acting out." He walked across the living room to the bookshelves. "I've read all of these stupid things," he said, pointing at the rows of parenting books. "And I still managed to screw it all up."

"No you didn't, Kevin." She followed him across the room. "You have a wonderful daughter and son who love you more than anything. Just because one of them is going through a hard time doesn't make it your fault. I may not know much about parenting, but I know all about guilt. And right now, your guilt isn't helping."

"I can't just stand here and wait for him to come home. What if he's hurt?"

Seeing the anguish on his face, she reached out to him. Her palm cradled his cheek. "If you needed proof you're a good father, there it is, Kevin. If you were as bad a father as you think you are, you wouldn't care. You wouldn't be worried."

"What can I do, Heather? I need to protect him."

She lowered her hand and it felt deprived of him. "Right now you need to trust him. I know it's hard. I know. But he'll come home. When he does, you need to be here for him and, most importantly, you need to talk to him."

His pain was palpable and no matter what she said it didn't seem to subside. In fact, the more she spoke the darker his eyes grew.

"Why does everything have to take a turn for the worst?"

She laughed. "Call me a cynic, but isn't that what life is? Constant upheavals only broken up by quick glimpses of what could be?"

Her face burned as she stared at him and she was struck by her dreams of what "could be."

Some of the darkness in his eyes dissipated. "I don't know what I'd do without you."

"You'd definitely have less to deal with." She smiled.

"That's not true. I would just have to deal with all this alone."

The floodgate seemed to break within him and he rushed to her and took her in his arms. His lips pressed against hers in a glorious cloud of want, the pheromone-laced heat of his tongue flicking against her lower lip, coaxing her to open. His hand moved down her back, his thumb rubbing the skin of her back as it moved lower to her jean-hugged curves.

He pulled back, his forehead against hers, the moisture of his breath dampening her lips. His breath was ragged when he finally spoke. "I know this is wrong, but I've wanted this for so long."

They were the words she longed to hear. No response

she gave him could convey her desire. Instead of speaking, she took hold of the waistband of his black uniform pants and led him down the hall toward his bedroom.

When they entered the darkened room, she locked the door behind them.

Pressing her back against the door, she stopped and stared at him. "I want you, Kevin. I've wanted you for so long."

"Are you sure that you want to do this?"

She wasn't sure of anything the way she sure of that. Her life was in turmoil, rocked by a brutal storm, and the only safe harbor was the one she'd find in this man's arms. She needed to feel him inside her. She needed to know someone cared about her, someone wanted her. If they were going to sleep together, it was a risk, but she couldn't believe it would be a mistake. Not with Kevin.

She nodded at him. "Just be quiet," she said, pushing him down on the bed and climbing on top.

"As you wish." He laughed, pulling her down to him, her body supported by his. His kisses moved down her neck as he lifted up her shirt and then unclasped her bra. Her entire body ached as she yielded to his firm touch and the gentle movement of his lips over her skin.

His hand moved up and he cupped her breast, his thumb gently rubbing over her responding nub, making her desire deepen.

She stood up again so she could open his pants and boxers and, in one swift motion, pull them down his legs and drop them to the floor. His legs were covered in a fine layer of caramel-colored hair and higher up his thigh, the color of his hair darkened.

Kevin unbuttoned her pants. He slipped them down her legs in a slow descent, and with each slip of the fabric he followed with a kiss to her fevered skin. She had never wanted a man like this, not with every cell of her being. And no other man had made her feel what Kevin was making her feel now. For once she felt alive. Her body quaked and heated as Kevin's mouth traveled over her hills and valleys.

He stood up, wrapping his arms around her, and lifted her body to meet his. As she linked her legs behind him, he moved her against the wall, her back pressing against the cold paint, making the heat of him inside her intensify.

She felt guilty about many things, but making love right here, right now was something she'd never regret.

Chapter Eighteen

Kevin ran his finger down Heather's side, tracing the slope of her hip, the naked arc he had always imagined but never thought he would see. Her eyes were closed and her body relaxed under his fingertips. She wasn't asleep, just reveling in the aftermath of a torrid love-making session.

He was a lucky man.

She looked so happy, happier than she had in a long time, and he had made her feel that way.

But she was still married to him.

He pushed back a strand of hair from her neck. She was so beautiful. He would never understand why David had treated her the way he did. How did he not realize what a special woman she was, or how lucky he was to have had her?

If Heather was Kevin's wife, he would never treat her the way David had. He would never cheat, never berate her or call her names. She would be his everything, not something to put down and kick around.

Then again, just because they'd had sex didn't mean that she was his. No. For all he knew, he was just a rebound to her, someone to help her forget about David.

Was it possible she knew about David's infidelity?

He couldn't tell her, but if the arson investigation went to court, it was likely Elke would be called to the stand and her whereabouts would be put to question. She'd have to tell the court where she had been, and with whom. David's secret would be out, and Heather would know Kevin had kept the truth from her.

She'd been lied to enough that, undoubtedly, if she found out he had been keeping it from her, it would be hard to make her understand why. There was no right answer, no right thing to do.

Maybe if he didn't push so hard, and if he listened to Hiller and swept the fires under the rug, it would be for the best. Heather wouldn't have to learn the truth, the chief would be happy and Kevin could concentrate on the kids a little more. If he pulled away from the investigation, maybe it would be for the best.

Then again, if he let it go there was no way of knowing what would happen next. Maybe the arsons would stop. But the feeling in his gut told him there would be more of the same—or worse—especially if the perpetrator made Heather a target now that she'd seen him.

She stirred beside him and for a moment he contemplated turning to her and making love to her again, this time at a slower, less frenzied pace. It was hard not to want it all, especially when she lay relaxed and smiling blissfully beside him.

His phone rang.

He jumped up and grabbed it midring. "Hello?"

"This is Lawrence," the detective said, his voice lower and more hard-edged than usual.

"Everything ready for the meeting?" He stood up and rushed to put his pants back on, then glanced over his shoulder to motion to Heather.

She lay there in bed, her perfect brown-tipped breasts rising and falling as she watched him hurry to get dressed. She frowned, but her expression was playful.

"What are you doing?" Lawrence asked. "You sound…off."

"Nothing. Just had to run home and take care of some urgent business before the meeting." He looked at Heather and smiled.

Heather brushed her hand lazily over her stomach, drawing loose circles around her belly button, reminding Kevin exactly why his mind had turned off and his body had taken over.

He stepped over to her and ran his hand down her naked thigh. Oh, the things he would do to her if life hadn't been waiting.

"Well, there's no need to rush," Lawrence continued.

Kevin looked over at the clock. The meeting was set to start in an hour. "Don't worry. I'm on my way."

"No really, Jensen, there's no need. I'm surprised you haven't heard. Your damned BC got your chief involved—I think he wanted to draw more attention, but the whole thing went up like an atom bomb. Your chief was pissed he wasn't involved and got into it with the mayor. Long story short, the press conference is cancelled. You can thank Hiller."

"You've got to be kidding me. There's an active arsonist and he let his ego get in the way?"

"Hey, this is your department, your chief and your BC, not mine." Lawrence chuckled. "Just let me know when I can bring over the marshmallows."

"What?"

"Yeah, I want to be prepared for the next arson. Hate to let a good fire go to waste."

"I'll let you know." He clicked off his phone and threw it down on the bed.

Damn that Hiller. He'd been against Kevin from the very beginning. Kevin should have known he would pull some kind of stunt.

"Everything okay?" Heather asked, pulling the sheet over her naked body.

"Don't do that," he pleaded. "That's the only thing going right." He pulled the sheet down, sat down beside her and ran his fingers over the sharp line of her collarbone.

"This spot," he said, stopping at the intersection of the clavicle and the shoulder where a soft little indentation hugged his fingertip. "This spot's mine." He leaned down and kissed her porcelain skin.

She said nothing as she ran her hands through his hair.

"I know I don't have any rights to, but—"

She sat up and pressed her lips to his, stopping him from finishing his sentence.

"Shut up, Kevin. Just shut up," she said, leaning back. She looked at him with the same expression she'd had while they were making love—soft, open and comforting.

Her breasts reminded him of all the other curves of her body, and all he wanted to do was fall back into her.

"Now, how can I help you?"

He smiled as he looked at her, but he let it fall away as he thought of the storm that waited for him outside of his bedroom door. "Detective Lawrence and I had put together a press conference to pull our arsonist out of the shadows, and then Hiller, the battalion chief who had worked on the cases—you met him at Brittany's—stepped in and the whole thing was canned."

He sighed. "Now I've got no suspect, no press conference, a missing son and a pissed-off battalion chief, chief and mayor. I'll be lucky if I don't get suspended—or worse."

"Why would Hiller want to get your conference cancelled? I don't get it. Wouldn't he want to catch whoever is behind these arsons just as much as you do?"

"You'd think so, but you know politics. Hiller and the chief are more worried about the financials than keeping people safe. If we keep this an open investigation it's going to cost the department money it doesn't have."

"But aren't they worried about it happening again?"

"Sure, but so far no one's been hurt. They're trying to argue against spending money on investigating little fires where the insurance companies will cover everything. Even if I nail down the perpetrator, the district attorney probably isn't going to take the case to trial. Knowing how Montana works, the guy will get a plea bargain and some slap-on-the-wrist sentence."

Heather nodded. "So why don't you just call it off?"

"Call what off?"

"Your investigation."

"I guess it would be easiest if I did. The honest truth is that a lot of the time it just feels like I'm phoning my job in. After Allison died, I couldn't…" He paused as he searched for the right words. "I couldn't be the man I had been. But this investigation was my chance, my opportunity to show not only the department, but the city and my family that I can stop bad things from happening. I may not have been able to save Allison, but maybe I can save someone else."

She sat up and wrapped her arms around him. "You can't feel guilty about Allison. You *couldn't* save her, not even the doctors could. You don't need to carry that weight."

He looked at her through teary eyes. "But I do. I have. This is my chance to make it—and me—better."

She reached up and cupped his face. "Then you need to fight for this. You need to do what you think is right. Don't let me or anyone stop you."

He reached up and took her hands in his, pulling them from his face. Her fingers wrapped around his hands as he lifted them to his mouth and softly kissed her skin.

"I can watch Lindsay and wait here for Colter. You go. When you get back, I'll be here waiting for you and *this*." She sat forward and kissed his lips.

He stood up, carefully putting distance between him and his dreams of something more.

"I'll be back soon. Why don't your order some pizza? And—" he paused as he carefully selected his words "—just so we don't confuse my kids, there's a spare bedroom downstairs. As much as I want you to stay here with me, I think it would be best for now if you stayed down there. Okay?"

She sat back against his wooden headboard and her face tightened. "That's fine."

"I'm sorry, it's just—"

"No. It's fine. I get it." She slid her legs out from the sheets and reached for her perfect pink panties. As soon as she slipped them up her legs, he wanted to pull them off again, but he resisted.

"I'll see you when I get home?"

"Yep. I'll be here. Lindsay needs me."

He had made a mistake. Kevin saw it in her eyes the moment he closed the bedroom door, but now it was too late to go back and make things right. He stood in the hallway and looked back at his room. There was nothing he could say that would make things better.

If they were caught, Lindsay would probably be okay about their "sleepover," but the same couldn't be said of Colter. Kevin was already having enough problems with his son; he didn't need to stoke the fire.

He stopped in front of Colter's door. After a momentary hesitation he twisted the cold metal knob. The room was a mess and it stunk of dirty shoes, teenage boy and the sulfur-rich scent of rotting food. A plate littered with unidentifiable food sat on his desk next to a glass of what must have been milk. He made his way over to the plate; at least he could take it to the kitchen and drop the stinking mess into the sink.

The desk was covered in a mess of candy wrappers, but near the top of the stack of papers was a receipt from Truck Boys, the local auto parts store. Picking up the receipt, Kevin read the items:

Mechanix Gloves…$14.99
TB Brake Fluid…$4.97

He gripped the back of the desk chair to steady himself.

Why would Colter need to buy brake fluid? He hadn't mentioned his car needing supplies.

His mind raced as he thought back to the night of Elke's fire. As usual these days, he and Colter had been at odds, maybe more so than usual, but was it possible Colter had snuck out in the night to start a fire?

He looked at the date of the receipt. It was marked the day before Elke's fire. The next day, Kevin had found his money missing; Colter had probably taken it the night before. Plus, the day of Brittany's fire, Colter had bailed on his morning classes.

Kevin carefully folded the receipt and slipped it into his pocket. Sure there were some connections, but none of it was more than circumstantial. Colter didn't fit the profile of the man Elke's neighbors had seen walking away from the fire, but Mrs. Jones *had* admitted it was dark and she hadn't seen the man's face. As much as he hated the thought, there was a chance Colter could be the arsonist. With a father in the department, he certainly had enough resources to learn how to make a chemical fire.

Maybe he needed to feel in control. Maybe the fires were set to get back at him.

Kevin walked toward the mess of clothes on the floor and picked up one of Colter's discarded shoes—size ten.

No...

Colter would never do something so stupid.

He'd never try to hurt anyone.

Not his son.

Chapter Nineteen

Heather buttoned her shirt as she glanced into Kevin's bathroom mirror. She'd washed up and dressed, and except for the new ache in her gut, everything was as it had been just a few hours before.

The front door shut and Kevin's truck roared to life.

She slipped out of his bedroom and into the hall. Lindsay's music was playing and Heather tapped on her door. "Lindsay?"

A crescendo of her footsteps moved toward the door. She opened it a crack and looked out. "Huh?"

"Everything okay?"

"Yeah, I'm fine, just watching videos on YouTube. You should've seen this one I just watched. The cat can *actually* talk. I swear. It says 'no' and you would swear it was a person. Wanna see it?"

Heather laughed. "Sure."

Lindsay opened the door and, taking her hand, led her to the computer. She clicked a button and a gray cat took over the screen.

The cat started to caterwaul, but Heather barely paid attention; instead she couldn't take her gaze off Lindsay. As Lindsay watched the silly cat, her eyes bright-ened and she laughed from a deep place in her belly, the sound so rich that Heather couldn't resist joining her.

The sound was so strange. It had been so long since she'd heard that specific sound—real, true delight.

For a moment, Heather imagined her life being just like this. She and Kevin could get married; they could raise Lindsay and Colter together. They could be each other's rocks.

The front door opened and slammed shut.

"Kevin, is that you?" She stood up and patted Lindsay on the shoulder. "Have fun, kiddo. I'll be right in the living room if you need me."

"Okay, Mrs. Sampson." Lindsay didn't look away from the cat.

Heather closed the girl's door as she made her way down the hall.

Standing in the middle of the living room was David. His eyes were bloodshot, as if he had been crying.

"David, what's the matter?"

"I made a mistake, Kitten."

She cringed as he used her pet name. "What do you mean?" She tried to steel herself. He wasn't the type to admit any wrongdoing.

"What did Kevin tell you?" He stepped closer to her, forcing her to take a step back.

"He didn't tell me anything."

David looked away from her, but not before she noticed a slight smirk flash over his face.

"What did you do? Is there something Kevin should've told me about?"

David paused for a second. "I… He came over and… then…" He looked around the room as if somewhere in the air hung the words he was looking for.

"What, David?" She crossed her arms over her chest.

"I told him about the divorce," David said, glancing at her with the puppy-dog eyes he always used when he rounded this curve in his emotional cycle—the same abusive cycle she fell for every time.

"I told him how bad I felt. I never should've asked for the divorce."

"What?" The word came out no louder than a breath as the floor seemed to disappear from beneath her.

He couldn't be serious.

"I'm sorry, Kitten. I made a mistake. Come home."

David had to be kidding. He had been thoughtless, sadistic and unforgivably cruel.

"No, David."

He reached out for her and took her hand. She started to pull away from his grip but stopped. If she acted petulant, he would know what she had done. He always knew when she had done something wrong. If she wanted to get anything in the divorce, he could never find out about her tryst with Kevin.

"*No* what, Kitten? You wouldn't refuse me. You love me." He stepped closer and draped her arms around him and pulled her close against him. His chest was warm against her cheek, so warm it made her start to sweat.

She pushed him away. She had loved him when they'd first met, when she had known him as a man of integrity, a man who wanted to help people. He was no longer that man. He was something far more sinister and manipulative.

"You're wrong. I don't love you."

He laughed, the sound dangerous. "Come on now. We both know that isn't true. You're just mad. I get it.

But please… You know I go crazy like this every once in a while. You know how bad I feel."

"If you feel so bad, then why do you keep treating me like this?"

David took her face in his hands. "I don't know, Kitten. I'm sorry. I wish I could be perfect for you. I do. You deserve the best, but sometimes you just make me so mad. Maybe it's the stress of work. Maybe it's the fear you'll leave me that makes me want to push you away first. Who knows? All I know is that I want you to take me back."

He rubbed his thumbs over her temples, the motion both placating and annoying.

She reached up and took hold of his hands, trying to move them from her face, but he held strong.

"I know you live for me," he said with a sick smile.

She gripped his hands hard. He had meant the words as some kind of compliment, but behind them she could read what he really meant—she couldn't live without him. More than that—that she wasn't good enough for anyone else.

Her father had been the same way with her mother. They had constantly fought, mostly about money, but even as a child Heather had known there was something just under the surface—there was always some kind of hidden meaning behind the words her father had spoken. Now here she was, reliving the same fights, the same berating behavior and the same phases of abuse that her mother had gone through. She was perpetuating the cycle.

"What do you want from our relationship?"

"I know I always said I wanted kids, but the last few days I've been thinking and I don't know if it's right for me. I mean look at Kevin," he said, motioning around the living room. "He has his hands full. Brittany told me about what's happening with Colter. I don't want to have to deal with everything that comes with kids. Think about it. If we bypass the whole thing, we could spend our time and money doing what we really want— we could travel, we could get lost in the world."

"Kids are something I *really* want, David."

"Why? They just eat, poop and destroy everything."

She stepped back from him and turned to go. She didn't want this… She didn't want him. Kevin waited.

"Wait, Kitten, if you want kids… Fine. Whatever. Just come home. You have to come home. If you don't… I don't know what I'll do," he said, with a dangerous edge to his words.

She turned back to him. His face was tight and he glared at her—his expression almost bloodthirsty.

Her gut tightened. He hadn't meant he would *hurt* her, had he?

"You… Why are you threatening me?"

"I'm not threatening you," he said with an alarming laugh. "I'd never threaten you, Kitten." He reached out and took her arm and gave it a tight, painful squeeze. "You'd never make me go that far. Would you?"

She tried to pull out of his grip, but he only gripped harder, making her arm throb with pain.

She had to stay with him. If she didn't, it was clear from the look in his eye that he would do whatever he needed to do to keep her from leaving him.

"I can't leave Lindsay here by herself," she said in a panic.

"Where did Kevin go?"

"Why are you worried about where Kevin is, David?"

He smiled the smile of a politician. "Don't worry your pretty little head about it."

She hated when David spoke down to her like that, like she couldn't think for herself.

David pinched the back of her arm, as if he was measuring her. "You know, Kitten, you could lose a little weight. You aren't what you used to be." He looked her up and down, stopping for a second at the little roll of skin that spilled over the waist of her jeans.

She recoiled from him.

He was such a jerk.

"If that's true, David, I don't know why you want me to come back."

He pinched her arm. "You know, if you were easier to live with, none of this would've happened. This is all your fault. I've tried my best to get you back. If you walk away, you won't be under my protection any more. You won't be safe. You'll never be safe. You'll have no one."

Her skin crawled as his words scuttled over her. She had to play along at least until she knew she was out of danger.

She turned back to him. "If I come home, you need to prove to me you're going to change. You have to be nicer. And I'm going to need access to everything. You can't go on controlling my life."

He tilted his head and smiled. "Kitten, everything will be fine as long as we can just put this divorce talk behind us."

"I'll get Lindsay and have her come over and wait with us until Kevin gets home." Her throat tightened as she said Kevin's name. He would never understand what she was doing or why, but he'd never lived with David. He didn't understand how terrifying he could be.

Chapter Twenty

Every time Kevin closed his eyes, he was back in bed with Heather. Her long brown hair lay around her in a halo as if she was his personal angel. It had been so long since he'd been with a woman; in fact, the last woman had been Allison.

For a moment, he wished he was eighteen again and he could just appreciate the moment with Heather without adding the weight of all of his baggage. Nothing in life was easy anymore.

He reached for his phone and tried to call Colter again.

This time, his voice mail was full.

When he found him, Colter was going to be in trouble.

He looked over at the clipboard in the passenger seat of the truck and thought about the receipt he'd stuck inside—the evidence his son might not be the boy he'd thought he was.

He gripped the steering wheel tight as he drove toward the fire station.

There was no way Colter could be the arsonist. Sure, he knew Brittany, but Colter didn't know Elke. Did he?

Even if he did know the waitress, that meant nothing. His son didn't have a reason to pull some stunt like this. It didn't make any sense. It just didn't fit.

Then again, he couldn't dispute the receipt. He had proof Colter had bought the same brake fluid used in the fires immediately prior to the arson. He had the same size feet. But so far everything was circumstantial, even the fact his son wasn't accounted for at the time of the ignition. Then again, at a certain point, when everything was pointing one way, there was usually only one answer.

If he had just had his life together, if he had just been a better father, none of this would have happened. He wouldn't have a son that was a criminal. If he could have helped him, he could have stopped Colter from going down this road.

He pulled the truck into the parking lot of the station. Through the sliding glass doors he could see Hiller sitting in the lounge, his feet up on the ottoman as Kevin parked. He needed to file his findings, but if he put his most recent notes into the computer, the department would have access. If he put in his thoughts about Colter, everyone would know his son was a suspect before tomorrow's breakfast.

Hiller turned in his chair and, noticing him in the parking lot, got up and opened the door.

Screw it.

He threw the truck into Reverse. Hiller could wait, filing the papers could wait, but his son couldn't. He couldn't let his thoughts about his son's guilt go any further. It was his job to keep his family safe, even if that meant just getting to them first.

He hit the gas and sped out of the parking lot.

As he raced down the road, he dialed Colter's best

friend, Shawn. He glanced down at the time. Shawn was probably still at the baseball game, but it was worth a shot.

He wasn't surprised when the phone went to voice mail. He hung up without leaving a message. Shawn wasn't the type to rat out his friend anyway. If Kevin didn't find Colter by dark, he would call again. Heck, he'd show up at Shawn's door.

He drove toward the high school. Maybe Colter was under the bleachers with some girl. Maybe that was what all this was about, why he was so secretive. Maybe he was using his testosterone to do his thinking. Whatever it was, when Kevin found him, they were going to have a long talk.

The school parking lot was mostly empty. The only cars were parked near the baseball fields and a few were scattered in the teacher's lot. Colter's blue 1994 Honda Accord was nowhere to be seen.

He drove around back and turned down the little alley that led to the rear of the building. The doors leading to the kitchens were closed, but the auto shop's garage door was open. Inside, up on the car lift, was Colter's Honda. The big industrial-strength lights were on under the car's undercarriage. In the spotlight was Colter, his coveralls spotted with black grease and a wrench in his hand.

Kevin parked his truck in front of the garage doors and got out. "Why didn't you answer your phone?"

Colter turned, giving him a confused expression. "Huh? Dad? What're you doing here? Aren't you supposed to be at a meeting?"

"I'm here because you don't answer your phone. Everyone has been worried about you. *I've* been worried about you. I thought you were studying for a Spanish test."

Colter walked out from under the car and wiped his hands on a shop rag. "I didn't tell you cause I thought you'd take it…well, just about as well as you are."

"I'm pissed because I didn't know where you were."

"One way or another, Dad, I was at school. It wasn't a complete lie. You don't have to be so pissed."

"Why didn't you answer your damn phone?" Kevin tried to pull back his temper, but there were still so many unanswered questions.

"Are you really going to come down on me? You're the one who's never available. So sue me that I decided I wasn't gonna sit around and wait for you so we could talk about me getting pulled from the game."

Kevin walked into the shop and put his hand up on the car's tire. "I had no idea where you were. Do you know how worried I was about you? How worried I *am* about you?"

"Wait, Dad. If that's true, tell me, did you even *remember* I had a game today?"

"Of course I remembered."

"Did you stop by?"

Kevin felt swamped by guilt.

"You didn't. Did you?" Colter threw down the wrench in the box of tools with a loud clang. "I can't believe you didn't even bother to show up for the game. You don't care, so why should I?"

Kevin's anger melted away. "I do care, bud. That's why I'm here. Don't quit chasing your dreams because of me. You're not a quitter. You're an amazing baseball player and a good student. We just need to work together to get you back on the right track."

"You think I'm good?"

"I think you're awesome, bud. You're just making some bad choices." Kevin sighed. "Tell me, what's going on with you?"

"You mean why did I get benched?"

"If that's what you want to talk about. Yeah, what led up to that?"

Colter turned his back to him and picked up a few different tools, as though he was looking for exactly the right one to get him out of this jam.

Kevin waited, but Colter didn't answer.

"Okay, bud, let's restart. Why did you steal money from me? All you ever have to do is ask and I'll give you what you need."

Colter turned to look at him. "I didn't mean to steal your money. I've just been trying to fix my car. I was hoping I could get it fixed before you found out about it. I didn't want you to get mad."

"Is this where you were the other day when the attendance secretary called?"

Colter nodded.

"If you were skipping to work on your car, why did you to lie to me and tell me you were in class?"

"Well… Okay, yeah. It was a lie, but I didn't want to tell you my car broke down."

"Again, Colter, if you just tell me the truth, I won't get upset. But all these lies… How can I trust you when you've been lying to me?"

"You have to trust me, Dad. I had to replace the lines. That's why I needed your money."

"Where were you on Wednesday morning?"

"At school."

"How about before school?"

In all honesty, Colter could have been gone in the hours the fire took place and he wouldn't have known. If Colter was pressed in court for a strict timeline, there would be little Kevin could do to corroborate.

"You promise me you didn't go anywhere before school, and the only day you skipped was the day you went to Truck Boys for brake fluid and when you were working on your car?"

"Wait a minute. I didn't tell you I went to Truck Boys."

He waved him off. "Did you go anywhere else? It's important you tell me the truth, Colter. Very important."

Colter looked down at the floor. "How do you know?"

His gut tightened. "Just tell me what you did, Colter. I can't help you if you don't tell me the truth."

Colter looked up. "Fine. I skipped some of my classes over the past few weeks. Shawn and I have been going up to Deep Creek to go mudding. I just… I didn't think it would mess with my baseball."

"You went mudding with this car?" No wonder the thing had broken down.

"Yes, sir." Colter stared at the wrench in his hand. "I know it was stupid."

Colter had lied so many times—was it possible he was lying again? Was he trying to cover up the fact that he'd committed a crime?

"But you were at school part of the time this week?"

"Yeah, I was here most of the week. After I tore up the lines, it wasn't like I could keep going up there. I just missed a couple of hours to run to the auto parts store, and yesterday I skipped English to go to Taco Bell with Shawn. I was hoping I could get it fixed and make up my classes before semifinals, but Mr. T found out I skipped more classes so he benched me."

"I hope you learned your lesson." Kevin shook his head as he heard his own father's words coming out of his mouth.

"I'm sorry, Dad. I shouldn't have hidden it from you."

Kevin stepped next to Colter and drew him into his arms. "Bud, I love you. We all make mistakes. God knows I have. I'm sorry, too. I promise I'll try harder to be available."

For a moment all he could think about was the afternoons Colter had waited for him on the porch. For a split second, he was back there and Colter was five years old and clinging to him.

Colter stepped back. "I got to get this fixed, Dad."

Kevin nodded. "Sure, but one more thing… Can you promise me you weren't at Elke Goldstein's house the morning of her fire?"

"Who's Elke Goldstein? What are you talking about, Dad?" Colter frowned.

"Where were you the day of Brittany's fire? About 1:00 p.m.?"

Colter frowned. "That's when Shawn and I skipped to go to lunch."

"So you were never near her house?"

Colter looked away, picked up a hammer and spun it in his hands. "Actually, I did come home."

"So you drove by her house around one?"

Colter nodded. "Yeah, but I didn't stop. There was something weird."

"What?"

"Well, on the way home we passed one of your guys' trucks."

No one had arrived on scene until one-thirty. It's not possible one of the city's fire trucks was there before.

"Was that about one-thirty?"

Colter shook his head. "Nope, I had Chemistry at one-thirty. I was back in time. Had to be before."

Kevin's hands shook. "Did you see who was driving?"

"Well, that's the weird part. I'm pretty sure it was one of the guys you work with, but when I waved, the guy didn't seem to see me."

Chapter Twenty-One

Heather rolled her suitcase to the bottom of the steps, but instead of taking it up to her and David's bedroom, she dropped the bag by the landing.

Lindsay walked into the living room. "I'm going to go outside and play. Okay, Mrs. Sampson?" She looked back over her shoulder at David, her lip quivering slightly.

As much as Heather wanted to reach out to Lindsay, she knew it was best to let her go.

"That's fine."

As the door clicked shut behind Lindsay, David walked up behind Heather. "When are you going to cut those kids loose? Lindsay's old enough that she doesn't need a babysitter, or a nanny, or whatever you are."

"I don't want to *cut them loose*. I love those kids."

"That's stupid, Kitten. They're not even your kids. You don't mean anything to them. You are just setting yourself up to get your heart broken."

"No." She paused. "No… That's not what matters. What matters is that they know they have someone who loves them, someone who will always be there when they have a problem." She glanced out the back window and watched as Lindsay sat on the swing. The previous owner had installed a play gym in the yard, and Heather hadn't had the heart to take it down. She'd always hoped one day her child would find it a perfect place to play.

"I love you so much. No one could ever love you as much as I do," David whispered.

He took her by the waist. She flinched under his touch.

"No, David." She pushed his hands off. "Stop."

"What? Doesn't it make you happy that I want you? That I wanted you to come home? Didn't I show you I was sorry when I came to get you?"

"That's what I don't get, David. Why did you come to get me?"

"Because I wanted you. I needed you."

"But why, David? And don't tell me you suddenly just decided you love me. If you loved me, you would never have left a note to tell me you were leaving. You never would've treated me the way you have."

"You are so damn frustrating." He took a step back.

"And you think you are some kind of daisy to live with? You don't think I get frustrated with you? But you don't see me walking out that door at the first sign of trouble. You don't see me leaving you notes."

"You would never leave me. Come on, where would you go?"

"I'm stronger than you think."

He tried to reach out toward her, but she batted his hand away. "Kitten, I never said you weren't strong. That's one of the reasons I fell for you." He gave her a placating smile. "When I first met you, you were so vibrant, so full of life…"

"And now?" She should've never asked the question, but from the way he spoke it was obvious that he wanted to deliver the blow.

"You know. You've changed. It's like your light or something has gone out. That's why—"

"You left me," she said, finishing his sentence.

He looked her in the eyes. "I just want you to be the girl I once knew."

She thought about all the times he had put her down, the times he had called her stupid, fat and lazy... Those were the moments that a little bit of her died. And now, when push came to shove, it was her fault she had changed?

"Thanks to you, David, that girl is gone." She held his gaze.

David looked away. "You're pissed. I get it, Kitten. Why don't you go upstairs, take a little nap and we'll talk about this later?" He gave a smug chuckle.

Her hands balled into tight fists. She wasn't stupid, and that was something he was never going to understand.

Confronting him again wasn't worth the fight. He was too narcissistic to care how she felt, or to try to understand what he did that bothered her. Nothing was ever his fault.

"Don't bother coming upstairs tonight. The door will be locked." She turned away from him, leaving David to stand guppy-mouthed and blabbering things she didn't bother to hear.

She made her way outside. Lindsay sat on the swing, her feet digging into the dirt, creating little clouds of dust as she swung.

"You okay, honey?" Heather asked, sitting down in the swing next to her.

"Yeah." The tone of her voice made it clear she wasn't.

"You know, you can always talk to me. I'm here for you."

Lindsay looked toward the door, where David stood at the window, staring out at them.

"Why does everything have to be so hard?" Lindsay shifted in the swing, making the chain clang.

Heather sighed. "I'm sorry you keep seeing the worst between David and me. We're going through some tough stuff right now, but it's almost over."

"I know. He doesn't make you happy... Not like when you're with my daddy. I love watching you with Daddy. You look so pretty. You're always smiling."

Heather stared at the girl.

Out of the mouth of babes...

"Would you be okay with it if I was your daddy's girlfriend?"

Lindsay rushed to her and threw her arms around her. "Colter and I have talked about it... We've always wanted you to be our mommy. We'd be a whole family."

THE COLD CHEESE pizza sat on the island as Lindsay, David and Heather sat watching *Frozen*. Lindsay's body was pressed against Heather, and she had her arm wrapped lovingly around her.

David's phone beeped with a text message. He looked almost relieved as he read the screen. He glanced over at Heather. "I have to run to work. Looks like I have a late-fifties male with possible CHF coming in from the ER."

"Go ahead," Heather said, thankful that with his departure some of the tension would go with him, as well.

He ran upstairs and, a few minutes later, made his way out through the garage without a good-bye.

Heather gave Lindsay a hug. "Want any more pizza?"

Lindsay shook her head, her attention still on the movie.

She never wanted to lose this—the time with Lindsay. It was just too bad Colter wasn't there, and Kevin. If they were, she would have everything she needed to be happy.

There was a knock at the door.

Getting up, she made her way over and opened the door. Almost as if thinking of them had beckoned them to her, Kevin and his son stood on the front porch. Kevin's arm was over Colter's shoulders.

"Hiya, Mrs. Sampson," Colter said with a smile. "Sorry you were worried about me—I was at school working on a project. And sorry I forgot to tell you about the game."

She looked at Kevin, who gave her a reassuring nod.

"I'm just glad you're okay. Is everything all right with baseball?"

He nodded, but looked to Kevin.

"We're going to talk to his teachers about doing some makeup work and then try to make things right with his coach. I'm sure we can get him back on track for college and the Huskies. Right, Colt?" He squeezed Colter's shoulders in a side hug.

Colter smiled, his eyes lighting up with his father's hope.

"Why don't you guys come in?" Heather asked, motioning toward the couch and Lindsay.

Kevin frowned. "I thought you were going to be staying at our place for a while?"

She looked away. "Well…yeah… David came over and apologized. I—"

"Oh." Kevin took a step back from her. "I get it."

"No. It's not like that," she said, but Kevin's smile disappeared.

"Lindsay," Kevin called. "We need to get going. Mrs. Sampson's probably tired."

"You don't need to go. I wanted to talk to you."

"Actually, I do need to go, Heather." He finally looked at her, but all the softness was gone from his eyes. "My family needs me."

She stopped. He needed to be with his family, to fix things that needed to be fixed, and no matter how badly she wanted to be a part of their lives she couldn't. David had been right—they weren't her family.

"How about coffee tomorrow?" she urged, trying to stop Kevin from thinking the worst.

"Fine. Text me, but as you know, I'm kind of busy. I may not be able to drop everything." His tone whipped through the air between them, lashing her with his words' true meaning—he regretted sleeping with her.

"Oh… Okay," she mumbled.

Lindsay walked outside and Kevin turned away.

"See you later, Mrs. Sampson," Colter called into the night.

She waved after them, but they weren't even out of sight before the loneliness crept in.

THE BED WAS cold when she finally slipped between the sheets, but the chill of the bed was something she had long ago grown used to. At least she hadn't had to follow through on locking David out of the bedroom; no, he hadn't even bothered to come home.

It was funny, the second he thought she had come back into his life, he had slipped back into his old habits. If she stayed it wouldn't be long before she received another note.

David's side of the bed was a sea of white. His pillow was fluffed, but there were tiny wrinkles where his head had lain. The loneliness crept a little deeper.

This feeling, this emptiness in her center, was something she was going to have to get used to. Maybe with therapy, she could learn to get through this…or better, learn to be happy being by herself.

Happy being by myself…

As the thought echoed in her mind, she reached over, picked up David's pillow and threw it to the floor.

I don't want to be by myself. I want to be with Kevin.

Yet, until she was healthy, she couldn't pull him any deeper into her life. Maybe after the divorce was finalized and she'd gone through therapy, maybe then she would be ready. Maybe then, she could not just make him happy, but have the strength to be happy with herself.

She smiled as she moved her body into the no-man's-land that was the center of the bed. She stretched out her arms and legs like Da Vinci's *Vitruvian Man*. Snuggling deeper, her foot touched something silky.

She threw back the comforter and sheets. Tucked deep in the bed's corner on David's side was a tiny wad of black fabric. She picked it up, and the satin unfurled revealing a woman's G-string.

Heather jumped out of bed and dropped the panties. She hadn't owned a G-string since…well, never.

Unless David was experimenting with women's clothing, she had her evidence for an equitable divorce.

She took a picture on her phone and sent it to Ms.

Kohl with a note: Found these in my bed. Evidence of David's cheating. Prenup nullified?

She ran downstairs and got a plastic bag and a pair of tongs. When she got back to her bed, she picked up the disgusting panties with the silver tongs and stuffed them into the bag. The black plastic-wrapped *thing* looked out of place as she dropped it onto his dresser.

Next she pulled the sheets from the bed, letting them fall to the floor. She could deal with the mess in the morning.

Lugging a new blanket and pillow from the closet, she lay down on the unmade bed. As she slipped away to sleep, she couldn't help but think about how her life was just like the bed—full of secrets, lies and defilement…and it, too, had been left in total disarray.

Chapter Twenty-Two

He looked down at Heather Sampson as he pulled the matchbox from his pocket. The box dropped from his hand, spilling matches on her bedroom floor in a heap of deadly promise. Crouching down, he scooped them back into the container, careful to move quietly, afraid that at any second she would awaken and find him standing over her.

Her eyes were closed and her lips slightly parted, as if she waited for a kiss from her Prince Charming. She should have known better. There was no such thing as Prince Charming. There were only toads and a precious few men like him—men who worked to make everything just.

The sad truth was that there was no justice in marriage—at least not in any of the marriages he had witnessed. No. Marriage was one lie after another. One hurt feeling masked with a fake smile, only to have another lie strip it away. It was an endless cycle of pain.

What was the point? What was it all for?

As far as he could tell, it was for nothing more than ego and some idealistic hope that if they acted happy, if they faked it well enough, maybe they could finally believe it themselves.

He was here to make her a martyr, not that she would understand, but this was his chance to show her and the world what her marriage truly was—nothing more than smoke and ashes. A fire that had yet to burn itself out. But at last the time had come. The hour was here for him to stoke the flames and let them consume every crumb of her failing marriage.

The inferno could have it all.

He walked out of her bedroom and made his way downstairs where the glorious scent of gasoline filled the space. Unlike the others, Heather's house would go up in a flash. In one giant fireball the whole charade would be over—the secrets, the lies, the fake smiles and hurt feelings. It would all be gone, and all her pain could be for a higher purpose.

The night air blew into the house, diluting the gas's perfume. He made sure to leave the door open as he stepped out and walked toward the garage. A puddle of gas sat on the sidewalk, just waiting for him.

He struck the match.

It was so much easier this way.

The fire's smoke curled skyward, creating a trail that led to the heavens. If he had his way, life would be better and she would be free.

THE AIR WAS thick with smoke, choking Heather as she rolled from the bed and onto the floor. Flames licked up the walls as her smoke detectors screeched.

She screamed, hoping someone would hear.

Stay calm. I have to stay calm. I need to save my oxygen. I need to get out of here.

Her knees rubbed against the hot carpet as she

crawled toward the door. A path of fire ran through the middle of the door frame, blocking her way. The only other way out of the room was through the window, but it would be a two-story fall.

Her body froze with indecision. No one was going to come for her. She was going to die. Right here. Right now.

Tears spilled down her cheeks.

I don't want to die...

The lights flickered around her and went out, leaving her alone in smoky darkness.

She forced herself to move across the floor. She drew in a breath of the tarry smoke and the heat of it penetrated her lungs, seeming to cook her from the inside. Her mind blurred, as if she was choking, not breathing.

If she didn't hurry, the gases and heat would kill her.

Just keep moving...

The alarms blared overhead, barely audible above the roar of the fire.

She hurried by the flames in the doorway, careful to keep out of reach of their touch. The fire cascaded down the top of the steps and spilled up the walls.

Someone wanted her dead.

She couldn't let them win.

The stairs were too steep and the flames too close for her to crawl down, but if she stood, her head would be in the deadly smoke.

She crouched as she tried not to inhale the black haze that filled the stairwell. She rushed down the stairs, carefully avoiding the line of fire. Reaching the bottom, she got back onto her hands and knees.

Her lungs ached as she pulled in a deep breath of sooty air.

The living room was black, but the front door had to be close.

If she could just reach the door.

Her hands searched the floor that in daylight was familiar but, in the blinding darkness, seemed like the surface of the moon. Her hand brushed a hot wall to her right.

The stairwell didn't reach the wall where the front door was located. If she was going to have a chance of getting out, she would have to cross the floor…and keep from getting disoriented.

She had to move. The smoke was getting thicker. Soon there would be no air left to breathe.

She crawled low in the direction of the door. The metal door was warm, but she pulled it open, pulling fresh air into the room. The cloud of smoke and flames rolled out over her as it searched for more oxygen. She rushed outside into the night. The heat followed her like a grasping hand, wanting to pull her back into the deadly furnace.

The street was empty. The only lights were from the streetlamps. No one knew. No one had seen what was happening to her.

She ran to Kevin's house and banged on the front door.

"Kevin!" she screamed.

The door opened and Kevin stood there, his eyes wide and alert. "What's the matter?"

"My house is on fire!" She pointed toward her house as smoke roiled from the front door.

"Get inside. I'll call 911." He turned and ran to the

phone and dialed as she followed him into the house. He talked fast to the operator, his words muted and monotone.

She leaned against the wall by the door, her body numb with shock.

He hung up the phone and walked toward her. "Sit down." He took her by the arm and led her to the couch.

The leather was cold against her skin, making her scorched flesh burn.

"Are you okay?" he asked, getting down on his knees in front of her.

"It was so hot."

"You're okay. Everything's okay." He looked over her arms, turning them as he looked for serious burns. "I *knew* I shouldn't have left you alone… Damn it. Does anything hurt?"

"I'm fine."

"Where's David?"

She started to speak, but her words turned into a jumbled mess as her tears took over. Had David done this to her? Had he acted on his threat?

He wrapped her in his arms. Her face pressed into his neck as she sobbed and her body shook with terror.

"You're okay. You're with me," he whispered. "I have you. You're safe with me."

Chapter Twenty-Three

If David was behind this, he was going to kill him with his bare hands.

Kevin dialed the number for the front desk of the Heart Center.

"Hello, Community Medical Center Heart Center, this is Patty. How may I direct your call?"

"Hi, Patty. I need to talk to Dr. Sampson."

"One moment, please." The line switched to elevator music that sounded like something from a funeral home.

Finally the line clicked back. "May I ask who is calling, please?"

"This is Inspector Jensen with the Missoula Fire Department."

"Well, Inspector, Dr. Sampson is currently in surgery."

"How long has he been in there?"

"Well, due to HIPAA regulations—"

"I don't care about the patient… Well, I do, but I just care how long he's been in surgery. It's important."

"I, uh… Well, he's been in there for at least the past three hours."

David wasn't his man.

"Thank you, Patty."

"Would you like me to give him a message?"

"Tell him his house is on fire."

He clicked the phone off and stepped out in front of the house. The firefighters had arrived and now struggled to gain control of the blaze. The windows of Heather's house were gone and flames licked up the siding.

A few feet from him, he saw Lindsay wrap her arms around Heather's waist as Colter stepped to her side. "I'm sorry, Mrs. Sampson."

She nodded. "Call me Heather, guys."

Lindsay hugged her tighter.

If Kevin had his way, they would call her something else entirely, but Heather wasn't ready for such a commitment. No, she had moved back in with David...not long after they had made love. He just didn't understand how she could go back to her old life and a man like David.

Then again, when she'd run from the fire, it wasn't David she had run to.

Her jaw was set as she watched her house burn. She was so strong. If he had been through everything she had, he would've been at the bottom of some bottle—or worse.

Hiller pulled up to the house and, when he noticed him, gave Kevin a shallow dip of the head.

"You guys stay here. I need to handle something," Kevin said.

Heather nodded, but as she looked at him, he could see the tired circles under her eyes. Whoever did this to her, whoever was responsible for hurting her, was going down.

He walked over to Hiller as he stepped out of his truck.

"Guys say it looks like arson. Liquid accelerants, huh?" Hiller asked.

"What took you so long to get here?"

Hiller grabbed his notebook and stepped past him, barely glancing at him. "Are you really going to talk to me about being on time, Mr. King-of-the-Barbecue?"

"That was different and you know it. This time a woman's life was at stake. Heather could've died."

"But she didn't."

"Yeah, and we're just lucky." Kevin shoved his fists into his pockets in an effort to stop him from hitting the BC.

"You know, Jensen, you've a hell of a reputation when it comes to women."

"What's that supposed to mean?"

"Well, look at you. Any woman you have in your life seems to be doomed. First your wife...now Heather." Hiller motioned toward her.

Kevin drew his fist tighter. "Who are you to judge my life?"

Hiller chuckled. "At least I don't screw up people's lives just in an attempt to get laid."

He lunged toward Hiller, but stopped as a black SUV parked in front of the house.

Detective Lawrence stepped out and looked over at Hiller and then him. "Hey, Jensen. I got something you're going to like."

Unless it was a bat to pummel Hiller with, he was going to be disappointed.

Hiller barked instructions as he walked toward the firefighters. "Hose one needs to be moved around back!" he yelled, pointing toward a west-facing window.

Kevin walked over to Lawrence. "What is it?"

"You and Hiller making nicey-nice again?"

Kevin flipped him off. "What did you find?"

"I just left Truck Boys. I have all of their security footage from the past two weeks. I'm thinking you'll find what you need in it." Lawrence looked over at Heather's house. "You think this one's connected to the others?"

"I haven't had a chance to get in there yet, but based on the fire pattern and Heather's observations, the perp may have used gas. Ran the fire all the way to her bed. Whoever did this wasn't trying to scare her. This time I think they were going for the kill."

"Why do you think they didn't just kill her outright? A gun's a hell of a lot easier than setting a fire."

Kevin nodded. "Whoever set this fire is angry about something and they want to get back at someone, but they aren't the type who wants blood directly on their hands."

"If they kill someone in a fire, their hands aren't clean."

"No, but it's a passive kill. God's will kind of thing."

"You think whoever's behind this could be a woman?"

Kevin thought for a moment. "It could be, but I doubt it. Besides, Heather doesn't have any female enemies."

"No, but based on what you told me about her husband, he might. Maybe it was one of his spurned lovers. Someone who wanted him all to herself?"

"It would make sense, but it doesn't feel right."

Lawrence leaned against his car, crossing his arms over his chest. "You think it's the husband?"

He shook his head. "I think he's in the clear. He's been in surgery for the past three hours. This has to be someone else's work."

"Was Heather sleeping with another man?"

She was sleeping with someone, all right, but he was never going to tell Lawrence.

"She's in the clear."

Heather was talking to Lindsay, but she glanced over at him as if she could tell he was thinking of her and what they had done...and what he wanted to do again.

"What are you thinking?" Lawrence continued.

"I'm thinking Heather's lucky to be alive." He paused. "Whoever's behind this wanted to show their strength. Show they were in control. They want us to fear them—and they wanted to get rid of any possible witnesses by taking Heather out. If we don't get him, I doubt Heather will make it out of this alive."

Lawrence looked toward Heather and a grimace flickered over his normally stoic features. He pulled out a DVD case. "We'll find something."

"We may not. Whoever is behind this is smart. He knows what he's doing."

"But he still made a few mistakes."

"Yeah, but we'll see how far that takes us."

"WHAT'RE YOU GOING to do, Heather?" Lindsay asked, letting go of her waist.

She shrugged. She didn't have a clue. Everything she owned was in that house. Even the G-string she'd found was gone. Now there was no chance of her getting her life in order for the divorce. Add to that the fact that Kevin must think she hated him. And now someone was trying to kill her.

She gave a hysterical laugh.

"You okay?" Colter asked, frowning.

She laughed harder. "I'm fine. Really."

"Then why are you laughing? This can't be funny."

"It's not funny at all. But sometimes when things are this—" She stopped before she said "terrible." Lindsay and Colter didn't need to worry about her. "When things are this *crazy* all you can do is laugh. All I can do is roll with the punches."

Things couldn't get worse.

Lindsay looked at her as though she'd lost her mind and she tried to gain control of her hysterics. This wasn't her. She didn't just lose it. She bit her lip until tears welled in her eyes and there was an iron taste in her mouth.

"You need to take a break. I'll call Brittany," Colter said, taking her by the arm as he led her toward his house.

She sat down on Kevin's couch.

Colter took Lindsay by the hand. "If you need us, Mrs. Samps—Heather—we'll be outside."

She nodded as the door closed quietly behind them. As it clicked, she slumped down, pressing her face into the pillows. All she could smell was tarry smoke. It attacked her senses, its odor reminding her of exactly how powerless she was.

She got up and made her way down the hall to Kevin's room. She grabbed a T-shirt and a pair of shorts that were heaped on the end of his bed. She lifted the clothes to her nose and took in his scent, manly and strong. He smelled so good.

His bed was unmade and wrinkled where their bodies had melded. If only that moment could've lasted, if life had taken a break and let her recover. Instead it had pounded on, wrestling her to the ground.

She sat down on the edge of the bed and ran her fingers over the ridges of his sheets. Kevin could never love the mess that was her and her life. He deserved so much better.

Making her way to the shower, she set his clothes on the sink and turned on the water. The steam rose around her, making the world disappear. She stepped into the water and let it run down her back and over her heated flesh. Her legs were red where the fire had tried to nip at her, but luckily she had no serious burns.

She had been lucky.

She watched as the ashy remnants of her former life swirled down the drain.

There was a knock on the door.

"Yeah? Kevin?" she called, trying to wipe the water from her face.

The door opened.

"Kevin, is that you?" She rubbed her eyes.

She got no answer before the shower curtain was pulled back.

Stephen Hiller stood looking at her with a double-headed ax in his hand.

Heather gasped.

"Get out. Put on a towel," he ordered.

She stepped out of the shower, water dripping from her and pooling on the floor. She pulled a towel from the rack and wrapped it around her. "What're you doing? The fire's not here." As she spoke, fear crept through her.

"I didn't want to do this." Hiller gave her a desperate look. "Why couldn't you just die?"

"I...I..." she stammered. "I don't even know you. What did I do?"

The man snorted. "You wouldn't understand. Your death... It makes sense."

"What're you talking about?"

"Come on now, I've been watching you. Your marriage is a joke. Your husband's a liar, but you buy into it—you're just like him. You are part of the problem, Heather. Don't you realize all those fake smiles and attempts to appease him can come to an end? You don't have to hurt anymore. You can be free of everything. You can make a real difference. You can die for a higher purpose."

"I don't understand," she said, her voice frantic.

"It would help so many people, Heather. You could be a martyr."

She inched toward the door. If she could just get out, maybe she could survive.

"I don't want to be a martyr. I want to live." She inched forward. "You're a fireman. Don't you want to save lives?"

"That's the point. Your death would raise awareness. People would be called to action. Right now, fires happen to *other* people, not them." Hiller twisted the ax in his hands. "Because of this head-in-the-sand attitude, the city and taxpayers don't want to fund us. The people don't understand."

He looked her square in the eyes. All she could see was darkness looking back at her. "You could fix all that. Your death would make people realize arson could happen to them. They would fund our programs and we could really help people instead of getting caught up in bureaucratic games."

"Is that why you chose Brittany and Elke? To send a message?" She slid her foot closer to the door.

He chuckled. "They're nothing but sluts."

She jerked. Brittany wasn't a slut, but she bit her tongue. She wouldn't argue with a potential killer.

"They needed to know fear. They need to always look over their shoulders for what they've done."

"Everyone makes mistakes."

"They were sleeping with your husband. That's one hell of a mistake." He laughed, setting the head of the ax on the floor. "The other day, when you came home and David was on the couch, Elke was upstairs. She was hiding in the guest room."

"How do you know that?"

Hiller gave a large toothy smile; his canines glistened like a carnivore's who was waiting to feast. "I've been watching... Always watching. When Brittany has sex with your husband she likes to be on top."

The man was lying. Brittany wouldn't have slept with David. She was her friend. She had tried to help her win David back.

"You're lying."

"No, I'm not. I thought you'd see Brittany's underwear and figure it all out... Didn't you?"

She looked down at the floor as she thought about the panties she'd retrieved from her sheets. This man had put them there. He had been in her bed. Goose bumps rose on her arms.

"It wasn't just that slut Brittany's fault. No. It all started with that stupid waitress. I gave her so much money, so many tips...but did she even look at me once? No. But in walked your husband and all of a sudden it was like she flipped. She became a teenage girl, giggling and laughing at all his stupid jokes. She couldn't get enough of him. It didn't take long before she took him home."

"So that's why you set the fire at Elke's—you were jealous?"

"I told you," he growled. "She needed to be taught a lesson." He picked the ax up. "Just like the city does."

"Were you in love with Brittany, too?"

"I didn't know her until I started watching David. She was a useful tool to get back at your husband for stealing Elke."

"What about your message to the community?"

"Two birds with one stone, Heather. Two birds." He stared at her. "If things had gone like I planned, no one would've ever known I was involved. No one would've guessed. Then you saw me at Brittany's. Why did you have to look out that window?"

"I didn't see you. I only saw a shadow."

"No, you saw me. Don't lie. It's too late to save yourself."

"If you let me go, I won't tell anyone. I promise. No one has to know you're behind this."

"You know that's a lie. You're friends with Kevin. You could never keep something like this from him. You're just like Allison. That's why he's in love with you."

"He's not…"

"You know he loves you. You have to. Even I can see the way he looks at you. Why do you keep trying to lie to me? I told you. I don't want to kill you, but every time you lie it makes it a little easier."

"There has to be another way. Tie me up. Leave me here. Run. No one will find me for a little while. I'll give you twenty-four hours before I talk to anyone. Even Kevin. I won't say anything. I promise."

Hiller shook his head as he raised the ax. "Let's just get this over with."

She moved fast, unthinking, her fist connecting with his nose with a dull crunch. He stepped back and bumped against the sink as he put his hand to his face. Blood poured from his nose, but he looked up at her with pain and fury in his eyes.

She rushed past him, but as her hand touched the doorknob, his foot connected with the middle of her back like a steel ram and slammed her down to the floor.

"I was wrong, Heather. Killing you is going to be easy."

Chapter Twenty-Four

The video from the tool store was grainy, and if it hadn't been on a DVD Kevin would have been convinced it was a video from the 1980s. He sat in Detective Lawrence's SUV with a laptop on the dash, looking through what felt like a hundred hours of video before he noticed a man walk in the main door that fit the perp's description—dark-haired, stocky, mid to late forties. But his back was to the camera as he walked down the aisle and stopped in front of the brake fluid.

Lawrence tried to zoom in on the man, but there was a glitch and the man in the video went out of focus. "Damn it. Why don't these stores spend a little more money on their security?"

"It's easier and cheaper to let people steal a few bottles of oil than to integrate a new system."

Lawrence huffed. "Ridiculous."

The man in the video turned, keeping his head down, and walked to the counter. It was almost as if the man knew he was being videotaped and was trying to keep from being identified. However, as he moved to hand the cashier some bills, his head rose just enough to glimpse his face.

"Stop. Right there," Kevin said, pointing to the video. "That's our man."

"How do you know?" Lawrence asked with a frown.

"He knows he's being watched. Look at the way he walks." He skipped backward so Lawrence could see the man move.

"You're right. He won't look up."

"But he does…right…here," Kevin said, pausing the video. "Can you pull up a larger image of his face? Anything that would distinguish him?"

Lawrence pressed the buttons on the computer, zooming in on the image and trying to sharpen it as he went. This time, the face came into focus.

"Holy crap," Lawrence whispered. "Can you believe it?"

Before him on the screen, zoomed in so close that he could read the last name on the man's coat, was Stephen Hiller.

He looked out the car window trying to spot the BC, but the man wasn't in the Sampsons' yard. "Where the hell is he?"

Lawrence saved the image and slammed the computer shut. "Isn't he out there?"

Kevin jumped out of the SUV, his eyes searching for one other person. "Heather's gone, too. We need to find her."

"I'll take a look around the house."

Kevin barely heard him.

"Heather!" he called into the mass of firefighters, police officers, neighbors and bystanders who milled around the scene.

There was no answer.

"Heather! Has anyone seen Heather Sampson?"

Colter strode toward him. "It's okay, Dad. She's fine. She just needed a rest. Lindsay and I took her into our house."

He pushed past his son.

"What's going on?" Colter called after him.

"Stay outside with Lindsay."

He rushed across the yard and to his house.

The shower was running in the master suite. "Heather?" he called as he made his way into his bedroom.

Hiller wasn't the kind to kill an innocent woman. Then again, he never thought Hiller was the kind who would be behind a string of arsons.

"Heather?" he called again.

She must not have been able to hear him.

Steam crept out from under the door of his bathroom.

He tapped on the door. "Hey, you in there? Answer me," he yelled.

"Yep… I'm here," she called back, but her voice was hoarse and tight.

"You okay?"

"Fine," she said stiffly.

"Do you need anything?"

There was a long pause and the sound of some muffled movement from behind the door.

She must have been drying off.

He was freaking out over nothing.

"Heather?" he asked, trying to sound calm, but his voice came out strangled and high. "I just found out some things I think you'll want to know. Is it okay if I come in? You decent?"

"No!" she shouted. "Don't come in!"

Something was up. He could feel it. She sounded wrong.

He reached down and twisted the handle. Locked. "Open the door."

Something inside the bathroom fell to the floor, followed by the sound of a body hitting the wall.

He threw his weight against the door. It cracked, but the lock held. He threw himself against it again.

Her scream pierced the air as something smashed to the floor.

Throwing all his power into it, his body connected with the door one more time, and the frame gave way.

Heather was pinned against a wall, wrapped in a towel, her body pressed against the towel rack. Standing in the middle of the bathroom, blood running down his hand, was Stephen Hiller. The bathroom mirror was broken, its glass sprayed around the floor, and an ax was wedged into the wall where the mirror had once been.

"Hiller... What're you doing?"

The man's eyes were dark and swollen, as though he'd taken a hit to the nose, and there was a smudge of blood where he must have wiped it away.

"I didn't want to take things this far. I never wanted to take things this far," he mumbled. "Now you're going to have to die, too. I didn't want to have to kill anyone." He turned to reach for the ax wedged in the wall.

Kevin lunged toward him. Hiller's fist connected with his cheek, making his head spin. Everything around him slowed as he struggled to remain conscious. Only one thought kept him from slipping into oblivion. Heather needed him.

He swung his fist blindly, glad when it slammed into Hiller's gut.

"You're under arrest," Kevin said, even as he struggled to regain his balance.

But Hiller would not be stopped. He rushed at him. His head connected with Kevin's sternum, sending him to the ground, his breath exhaling in a whoosh. Heather screamed as Hiller moved for the ax.

Hiller grunted as he tried to dislodge the ax. As he struggled, his new boots slipped in the puddle of water on the floor. His feet slipped out from under him. As he fell, his eyes were wide and searching. His head connected with the porcelain toilet with a sickening crunch that reverberated in the bathroom. When his head jerked back, the hatred in his eyes had disappeared, replaced by a lifeless void.

"Heather." Kevin rushed to her and pulled her into his arms. "I should've never let you go. I'm so sorry. I didn't know."

"I'm okay," she said in a voice no louder than an exhale.

He pulled back and he looked her over. The only blood on her seemed to come from her feet, where she must have stepped on the glass from the mirror.

He picked her up, taking her in his arms and carried her out of the house and to the safety of the crowd.

An EMT ran toward them. "Here, I'll take her!" the man offered.

Kevin shook his head. "I'm not letting her go. Not until she's safe."

Lawrence ran around from the back of the house. "Did you find Hiller?"

"He's in my bathroom. He…he's dead."

Epilogue

Six months later

The snow was falling as Heather made her way across the street. Kevin stood by his truck, waiting with a black bag in his hand. She waved, the cold nibbling at her fingers as she made her way toward him.

"How did it go?" he asked as she stopped beside him.

"Good." She hopped from foot to foot trying to stave off the cold. "But I'm starving," she said, pointing down the street toward the restaurant.

Kevin took her hand, his sudden warmth penetrating the thin cloth of her glove. "What did the judge decide?"

"The divorce is final. All assets are going to be split evenly. David has to pay me alimony for the next five years, long enough for me to go to school." She wrapped her fingers in his, as her excitement filled her. "As for the house, now that everything is fixed, I get it free and clear. I think I may keep it."

"So you're staying there just because it's paid for? No other reason?" Kevin asked with a mischievous grin. "It has nothing to do with who it's next to?"

She returned his grin. "What can I say? Location, location, location."

"I'll take what I can get, but you know you could always move in with me."

She wrapped her other hand over their entwined fingers. "Are you sure you're ready for that? Sure the kids are ready? The therapist said—"

"I know it's fast. If you're not ready—"

"That's not it," she interrupted. "It's just that—"

He stopped walking, the bag in his hand swinging heavily to a stop against his thigh. "I love you, Heather. The kids love you."

Her heart skipped a beat. She had waited for him to say that for so long. "I...I..." she stammered.

"Don't feel like you have to answer now, but..." He got down on one knee and reached into the black bag. He drew out a large, pink box with a black ribbon on top.

"What's that?"

His hands shook slightly, making the box quiver. "Would you please have a piece of cheesecake with me?" he asked with a nervous laugh.

She laughed, cupping her hands over her mouth. "You're crazy. What made you think of that?" She could hardly believe he remembered how much she loved cheesecake.

"Will you?" he repeated, lifting the box higher.

"Absolutely, but you didn't have to get down on your knee for cake."

"Actually, I think I do." He opened up the box.

Inside, on top of the white, creamy cheesecake was a small black velvet box. He set the cake box down on the sidewalk and drew out the smaller box.

"Heather, I know this is fast. You don't have to say yes, but I can't stand it anymore." He opened the box to reveal a diamond solitaire engagement ring. "I love you. I will always love you. I want you in my life. You've been my best friend and helped me through things I never would have made it through if it hadn't been for you. You are the first thing I think of in the morning and the last thing I think of at night. I want you to be my forever. We don't have to do it right away, but… Will you marry me?"

A crowd of people started to form around them on the sidewalk, but she didn't care. She stared at him, at the soft lines around his mouth as he spoke and the glimmer of hope in his eyes. She loved him. She'd loved him almost from the first moment they had met. Her dreams were coming true. It was so surreal.

"Yes… Yes… I love you, too. I will marry you."

He slipped the ring on her finger and stood up. Their warm breath mingled together in the cold, creating a misty cloud around them. She stood on her tiptoes and kissed his lips as he wrapped her in his arms.

He tasted like fresh air, frost and new beginnings.

She leaned back. "I love you so much," she whispered.

His lips took hers, tender and hard in their need, a need that echoed hers.

Life was messy, and things wouldn't be easy, but she was ready. No matter what was to come, they could rise up from the ashes and create a life filled with happiness and possibilities—a world of dreams.

* * * * *

MILLS & BOON®

Mills & Boon have been at the heart of romance since 1908… and while the fashions may have changed, one thing remains the same: from pulse-pounding passion to the gentlest caress, we're always known how to bring romance alive.

Now, we're delighted to present you with these irresistible illustrations, inspired by the vintage glamour of our covers. So indulge your wildest dreams and unleash your imagination as we present the most iconic Mills & Boon moments of the last century.

Visit **www.millsandboon.co.uk/ArtofRomance** to order yours!

ß OB